Christina Koning was
Borneo, and spent he
and Jamaica. She reviews fiction fo
has taught creative writing at the University of Oxford and Birkbeck, University of London. Koning's first novel, A Mild Suicide, was published by Lime Tree in 1992, and was short-listed for the David Higham Prize for Fiction; her second novel, Undiscovered Country (Penguin) won the Encore Award for fiction and was long-listed for the Orange Prize for Fiction. Fabulous Time (Viking) was awarded a Society of Authors Travelling Scholarship. Her most recent novel is The Dark Tower (Arbuthnot Books), which, like much of her earlier work, touches on colonialism and its legacy.

VARIABLE STARS

Christina Koning

To Patsy,
best wishes,
Christina.

ARBUTHNOT BOOKS

ARBUTHNOT BOOKS

Published by Arbuthnot Books

This edition published by Arbuthnot Books 2011
ISBN 978-0-9565214-4-6

www.arbuthnot-books.com

For Anna and James

Bright star, would I were steadfast as thou art—

John Keats: Written on a Blank Page in *Shakespeare's Poems*, facing 'A Lover's Complaint', September 28th, 1820

Nebulae

I

Hannover, 1764

At the bottom of the bucket is the Sun. There it lies, a drowned Star, in the water. Not that she is foolish enough to suppose it to have fallen from the sky; it is of course still up there, in its accustomed place—nor, despite appearances to the contrary, does it really disappear during the minutes that follow. That is simply the effect of the Moon's shadow, passing in front of it, her father says—a phenomenon she and her brothers are now about to witness. For they must never stare directly at the Sun, he goes on; if they did so, it would turn them stark blind. Today, April 1st—the Day of Fools, she cannot help but remember—he has called them out into the courtyard, to observe the Eclipse, having filled the big iron tub with water for the purpose.

So she keeps her gaze fixed on that. There, reflected in that improvised mirror, she sees a yellow disk, being slowly eaten up by a disk of blackness. The blackness is the Moon. Soon there is nothing left of the Sun but a fiery rim, around that circle of darkness. If they watch closely, their father says, they will see the 'diamond ring' appear...

Then the noonday world is plunged into a strange grey twilight. Even the birds have stopped singing. In the eerie hush of that moment, she feels her little brother take her hand.

'In the old times, they would bang the drums and shout and sing until the Sun came back,' says her father. 'Now we understand these things better.'

Even so, she hardly dares to breathe, until the ring of fire thickens to a sliver of yellow, like a rind of cheese. On the ground at her feet, the same shape is repeated, in the spots of light—now turned to tiny crescents—which fall through the leaves of the chestnut tree. After a minute or so, the cheese-rind becomes a slice; then a quarter, then a half; then the whole round cheese itself. And there it is once more—the dear familiar Orb—without which, she knows, the Earth would be in perpetual darkness: a lifeless lump of rock, adrift in the wildernessness of Space.

'For without the Sun, we would not have Light,' her father says. 'And Light is what gives us Life…'

In times past, he goes on, people had thought Eclipses of Sun or Moon to be harbingers of terrible events. Battles had been lost and won, kings crowned or overthrown, on account of such phenomena. Now, he says—thanks be to God—they are not so credulous. Now they are guided by Reason, not superstition.

Nonetheless, she half-expects him to call out 'April Fool!'—the way he used to when they were little, and had found their breakfast eggs to be nothing but empty shells, up-ended.

The day after the Eclipse, her brother Friedrich Wilhelm comes home, after eight long years in England. She has been kept busy right up to the moment of his arrival, making cakes and puddings for the feast there is to be in his honour; she has only just taken off her apron when the carriage is heard outside. There is no time for anything but to rake her fingers through her curls to smooth them, and to shake out the creases in her best blue Holland frock, before she must face him. Mingled with her joy at the prospect is the fear that, after her illness, he might not know her.

Examining her face in the looking-glass that morning, she had thought that the marks of the smallpox were not as bad as they had once been. In some lights, they were hardly visible. The wasting effect of the fever was only too apparent, however. It had spoilt her looks, and stunted her growth, so that she would never grow any taller than she had been at twelve years old. Turning away from the unpleasing sight of herself, she began, with short, fierce, strokes, to brush her hair. It had been impossible to stop her eyes filling with tears, at the thought of Wilhelm's seeing her like this…

Now, as she stands waiting for him to appear, she feels almost sick with dread. How fast her heart is beating! When she hears the sound of his voice in the hall, it takes all her reserves of courage not to run away. Although why she should feel like this, when it is Wilhelm—dearest of brothers—coming back to her, she cannot say.

As he comes into the room, she risks a glance at him. How handsome he is, in his smart new English clothes! If she had passed him in the street she would not have known him. His voice, though, is just the same, even after all these years. Years during which not a day had passed but she has thought of him, and longed for his return. And yet now she hangs back, letting her sister and brothers and Sophia's little ones go ahead of her to greet him. Her mother and father are of course the first to embrace him; Anna Ilse weeping loudly all the while. Still she herself hesitates.

She need not have been afraid, however.

For—after he has clasped their father in his arms and kissed their mother, and lifted Sophia's youngest up into the air—he looks for her, over the heads of their older brothers.

'Carolina?' he says. 'Am I not to have a kiss from you, after so long?'

She goes to him, then, and throws her arms about his neck.

'I am very glad to see you,' he whispers.

She is surprised, nonetheless, to see tears in his eyes when they move apart; although whether this is from the emotion of the moment, or some other cause, is impossible to say.

After he has been made to sit down, and has been given a glass of beer, and has been served with some of Anna Ilse's home-cured ham, and a dish of pickled cabbage, and then the cinnamon cakes she herself has made (which he says are the best he has tasted since, O, the last time he was in Hannover), Wilhelm pronounces himself content at last.

'For is not a man's home the seat of all contentment—and am I not home at long last, after wanderings almost as lengthy as those of Aeneas?'

He then proceeds to unpack the presents he has brought: tobacco for their father and Jacob, a box of China tea for their mother, a pocket-knife for Alexander, and a strange English cake full of plums for Dietrich. For Sophia he has brought a bolt of yellow silk, to make a new dress. When it comes to Carolina's turn, he smiles.

'I am afraid you will not think much of this, Lina—for it is not good to eat, nor useful—nor is it pretty, like Sophia's gift. And yet it is the most precious thing I could think of to give you…'

She replies that she does not mind what it is. What she means is, she will be happy with whatever he chooses to give her.

'Here you are.' Into her hands, he places a sheaf of music. 'It is all the latest pieces from the Italian opera. They listen to nothing else in London. There are some of Signor Galuppi's songs, and one by Signor Piccinni, which I think you will like…'

She thanks him with all the emotion she feels at being thus singled out, in a family of musicians, as the one most deserving of a gift of music. And yet her heart is heavy, knowing—as he does not—the unlikelihood of her ever being able to benefit from his generosity.

It is her mother who saves her the trouble of explaining.

'O, Carolina will have precious little time for singing,' says Anna Ilse. 'Now she has left school, she will be busy improving her skills as a seamstress. For she is to go to Fräulein Kuster's next month, with that end in view.'

At this, Wilhelm is unable to conceal his dismay.

'Is this true, Carolina? You have left school?'

She hangs her head, and admits it is so.

'I am very sorry to hear it,' he says gravely. 'Very sorry indeed. I had thought to assist your education—not to hear of its coming to an end.'

If the family had not all been present, she would have cried out that it had not been her choice to have her studies thus curtailed. As it is, she says nothing.

'Carolina often sits in on her youngest brother's violin lessons,' says their father, with his usual mild and conciliatory air. 'That is, when her mother can spare her from her domestic duties. She has quite a good ear, I believe, our Carolina. Yes, yes. I am sure she has a good ear…'

All that day, and the next, and every other day of that all-too-brief fortnight's visit, she follows Wilhelm around, delighting in his presence, and listening to his talk. And how brilliantly he could talk, on such a range of subjects, from Newton's theories on the refraction of light, and Euler's calculations concerning the orbiting of comets, to the merits or otherwise of the opera buffa he had seen the previous month at Covent Garden. It is not to her he talks, of course, but to their father and brothers. She manages to find some excuse to be there, however—bringing her sewing to her favourite seat on the parlour windowsill, and making herself as inconspicuous as possible, so as not to cause comment from any other quarter. Even so, she is soon tagged with the name of 'Shadow'—their brother Jacob being quick both to observe and to condemn.

'One would think she had never laid eyes on our brother Wilhelm before, the way she keeps staring,' he says, well aware that she is listening. 'Has the little wretch nothing better to do than eavesdrop on our conversation?'

'Leave her alone,' is Wilhelm's reply. 'I am sure we have nothing to say that Carolina may not hear…'

At this, Jacob can only subside into muttering about the miserable state of his linen under Carolina's care:

'For look,' he exclaims disgustedly, snatching up the shirt she is presently working on, 'she has left spots of blood all over the sleeve from pricking her fingers…'

'Then we must take care to say nothing that will distract her too much from her sewing,' says Wilhelm, with a wink at Carolina.

With Wilhelm there to defend her, she feels equal to anything. Neither their elder brother's unkind comments, nor their mother's complaining that all this talk of things she does not understand will turn Carolina's head, can hurt her. How she will manage when Wilhelm is gone, is another matter.

As she lies in bed later that night—her little brother Dietrich Johann on the truckle-bed beside her, and Sophia's youngest (who is teething) snuffling in the cot at her feet—she thinks of all that Wilhelm has told her about England. The countryside in Yorkshire, where he has been living, is very wild, he says. He is often obliged to ride fifty miles, across dark and deserted moorland, in order to fulfil his various obligations. The houses in Yorkshire are very fine, however; when he was tutoring Lady Milbanke on the harpsichord, he had spend several months at Halnaby Hall—Sir Ralph's country seat, and one of the grandest houses to be found in that region. Why, it was not unusual for there to be thirty sitting down to dinner. He was often obliged to play to the company, when the ladies were too tired.

Was there dancing? Carolina wants to know. O, a great deal of dancing, says Wilhelm. Lady Milbanke liked nothing better than to have four or five couples stand up together of an evening, when their elders were engaged at cards.

'You would like it there, Lina, I am sure,' he goes on. 'For there is a library full of books where you could read to your heart's content, and no end of pretty walks about the grounds.'

The picture he conjures up is so agreeable that she returns to it many times in imagination, thinking what it must be like, not only to have a library at one's disposal, but also the leisure to enjoy it. Were she to have a house of her own she would fill it with books, she decides. There would be a harpsichord, too; and she would do nothing all day but play and sing. In the evenings, there would be dancing. She would never have to sew another shirt, or scrub another kitchen floor. She and Wilhelm would live together, perfectly content for the rest of their lives.

She thinks of the day, eight years before, when Wilhelm went away. She was six; she remembers it well.

He had just turned eighteen, and—at their father's instigation—was to play the hautbois in the military band, which was going to England with the Hannoverian Guard. She remembers how proud he was of his new uniform. She had stared at him, suddenly shy at the sight of him, tall and handsome in his blue-and-gold; although, only that morning, he had given her a piggy-back around the stable-yard, and had pointed out a swallow's nest under the eaves.

Now the drums are beating so loud it seems to make the air shake; the flags are flying all along the street; and her mother is weeping as if her heart will break.

'What shall I do? What shall I do?' cries Anna Ilse, half-distracted with grief, so that nothing can be done to quiet her. All Carolina can do is to fetch the handkerchief she has been hemming from the stool, and put a corner of it into her mother's hand, whilst with another, she wipes away her own tears.

'*Ach*, poor wretch, what will you do, now your father is gone to war?' is Anna Ilse's response to this, in a kinder tone than she is accustomed to use to her small daughter. Then she falls to weeping once more—which rouses the baby, Dietrich, from his sleep, so that his wails drown out even the sound of the drums. It is left to Carolina to soothe him, by pinching his cheeks and making faces at him, for her mother takes no more interest in him than in any of her children, save Jacob.

He—having found fault with everything that has been done for him, from the way his coat has been brushed to the polish on his boots—is also going to England with the regiment, though to hear him talk, you'd have thought he was at least a sergeant, instead of just a musician in the regimental band.

'O my poor boy, my poor boy!' weeps their mother, when he comes to take his leave, all dressed up in his finery and impatient to be gone. 'When shall I ever see you again?'

As ill-luck would have it, Jacob is the first of them back; although he is obliged to return to England double-quick, to avoid being pressed for a soldier. Would that he had stayed abroad for good—for on his return two years later, he has grown into even more of a tyrant than when he left. From that time on, Carolina has nothing but kicks and curses from him. His beefsteak is too tough; his tea is stewed; or the knives and forks have not been cleaned to his liking. How he likes to box her ears! It is a wonder she is not half-deaf, as well as half-blind from the smallpox.

Almost as bad as the slaps and pinches are the unkind names—*Dummkopf. Hässliches Weibchen*—and the constant jibing.

She will never get a husband, with a face like that. It makes him sick just to look at her. As for her cooking—it is not fit for the dogs to eat.

Sometimes it gets so bad that their father is moved to remonstrate with his eldest son.

'That is no way to speak to your sister.'

His voice trembles a little, for it is an effort for him to speak harshly to any of his children, even one who so richly deserves it.

Jacob replies with a scowl, muttering that it is not his fault if Carolina persists in scorching his shirt-cuffs.

'A sister is worth more than a shirt-cuff, my son,' Isaac says, with a quelling look. Of course it does no good; but she is glad that one person in that house at least cares enough for her to take her part.

It was her father who first showed her the stars.

She cannot have been more than seven or eight years of age; he had taken her by the hand and led her out into the street, to look at the Comet, which was then visible. She remembers the way the cobblestones rang under their feet, hard as iron in the bitter cold, and how their breath smoked in front of them, as he pointed out the constellations to her, one by one.

There was Andromeda. Al Sufi mentioned a nebula in that constellation, on the boundary near Pisces—could she make it out? There was Perseus, and, overhead, Cassiopeia. It made a shape like a 'W'—for Wilhelm. There was his own favourite, on the other side of the Milky Way—the Lyre. It was the instrument played by Orpheus—did she know the story? Orpheus was a musician, like himself—although of course a far greater one. He could charm the birds of the air with his music, and even the wild beasts...

She remembers the gentle sound of his voice, and the light touch of his hand upon her head.

Schauen Sie, Carolina! Das ist Coma Berenices...

This last was named, he told her, for a princess's beautiful hair, cut off and flung into the sky in a shining mass, to remain there for all eternity. Her hair was beautiful, too—like her mother's—he told her kindly. Although later he was to speak more frankly about her looks, or lack of them.

For it is all too true that she has nothing to recommend her—neither beauty nor accomplishments. All her brothers, even nine year-old Dietrich, can play at least one instrument, and—thanks to their father—are well-versed in the rudiments of Natural Philosophy. Her sister, being beautiful, has no need to know such things; nor does she care to know them. That her name means 'Wisdom' is neither here nor there.

But for Carolina, to be denied the chances that are offered to the others is to be denied all that makes life worth living—like a plant starved of the Sun's life-giving light... So that when Wilhelm, on one particular afternoon towards the end of his visit, asks her—is she happy, now that she has left school?—it takes all her reserves of self-control not to break down.

'I am happy enough.'

They are walking by the river; the water-meadows are scattered with daisies and cornflowers, and the sky above their heads is a pure, clear blue. They stop to listen to a skylark singing, so high up in that cloudless vault that it can scarcely be made out—the shrill, sweet, bubbling notes seeming to come out of nowhere. For at that moment, it is true: she is happy. On such a day, and with her dear Wilhelm beside her, how could she have been anything else?

She breaks off a spray of wild roses from an overhanging bough, and fastens it in his buttonhole.

'But Lina,' he persists. 'Would you not care to have singing lessons, or to learn to play an instrument, like the rest of us?'

'Sophia does not play an instrument.'

He gives an impatient shrug. 'Sophia is married, with little ones to care for. I do not see that Sophia has anything to do with it...'

She is silent a moment.

From across the river, comes the silvery chimes of the Marktkirche clock.

'Well?' He gives her an encouraging smile. For a moment she is seized with an impulse to tell him everything. How miserable her life has become, now that there is not even the consolation of her daily lesson with the Pastor's wife. How much she would have loved to sing, and play—and how unlikely it is that she will ever be given leave to do so.

'I have not thought much about it.'

A look of disappointment crosses his face. She cannot bear to have him look at her like that.

'Then perhaps you *ought* to think,' he says, with a reproving shake of the head. 'To be able to sew and cook is all very well, but you should not neglect your studies.'

At this, she feels the tears start to come, so that she has to turn her head away quickly, to prevent him from seeing. For it was not *her* idea that she should leave school; nor is it her fault that she has not developed her musical skills.

'Why,' her brother says, warming to his theme, 'in my opinion there is no reason why women should not be as well taught as men—in music, art, and science, too. I have met several young ladies during my stay in England whose command of Latin and Greek is as good as—if not better—than my own. Indeed, there is one I could mention—the sister of a pupil of mine in Pontefract, you know—who is not only as learned as any man, but can play very sweetly upon the guitar...'

Here he colours slightly, and clears his throat, as if a fly had got stuck there.

'So you see, Lina,' he goes on, 'there is no reason in the world why you should not be educated. A woman should have at least the rudiments of languages—French and English will do to begin with. And mathematics, too. I will write to you on the subject, as soon as I am back in England...'

At this—the thought of his imminent departure—she is so cast down that she says not another word. And if she had, what could she have said, that would have conveyed the utter dreariness of her life?

For this is the pattern of her days: after rising at five, from the bed she shares with Hildegard, the servant (a country girl, who snores, and kicks, and is not overly particular about washing), she lays the fires—it is Hildegard's job to sweep out the ashes—and makes the porridge for the younger ones' breakfasts. Mornings are spent at the market—searching out the cheaper cuts of meat, or begging for fish heads for a soup from the fishmonger. Afternoons are consumed in darning and mending, or cutting out ruffles for shirts. Evenings she likes the best, because it is then—the housework being done—that she helps her father copying music, a task for which her neat hand (Isaac says) makes her particularly suited.

Monotonous as it is, all this would not have been so bad, if it had not been for her brother Jacob.

How she comes to hate him, during those years of her servitude, for his vanity and his spendthrift ways (nothing is ever too good for him—no matter that the rest of them are living on stews and slops); above all, for his cruelty to her. Not that her mother is any less sparing with the rod; but she, at least, has the excuse of having been treated with similar harshness by her own parents. Jacob—her mother's darling—has never suffered so; and yet he does not forbear to punish his sister whenever he sees fit.

Later, she comes to see that he was just a spoiled young man, whose chief fault was that he lacked imagination. To him, a sister was of no more interest—indeed, of considerably less interest—than his horse or his dog. Unlike Wilhelm, that Paragon amongst brothers, Jacob never said two words to her that did not concern his dinner or the state of his shirts. That she might have a mind—a Soul—above such matters would never have occurred to him.

II

Hannover, 1772

When she is seventeen, her father dies. Worn out by years of privation, and the demands of an ever-rapacious family (for there are Sophia's children, as well as his own, to provide for), he gives up the ghost at last. Terrible as it is, his death sets her free; for after that, there is nothing to keep her in Hannover. That city, whose miseries have been alleviated only by Isaac's presence, becomes Hell indeed. Now there is no one to stand between her and her mother's black moods, or her brother's rages. Tyrannised over by both, and made the drudge of the rest of the family, she finds comfort in nothing but the letters which come from England, and the glimpses they afford of a world beyond her experience. Five years pass, each more wretched than the last.

It is from this torment that her brother Wilhelm rescues her.

It begins as an almost casual enquiry in a letter. Would she care to come to Bath, to train as a singer? There is room in the house, he tells her—for their brother Alexander (who had moved to Bath two years before) does not need a whole floor to himself. If she likes the idea, he adds, he will broach it to their mother... Of Jacob he makes no mention; but it is understood that Jacob will have to be consulted. *He*, predictably, thinks the idea ridiculous, and loses no time in saying so. If his sister's voice is as ugly as her face, she will soon be the laughing-stock of two cities, instead of one...

Not that Jacob has ever heard her sing; she has made sure of that. Now, when she practises at home, she holds a gag between her teeth, to muffle the sounds. Only when she knows herself to be alone, does she allow her voice full rein. Nor is her routine of housework disrupted by this new enthusiasm. A floor can be washed just as easily whether one is singing, or not. A sock can be knitted just as fast to the accompaniment of scales, as in silence.

So she prepares in secret for the day when her Liberator will come. The weeks go by; she crosses them off on the calendar. Now that she has tasted the idea of freedom, she cannot bear the thought that Wilhelm's plan might not, after all, succeed. She will fall at his feet when she sees him, and beg him to carry her away. She will implore him not to desert her.

Another year—another *day*—in this hateful place might be her last.

Her mother, of course, is unhappy with the idea—for how is she to manage without a daughter to scold? Who will do the rough work, in Carolina's absence? Wilhelm, fortunately, is equal to this: they will engage another servant, he says; he will put up the money himself. (Jacob, even more fortunately, is out of town. What *he* would have said to all this is not hard to guess.)

'You need not fret yourself, *Mutti*,' Wilhelm goes on, winking at his sister over Anna Ilse's head. 'For it will only be for a year—two at the most. If it turns out that Lina's voice is no good, I will send her back...'

Meeting his laughing eyes, Carolina wants to weep for happiness. She is free at last. If she has to crawl all the way to England on her knees, she will do so, and gladly.

And indeed the journey is not without its share of discomfort. For six days and nights, they travel across Holland in an open coach. Wilhelm takes the opportunity to point out the constellations to her, since there is little chance of sleep (*Look, Lina! That is Ursa Major... There is Auriga... Do you see Pegasus?*) Her hat is blown off her head into a canal (*Never mind. I will buy you another when we get to England*). The sea is stormy during the crossing; great grey waves threaten to overwhelm the packet, and one of the masts is carried clean away. Most of the passengers are sea-sick; the smell is disgusting. She is not sea-sick, however.

A mile or so off the coast of England, they transfer into an open boat. Two brawny English sailors pick them up and 'toss them like balls' (she notes in her journal) upon the stony English shore. On the road to London, the Diligence is upset, and they land in a ditch. Fortunately, the ditch turns out to be dry.

London she thinks very beautiful—if rather dirty and noisy. Instead of Hannover's narrow streets and crooked, half-timbered buildings, there are broad streets of fine new houses, built of red brick, and pale stone, and shining white spires of churches. They visit the new Bank of England, which Wilhelm (William, as she must now call him) thinks very fine, but which she herself thinks rather too plain. They also visit St Paul's Cathedral—which, whilst it was being built, was used as an Observatory for looking at the stars, her brother tells her. 'Unfortunately, the architect was obliged to put a roof on it…' Since William appears to have forgotten his promise about the hat, she borrows one from their landlady's daughter. There is no opportunity to do more than look at the shops, with their lighted windows and trays of fancy goods, because they are on their way to Bath the next day—and in any case, the only such establishments her brother cares about are Opticians' shops.

Anything not connected with mirrors and lenses interests him not at all.

On their last day, he insists on taking her to the Monument. For it was designed as a giant telescope, he says—though never used as such. An Observatory was to have been constructed below the ground, from which astronomers would have viewed the heavens though a central gap in the spiral staircase, which formed a tube two hundred feet high…

'Think of it Lina!' he cries, when—more than a little out-of-breath—they arrive at the top of a seemingly endless flight of steps, and stand looking out over the rooftops. 'If Wren and Hooke had had their way, we would have been star-gazing in the middle of London, instead of only at Greenwich.'

'But how would such a telescope have worked?' she asks, feeling a dizziness overcome her as she looks over the edge. 'Since the structure does not move—or at least'—feeling herself caught by a gust of wind—'not very much.'

'It is a zenith telescope,' he replies, 'and therefore not designed to move. Being fixed, you see, on the moving stars…'

He waves his hands about to simulate this astral movement.

'I am very glad to have seen it,' she says, although in truth she would much rather be safely back on solid ground.

But William seems strangely reluctant to leave the place.

'To think,' he murmurs, 'of all that one might see with such an instrument...'

In the middle of the following day, they arrive in Bath. She is dusty and hot after being shaken about in the rattling coach for hours, and falls down upon her bed (as she confides to her journal) 'almost annihilated.'

The house to which William brings her resembles neither a castle or a palace; nor is it very like the picture she has constructed, from William's description, of Sir Ralph and Lady Milbanke's superior establishment, Halnaby Hall. Here are to be found no spreading lawns, no Yew Walks, or picturesque vistas; whilst the well-stocked library, in which she had envisaged herself, in those long-ago daydreams, idling away a pleasant hour or two, is present only in its essentials. (Her brother's house never lacks for books.) And although it is a decent enough establishment—one of a terrace, built of pale yellow stone, with long narrow gardens running down to the river—it is by no means large. They are, moreover, obliged to share it with Mr and Mrs Bulman—who have the ground floor—while she and her brothers divide the upper floors between them.

This, William says, is the way of it in England. Only the rich can afford whole houses to themselves.

But in those first few weeks in her new home, Caroline comes to love everything about it. For this, she feels, is where her life will begin. From the sunny garden, on account of which the house has been chosen—for, William says, mysteriously, there will be space enough for workshops—to the airy parlour, which is to be their music-room, she is delighted with it all. The best room in the house, to her mind, is her attic-bedroom, whose very plainness of whitewashed walls, and air of quiet seclusion, is in happy contrast to the cluttered dark rooms and incessant clamour of quarrelling voices she has left behind.

Waking early, on those fine Autumn mornings, she lies for a few moments, listening to the muted jangling of the harpsichord drifting up from the floor below, and marvelling again at her good luck. To have left behind *that* house, and all its miseries, to come to *this*, is wonderful enough; but to be allowed—encouraged, rather—to devote herself to Art, is beyond anything she could have dreamed of.

And certainly, in the beginning, there is time for music—sometimes as much as three or four hours a day. She so loves those hours, with Wilhelm—William, that is—by her side. She sings, and he accompanies her on the instrument, breaking off from time to time to get her to repeat a phrase.

'You have a sweet voice and a true, dear Lina,' he tells her, after one such session. She has been singing Cecchina's song from *La Buona Figliuola*—the music for which had been his present to her, on that long-ago visit to Hannover. 'It lacks strength, to be sure—but I think we might improve that, with practise...'

How she glows with pleasure at his praise! She vows then and there that she will prove herself worthy of his trust in her. If she has to practise five hours a day, or six, she will do so, and gladly. She will gargle with salt-water, to strengthen her vocal pipes, and sleep with the window open, in midwinter, to expand her chest. Of course, her practising will have to be fitted in between all the other things expected of her, during this first phase of her new life. For as well as being trained as a singer, she is also, she finds, to take charge of the household arrangements.

This useful function—though by no means new to her—is complicated by the fact of her knowing no more than a dozen words of English.

Fortunately, there is their neighbour, kind Mrs Bulman, to turn to. She it is who accompanies Caroline to the market-place, and encourages her first, halting, attempts at buying foodstuffs. For the market traders in Bath, it transpires, are just as likely to try and cheat one as their counterparts in Hannover... From Mrs Bulman she has lessons in baking—for pies and puddings are what the English love best—and is taught how to lay up a good stock of pickles and preserves. If she thought her days of scouring pots and chopping vegetables were over when she left Hannover, she was mistaken.

Still, there is a great deal more to her life besides chopping vegetables.

Breakfast times are devoted to the study of mathematics—for, William says, he is much too busy with his students to spare her any more time than this, and it is essential that she knows the rudiments of the science. Each day there is another of what he calls his 'Little Lessons for Lina' in geometry, trigonometry, or algebra. Each day she shows him how she has got on with the exercises he has set her on the previous one, and he congratulates her—'Bravo, Lina! You are right!'—when she hits the mark; or frowns and shakes his head when her answers fall short.

At dinner-time, one day, she has just brought in the pudding—a particularly fine one, full of currants—when he tells her to pay close attention.

'Now, Lina,' he says, brandishing the knife with which he is about to serve this delicacy, 'I must ask you to tell me as near as you are able what angle it is that I am cutting. For you know we have gone over and over this, and I am determined that you will get it right…'

She starts to laugh, thinking he must be joking; then she sees that he is not. Trigonometry has never been her favourite subject. Now she gazes at the pudding, which glistens enticingly as the knife slides through it, releasing a fragrant puff of lemon-peel scented steam.

'Mind, you must tell me the *exact* angle,' says William, having completed the operation. 'If you are 'out' by even a few degrees, I am afraid you will go without pudding. And it promises to be'—he gives an appreciative sniff—'a very delicious one.'

Caroline stares at the pudding in despair.

'I think, perhaps…'

'Take your time, Lina. For geometrical accuracy is more important in life than pudding, do you not agree?'

She does not, as it happens, but she knows her brother well enough not to argue the point with him just now.

'Can it be forty degrees?'

'Bravo, Lina! We will make a mathematician of you yet. It is indeed a forty degree-angle slice.'

He levers it onto her plate, and then cuts another, just the same, for himself.

'For a minute, I thought I might have to eat both of them myself,' he says. 'But you have learned your lesson well, and so I must be the one to go without…'

If her mathematics is improving, her singing is increasingly catch-as-catch-can; for with all his concerts to prepare, and scholars to instruct in the violoncello, her brother has not much time left to give her. Two or three hours' instruction a day dwindle to a snatched half-hour between engagements. In the evenings he is often too tired to act as her accompanist.

'You must practice, Lina! Practice!' he nevertheless exhorts her. 'For we have not much time before the Season begins, and I will need you to rehearse the sopranos for me…'

They are doing *Judas Maccabaeus* in the New Rooms that year. If it proves a success, they will take it on to Bristol.

Then there is William's latest enthusiasm to contend with…

One day she comes home from market to find the house in an uproar. A dreadful hammering comes from the drawing-room. When she investigates, she finds William, assisted by two men in carpenter's aprons, busily engaged in building a structure out of wood. The floor of the room (which she has turned out only the day before) is now strewn with shavings and sawdust.

'*Ach, was ist los?*' she cries, forgetting her English in her amazement at seeing the house given over to such activity.

'Lina, this is Mr Stanley and his son,' says William calmly. 'They are helping me to build the stand for the seven-foot telescope… Why, Lina, where are you going?'

For an even more unpleasant sound than the banging of hammers upon nails now forces itself upon her. Leaving her basket at the bottom of the stairs, she follows the shrill complaining note to its source, in the front bedroom. Here, she finds the furniture all topsy-turvy, and her brother Alexander grinding an eye-piece out of brass. As she watches, in horrified fascination, sparks fly out from the turning-machine, and a smell of hot metal arises.

'How are we to live, with such a riot going on?' she demands of William, who—typically—sees nothing amiss.

'Come, Lina, do not distress yourself,' he replies. 'You know it is only for a few weeks, until we have completed the trials for the new telescope. Besides,' he adds, with his customary air of sweet reasonableness, 'we have left the kitchen quite clear...'

Of course, that does not last long. Soon she is obliged to prepare their dinner surrounded by the impedimenta of the instrument-maker's trade. One day, searching for her largest saucepan, in which to make soup, she finds it has been put to use as a receptacle for some noxious substance.

'*Lieber Gott*! What is it?'

She shoves the treacly mess under William's nose. He seems unperturbed.

'Oh, that. A mixture of copper, tin, brass, silver, and arsenic. The constituents needed for coating mirrors,' he adds helpfully. 'Unfortunately, I seem to have got the proportions wrong.'

How they do not all die of poisoning she cannot say.

But even though what was once a gentleman's home is now transformed into a Factory, there is still room in it for music—William sees to that. Indeed, he has little choice but to see to it, for there is no income to be had from star-gazing. Throughout that summer of 1773, he is working harder than ever, rehearsing the soloists for the winter concerts, as well as taking on more pupils for violin and hautbois. One day, Caroline comes in, all over dust from the walk home, to a sound so exquisite and unearthly it seems as if an angel must have descended from heaven to give voice to it.

She stands stock-still in the hall, listening to the notes floating down from above; unable to breathe for the beauty of it.

In the parlour, she finds her brother, and Miss Farinelli. She has had only glimpsed the famous singer once before, during rehearsals at the Rooms. Then, Miss Farinelli was decently clad; it is a little startling to see her legs in breeches. Her face is very pretty, thinks Caroline: round and girlish, with a fresh colour, that appears to have nothing to do with rouge. And how tall she is! Such long-limbed elegance cannot but make Caroline feel the inadequacy of her own stature.

'How beautifully you sing...'

'*Grazie*.' The large dark eyes regard her thoughtfully. 'Your brother tells me you sing very prettily, too.'

Caroline feels herself blushing. 'My brother exaggerates. I am but a beginner.'

'Ah.' The rosebud lips make a charming little *moue*. 'We were all beginners once, no?'

After their distinguished visitor has gone, Caroline remarks on the former's attire: is the lady performing Cherubino, perhaps? 'For she is much too pretty to play a boy, in my opinion…'

William stares at her for a moment; then he bursts out laughing.

'O Lina, Lina,' he gasps, when his fit is done. 'What a precious goose you are…'

He wipes his eyes, and tells her the truth about Farinelli.

When she understands what it is he means (for he is obliged to be circumspect in his account), her eyes fill with tears.

'O, the poor creature! I cannot believe that anyone could be so cruelly used in the service of Art…'

William shrugs. 'It is the way of things in Italy. And what a voice! You heard it, Lina. Did you not think it miraculous?'

'I would not call it a miracle, after such a sacrifice,' she says.

Aside from her mathematical studies and her singing, there are also dancing lessons to contend with. These, she suspects, are all part of William's campaign to drill her into becoming a Gentlewoman—and as such, she at first resists them. For although she has always been light on her feet—a consequence, no doubt, of her small stature—and had danced, as a child, at family weddings, still she feels awkward when anything more complicated than the country dances of her youth is called for. The idea that she might have to display her dancing skills—or lack of them—at some fashionable evening party fills her with dread.

'But *why* must I learn dancing?' she cries. 'I will have no call to dance, if I am to make my living as a singer…'

'All ladies must know how to dance,' William tells her, with uncharacteristic severity. 'You are no exception. If you are to live here with me in Bath, I cannot allow you to be thought deficient in anything.'

And so, with the excellent Miss Fleming's help, she is adding to her repertoire of steps the circling mazes of the minuet, the leaping steps of the gavotte, and the stately advancing-and-retreating of the sarabande. In truth, these are not so very different from the jigs, polkas and mazurkas she can recall her father playing to her on his violin. Before long, she finds that dancing, too, has gone from being a unwelcome duty to being a keenly anticipated pleasure.

Her transformation into an exemplary member of her Sex is further advanced when, at William's insistence, she is sent to London, in the care of Mrs Colnbrook. They are to attend the Opera every night for a fortnight—or, failing that, the theatre. Only thus, in her brother's view, will she come to understand what will be expected of her, as a performer. In addition, Caroline knows, he hopes that exposure to the icy correctness of Mrs Colnbrook's conduct might have a beneficial effect on his sister's behaviour. For there are times when (she suspects) he thinks her manners lacking in polish.

Her London trip begins promisingly enough, with visits to Covent Garden (where she sees a new comedy by Mr Goldsmith, which perplexes her extremely) and Drury Lane (where she is disappointed not to see Mr Garrick play King Lear). There are concerts at the Pantheon, featuring the famous Leoni, and Mr Crosdel, on the Violoncello. As for the opera—there are performances twice a week at the King's Theatre. At William's insistence, they go to hear Millico sing.

This time she knows enough not to confuse his voice with that of a woman's.

In addition to these refined pleasures, there are other, less elevated, amusements. They walk up the Mall in St James's Park; she ruins her shoes on the gravel. They go to look at the Palace, but the King and Queen are not at home. They go shopping for silks in Covent Garden for Mrs Colnbrook's new gown. They drink tea with Lady This, and Mrs That, and attended at least one fashionable *ridotto*.

London—when she is able to evade Mrs Colnbrook's censorious eye—amuses her very much indeed. She likes the people, who seem a lot more extreme in their affectations, and extravagant in their dress, than the citizens of Bath; and she likes the buildings, which seem to be going up overnight, so rapid is their construction all over the city. When she remarks on this, Mrs Colnbrook says that it is because so many of the older buildings are unstable—some quite dangerously so. Why, only the other day a whole row of houses collapsed in Cheapside, killing several of the inhabitants, it was said. Not that that, Mrs Colnbrook adds, with a supercilious smile, is a very great loss, it being such a very *low* district.

Still, it will be an advantage to everyone when such horrors are all pulled down.

For her own part, Caroline likes the mixture of old and new; the co-existence of splendour and squalor. It seems a city always on the brink of re-inventing itself; full of coarse life, of vigour. Of course, elegance is also to be found here, in the broad sweep of Nash's terraces, or in the magnificence of Hanover Square. But there is vulgarity, too—of a kind seldom to be observed in Bath: the gold-painted railings of the houses in Berkeley Square, which seem designed for no other purpose than to advertise their owners' wealth; the no less gaudily-painted faces of the fashionable ladies one encountered everywhere—in the arcades at the Royal Exchange or at Covent Garden. She thought they must be women of the town, until Mrs Colnbrook put her right...

Here, it is as if everything and anything were possible.

In the pleasure gardens at Ranelagh one night, she and Mrs Colnbrook and the Fishers watch the fireworks. Green, red, gold, and violet, they burst upon the night sky in a shower of artificial stars, to appreciative gasps from the crowd. It is bitterly cold. Even wrapped up as she is, in a fur-trimmed cloak she has borrowed from the youngest Miss Fisher, she feels her face and hands turn to ice. She cares nothing for this. All she cares for is to stand and see the coloured stars fly up, in a whirl of dazzling light. One, shooting higher than the rest, traces its silver arc above the dark city, as if a hand swept a pen across a page.

How could she ever grow tired of such sights?

But the proposed two weeks lengthen into six, owing to heavy falls of snow, which make the roads impassable beyond Devizes. Thrown together as much as they are, she and Mrs Colnbrook grow weary of one another's company. Then there is the question of money. William has given her an allowance—to be spent, as far as possible, on educating herself, he says. By which he means attending as many concerts as possible—what could be more agreeable?

Being a man, he has not thought to consider the additional expense that such occasions necessitate. The hiring of chairs, and post-chaises to convey one to the entertainment, and the running-up of hairdressers' and dressmakers' bills (for one cannot wear the same dress fourteen nights in a row) are just some of these hidden costs. Added to which is the fact—unfortunate, but true—that one cannot exist upon air, least of all in London. Her appetites are modest—but even she requires more than a cup of tea in the morning, and a bowl of bread-and-milk at night. Chophouses are expensive, for one on a meagre budget.

She takes to smuggling a slice of cold tongue or a piece of pie left over from dinner back to her room each night, for breakfast the next day; until Mrs Colnbrook complains about the smell.

One day she contrives an escape—for Mrs Colnbrook has woken up with the toothache—and, leaving the polite environs of Bruton Street behind, walks through Covent Garden and along Fleet Street to St Paul's. It is a clear, cold, day; the snow-clouds having lifted at last to reveal a sky of brilliant blue, and a pale sunshine washes the stone fronts of the fine new buildings along the Strand. Although it has not yet struck eight, the streets are crowded—mostly with roughly dressed working people, it being too early in the day for fashionable Society. She is glad of this, being plainly dressed herself, and thus inconspicuous among them.

At Aldwych, she buys a paper screw of hot chestnuts from a street seller, as much to warm her frozen hands, as because she is hungry—although she is hungry. But the joy of being out-of-doors on such a morning makes up for her inadequate breakfast.

She feels light, untrammelled, *happy*, for the first time in weeks. To be here, alone and free, in this glorious city, is more than she could ever have dared to hope for. Now, with a whole morning at her disposal, she will revisit Wren's masterpiece, whose airy dome had so captivated her the day she arrived in London—already two years ago, although she can scarcely believe so much time to have passed since then. Already, she can see its distinctive ice-blue Shape rising against the bluer sky. Its beauty, William said, was as much the result of mathematics, as of artistic vision.

'You see before you a marvel of engineering, Lina,' he had told her, on that first, never-to-be-forgotten visit. 'For they said it could not be done—to build so large a dome, unsupported by pillars or buttresses. They said it would fall—but it did not fall,' he had added, with a satisfied air.

But Ludgate Hill proves impassable, for a horse has slipped on the icy cobblestones and broken its leg, tumbling cart and driver into the street, and preventing any other vehicle from getting through. The noise is intolerable—the screams of the poor injured beast mingling with the shouts of coachmen urging their horses on. Though her six weeks in the city has made her more used to crowds than before, she still dislikes such scenes, whose volatility too often leads to violence. Only last week, returning from drinking tea in Brook Street, she and Mrs Colnbrook had been trapped in their carriage for half an hour by the mob on its way to Tyburn.

They were going to see Gentleman Jack sent to his Maker, said the coachman. It promised to be a fine show. For in addition to all the gold watches and diamond rings he had stolen, the rascal had married his wife's sister, without waiting for his wife to die first. Ever so many songs had been written about him, and he himself was to give a speech at the foot of the gallows...

He seemed surprised that they were not inclined to view the entertainment for themselves.

Intent on getting out of the press of the crowd, Caroline turns down Bride Lane, intending to skirt around the main thoroughfare, and thus emerge—if her calculations are correct—in St Paul's churchyard. Here, the houses are narrower and closer together, and the sunshine which has made her walk so pleasant up till now is suddenly extinguished. She likes London—but this dank and gloomy passage is the worst of London. The sooner she is out of it and back in broad daylight again, the better...

It happens before she has time to think.

A figure comes hurtling out of an alley. It collides with her, knocking the breath from her body. Fearfully, she turns to confront her assailant—and sees it is in fact a child: a boy. For a moment they look at one another. He is very dirty, she sees; but young. No more than seven or eight years old. His eyes are large, and frightened—which amuses her, a little. For when had she ever frightened anyone?

Under one arm, this strange frightened boy is holding a dirty bundle. When she gestures at him to reveal what it is, he at first tries to run away. But, small as she is, she is more than a match for him; she holds him fast.

'Now,' she says firmly. 'Show me what it is that you have there.'

Unwrapped, the bundle turns out to contain a scrawny-looking chicken, missing its head.

'I see,' says Caroline. 'You have been shopping for your mother—not so?'

The boy stares at her blankly. Her accent is not good, she knows, but even so…

Just then, comes a shout from the alley: a man's voice, raised in anger. A look of terror crosses the child's face, and he squirms away.

Suddenly, she sees it all.

'Quick!' she cries, letting go of him at once. 'You must go that way! There are many people. It is safer, so…'

She points back at the way she has come—and this time the boy catches her meaning, for—clutching his stolen chicken—he runs, as if the Devil were at his heels, towards Ludgate Hill.

He is barely out of sight when a large, unshaven man in a stained butcher's apron bursts out of the alley.

'Seen a boy?' he shouts. His face is red, his eyes bloodshot: a man easily provoked to acts of violence, she surmises.

Caroline's experience of men like this—that is, of one man in particular—has taught her to command her feelings, even when afraid.

Calmly, she points in the direction of the river.

'He went that way,' she says. 'But I do not think that you will catch him now.'

III

Caroline's English, though a good deal better than when she first arrived in Bath, is still awkward, as far as making conversation goes. On the rare occasions when she voices an opinion in company, she is all too aware of the halting pace of her utterances, and of the barbarous accent she brings to them. Her interlocutors are usually kind—she is very much improved, says Mrs De Chair—but there is a condescension in such remarks; and in the sly looks and amused twitches of the lips to which her more inelegant sentences give rise. Thus she is wary whom she speaks to; and careful not to overreach herself.

She cannot bear the thought that she might look a fool.

The intimacies of friendship are therefore unavailable to her—for how can she express subtleties of feeling, without the words to express them? Used as she is to her own company, she still feels the want of an intimate friend, in whom to confide. In Hannover, Fräulein Carsten had been her friend, but she had died of a Consumption, at the age of eighteen.

What had they talked about, the two of them? She cannot remember, now. Girls' secrets, she supposes. A shared partiality for the handsome young Pastor, or for the poetry of Schiller. What she does recall is the sound of Ottilie's cough, beneath her window. Poor Ottilie! She had been ailing, even then. There had been days when she had not the strength to do more than lie on the sofa, her face as pale as wax under her golden curls.

'What a tiresome creature I am,' she would say, patting her lips with the lace handkerchief she always had about her. 'I am sure you must be tired of spending your time with such a one as I.'

After she was gone, Carolina had wept bitter tears—as much, she sees, for herself, as for her lost companion. For without Ottilie, there was nobody to whom she could tell her sorrows; no kindred Soul to make bearable the humiliations of her life.

With Ottilie gone, she was more alone than she had ever been.

Now she has come to England, there is no one she can call her friend. With her brother alone is she able to unburden her heart. They share, of course, both a lineage and a language; although William prefers to converse in English most of the time. But when a word or phrase proves elusive (as it often does, for Caroline) he is willing to switch between their native and adopted tongues.

'Concentrate, Lina—concentrate!' he exhorts her, as she struggles to express what it is she wants to say. 'For you know the words are all locked up inside your head, waiting to come out. You need only reflect a moment, and the word you require will come...'

That is all very well, she thinks but does not say, when one has all the time in the world to reflect. But conversation is like dancing: to think on it too much is to inhibit performance.

She is tired of the patient smiles which attend her efforts to give expression to thoughts more complex, say, than the continued clemency of the weather, or the pleasing effect of new ribbons on a bonnet. So she confines herself to banalities—or says nothing at all. At least William does not talk to her of bonnets.

But with her brilliant and unworldly sibling, one seldom gets to dictate the choice of topic. He will discuss music, it is true—but generally only with regard to some technical problem to be surmounted; and even this, of late, cannot hold his interest for long. No. If one wishes to engage William in conversation, one is limited to the universal. With the petty details of human feeling, he is not unduly concerned. But with the stars; with the movements of the planets and the measurement of celestial objects as yet unrecorded, he is entirely enthralled. Everything that has been written on the subject he has read, and will eagerly discuss.

If the universe were the face of a loved one, and he an ardent suitor, he could not have pored over its every feature and contour with more assiduous devotion.

But if Astronomy is a beloved mistress, stealing all her brother's leisure time, Music is a demanding wife. Having taken over from Mr Linley as Director of public concerts, with a full programme of oratorios and other entertainments to prepare, William has his work cut out for him. But it is half-heartedly done. Much of the time, he seems distracted, as if the effort of dragging his attention back from the contemplation of celestial matters to the intricacies of rehearsing a choir, or performing a Sonata on the harpsichord, were altogether too much for him. Thus he will come in, after a day of such activities, and sit straight down at his grinding-stone, without even taking time to change his dress. When remonstrated with for the consequent ruination of his shirts—which become spattered with pitch, and have their lace ruffles torn—he will shake his head in mild surprise, as if he has only just that moment noticed that he has his best clothes on.

Disappointing as it is for Caroline to see her brother so preoccupied with scientific matters, to the neglect of her own studies and the detriment of her musical career, still she cannot but find his enthusiasm contagious. Whatever she herself has in hand—practising a solo part or skinning a rabbit—she will set aside, in order to admire her brother's latest endeavour... which is becoming, increasingly, *her* endeavour, too.

One night he calls her outside to look through the new telescope. It is at Walcot, whence they had moved in the summer of '74—for there is a large garden behind the house, which is ideal for the twenty-foot instrument. The construction of this had taken many weeks, and had turned the garden into a trampled mess of towering spars and ladders rising overhead, and of mud and sawdust underfoot. Flowerbeds—not to mention her poor rose-trellis—had had to be sacrificed. For, William said, there was only just enough room for the scaffolding that supported the telescope, as it was.

But he professed himself delighted with the finished article—although to Caroline it resembled nothing so much as a great cannon, with its muzzle pointed at the sky.

The first time she had ascended the ladder, at William's insistence, she had been terrified that she would fall. To be fifteen feet off the ground, on a rickety wooden structure, with the wind whipping her skirts about her, was not an experience anyone with the smallest sense of self-preservation could be expected to enjoy.

'Hold on, Lina—hold on!' she had heard William crying from below. And—no less superfluously—'Do not look down! Keep looking straight ahead, and all will become clear…'

In the event, she had been trembling so much that it was an effort to keep her balance, let alone to see anything through the eye-piece of the instrument. One needed two hands to adjust this; and she found, on this occasion, that her hands could not be spared from holding on. Despite William's exhortations to her that it was quite safe—she would not fall—she had found herself quite unable to make any kind of observations at all.

'Never mind, Lina. You will get used to it in time,' William had assured her, when—to her enormous relief—she felt the ground beneath her feet once more. 'You will soon be running up and down the ladders with no more thought than if you were climbing the stairs at home. It is a great pity,' he had added, as if the idea had just occurred to him, 'that we cannot dress you as a boy. It would be a great deal more practical for the purpose.'

She had said nothing to this, thinking that she already looked enough of a fright as it was, with her frock all torn and dusty from her exertions, without being made to wear breeches. With William, one never knew what a chance remark might lead to. To him, nothing mattered except to achieve what he had in mind; everything else—even a sister's modesty—could be sacrificed to that end.

On this particular evening—some weeks after that unsuccessful first ascent—he has been testing the instrument's light-gathering power. It had just been fitted with a newly polished twelve-inch mirror.

'Come, Carolina, come!'

She knows at once from his tone of voice that he has found something that pleases him.

Dropping whatever it is she is doing, she follows him outside, to where the immense bulk of the telescope stands silhouetted against the night sky. Even now, it is a shock to see how high it towers over everything around: the house, the garden wall, the neighbouring houses…

William seems barely able to contain his excitement, half-dragging her across the frosty grass—for it is now midwinter—and hopping from foot to foot in his impatience, as he waits for her to ascend the ladder. She is more confident now than at her first attempt, but still she does so with caution.

'Tell me what it is you see.'

She adjusts the angle of the eye-piece (for she is a good head-and-shoulders shorter than he is), and puts her eye to it, looking first out of the corner of her eye, to accustom her gaze to this mode of seeing.

At first she can see nothing; then a cloudy shape comes into view.

She frowns; blinks; looks again.

'It looks like a kind of mist… a luminous mass.'

'Yes.'

She can hear the satisfaction in his voice.

'It is not very distinct…'

'It is not. Wait a while. Then you will see.'

As her eye grows dark-adapted, she is able to make out the object in question more clearly… or rather, the *objects* in question. For that there are many—perhaps too many to enumerate—is now apparent.

'Could it be a mass of stars?'

'Bravo, Lina! You are right! It is indeed a mass of stars. That is what we call a nebula, a formless cloud. Is it not beautiful? See! It appears at first to be a single ball of light, but it is made up of a great number of smaller objects. The scattering of loose stars around the edges is what gives it that misty look…'

'It is very fine,' she says.

'It is more than fine—it is magnificent!'

She laughs, suddenly struck by the absurdity of it all: to be standing fifteen feet up, in the middle of a garden in winter, looking at the stars… How strange and wonderful my life is, she thinks.

'It is, as you say, magnificent.'

Her feet, in their thin-soled boots, are beginning to lose all feeling. It would not do to lose her balance, at this height. Gingerly, she begins to descend.

'I believe that all of these as yet unknown nebulae will eventually fall to the power of my new telescope and resolve into stars,' her brother goes on. 'There are many such in the heavens. Messier lists them, in his Catalogue.'

He takes her by the shoulders and draws her away from the foot of the scaffold, then, scrambling up the ladder once more, reapplies his own eye to the glass.

'There are forty-five in his latest catalogue. But not, I think, this one. *This*'—his voice shakes slightly, with excitement—'has never before been seen by human eye.'

Even in the darkness, she can tell that he is smiling.

'Messier's list is a Frenchman's conceit,' he says, his voice drifting down faintly from above her head. 'It is merely a collection of what he has come across while following comets—the brighter coloured pebbles he has found upon the beach as he looked at seashells. I am convinced there may be hundreds, even thousands, like it.'

He returns to earth at last, and they begin to walk back towards the house, her brother still talking with animation of the discoveries he has made, and of those he would make in the future.

'The way we can seek them out—these remarkable nebulae—is not to chance upon them while looking at something else, but to search diligently everywhere in the sky and record everything that we see. For indeed everything in our survey will have its turn to be discovered—nebula, double star, comet... And if we look at everything, we will in due course discover the rare and valuable. With an instrument of such power, we will be able to explore the furthest reaches of the heavens.'

'There is no one else who could do as much,' she says loyally—although it is no more than the truth.

'Think of it, Lina!' She has never known him so delighted with a night's work. 'We may even come across nurseries of new-born stars!'

She smiles at the image this conjures up, of the baby-stars in their cradles; although later she comes to understand that this, too, is an example of her brother's genius. For if there are newborn stars, then there must also be stars of middle years. Ageing stars. Dying stars. Stars reborn out of that dead matter...

That the Universe is born, grows old, and dies—is subject to change, in fact—may turn out to be the most far-reaching of William Herschel's discoveries. And she, it seems, is to assist him in this—becoming in the process (who can say?) a Discoverer in her own right.

They do not remain long at Walcot, as it turns out—the house being too far out, and not roomy enough for workshops. By the following winter, they have returned to New King Street. Caroline, for one, is glad. Being here, at the centre of things, is what she prefers. And they are certainly at the centre of things...

For William's circle of scientific friends is increasing rapidly. Foremost amongst these is Nevil Maskelyne. 'The very devil of a fellow,' William pronounces him, after their first meeting, at which she has not been present. 'I should like to know what you think of him, Lina.'

With this report of the eminent astronomer's character ringing in her ears, she feels some trepidation when he is presented to her.

But in fact there is nothing devilish in his manner at all.

'Your brother tells me you have been assisting him with his sweeps,' he says, with what seems to her the utmost civility. 'He is fortunate to have so assiduous a helpmeet.'

'You are kind. But I do very little except write things down,' she demurs.

The Astronomer Royal smiles.

'So much of what we do consists in exactly that,' he replies. 'For without accurate records, what use would any of our observations be?'

Sir Henry Englefield is another regular visitor to New King Street; as is Mr Bryant, Dr Blagden and Dr Lysons. These are now in the habit of turning up most evenings—either singly or in pairs—to sit talking, late into the night, about the best method for calculating distances between stars, or measuring the rings of Saturn. Sometimes, the conversation gets so heated it sounds to her like quarrelling.

On one occasion, she knocks at the door of William's study, to ask if the gentlemen want coffee, and hears her brother shout,

'No, no, no! You *haff* not understood...'—excitement making his accent more pronounced than usual, even to her ears.

She knocks again, a little louder. This time, there is silence.

The door opens, and William looks out.

'Ah, Lina. Come in, come in...'

She would rather not go in. She has only come to ask about the refreshments...

But he insists.

'You know Dr Maskelyne of course... and Sir Henry, and Dr Blagden...'

She curtseys, wishing the ground would swallow her up.

'Dr Maskelyne takes exception to my idea that the Moon must be inhabited,' says William. 'Indeed, he has called me a Lunatick to my face...'

'My dear Miss Herschel, I assure you I said no such thing...'

'But I am in hopes of convincing him—with your help, Lina.'

She stares at him in horror. What is he saying?

'If you would summarise for the benefit of these learned gentlemen my reasons for believing that the Moon is habitable, I am sure they will admit the error of their ways.'

'I...' She feels herself growing red as fire. 'I believe it is because the similarity of the Moon's geography to our own—with mountains, and rivers, clearly discernible through a powerful telescope—makes it entirely likely that... that it possesses a breathable atmosphere, and that there are Creatures upon it resembling ourselves...'

'Excellently put, Lina...'

'And convincingly so,' says Dr Maskelyne, with the ghost of a smile. 'I can see I shall have to reconsider my view—shall not you, Blagden?'

'Indubitably,' replies that gentleman.

'Now, Lina, since you have finished dazzling us with your learning and good sense, I think you might fetch us some coffee,' beams her sibling, his good humour restored by the general concurrence with his opinion.

To the great credit of these learned gentlemen, there is never an eyebrow raised at the fact that her opinion should be thus solicited. If, indeed, any of them wonder at it, they are much too polite to say so. Even in those early years, before she has done anything in her own right to deserve such notice, she is listened to—although as a rule she is reticent; not wanting to be thought ridiculous, either because of her meagre understanding, or on account of her Sex.

On her birthday that year, William presents her with her own telescope: a pretty little thing of turned wood and brass, in a shagreen case.

'I designed it with you in mind, dear Lina,' he says, with such obvious delight in his own ingenuity that she feels quite ashamed of her own more subdued reaction to the gift. 'For you see, it is small and light enough for you to handle without effort.'

Touched as she is by his thoughtfulness (for when had she ever received such a handsome present? The only 'presents' she ever had from her brother Jacob were kicks and curses), privately she wonders what use, if any, she will make of it. For she is busier than ever with copying music—most recently, the vocal parts of Samson. Her practising she fits in when she can. There is precious little time for observing the stars.

She knows she is not beautiful, although her figure is not unpleasing—slender as a young girl's; and she has always been proud of her hair, which is copious, and naturally curling. But the smallpox has ruined her complexion; even though the scars are much less than they had been.

'My poor little *mädchen*,' her father had said to her one day, when she was sixteen, or thereabouts. 'You must never expect to marry, for you have neither face nor fortune... Unless, perhaps,' he added, by way of softening the blow, 'some elderly man will take you in later life, as his companion, on account of your good heart...'

At the time, the words had stung; although she sees now that he was merely trying to prepare her for the disappointments which must follow. In his fondness for her, he had perhaps forgotten that she was a young girl, like any other, with a young girl's vanity. He had not meant to hurt her, of that she is sure.

Still, her face will never be her fortune...

That there are women far more ill-favoured than she—even in Bath, that Temple of Fashion—she is well aware; she has not the resources at her command to make the best of herself, however. What little money there is coming into the household, cannot be spent on fine clothes and jewels. A new ribbon to tie in her hair, or a bunch of violets to pin at her breast, are all the concessions she is able to make to Love.

Not that she has ever thought very much about Love, until that moment. Her father had said she would not marry, and so she does not expect to; nor does she expect to enjoy the pleasures that precede marriage. The smiles and nods, and the sending of little notes between interested parties, with which most other young women seem to concern themselves, are of no concern to her. She does not expect Love, and so her heart is undefended against it; and Love's arrow strikes her with a force all the greater…

IV

It is William who introduces her to Edward Pigott—just as he had introduced her to every other passion of her life. It is at the house in New King Street. She walks into the parlour, where William is sitting with an unknown gentleman, to ask what her brother requires for dinner. She is all over flour from the baking (afterwards, she is mortified to find a smudge on her nose), and wearing her oldest gown. Not fit to be seen in company, in fact—especially by such a one as this elegantly attired visitor, who favours her with so charming a smile, as he rises to make his bow.

She would have made her escape at once, muttering something about having to see to the pie, but William will not hear of it.

'Come in, Lina, come in,' he says. 'Sit down and rest a moment. I was just telling Mr Pigott of our recent discoveries in the matter of variable stars. My sister is my assistant in all my researches,' he explains to their guest. 'Indeed, she is shaping up to be a very creditable astronomer in her own right, are you not, Lina?'

She blushes and denies it, conscious all the while of the stranger's bright brown eyes upon her.

Then William, bless the man, goes on to embarrass her further:

'But it is as a musician that my sister presently excels. You must be sure to come and hear her in *Messiah*—she is our principal Soprano, you know...'

'Miss Herschel is evidently a woman of many accomplishments,' says Mr Pigott, with a smile.

How handsome he is! She can hardly bring herself to meet his eyes, for fear their glance will undo her.

'Lina is an angel,' says William (ridiculous man!), 'for she sings like one—and she also cooks like one...'

This, a timely reminder of her duty, gives her an excuse to escape. She begs the gentlemen not to get up, but she has to see to her baking...

Disregarding this injunction, Mr Pigott rises to his feet once more.

'A great pleasure to make your acquaintance, Miss Herschel,' he says.

She ducks her head and mutters some reply—she can't now remember what.

That night, as she lies awake in her narrow bed under the eaves, she goes through the conversation once more in her head: the sound of his voice; the turn of his head as he had looked at her; the way he had smiled as he took his leave... He is quite unlike any other man she has met before, she thinks—for though young, he is evidently far from foolish, as are most of the young men she has met so far.

She allows herself to hope that she might see him again; although that will depend, of course, on William.

William has given her ten pounds to buy a dress; for she is to make her debut a few nights later as principal Soprano, and all eyes will be upon her. 'O but Lina—I insist,' he says, when she protests (knowing as she does only too well how far such a sum could be made to stretch in their monthly budget). 'I cannot have it said that the sister of the Director of the Bath choir is dressed worse than the other ladies. Miss Cantelo will be there, you know,' he adds, perhaps unhelpfully—for that lady is renowned not only for her voice, but for her beauty. *She* has no need of a fine frock to enhance her looks...

'Here. Take it,' William goes on, his good humour turning suddenly to impatience. 'And do not say that I never indulge you in frills and fripperies. For I know you women like such things,' he concludes, giving her a kiss. Although *how* he knew it was hard to fathom, given that there is no woman—apart from herself—in his life, and she can hardly be accounted a typical specimen of her sex.

The dress is black silk, quite plain, and very becoming. Having no diamonds to display upon her bosom like Miss Cantelo, she makes do with a plain gold locket, which looks very well. Her hair she leaves *au naturel,* which is becoming the fashion.

'Miss Herschel! I declare I hardly knew you,' says Mr Palmer, when she arrives at the Rooms. 'Upon my Soul, you are an Ornament to the Stage.'

She had not thought herself nervous until that moment. Has she not rehearsed her part until she knows it backwards? William has seen to that. Five hours, six hours a day she sang—until it seemed as if she must lose the power of ordinary speech altogether, so attuned has her voice become to singing.

'I fear I will shortly grow feathers and become a bird,' she says to her brother, after one such session, at the end of which he pronounced himself satisfied with her first solo.

Distracted as he is—for there is but a week to go, and fifty singers to rehearse, to say nothing of the orchestra—he smiles at that. 'As long as you do not fly away from me, little Bird, I shall be content,' he replies. 'For without you, all my efforts will come to naught.'

This is, of course, untrue; with or without her, he would have achieved what he wanted to. Although she is willing to accept that her contribution might have helped him achieve it rather sooner…

'You are my right hand, Lina,' he is in the habit of saying. 'With you by my side, there is nothing I cannot do.'

Well, she will admit that much at least. As a 'right hand', she has her uses—whether it is copying parts for singers (eighty, at the last count), turning the pages of his score, as he sits at the harpsichord of an evening, or fashioning a pie-crust (for no one else, her brother insists, has such a light hand at pastry as dear Lina). Manual dexterity is certainly required in the furtherance of William's latest enthusiasm—that is, for telescopes. For he has pronounced himself dissatisfied with the mirrors of all that he has tried. The only solution is to grind his own.

This can take up to sixteen hours. An inhuman length of time, for any task—let alone one which makes the shirt stick to the labourer's back with the exertion, and the muscles in his arms seize up with pain, when at last it is over. So arduous is the exercise, that the sweat often drips down his face, as he sits at the grinding-stone, so that the drops sizzle onto the hot metal. *Then* her 'right hand' is required to wipe the salty liquid from his eyes, and to bring sips of water to his parched lips. Morsels of food, too—for after eight hours or so, with another eight still to go, he is faint with hunger and exhaustion. Other bodily necessities she is not able to attend to, for even William baulks at asking her to hold the bucket for him, and—worse—unbutton his breeches, so that he might achieve relief.

Fortunately, their brother Alex is on hand to provide at least this service, while William keeps both hands on his precious mirror.

'It is gratifying to know that that I am so indispensable,' says Alexander.

Caroline also needs her hands—right or left, it does not matter—and her eyes as well, to read to William as he labours, for it is tedious, as well as tiring, work. So far they have got through *Don Quixote*, the Arabian Nights entertainments, and several novels by Mr Fielding and Dr Sterne.

O, she is a dutiful apprentice in all of this.

Although, knowing, as she does, that mixture of charm and obduracy with which her elder brother drives all before him, she is also aware that, had she and Alex not been there to serve him, others would have done as well in their place. Certainly, William is not deterred by the difficulties of anything he sets out to do; indeed, it might be supposed that he does not perceive them. It is as if all the optimism of their father's character has survived in him unchecked, with none of their mother's black humours—from which she herself, she knows, has not escaped entirely...

Now, something of that darkness threatens to overwhelm her, as she stands there, in the wings, listening to the unmistakable sounds of a theatre filling up with people: the buzz of voices, as those taking their places greet one another, mingling with the nervous twanging of strings and tremulous fluting of wind instruments, as the orchestra begins its tuning-up.

All of a sudden, her palms are wet. Why had she ever agreed to go through with this? Beside her, she can hear Miss Cantelo going through her last-minute vocal exercises, their *Oo-Aah-Ee* masked by the noise of the choir taking their seats. In a moment, it will be their turn...

She glances at the girl—her technique is good; which is only to be expected from a pupil of Miss Grassi's—and receives a smile in return.

'Good luck,' mouths Miss Cantelo.

It is on the tip of Caroline's tongue to say that she does not need it; for she is well-prepared enough. But the words die on her lips, as there comes a another sound from beyond the curtain: the ripple of applause as the Director—that is, William—takes his place at the harpsichord, from where he is also to conduct.

It is their cue.

Stepping out from behind the curtain, she is momentarily dazzled by a blaze of light and colour; the applause which accompanies it seems, to her heightened senses, like a clap of thunder. Somehow, she manages to find her chair without stumbling; Mr Brett and Mr Wilson then resume theirs, and the first, stately chords of the Overture sound. She closes her eyes a moment, letting the music flow over her. How beautiful it is! Although she has heard it a thousand times, it never ceases to move her.

Then Mr Brett stands up again for his first solo—

Comfort ye, comfort ye, my people...

—and from that moment on, everything is as it should be. For are they not, all of them—singers, musicians, and audience alike—caught up in a world of sound: a perfect, glittering structure, which moves according to the same principles as the Universe itself? Its harmonies are expressed through them, in the plucking of strings and the sounding of flutes and the blending of voices, just as those of the celestial realm are expressed through the movement of the stars and planets, which—so Kepler says—produces a music of its own.

And the glory, the glory of the Lord...

Behind her, rise the sweet voices of the Trebles. Training them has fallen to her, and so she knows their part as well as her own. She is glad, at least, that they have not fallen short on F Sharp…

Raising her eyes from her score (for her own moment of glory will not come for quite some time), she meets those of One she had not thought to see. A sensation as of falling overwhelms her momentarily. Perhaps she is imagining things… She risks another look, and is rewarded with a smile. It is certainly he—looking handsomer than ever, in a coat of French blue. But why has William made no mention of the fact that Mr Pigott was likely to be among the audience?

Unless Mr Pigott has other reasons for attending, than just to please his friend…

She feels herself begin to blush, as if she were eighteen, not eight-and-twenty. What a spectacle she is making of herself! She dares not look up again, for fear of encountering those bright brown eyes. Can it be that he has come to see her? She hardly dares to think it; and yet what other conclusion could she come to? Now Mr Wilson is clearing his throat for 'Thus Saith the Lord'. All too soon, it will be her turn to rise.

But who may abide the day of his coming?
And who shall stand when he appeareth?

Ridiculous. She is shaking like a leaf. How she is ever going to get through the whole performance without falling down in a dead faint she cannot say…

Except that, when the moment comes, all her nervousness falls away. She knows it the moment she opens her mouth, for the recitative. It is (she thinks afterwards) as if she were possessed by something greater than herself—as if she has become, in that instant, a mere vessel—a conduit for Sound. She has never sung better. Singing seems as natural as breathing—the pure notes flowing through her and out of her into the enraptured air.

And the angel said unto them, Fear not:
For behold, I bring you good tidings of great joy…

It is Joy she feels, in that moment—both in the unfettered expression of her Art, and in the knowledge that the one she loves is a witness to it.

It is for him—and him alone—she sings.

Afterwards, when the performance is ended and the crowd beginning to disperse, Edward Pigott comes over to offer his congratulations.

'I have enjoyed myself very much this evening,' he tells her.

'I am glad, Sir.'

'You have a beautiful voice,' he says- and it is as if he has complimented her person.

She blushes, and looks away, so that he should not see that she is blushing. Surely she does not imagine the admiration in his eyes?

'I am but one of many voices here, Sir...'

'Yes—but not all of them are singled out, as you have been, for so demanding a part...'

'Miss Herschel! Miss Herschel!'

It is Mr Palmer, the proprietor of the Bath theatre. She has never been less pleased to see him, although he is a pleasant enough gentleman. Now he rushes up to them, with another gentleman in tow.

'Miss Herschel... excuse my interrupting. But I was sure you would be glad of such an interruption...'

She composes her features into the semblance of a smile.

'Allow me to introduce my good friend Mr Simkins,' he goes on, indicating his companion. 'Mr Simkins is the manager of the Birmingham theatre...'

Mr Simkins, a portly gentleman, favours her with a bow.

'He has some good news for you, do you not, Mr Simkins?'

'I will leave you,' says Edward Pigott, in an undertone.

'O, do not go!' she cannot refrain from saying. 'I am sure my brother wants to speak to you...'

For there is William, coming towards them through a crowd of admirers, all wanting to press his hand.

Mr Simkins clears his throat, by way of recalling her attention to himself.

'I have much admired your singing tonight, Madam.'

'You are all politeness, Sir.'

'And I am come to offer you a contract to sing at our Festival this summer.'

'There!' cries Mr Palmer delightedly. 'Did I not tell you it was good news? Mr Simkins here wants Miss Herschel to sing for him in Birmingham,' he tells William.

'That is wonderful, Lina.'

'O, no!' she cries. 'That is... You are very kind, Sir. But I cannot leave my brother...'

'Nonsense, Lina.'

'I mean,' she goes on bravely, conscious of Edward Pigott's eyes upon her, 'I prefer not to sing except where my brother is the Conductor.'

'Very commendable, I am sure,' says Mr Simkins, although his disappointment is plain. 'Well, if you change your mind...'

Then he and Mr Palmer are gone, the latter throwing a reproachful glance over his shoulder.

'You need not have refused on my account, you know, Lina,' says William. 'It would have been a great chance for you—do you not think so, Pigott?'

'I am sure Miss Herschel knows her own mind,' replies their friend. 'And she will doubtless have singing engagements enough in Bath to fill her time.'

Caroline throws him a grateful glance. How well he understands her! Although there is one other reason why she has refused Mr Simkins's offer... For if Birmingham is a long way away from Bath, and her brother, it is even further from London, and Edward Pigott. Even for the sake of her music, she cannot bear the thought of being thus doubly exiled.

A week after the concert, there is to be a ball at the Assembly Rooms, to which all of Bath will be going—or so William says. He, still flushed with his success—for there have been kind remarks about the performance from the Marchioness of Lothian and others—is determined that the Herschel family should be well represented.

'Our brother Alexander is to be there—and you know he does not like dancing. Come, Lina, this is very remiss of you, to say you will not go—when you have been the toast of musical Society...'

'I have not said I will not go—only that I will not dance,' she replies.

'And why not? I defy anyone to find fault with your dancing. You are a credit to the estimable Miss Fleming.'

'Yes, but...'

'No more "buts", Lina. There is no need for you to be shy. Why, Miss Mahon will be there, with all her sisters—and Mrs Bates, too. You know you like Mrs Bates—you can talk to her about music. Mr Dubellomy is also to attend, and many other good friends...'

That is what she is afraid of. For of course, he will be there. Although he has heard her sing—which is the thing above all else that she does best—she is not sure she can bear to let him see her dance. Then she will be one amongst many young ladies—all doubtless far more accomplished (and prettier) than herself.

She would rather spend the evening star-gazing, when at least she can be sure she will not be *looked at*.

It is after eight when they arrive, and the country dances have begun. She has seldom seen the place so full. There are at least fifty couples dancing the Cotillion, and the chairs on either side of the ballroom are filled up. It seems as if, after all, she and her brothers will be spared the dancing. Alexander immediately announces his intention of going to watch the card-playing, while William goes to order their tea—for if they are not to dance, he says, they must have somewhere to sit down...

So it is that she is left alone for a moment. Idly watching the pairs of dancers, as they move along the floor—each crossing and re-crossing with the facing couple, to pleasing effect—she is unable to suppress a start at the sound of a familiar voice:

'Why, Miss Herschel, are you here?'

'I and the rest of Bath, it would seem, Sir,' she replies, without a tremor.

How strange that she is able to stand and talk to him like this, when all the time her heart is hammering like a mad thing...

'Will you dance—or do you prefer to watch others dance?'

'I...'

She is prevented from replying by the reappearance of William.

'Ah, Pigott. If you are not dancing, you might take my sister out. For she has a foolish notion that she will never get a partner...'

'I assure you...' She is almost too mortified to speak.

'Nothing would give me greater pleasure,' says Edward Pigott.

The musicians are tuning up for the next dance: a Sarabande. She remembers the patterns it makes—for it is all about patterns, Miss Fleming had said. Once you had those in your head, your feet would follow.

She holds out her hand to her partner. He smiles at her. In a trance of happiness, she lets him lead her onto the floor.

And while the dance lasts, she feels only that she is floating—as if her feet, instead of touching the floor, were gliding a little way above it. Aware of nothing but Edward's eyes; the feel of her hand in his; the elegance of his gestures, as—slowly, gracefully—they progress along the line of dancers. Intent as she is on the movements she herself is making, still she has leisure to notice the movements of others: the repeating patterns their bodies form—patterns doubled in the mirrors on the facing wall.

At last the music stops, to allow the dancers to catch their breath; she murmurs her thanks, and makes as if to rejoin her brothers.

'I hope you will permit me to have the next dance?' says Edward Pigott. 'Unless of course you are tired...'

'O no!' she says. 'I am not tired.'

'Then I am fortunate.'

The music starts again: an *Allemande*, in C Major; one of Haydn's. It is a favourite of hers; she has played it often enough on the harpsichord at home. Whether it is this happy familiarity, or the proximity of her partner, which effects the change, she cannot say—only that her dancing ceases to be a matter of steps remembered and patterns memorised, and becomes instinctive; a no less delightful mode of expression to her than her singing has always been. Now, it is as if the old familiar airs of her childhood have taken possession of her feet; she feels light, released from care.

She wishes she could go on dancing forever.

'Bravo, Lina!' says William, when—Hayden's mellifluous strains having come at last to an end—her partner returns her to her brothers' keeping. 'You see—you are not as bad a dancer as you had feared...'

'Sir, I must protest—Miss Herschel is an excellent dancer,' says Edward Pigott.

'Well, well, she is far from being the worst,' laughs William. 'Now, Pigott, will you join us for some tea? It is the least I can offer you, now that Lina has danced you off your legs...'

'Thank you,' replies the young man. 'That is, if Miss Herschel has had enough of dancing...'

She would much rather dance, of course; she cares nothing for tea. But to say so would be tantamount to throwing herself at his head...

She murmurs some reply.

'Perhaps,' goes on Edward Pigott, with the diffident air that so becomes him, 'when we have had our tea, Miss Herschel would favour me with the dance after that? Unless, of course, another gentleman has claimed that honour already?'

'O, she has all the gentlemen in Bath at her feet, do you not, Lina?' says William, with a wink at Edward.

She knows her brother does not mean to vex her; nonetheless, she wishes he would refrain from teasing her in front of friends—in front of this particular friend especially...

'I would like that very much indeed,' she replies with as much dignity as she can muster.

For she would not like him to think her desperate—a woman who cannot get a partner, at any price. She wishes now that she had not been so very insistent at the start that she would not dance, so that someone else—that nice young curate, Mr Smythe, who had smiled at her when they arrived—might have plucked up the courage to ask her. To have had at least one other dance reserved would have made her feel the awkwardness of her situation less.

Had she cared nothing for Edward Pigott, she would have danced every dance on the card with him, without giving it a single thought.

But, when the time comes, and he leads her out onto the floor, such considerations do not matter. All that matters is they are together, moving in harmony, to music she loves—a minuet, this time. In that moment, she is entirely happy, lost in the pleasure of the exercise, and in the bliss of his company.

That night she lies awake, too tired and happy to sleep, thinking of everything that had passed between them that evening. Was she too hot? he had asked her at one point, while they were dancing. It was very hot in here, with such a crush of people—did she not find it so?

She was perfectly comfortable, she had replied—which indeed she was. She had never been more so in her life.

Would she care for an ice? he had then asked. He would fetch it, if she would like one. Dancing tended to make one thirsty, did she not agree?

A few minutes later he asked her: did she prefer Bath to London?

She had replied that she knew so little of London; it was not possible for her to say. But on the small acquaintance she had had, she thought London in all probability the finer city.

'Ah, but the scenery in Bath is so delightful!' he had replied; and she had agreed that it was.

These and other remarks, trivial in substance, had occupied most of their time together. And yet she would not have changed a word. Hours of conversation on serious topics with the most eminent men in the land—and she had conversed with not a few—could not compare with such sweet nothings.

O, if he could love me...! she falls asleep thinking. Surely there had been a look of love—or at least of admiration—in his eyes?

There had been no arrangement made that he should call the next morning, and so it is surely unreasonable of her to feel disappointed when he does not? But she cannot help herself. Having enjoyed so much in the way of happiness for those few, miraculous hours, it is hard to return to the dullness of household tasks. After dancing half the night away with such a man, all other activities—setting the bread to prove; or washing dishes—can only seem uninteresting. Not that she *sees* the particular task in front of her, nor *hears* anything that is said to her, while she is thus engaged. All her thoughts are of him, as he looked last night. The way he had smiled at her. The touch of his hand...

'Why, Lina, I declare you must still be half-asleep, after your efforts on the dance-floor last night,' says William, interrupting these private reflections. 'I have been speaking to you these past five minutes, and you have not heard a word.'

She stares at the plate she has been washing as if she had never seen such an object before.

'I was just...'

'...only I wanted to remind you to make sure when you are making our supper this evening, that there is enough for three,' he goes on. 'For Mr Pigott will be joining us in an hour or so. He has a mind to look through our telescopes, for double stars and the like. And we shall be in need of some refreshment, later, I collect.'

'Oh!'

'Do not look so dismayed, Lina. Bread and cheese will do, you know—and a dish of coffee.'

Bread and cheese! It is all very well for him to talk of bread and cheese. She knows there is only a stale heel of bread to last until the next batch of loaves is ready. As for the cheese, there is nothing but a bit of dried-up Cheddar not fit for the mouse-trap.

One cannot offer such fare to gentlemen—least of all this particular gentleman...

'I will see what I can find,' she manages to say.

She is suddenly breathless. He must not see her like this! In her oldest dress, with the sleeves rolled up, and grease-spots all over her apron... She must change at once. Although what has she to wear that becomes her as well as her beautiful gown of apricot coloured lutestring—the one she had worn last night, and which she would always love, because she had been wearing it when he asked her to dance?

Yes, yes, she must change. First, though, she must see about the dinner…

In the pantry, things are better and worse than she fears. Worse, because the bread, as well as being stale, is now spotted with mould, and the cheese so hard you cannot get a knife through it. Better, because there is, after all, the remains of the chicken from yesterday—which, with a piece of the ham she had intended for tomorrow, and a dish of pickled cabbage, will do very nicely.

Then she runs up to her room, to settle the question of what she should wear. Her heart is pounding, and the breathless, excited feeling still possesses her. He will soon be here! Catching sight of herself in the looking-glass, she sees that there are round spots of colour on her cheeks, as if she had daubed herself with rouge. She thinks, I am in good looks tonight, and the thought makes her smile. But now—what to wear? She flings the closet open. There it hangs, her golden gown—colour of the Harvest moon—amongst the drab brown worsted and striped Holland of her everyday frocks. Next to it, is her good black satin, which she wore to sing *Messiah*. Neither will do for an evening's observing. For although it will soon be summer, the nights are still cold.

But with Edward Pigott coming, her warmest dress—which is also her oldest—is out of the question. The well-worn cloak she had thought to wear would not do, either. As for the ugly thick boots, which are all too necessary, if one's feet are not to be wet through from standing all night in the long grass—they, too, are not fit to be seen.

She knows, as she hesitates between the snuff-coloured dress or the blue, that such considerations are trivial, if not actually light-minded. How often has she scoffed at other women—her sister Sophia, for one—with their endless fussing over frocks and bonnets! As if it matters what one wears, as long as one is decent, and comfortable…

Now she sees that it might matter very much indeed.

Hastily stripping off her work-worn clothes, she washes herself as best she can in what remains in the jug from that morning; then begins on her tangled hair. Although it is her chief beauty—

being of a pleasing colour, and full of curls—it requires a good deal of taming. She seizes the brush, and begins.

'In an hour I shall see him,' she murmurs, with every stroke.

Lavender water behind her ears, and in the hollow of her throat. Clean stockings. A clean chemise. Then the dress…

Descending the stairs at last, at the sound of voices, she finds her brother and Mr Pigott already deep into variable stars, so that they do not at first look up when she appears. In the end, she had decided upon the blue frock—the prettier of the two—with her new cloak, usually kept for Sundays, over it.

The boots will have to do, for she has no others sturdy enough to keep her from catching cold. Perhaps, it being dark, he will not notice…

'I think we might start with Gamma Draconis,' William is saying. 'And compare it with Gamma Ursae Minoris… Ah, there you are, Lina. If you have your notebook ready, we will begin…'

'Good evening,' says Edward Pigott with a bow.

Even though it is only a few hours since she last saw him, she has forgotten quite how beautiful his eyes are; how warmly caressing his voice…

Unable to say a word in reply, she curtseys instead.

'I trust,' their guest goes on, 'that you are not too tired, after last night's exertions?"

She murmurs that she is not tired at all.

'O Lina has been quite stupid all day,' laughs William. 'I have not been able to get a sensible word out of her. Come! Let us get started. It is to be hoped that my sister will be awake enough to do what is required of her…'

And, as they troop outside into the garden, where Mr Smith's boy has already set up the instruments, her brother explains his new system to his fellow astronomer. For he has found that his observations proceed much faster if he is not obliged to write his own notes, he says. With Carolina at his side—or seated at her desk at an open window, as occasion requires—he need only call out his findings to her as he goes along, without moving away from the telescope. No longer does he have to take his eye away from the eye-piece, losing valuable time through having to write things down; and then being obliged to wait until his eyes grew once more accustomed to the dark…

'It is a splendid system,' exclaims William, 'and altogether more productive of results. Why I did not think of it before I cannot say.'

So that night, it is Caroline who records all that is seen by the others, in the hours from ten till three or four in the morning, when it grows too light—or too cloudy—for good observation. As each calls out to her his observations, she writes them down. Her own observations are confined to what she can see with the naked eye, as the constellations move in slow procession across the sky.

Once or twice, it is true, her brother calls her across to his telescope to show her what he is looking at:

'Lina, let me have your opinion as to the relative magnitudes of Deneb and Vega…'

and, after an hour or so,

'Tell me, sister, can you make out the nebula in Draco?'

Edward Pigott says little to her at first—beyond calling out the co-ordinates of certain objects he is presently observing—and this, only after William has urged him to do so:

'For with only two telescopes set up, there is nothing else for my sister to do; and she does prefer to be occupied—do you not, Lina?'

She says that she does.

'It is a far slower process if one must continually be stepping away from the instrument to write down one's findings, instead of calling them out as soon as one sees them,' William says.

Edward Pigott agrees that this can be very time-consuming.

'Although,' he murmurs, 'it seems to me that *someone's* time is still being consumed, if mine is not—is it not so, Miss Herschel?'

She says that she does not mind in the least; as indeed she does not. If she could spend every waking hour at Edward Pigott's side, as she is now, she would do so, and gladly.

Added to which sense she has of being of use to the one she loves, is the pleasure to be had from looking at him, when he is unconscious of being looked at. For the eye, which adapts to the dark after ten minutes or so, allows one to see a great deal more than might be expected in the darkness. Not only stars, but the Shape of one looking up at them; the outline of a profile, the silvery gleam of an eye. The great dark sky, thickly strewn with stars, is to her that night no more than a jewelled backdrop, against which the Object of her affections can be admired. Unrestricted by daylight proprieties, she can gaze and gaze, and no one will ever know.

If there is any greater happiness than this, she does not know of it.

At a quarter to twelve, having ascertained that her brother and Mr Pigott can manage for a few minutes without her, Caroline goes to set out the little supper she has prepared. This, with a glass or two of wine to keep out the cold, is received with much appreciation by their guest:

'I am already convinced of your talents, both musical and astronomical,' he says, bowing to her over the rim of his glass. 'Now I must add to those another—which can only be called magical. For you have conjured up a delicious feast out of nowhere—and at midnight, too! It is like the invisible fairy hands, in *La Belle et la Bête*...'

'O, I am convinced that Lina is part-fairy,' says William. 'Or at least a changeling. She is so very unlike the rest of our family in looks—being so very little, you know, where the rest of us are tall...'

Edward Pigott must have observed her embarrassment, for he says quickly, 'Likenesses in families are often hard to fathom. I myself take no account of such things at all. For whilst it is often thought preferable for a son to resemble his father, I can think of at least one instance where the son is very glad that he does not.'

'I, too, feel such things to be of little consequence,' she replies bravely, not quite meeting his eye. 'For if sons are supposed to favour their fathers, then daughters must equally take after their mothers. I am not at all like my mother, in looks or disposition...'

'Without having had the honour of meeting that lady, it would be impossible for me to judge,' says Edward Pigott. 'But I feel sure that any mother would be only too proud of such a daughter…'

There is no way of replying which does not seem disloyal to her mother, and so she merely smiles. The short silence which ensues seems, to her heightened senses, to be full of meaning.

But William, who has paid little attention to this exchange, is already wiping his mouth, and pushing his plate away.

'Come, Lina. If you are ready, I am sure Mr Pigott here is as anxious to be back at his telescope as I am. We should have a good two or three hours' viewing, if the night remains fine…'

V

All that Spring and Summer, they are observing variable stars. These are stars whose brightness is not constant, but which varies according to regular or irregular patterns—the cause of which is as yet obscure. Stars have been identified as variable before now—Fabricius observed Mira's changes as early as 1596, and Maraldi had noted the variations in Algol; what has not yet been ascertained are the *causes* of the phenomenon. William himself has a particular theory, which he will explain to her when they are at leisure, he says; his good friend Pigott has advanced another. That the periodical dimming and brightening of a star might be caused by its being eclipsed by another star—a companion, revolving around it—is one possible explanation. It has yet to be proved, however.

For not all variable stars vary in the same way…

That it had been Edward Pigott's enthusiasm for the subject which sparked her brother's interest is not lost on Caroline. Being William, of course, he has to make that enthusiasm his own. Every star in the sky which can be examined with the naked eye—and without—he forthwith sets out to examine, listing those which prove to be 'double'—that is, pairs so close they seemed like a single star. The Pole Star is one of these, observed on his very first night. After this, there is no stopping him. William is never one to do anything by halves.

For those few short blessed weeks, this is the pattern of their nights: the weather being fine (and it proves miraculously so), they set up the instruments in the garden; she fetches her notebook and pen; and Edward Pigott joins them, at a little after ten o'clock. Having been surprised the first time, she is now prepared. Never again will she be caught out with regard to victuals. Stale bread and rinds of cheese are a thing of the past. Game pies, hocks of ham, and fine clear soups, are now the order of the day. Even William—who seldom notices what he eats as long as there is a sufficiency of it—is moved to remark on the excellence of her cooking.

Where her own appearance is concerned, she is obliged to exercise a similar vigilance. Once, a swift plunge of her face into cold water, before pouring in the hot water brought from the copper for her bath, had been the extent of her toilette. On some days—William being in urgent need of her assistance for some reason or another—she barely has time to pull a comb through her hair, before hurrying into her clothes. These are days when, half-dead with fatigue after a night of polishing mirrors, she observes with dismay that her hands are grimed with black, her fingernails broken and dirty, and her face all over smuts.

Such days are gone. Now, she rises half an hour early, to get the water hot enough for a thorough soak in the big tin tub. Scrubbing her poor, blackened hands and arms with salt gets rid of most of the stains, she finds. Salt also helps to whiten the teeth. A handful of lavender-heads, thrown into the bath-water, imparts a pleasant odour to the body; while a dash of vinegar in the basin, when she washes her hair, gives a pleasing shine.

As to clothes—well, there is not much to be done, other than to make the best of what she has. Money spent on ham-hocks cannot be spent on fripperies. Luckily, she has always been clever with a needle—sewing having been one of the few accomplishments her mother had not objected to her being taught. So she turns collars, and unpicks bodices, in order to re-make them in a more fashionable style. She becomes extremely ingenious with lengths of ribbon and pieces of lace.

If the One for whom this modest display is intended is aware of her partiality, he gives no sign of it—although his behaviour towards her is never less than polite. Indeed, if she could bring herself to criticise anything in his manner towards her, it is that it is perhaps a little too polite. Never, in all their conversations, does he stray beyond the realms of propriety—never remarks on how particularly *well* she is looking, or takes the liberty to admire (as some less well-behaved gentleman might) the way a certain colour sets off her eyes.

Perhaps (she forces herself to think) he does not like her? And yet she flatters herself that it is not so. When he looks at her, there seems to be a real warmth in his expression; an interest amounting almost—she dares to hope—to affection.

Even William notices something.

'Why, Lina, I believe our friend Pigott has taken quite a shine to you. I have seldom heard him so loquacious about himself as he was last evening—for you know when he and I are together, all we talk of is the stars...'

'Mr Pigott is pleasant to everyone...'

'Yes, but you are his favourite. "Is Miss Herschel to join us this evening?" he is sure to ask me, when we meet...'

'Now I know you are teasing.'

She makes light of it—but privately she is aghast. Are her feelings then so obvious? She cannot bear the thought that he—Edward—might know of her love, and yet choose not to respond to it... Can it really be that he does not care for her? And yet no one could be more attentive, nor quicker to consider her comfort in all kinds of ways...

Lying awake at night, she considers the question of what exactly Edward Pigott's feelings might be towards her, but finds herself unable to reach a conclusion.

Does he love her, or does he not? Each separate encounter offers fresh evidence, one way, or the other...

The talk that night, for instance, had turned to foreign travel, William having referred in passing to their birthplace, Hannover: 'A place which holds the tenderest memories for me...'

But not for me, thinks Caroline, although she says nothing.

'I have never yet had the pleasure of visiting that city,' Edward Pigott says. 'Although I have heard it is very fine. My own travels upon the Continent have been limited to France and Belgium—where I was brought up, you know, for my dear mother is from that region.'

So he, too, is a foreigner, like herself—and William. She wonders that she had not divined it at once.

'When were you last there?' she asks.

'It must be five—no, eight years ago,' he replies.

'You must miss it very much,' she ventures.

For a moment, he holds her gaze.

'O, no,' he replies. 'I do not miss it—for everything I care about is here...'

She holds her breath, wondering if the remark can be meant for her; but then the talk passes onto other things.

He regales them with an account of the time when, aged a mere seventeen, he had surveyed the Flemish Lowlands, using astronomical calculations to do so. It had taken him and his father five months, at the end of which they had seen not a penny of the 7000 *livres* they had been promised by the Belgian government...

'Which did not please my father, you may be sure,' says he. 'For he is not a man who cares to lay out his own money, unless he can be sure of a speedy return. Added to which...' He pulls a wry face. 'He was encumbered with an assistant—I mean of course myself—whose knowledge of Surveying was rudimentary, to say the least. How he had to shout at me, to get me to pay attention—when the smallest variation in co-ordinates could mean the difference between, say, a hill-top's being located in one place, or at five miles' distance...'

'It is an exacting science,' says William. 'Lina, is there another slice of that plum-pie? When one thinks of what poor Maskelyne suffered, in his pursuit of the longitude question...'

'It makes one glad that there are now such things as chronometers,' says his friend, with a smile.

How it stops her heart, to see that smile!

'Growing up, as you did, in the Low Countries,' she persists, hoping to steer the conversation back to what interests her more than the longitude question, 'you must have spoken French before you spoke English, I suppose?'

'*Oui, mademoiselle—c'est vrai*,' Edward Pigott replies. 'Although my father was at pains to prevent it—preferring that my brother and I should speak English, you know...'

'English is the more practical tongue,' opines William, attacking his second piece of pie with gusto. 'For without it, we none of us would be conversing now... Though I write a letter in French as well as any man,' he adds.

'My command of German is no more than passable,' says Mr Pigott. 'Although I have cousins in Groningen...'

'O, Holland is quite a different matter,' says William. 'They speak a barbarous tongue, though they call it Low German.

Come, if you are ready, we will see what can be made out of the mountains of the Moon...'

Their Idyll cannot last. She has known this almost from the beginning—for had he not said his time was not his own? Yet it is still terrible to her when he has to go. For as well as their evenings observing the stars, there have been other meetings, of a more mundane nature, but no less precious to her. The time he arrives half-an-hour before his usual time, and strolls in the garden with her, while William and the boy are setting up the instruments. He much admires her border of red-and-white-striped tulips. The time he walks her to the shops and back (for it is really no trouble at all, he says). They talk of variable stars. After she has made her purchases, he insists on carrying her basket...

'All good things come to an end,' he says, at the end of one evening's star-gazing. It had not been a very productive one—the weather turning cloudy around midnight. 'I fear that as regards myself it is only too true. My father requires my presence in Glamorganshire—I had a letter from him this morning. For he has set up an Observatory, he tells me, which is to be the equal of Greenwich. At least such is my father's intention,' he adds, with the wry grimace he is wont to assume when speaking of that gentleman.

'You are fortunate,' says William, enviously. 'I mean, to have so remarkable an observatory at your disposal...'

'Indeed.' There is still a wryness about his expression, she notices.

'When must you go?' she asks. She is glad that her voice does not tremble, even a little.

It seems to her that he does not quite meet her eyes.

'As soon as possible, I am afraid.' He forces a smile. 'My father is not known for his patience...'

'I see.'

'What kind of telescopes has he got?' interjects William.

Sometimes she finds herself wishing that her brother cared less about such things.

'I believe Mr Sissons is building him a transit telescope,' is Edward's reply.

'Sissons is the best for that kind of thing, of course...'

'There is to be, in addition, a six-foot Dolland achromatic...'

'Better and better...'

'...a two-foot-five-inch achromatic by Watkins, and a two-foot-five-inch reflector by Heath & Wing with a five-inch aperture.'

'I confess I am quite jealous.'

Edward smiles. It seems to Caroline that the melancholy she is feeling is also to be found in that smile.

'My father will certainly be well-equipped for star-gazing. All he lacks is his Assistant Astronomer—that is myself. Which is why I must go...'

Is there an apologetic note in his voice? She cannot be sure. All she knows is that she wants very much to be alone, to cry out her misery in private.

'Well, we shall miss your companionship in our astronomical researches,' says William. 'Shall we not, Lina?'

'Yes. That is, I...'

'But you will visit us again, will you not, as soon as your father can spare you?' her brother goes on.

'With the greatest of pleasure,' replies Edward Pigott, with a bow.

How she manages to get through the rest of that day, and all the days and weeks after that, she cannot say. She moves about in a trance of wretchedness, dumbly going about her work—whether practising scales, copying music, or recording astronomical observations—as if she were a Doll composed of wood and wire, instead of a living Being.

For if to be with him is exquisite agony, not to see him at all is Death.

If he would only *write*, she weeps, time and again, over the sleepless nights that follow. But he does not write. Is their friendship—to put it no higher—worth so little to him, then? When at last a letter *does* come, it is addressed to William, and full of nothing but telescopes and star-charts.

In the event, it is more than a year before she sees him again.

It is a year during which a great deal else happens, naturally enough, for—however much one might wish that it would—Time does not stand still.

To begin with, there is a great deal of singing to be done—or rather, a great deal of encouraging others to sing. She herself never sings as Principal Soprano again. Her chance of making a life as a professional singer has come, and gone—for the affable Mr Simkins never renews his offer. That year, when they perform the *Messiah* at the New Rooms, she takes the part of Second Soprano, and Miss Cantelo—her so-charming rival, now engaged to marry Mr Harris—takes the First. Caroline's time, she now finds, is a great deal too much taken up with other things: rehearsing the choir's Trebles, and copying out scores for singers, being but two of them.

More than this, is the fact that her heart is no longer in her singing. The joy she once took in that expression has gone.

'I do not know what is the matter with you, Lina,' William says to her as they are rehearsing, on one occasion. She is practising one of the Italian Songs she has always loved for a concert they are putting on that Summer. 'You used to know this one so well. Now it is as if you had never sung it before in your life…'

He is surprised and not a little remorseful when she bursts into tears at the rebuke.

'There, there. Do not take on so. I only meant you are not in such good voice as you used to be. It will come again…'

Then, as she seems unable to stop crying:

'I know, I know. You are upset because Dietrich is going back to Hannover…'—their younger brother having taken it into his head to visit them that Spring. 'But he will not be so very far away, you know. When he and Fräulein Reif are married, they will be sure to come and visit us again…'

No, it is not surprising—all things considered—that her music has suffered.

Because, quite apart from all these other distractions, there is the fact that Caroline's time is now more than ever taken up with acting as her brother's Amanuensis. Noting observations. Calculating distances. Comparing magnitudes. There is little time left for anything else at all.

It is only at night—and at odd times of the day—that she has leisure to reflect upon Edward Pigott's unaccountable silence.

O, she receives news of him, from time to time, because he and her brother not infrequently meet, at one of the monthly meetings at the Royal Society—which are, of course, not open to ladies. Thus she learns that Nathaniel Pigott's famous observatory has not been a success. Neither he nor his son have made any observations worth the mention, William informs her, barely able to conceal his satisfaction at the fact. Now it has all been broken up, and its contents removed to York. There the family is to settle...

But about this piece of news—the most interesting to Caroline—her brother has nothing more to say. Instead, he regales her with details of the last meeting, at which Edward Pigott had described, for the benefit of the Society, his recent discovery of a nebula in Coma Berenices...

'His paper was much admired. I took the liberty of congratulating him. And—I hope you will not mind, Lina—but I have invited him to Bath.'

She stares at him, hardly daring to believe her ears.

'Of course I said that he should stay with us...'

Yes, yes—he must stay—but where to put him? Already, she is making arrangements, and turning out rooms. Maybe Alexander could be persuaded to put up at a neighbour's for a night or two...

'...but Pigott insists that he will stay at The White Hart—although from my own experience of that establishment, its beds leave something to be desired.' William seems struck, all of a sudden, by his sister's silence. 'You are very quiet, Lina. You are sure you do not mind?'

'O no,' she says. 'I do not mind.'

I will see him again, is all she can think.

That night she lies awake, turning over in her mind all that has passed between them—and all that has not. How will he greet her again, after so long? Will he be kind, or cold towards her—she has no way of knowing. But it is surely not in his nature to be cruel? Perhaps (she forces herself to think) he already loves another? That, then, might explain his silence; the puzzling shifts in his behaviour from warm to cool… With a bleak sense of having penetrated to the heart of the mystery, she falls asleep at last.

He arrives at five, in time for an early dinner—for William is of course anxious to show him the new instruments.

'Since you were last here, I have ground a new mirror for the seven-foot reflector,' says her brother, almost before their guest is through the door. 'If it remains fine tonight we will try it…'

'I had hoped as much,' is Edward Pigott's reply, as he shakes William's hand, and then Alexander's. 'How do you do, Miss Herschel?' he says, turning to her with a smile. 'It has been a long time since we met...'

'It has, Sir.'

'I hope I find you well?'

He is smiling still, but his eyes tell a different story. Something has changed, she thinks. He is the same—but not the same…

'I am very well, Sir. And you?'

'I have nothing to complain of.'

These polite lies having been got out of the way, the four of them proceed at once to the dining-room. For they must not waste too much time in eating and drinking, William says, when there are the heavens to be explored, and a fine night ahead… Thus an hour passes in much the same way as it would have done a year ago, with talk of developments, astronomical and musical, and of their mutual acquaintance. Having been afraid that she would be dumbfounded by Edward Pigott's presence, or that — worse—she would give away, by some unguarded look or word, the true nature of her feelings towards him, Caroline now finds that she is perfectly in command of herself.

Edward, for his part, seems more like his old self. The guardedness she had detected in the first few minutes of their meeting has given way to his usual ease of manner.

'Delicious soup,' he says.

Caroline smiles. 'A recipe of my mother's.'

'I can always be sure of a fine repast under this roof.'

'O, my sister has been busy with her preparations since first light,' says William.

'Our Lina is a not a bad little cook,' agrees Alexander.

'I believe congratulations are in order, Sir,' she says, cutting short this fraternal jocularity. 'My brother has told me of your findings in Coma Berenices...'

Edward Pigott's smooth brown cheek darkens a shade.

She thinks—'He is blushing'—and the thought makes her blush in sympathy.

'My nebula,' he murmurs. 'Yes. I was very glad the night I came across it, snared in the waves of Berenice's hair...'

'The constellation,' she says, 'is a particular favourite of mine.'

If her brothers had not been there, she might have told him about the night her father took her outside to show her the stars, when she was seven years old, and had pointed out that very constellation to her. She might even have repeated what Pappi had said about her hair being as beautiful as Berenice's...

But of course she does not.

'Perhaps you are familiar,' says Edward Pigott, 'with the lines by Mr Pope? A very good friend of my grandfather's, by the by:

A sudden Star, it shot through liquid Air,
And drew behind a radiant Trail of Hair.
Not Berenice's Locks first rose so bright,
The Heav'ns bespangling with dishevel'd Light...

She claps her hands with pleasure at the appositeness of the citation.

'*A radiant Trail of Hair*—that surely describes a comet—do you not think, William?'

But William is growing restive.

'I have no opinions about Poetry,' he says. 'But I know a very fine pie when I smell it. Carolina, make haste to fetch it, pray. You have not lived, Pigott, if you have not tasted one of Lina's rabbit pies...'

And so, once more, she finds herself star-gazing with Edward Pigott. It is all just as it was a year ago; or almost. There are the instruments set up in the garden, and there the fine night sky whose objects they are to study. Nor does their System vary. They look through the telescopes from nine until twelve, then break for supper, before resuming their observations. In honour of Mr Pigott's recent discovery, these are mainly of the nebula in Coma Berenices, comparing its magnitude with that of the nearest stars in Gemini, Leo, and Virgo.

Caroline finds it an interesting study, not least because it is Edward Pigott who has found the Object in question; still, she is unable to give her entire mind to it. For her thoughts will slide off in other directions—most of them unprofitable. The refrain—*does he love me, or does he not?*—beats like a dull insistent drum in her brain. Though he has been as charming to her as ever, there has been nothing in word or look to suggest that he means anything by it. He is charming to everyone—men as well as women—she has to concede.

It is one in the morning when he speaks to her at last. They are alone together for a moment—William and Alexander being busy with making adjustments to one of the instruments—and both stand silent, looking up at the sky, and all its dazzling points of light.

'Beautiful, are they not, the stars?' he says, in a low voice.

'Very beautiful.'

'One is apt to forget... that is, to overlook their beauty, in the pursuit of other matters...'

She says nothing to this.

'...by which I mean, scientific matters. Mathematics...'—his voice trembles a little—'...takes precedence, one might say, over Nature. Reason over Beauty.'

'I do not think one ever entirely forgets their beauty,' she says softly. 'Even when one's thoughts are taken up with calculating their positions in relation to one another, and so forth... One might see it as a consolation,' she goes on, emboldened by the surrounding darkness, 'for the difficulty of the endeavour. Given that our poor efforts are, for the most part, doomed to fail...'

She is glad that her voice, at least, does not tremble.

'When you put it like that, astronomy seems a futile enterprise indeed,' says Edward Pigott. 'I myself like to think that, in however insignificant a way, we are adding to the sum of human knowledge...'

'O, I do not doubt that. Even our failures are of some use, in that respect, one must suppose.'

'I am sorry to hear you talk of failure—you, who have always seemed to me to epitomise the virtue of striving...'

'O, I am diligent enough...'

'...for perfection, I was going to say.'

'Sir, I am as weak and changeable as any other mortal—for it is our nature, is it not, to be so?'

'Yes.' His tone is subdued. 'It is our nature.'

'And that of the stars, too.'

'Indeed. You are right. They vary as much as we.'

'So you see there is no hope for us,' she says, keeping her voice light.

'No hope at all,' says Edward Pigott, matching his tone to hers.

When the doorbell sounds, Caroline is alone in the house, for Alexander has gone to the saddler's to see about a broken harness, and William is instructing Mrs Lee's daughters in the violoncello at that lady's house in Laura Place. So it is she who opens the door to Edward Pigott. She had not expected to see him again, for had they not said their farewells the night before? All she is conscious of in those first, startled seconds, is that she is wearing her old brown dress, and that her hands are stained with ink from copying.

'My brother is not at home, Sir,' she stammers out at last. 'But he will return directly.'

Before she knows what she is doing, she has invited him in.

'Please to wait. For he will be vexed, I am sure, to miss you...'

She sees him hesitate. Then he smiles, and she feels her heart turn over.

'I should like that very well. If it would not trouble you too much..."

'O no. It is no trouble at all.'

She steps aside to let him enter. The blood is roaring in her ears, as if she were about to faint. She bites her lips, quite hard, to dispel the sensation.

'Won't you go upstairs to the sitting-room?' she says, in command of herself once more. 'There is a fire there. I will fetch some tea.'

'Well…' Halfway up the stairs, he seems to hesitate once more. 'As long as you are sure I am not keeping you from more important things…'

She almost laughs aloud at that. What could be more important to her than this?

'I was only practising scales. It is of no consequence,' she says.

This appears to give him the opening he is waiting for:

'I very much admired your singing, last year in Bath.'

'You are too kind, Sir.'

'No. Not at all. I am entirely sincere.' How full of feeling are his eyes! 'I have seldom been more moved by a performance.'

She lowers her gaze, afraid that if she does not, he might read the emotion written there.

'Thank you,' she murmurs. 'I'll just…' The rest of the sentence proves impossible to articulate.

In the kitchen, she breaks a cup in her agitation, and scalds her hand on the kettle.

O, why has he come? She must not suppose it is to see her… No, no. All such thoughts can only lead to despair. For if she has come to any conclusion about Edward Pigott's feelings for her in the course of the past few days, it is that they do not, in all probability, exceed those of friendship. If he loved her, surely he would have spoken out by now?

Or perhaps he has spoken, she thinks, remembering last night's conversation about the stars…

When she joins her guest in the sitting room, he is studying the pictures on the walls. There is one of her—a silhouette, cut out of black paper—taken when she was eighteen. The artist, Herr Gruber, had caught her profile very exactly. Also her curling hair, tied in its pigtail. She has not changed so very much since then, she thinks, although more than ten years have passed.

He sees that she has seen him looking at the picture, and smiles.

'A charming image,' he says. 'Although it does not show your best attribute—your voice.'

She does not know what to say to this, which seems both compliment and insult in one; and so she merely smiles, and sets down the tea-tray.

Edward Pigott seems pleased with his observation, however.

'Yes,' he says. 'Would it not be a fine thing if sounds could be recorded, as well as images? Only think—if we could hear Archimedes speak, or Homer... If we could capture a voice, with the same fidelity as an artist captures a face, what a fine thing that would be! Although...' He seems suddenly downcast. 'It would be of benefit only to the hearing...'

'That is true of voices in general, Sir,' she says, handing him a cup. She is glad to see that her hand trembles hardly at all. 'And of music, too. One must have ears to hear it.'

'Indeed. You are right,' he says.

A brief silence follows, while both sip their tea.

'Tell me,' says Edward Pigott. 'How goes your study of variable stars? Or periodical stars, if you prefer it. I recall you were compiling a list some while ago...'

'Why, yes.' She puts down her cup. 'If you wait, I will fetch it.'

'Please do not disturb yourself on my account. It is only that it is a particular project of mine...'

But she is already halfway across the room. Her study is on the floor above. She takes the stairs two at a time, nearly tripping over her skirts in her hurry, her heart pounding madly. Fortunately, the list is on top of the pile of notes. She seizes it, and returns, almost at a run. If it is true that he loves Another—although there has been nothing said to confirm or deny that suspicion—it is hard to believe that that Unknown Fair could share his enthusiasms to the extent that Caroline does.

In this one respect, at least, she can still be of service to him.

In the interim, he has risen from his seat, and now stands at the window, looking down into the street. When she walks in, he turns towards her abruptly, as if startled out of thoughts of something—or someone—else...

'Here.' She thrusts the pages at him. 'All the known instances of variable stars. I have noted Maraldi's comments, where applicable; and those of Fabricius, too. Tycho Brahe is mentioned, of course, regarding Nova Tychonis...'

He scans the charts she has made, a faint smile playing upon his lips.

'But this is wonderful! You have listed both known variables, and suspected ones. I could not have been more thorough myself.'

She feels herself grow warm with pleasure at his words.

'I see that I am myself mentioned here...' He indicates the entry for Andromeda. 'And here, and here...' His bright brown eyes have a mischievous gleam. 'If you persist in including me in such august company, it will quite turn my head, I fear.'

He makes to return the list to her, but she gestures at him to keep it.

'I have another copy.'

'But this is a generous gift indeed!' His face is alight with pleasure. 'When I show Goodricke what you have done, he will be delighted.'

'I am afraid I do not have the pleasure of Mr Goodricke's acquaintance.'

'No, indeed.' He is smiling still, as if at a happy recollection. 'He seldom ventures out of York, for his health does not permit it. Poor fellow, he is deaf and dumb. But a finer grasp of mathematics than his I have never encountered...'

There is the sound of footsteps on the stairs. A moment later, William bursts in upon them, rubbing his hands.

'Some tea! I must have some tea, or I will expire! Ah, Pigott, are you here? I hope my sister has been looking after you?'

'I have been royally treated. Miss Herschel has made me a present of her researches so far...'

'Researches?' William glances at the papers his friend is holding. 'Yes, she has a neat hand, has she not? It is why I can seldom spare her from copying...'

'Sir, this is more than fair copying,' Edward Pigott says. 'It is a perfect Digest of all the Authorities.'

'Yes, yes. You are right of course. My sister is a Prodigy in every respect...'

'William, *please*...'

Sometimes she finds his witticisms hard to bear.

'For with all her researches, and her singing, she is Science and Art combined in one person. Don't blush, Lina, for you know that it is true.'

'I must go,' says Edward Pigott, interrupting this heavy-footed teasing. 'I only stopped by to return this'—he takes a volume from his pocket, which he hands to William—'and to say farewell, for I return to York by the over-night coach.'

To prevent the dejection she feels from showing upon her face takes all her remaining self-possession.

'Goodbye, Mr Pigott.' She holds out her hand, and he touches it briefly to his lips.

The sensation of that glancing caress makes her tremble.

'Thank you again for this.' He holds the sheaf of papers to his breast. Would that she could have changed places with those poor, scrawled pages for a moment! 'I hope we shall meet again before too long.'

'I hope so, too.'

'Oh, I daresay we shall meet at the Society next month,' says William, escorting their friend to the door. 'Lina, is there any more of that tea?' he adds, returning. 'It is thirsty work conducting a choir, you know... Why Lina, what have I said?'

For she has melted into tears, the strain of the past hour having proved too much for her.

'It is nothing. I have a headache.'

At once he is all contrition.

'Poor Lina. You have over-tired yourself, looking after Pigott. You should have sent him away, you know, if you were not well. Come! You are to sit down in that chair and you are not to stir until I say so. If you tell me how to go about it, I shall make the tea myself...'

VI

They are moving house again—this time to Rivers Street. Here, they have barely finished unpacking, when William announces that he has bought his sister a share in a millinery business, which she is to run from that address. It will do her good to have a way of making some money of her own, he says. For she is clever with her fingers, and there is no shortage, in Bath, he has noticed, of ladies in need of hats to be trimmed, or remade into the latest style. He has also noticed, he says, that she has not been in her usual spirits. The move will do her good; and besides, the new house is just across the street from the premises of the Philosophical Society, which had been set up a month or so before, and of which he is now an honorary member…

But no sooner have they removed there, than the situation is found to be impractical; for it is not possible to set up the instruments within easy reach of the house. Undaunted (for he has a way of turning every situation to advantage), her brother sets up his seven-foot telescope in the street. It is thus that he first meets Sir William Watson, who is returning home late from the theatre. The two strike up a conversation, which lasts nearly till morning. Later, Sir William proves to be a great Supporter, in bringing his friend to the attention of the King.

That is her brother all over. He will talk to anyone, about anything under the Sun—or indeed, under the Moon, for it is of that Orb he and his new friend speak. William has been very much taken up, of late, with proving his theory that the Moon might be inhabited. For if one could measure Moon-mountains with the aid of a powerful telescope, he says, it might be possible to discern the traces of Moon-men…

It is not long after this that he returns to New King Street. Caroline remains behind, to wind up the business, which has, alas, not proved a success. Much of her stock of ribbons, feathers, jet beads and other such trash had been stolen—she has her suspicions by whom. (That Lizzie Barker, whom she had engaged to help out in the shop, is a bold piece. Her sister is worse. Hadn't she seen them parading about the town, with at least ten yards of scarlet ribbon about their persons, not a fortnight after shutting down the business?)

So it is that she is not, as it happens, at her brother's side when he makes his Great Discovery. He has gone ahead—not wanting to lose the advantage of the fine weather—while she stays put. Not the first and not the last time it falls out that way. For what is she, after all, but a Follower, where her brother is concerned? He leads, and she runs scuttling after. He gives commands, and she—gladly—obeys them. He makes discoveries, and she writes them all down in her book.

It is in fact the morning after the night of 13th March 1781—historic date!—that she looks up from what she is doing (working out the cost-price of some silk ribbon, to set against the actual price at which it had been sold) to see her brother walk into the room.

'Come, Lina—leave all that,' he says. 'Put on your hat, and let us walk.'

Seeing by his face that he has something to tell her, she does so at once, even though she has a thousand things to do, with the carrier due at noon to collect her boxes. But with William, attuned as he is to the movements of stars and planets, considerations of mere Solar Time are of little consequence.

'I must have your opinion, Lina,' he says, when they are scarcely out of the house. 'I have found something—I know not what. A comet, I believe…'

'But that is wonderful…'

'Or perhaps not a comet.' He frowns. 'I cannot be sure, although I observed it last night, for upwards of three hours, with the seven-foot. It is a pale greenish-blue in colour…'

'Does it have a tail?' she interrupts. A comet, she knows, should have a tail.

William shakes his head.

'That is what is so perplexing. There is no discernible tail. And yet…' Stopping dead in the middle of Catherine Place, so that a passing chaise almost runs him down—a near-catastrophe of which he seems entirely oblivious—he chews on a fingernail.

'I cannot help but think that this Object will prove to be more than just another comet... I have been so *thorough*, Lina,' he cries, as, steering him to safety, she draws him along beside her into Church Street. 'Night after night I have swept the skies, recording every Object I have found there...'

She, who has been the actual recorder of most of these, knows this all too well.

'...and yet *this* I had not found.'

'Until now.'

They have crossed into Crescent Fields, and now—safe from passing traffic—stroll towards the river. Pale Spring sunshine lights up the broad sweep of the grand new houses along the Crescent.

'Until now,' he agrees, still chewing his fingernail—a nervous habit from boyhood; although he is not, as a rule, a nervous man.

'May I see it?' she asks. 'It may be that another pair of eyes will help to resolve the matter.'

He turns to her, then, his smile lighting up his face.

'O, but you must see it! That is why I am come, to fetch you. You must be at New King Street tonight, without fail. Then'—he grows thoughtful again— 'we shall see what we shall see...'

What they *do* see remains obscure for several weeks. Although later William is to insist that he had known the significance of his discovery from the first. Has he not searched the heavens, month after month, and year after year, until he knows them as intimately as the pages of a musical score? Every star—variable, double, fixed—every planet and every nebula so far discovered, he has observed and noted down. Systematic as he is, there is nothing that can escape him in the end. If he had not found the Object sooner, he would have found it later...

For years afterwards, nothing is calculated to drive him to distraction more than the suggestion that his great discovery had been an accident. Such a notion was, he would say, absurd.

'There could be nothing accidental about it,' he cries, 'when every night I looked at a different part of the sky—every night at every season. Even if I had not found—what I found—*then*,' he insists, growing increasingly agitated, 'I should have found it *eventually*. This foolish idea that one stumbles across such things through simple *good luck*, has become, I very much fear, a modern Obsession.'

Caroline, who knows very well how much hard work has gone into everything they have achieved, is never one to contradict him. And yet... there *had* been something, if not exactly lucky, then certainly magical, about the finding of Georgium Sidus.

Her first sight of it is later that same evening, as they stand in the little courtyard behind the house where the seven-foot telescope is set up. Around them rises the scent of winter jasmine (this was before her poor garden had been wrecked by the building of the large telescope). She is shivering a little, out of excitement as much as cold. She puts her eye to the eye-piece and waits, until at last the strange new world swims into view.

'I see it now!' she cries. 'How beautiful it is! Pale blue. I do not see a tail,' she adds doubtfully.

'There is no tail. But do you *see* it, Lina?'

'I do.'

She feels his hand upon her shoulder. Gently, he draws her away from the glass.

'I am not sure what we have found here,' he says. 'But I know one thing...' His voice is not quite steady. 'Whatever it may prove to be, it has never before been seen by anyone else in the history of the world.'

Of course it is not a Comet William has discovered, but something much greater; although it is some weeks before this is established. Maskelyne's acknowledgment of the news, written in his usual slapdash hand, refers to 'your discovery of the present Comet, or Planet, I don't know what to call it'; while Sir Joseph Banks remarks with his customary wryness that

> some of our Astronomers here incline to the opinion that it is a planet, not a comet

adding

> if so you are of that opinion it should forthwith be provided with a name or our nimble neighbours the French will certainly save us the trouble of Baptising it…

A planet it turns out to be. As to the naming of it—why, what better name could it have than that of their Illustrious Monarch? Georgium Sidus it duly becomes.

From that time on, their quiet life in Bath is at an end. William has become a famous man, and the house is full of people, at all hours.

She writes in her journal:

> the interruption of Visitors which wanted to look through the telescopes at night were very numerous, for since the discovery of Georgium Sidus, I believe few men of learning or consequence left Bath before they had seen and conversed with its discoverer…

Many of these gentlemen have to be fed, for they have come from afar—from Antwerp, Munich, Copenhagen, and Stockholm. Those that do not need feeding require a dish of coffee, at the very least. She is kept busy all day long, fetching and carrying—but that is nothing new.

What *is* new are the commissions for telescopes—for suddenly, everyone wants a Herschel design. Since the mirrors needed are huge, and have to be mounted in long tubes—twenty foot long or more—there is no alternative but to turn the house into a foundry, to make the mirrors, and a carpenter's shop, to make the mountings. In addition to her other duties, Caroline is conscripted as a labourer in this endeavour, pounding vast quantities of horse-dung in a mortar for the moulds.

How the place reeks! You cannot air it out. Worse than the smell is the dust it makes, so that it seems as if they are living in a stable-yard, instead of a gentleman's residence. Everything—from the furniture to the very plates they have to eat off—becomes covered with a greasy film of dirt.

'But Lina,' William says, when, with tears in her eyes, she implores him to tell her when this dreadful Enterprise of his will cease, 'you know that we have no choice in the matter, if we are to succeed with the twenty-foot instrument…'

For he has set his heart on completing the trials for the telescope by the end of the summer. Nor do his plans stop at the twenty-foot; a thirty-foot is to be tested, and—why not?—in time, a forty-foot, too. Her brother's ideas never being having been subject to the limits imposed by mundane reality.

So she continues pounding horse-dung, and sifting it through a sieve, to get out the lumps—a loathsome task, which leaves the person engaged in it covered in filth from head to foot. Now, she might scrub herself with salt until her skin was raw, and yet still not get rid of the stench of it. She is like poor *Aschenputtel* in the fairytale, forced to lie in dust and ashes, while her proud sisters make eyes at the handsome prince. Not that any prince would ever seek her out—or if he did, he would recoil in disgust at the fright she has become: her hair thickened with dust, and plastered down with sweat; her clothes no less dirty—she will have to burn the dress; her body pungent with the odour of her exertions.

It is thus that Sir William Watson finds her one day, when he calls by to see William. She has never felt more embarrassed in her life.

Gentleman that he is, he insists on taking her place at once.

'For,' he says to her brother, 'this is no work for a lady, Herschel. I am quite surprised you allow it…'

'O, Lina does not mind,' William replies airily. 'She is my assistant in everything.'

'But still,' murmurs kind Sir William. 'The Gentler Sex, you know…'

There are times, Caroline feels, when her brother hardly seems to know she is a woman at all. 'I became in time,' she writes in her journal 'as useful a member of the workshop as a boy might be to his master in the first year of his apprenticeship…'

But she is not a boy. Nor has she left Hannover, with all its hardships and privations, only to come to this. To be driven hard, from daybreak until at last she fell into bed at night, is what she is used to. From her earliest youth, she has kneaded dough, and scoured greasy pots, and carried buckets full of water, and beat dusty carpets, until her arms ached. But these tasks—though taxing enough—have not made her repellent to herself. To go to bed stinking (despite all one's efforts to rid oneself of the stench) and rise stinking: it is too much! To be reduced to such an Object—unlovely and un-sexed—how can William permit it, she wonders?

It is the only time she has ever prayed that Edward Pigott would not take it into his head to visit them. The thought that he might see her in such a state—and worse, that he might *smell* her—is too dreadful to contemplate.

At last the vile task is over, and the mirrors for the twenty-foot telescope can be cast. These are to be the largest ever made: four feet in diameter (although this is later reduced to three feet). When ready, the mould—made from the hateful horse-dung—will be cast in a furnace, set up for the purpose in the back-kitchen. Alexander, together with Mr Smith and his men, is to assist—Caroline having been excused such hazardous duties. But even though William's calculations, as to temperatures and times, are as exact as he can make them. the firing does not prove a success.

At the first attempt, the mirror cracks on cooling. At the second, the entire party is almost killed, when the mould breaks, spilling molten metal onto the flagstones, and cracking them from side to side. The explosion blows William's eyebrows quite off, and half-chokes him, and his helpers, with black and noxious smoke.

After this, he is forced to admit that the dangers inherent in the process outweigh the benefits. Besides which, the cost is becoming prohibitive. Had it not been for the tireless efforts of his friends, his great Endeavour might have foundered. Now, thanks to Dr Maskelyne's intervention on William's behalf, he is commanded to go to London, to visit the King.

This honour, though delightful, could not have come at a worse time.

For—giant telescopes aside—there is still a living to make, and choirs to rehearse for the Spring season. They are supposed to be doing *Jeptha*; this—a work they have not performed before—is changed at the last minute to *Samson*, an old favourite; then to *Judas Maccabaeus*, an even older, and safer, choice.

With a hundred musicians and singers—all under-rehearsed—to coax a performance out of, and no time in which to do it, William is at his wits' end.

Caroline has never seen him in such a state.

'Kings and princes wait for no man!' he cries. 'I am commanded to go to London—and yet they tell me I cannot be spared tonight. It is impossible for me to be in two places at once. Indeed, it is not reasonable to expect it...'

It would have done no good to have pointed out that at least some of the difficulty in which he found himself was of his own making.

In any event, the performance turns out to be a disaster. Mr Tenducci, the tenor, refuses to sing, and so Mr Rauzzini takes his place. The famous Mr Rauzzini, however, is prepared to sing only one aria—which is all, he says, that he has had time to practise. The chorus is out of time, and loses its place at intervals—doubtless through being hurried through the score at break-neck speed by the conductor. Songs, duets, and whole choruses are omitted, and the orchestra thrown into confusion. Miss Storer, the soprano, is in tears, and Mr Croft, the bass, has a face like thunder. He has never, he is heard to remark afterwards, seen the like of it in all his born days... Long before the end, many of the audience have walked out in disgust, or suited their expressions of feeling—boos and catcalls—to the prevailing mood of Anarchy.

In short, it is an ignominious end to what had begun so brilliantly for both of them—she and her brother. Although of the two, Caroline suspects, only she will feel any lasting regret...

A letter comes the day after William's arrival in London, which should have left her in no doubt as to the way the wind was blowing:

May 20, 1782
Lincoln's Inn Fields

Dear Lina

I have had an Audience with his Majesty this morning, and met with a very gracious reception. I presented him with the drawing of the Solar System, and had the honour of explaining it to him and the Queen. My telescope is in three weeks time to go to Richmond, and meanwhile to be put up at Greenwich, where I shall accordingly carry it today. So you see Lina you must not think of seeing me in less than a month...

There follows an account of the dinner Dr Maskelyne has given in his (William's) honour afterwards, and the kind remarks of the Astronomer Royal concerning his protégé's discoveries. Perhaps afraid that she might think his head had been turned by such praise, her brother adds a postscript:

> You see Lina I tell you all these things. You know vanity is not my foible therefore I need not fear your Censure...

It is true enough. He has never been vain. Nor can he help it, if he is singled out for favour. It is not his fault that he is the greatest Astronomer of the Age.

William's visit, as he has predicted, stretches into weeks. Kings and princes could not, it seems, be hurried. Caroline is to explain to Mrs Lee and the rest of his pupils that he is unavoidably detained, he says—adding, with what in anyone else might have seemed false modesty:

> my having seen the King need not be kept a Secret, but about my staying here it will be best not to say anything, but only that I must remain here till his Maj. has observed the Planets with my telescope...

He has been star-gazing at Greenwich with a group of learned gentlemen, he tells her:

> We have compared our telescopes together, and mine was found very superior to any of the Royal Observatory. Double stars which they could not see with their instruments I had the pleasure to show them very plainly…

Of course he is not boasting—merely stating a matter of fact—when he adds, as if impatient with the fulsome praise he has already received:

> Among opticians and astronomers nothing now is talked of but what they call my Great discoveries. Alas! This shows how far they are behind when such trifles as I have seen and done are called great. Let me but get at it again! I will make such telescopes, and see such things…

'Our brother is doing great things in the world,' she says, to Alexander, handing him the letter across the breakfast table.

'Indeed.'

Alexander is a man of few words. When he does speak, his remarks often take a melancholy turn.

'You will think me ungrateful or perhaps unkind… but there are times when I cannot help wishing that things were as they were before… I mean, with just the three of us.'

'One cannot turn back the clock, sister.'

'I know.'

'Wilhelm is part of a greater world now.' Alexander sighs, and shakes his head. 'He will not wish to return to the little life he has had here with us.'

In her heart, she knows this to be true. Things will never be the same—how can they be the same, now that William is known to all the world?

A few days later, another letter comes:

> There is to be a Court mourning, which I believe will begin on Sunday; be so good as to send me my black clothes. I believe you may put them up in brown paper with a towel sewed about them as there will be no occa-

> sion for a Box. Let them come by the Coach that goes off either at 3 in the afternoon or, if you cannot have them ready so soon, by the evening Coach...

As she stands brushing the nap of his black velvet coat, before packing it up as he has instructed, she wonders if he will be much changed when she sees him again. She feels as she did when she was fourteen years old, and waiting for his return from his foreign travels. She hopes he will not think her dull, or provincial, now that he has seen the ladies of the court, and had tea with the King and Queen.

The demonstration at Windsor Castle proves a great success. William's telescope is set up beside a Refractor of Dollond's and a Reflecting telescope of Short's.

> My Instrument gave a general satisfaction; the King has very good eyes and enjoys Observations with the telescopes accordingly...

On the second night, it is cloudy. So as to avoid disappointing the young princesses, who have asked for a demonstration of their own, William sets up a pasteboard Saturn that he has prepared for just such an eventuality.

> The effect was fine and so natural that the best astronomer might have been deceived.

Their Royal Highnesses are most pleased by the artifice.

William's reward is not long in coming. He is to have a pension from the King of £200 a year (which Sir William Watson thinks cheap; but one cannot quibble with monarchs). He will give up teaching, and conducting choirs, and devote himself to astronomical research. The only condition is that he must live near Windsor, to allow his royal patron to benefit from the proximity of his tame astronomer...

Caroline had known something of the sort was in the offing, of course, even before he set off for London. Although the first definite news she has of it is when her brother arrives back in Bath. She goes with Alexander to meet the afternoon coach; they have hired a boy, in addition, to help with the luggage—for apart from William's traps, there will be the telescope to manage…

But when he gets out, she sees that he is unencumbered with any kind of baggage at all.

'Come, Lina, Alex—let us walk, and I will tell you everything,' he says.

He has found them a house in Datchet, in Berkshire, within sight of Windsor Castle, he tells them. They must be packed and ready to depart within a week.

'It is the most commodious spot—with stables that can very easily be converted to grinding-rooms, and a large grass plot, where we can set up the twenty-foot Reflector.'

'What more could anyone possibly desire?' murmurs Alexander.

'The house itself will need some fitting-out to make it comfortable,' William goes on, perhaps conscious, from his sister's silence, that more might be required to convince her of the appositeness of his choice. 'But I know that you, Lina, with your cleverness at all such things, will make it very snug and pretty, as you have done at every place we have ever lived…'

They have by this time, arrived back at New King Street. Dinner—William's favourite venison pasty, and cold mutton—is laid out in readiness for his return, and a fire is burning merrily in the grate. Dancing flames are reflected in all the polished surfaces of the furniture, and in the silver and glass upon the table. How she could bear to leave this room, in which she has spent so many hours—most of them happy—she does not know. To leave this house, which, of all the houses they had lived in these past ten years, she has come to love the most, will be painful in the extreme.

Was it not here—in this very room—that she first set eyes on him, dearest to her of all her brother's astronomical collaborators? *I am very pleased to make your acquaintance, Miss Herschel…* In this very room that, already two years past, he had kissed her hand. *I hope we shall meet again, before too long...* She feels her eyes fill with tears, both at the sweetness of these memories and at the sadness they brings in their wake—a sadness compounded of everything that remains unfulfilled in her life.

For the man she loves does not return her feelings. She has long ago come to realise that. But in the years since, she has—slowly, painfully—made a life for herself: a life in which music has taken the place of love. Now, it seems, even music must be relinquished...

'Only think, Lina!' William is saying, as he helps himself with relish to a slice of pasty. 'I shall be able to give up teaching for good and all...'

'A great relief, to be sure,' says Alexander, contentedly munching.

'No more tedious lessons, with pupils quite unable to sing a note. No more quarrels with egotistical soloists...'

'You will be able to devote yourself entirely to astronomy.'

She will not let her brothers see her cry, though every word is a knife-thrust to the heart.

'Pepper,' she says abruptly, getting up to fetch it.

In the kitchen, amongst the unwashed pots, she lets her tears flow freely. Tears for the man she loves, and for everything else she has lost. One by one they fall, with a tiny splash, into a sink full of dirty water.

VII

Nor are these the last tears she is to shed, before quitting Bath. For there are friends to be taken leave of—she had not known how many she had, until it came to parting. Farewells must be said to familiar walks she will no longer frequent, and favourite shops, that will know her custom no more. Added to these quotidian associations are others, of more particular significance. Streets she has walked down, in *his* company, seem to her now like hallowed ground. Places they once met and—on that one, glorious occasion, danced—have become sacred to her. As for all those nights, spent stargazing in the garden at New King Street—these, too, have left their traces on her mind and heart.

Compounding her misery, is the evident superiority of the place she has left to the one where she must now resign herself to dwell. For to leave Bath, with all its elegance and beauty, its rolling hills, and mildness of climate, to come to Datchet is a falling-off indeed! Instead of wide streets and spacious parks, there are little, low cottages surrounding a dusty patch of green, and a brash public-house of new brick, where they are obliged to put up on the first night, the beds at the house not having been properly aired.

When at last they reach the place, it is to find nothing but a Ruin of what was once a gentleman's house, but which is now barely fit for human habitation. Though it is midsummer, the walls blossom with damp, and there is a smell of mice in the servants' quarters. As for the garden, of which William had spoken with such satisfaction—it is a wilderness. Weeds four feet tall choke all the plots, and Alexander almost kills himself falling down a well, concealed by this vegetable mass. They will need a gardener—if not a team of gardeners—to dig the ground over. How they are to afford it is anybody's guess.

For, contrary to expectations, living in the country turns out to be a lot more expensive than living in town. The price of eggs is twice that of Bath. Coals are more than double the price. The butcher will not give honest weight. As for the cost of maintaining the property, with over thirty windows, and a roof that leaks—on a mere £200 per annum, it is not to be done.

If her spirits are low to begin with, on account of all these unlooked-for worries, they become more so after Alexander—resisting all attempts on the part of his brother and sister to persuade him to move in with them—returns to Bath. Suddenly, the isolation of their new home becomes glaringly apparent. In Bath, she had been the renowned Miss Herschel, sister of the Director of Music and distinguished in her own right, with a circle of friends that, whilst it could never have been called intimate, was at least extensive.

Here she is nobody.

When she goes into the local shops, she is stared at because of her eccentric appearance (is it her fault that she has no money for new dresses?) and sniggered at on account of her accent.

'Stingy German bitch' she is called—once to her face, by that rascal of a gardener.

What makes things worse, is that she is left so much alone. For William now spends most of his days—and nights, too—at Windsor, attending on his royal patron. The latter, no doubt wanting to get his two hundred pounds' worth, is forever requiring the presence of his astronomer, to demonstrate this or that for the benefit of visiting dignitaries. Caroline has accompanied him once or twice, at the invitation of their majesties, but—aside from the delights of the royal table, which is piled high with more food than she has ever seen in her life before (O, for a taste of those sugar puddings, sprinkled with gold!)—these are painfully awkward occasions. Queen Charlotte, attributing her guest's tongue-tied demeanour to a supposed difficulty with the language, insists on speaking German to her.

'Although I believe my English is better than hers,' Caroline says indignantly to her brother afterwards—a judgement with which he is wise enough not to disagree.

It may be that something of her dissatisfaction with their situation has become apparent. (Although what exactly does she have to complain about? Having dinner with the King and Queen is scarcely a hardship. Nor is conversing for three hours afterwards about the mysteries of the universe.) The very next day he presents her with a plan of work.

'For Lina, now that the house is set to rights'—it is not—'you will be in need of something to do.' Work being, for him, a Panacea. 'To be wrote down' he writes:

> Double stars that appear to be one, two, or three diameters asunder.
> Clusters of stars such as 5,6,7,8 &c. near together, all within a dozen diameters or so.
> Nebulas.
> Comets.

Adding, by way of putting her on the right track:

> In setting down such Phenomena they must be described by lines from certain stars and figures drawn upon paper-for example, 'I see a nebula, its situation is pointed out by a line drawn from A to B crossed by another line from C to D.'

Thus begins her career as a comet-hunter.

Sisterly devotion aside, there is another reason why she is inclined to take an interest in comets. A few months before they leave Bath, another letter with a York postmark arrives.

> York, Novemr 16th 1781
>
> Sir,
>
> It is with pleasure that I inform you that I discovered a Comet, last Wednesday the 14th, near the neck of the Swan, having no tail, a Coma of 3 minutes, and Small Nucleus, is visible to the Naked eye appearing like a Star of the 4th Mag:d…

A drawing follows, of the Swan's neck and head, showing the principal stars of the constellation, and the position of the comet in relation to them.

'There, Lina. You see that Mr Edward Pigott is already ahead of us in this,' says William, handing her the letter. 'Perhaps,' he goes on, 'you would like to observe his comet yourself, to give you an idea what to look out for?'

As if she needed an excuse to do so...

That night, she sits perched on a ladder twenty feet above the ground in the garden at New King Street, peering, first through the Finder, then through the eye-piece of the large telescope, as her brother shouts instructions from below. At first, there is nothing to be seen but blurred points of light; being suspended so far from the ground makes her nervous, and her fingers tremble so much that she cannot get the adjustment right.

But then she succeeds. Suddenly, there is the Swan, and there the comet—a beauty—beside it.

'I see it!' she cries, almost falling off the ladder in her excitement. 'O how wonderful to think we are the first to do so...'

'Well, you know, Mr Pigott was the first,' William reminds her good-humouredly, when she has looked her fill, and has descended to earth once more.

It is fortunate that the darkness prevents him from seeing her blush.

'I know. I only meant...' she stammers. But her brother is no longer listening.

'Just think, Lina, of all that we are going to do,' he is saying. 'I have such plans, Lina. I hardly know where to begin...'

'But we *are* the first to see the comet, you and I,' she says to herself; and it is not her brother she means. For if one looks at a star at the same time as another looks at it, might these two observers not be said to be united in that endeavour?

And that he, its Discoverer, *is* looking at it—and at that very moment—she feels... nay, *knows* in her Soul.

In the months since that momentous night, her brother has been interesting himself very much in double stars—a topic to which, she cannot help but recall, Mr Edward Pigott had drawn his attention in the first instance. Being William, he finds the work not proceeding fast enough for his liking. Having a sister on hand to train for an assistant therefore suits him very well indeed.

It suits her rather less well to be turned out in the hoar-frost and dew to spend the night sweeping for stars. But knowing her brother as she does, she realises that to protest would be a waste of breath. He has adapted a telescope for her use, which can be adjusted to either a vertical or horizontal position, by winding a string. On her first night, she finds only a double star, which William had already noted. Her second night is more successful, netting several more double stars and a nebula.

She begins to see that she might be rather good at this, after all.

As the nights grow colder—and thus better for observation, for the colder it is, the clearer the atmosphere—the volume of her clothing increases, so that when fully dressed she appears almost spherical. Her bird-like form is thickened by layers of petticoats, her warmest woollen dress, and a man's greatcoat (borrowed from William), tied round with her thickest shawl. A man's woollen cap, pulled well down over her ears, completes the ensemble, along with thick leather gloves, thick stockings and a pair of her stoutest boots.

Catching sight of herself one night in the looking-glass, she bursts out laughing; then finds herself as suddenly breaking out in tears.

'I am thirty-two years old, and no man loves me,' she thinks. 'Nor ever will, if this is how I must look.'

But she is glad of the shawl and the boots and the ugly hat, for it is as cold a winter as she can recall since she came to England. Winters are always cold in Hannover. Now, with the glass falling to well below zero these January nights, she can almost fancy herself back in her native land, with the ice cracking underfoot when she steps out across the grass, and the sky so thick with stars it seems as if a handful of rice has been flung down upon a dark blue tablecloth. 'Look'd at the Nebula in Cancer for half an hour' she writes.

> Saw nothing nebulous; but they are all very distinct little stars. Began at the above Cluster and made a horizontal sweep all around, I spent above an hour upon this sweep

> but found nothing remarkable. It was too cold, therefore could not continue my observations. A pretty strong frost.

Night after night she stands in the dark garden, shivering with cold, her teeth chattering so hard she can barely manage to keep the instruments steady. But she perseveres. In the space of a few months, she has got to know the skies and their changing constellations as well as her own face; or indeed, rather better. She has never cared much for looking-glasses.

On 26th February, she observes a nebula in the region of Canis Majoris. It is not, she finds, listed in Messier's catalogue. By early March, she has found several more, also previously unknown to Messier, and thus to the scientific world. She has to admit she is making progress.

William evidently thinks so.

'You see Lina—I was right! You are a natural astronomer...'

In place of the inadequate toy she has been using for her sweeps, he presents her with a far superior telescope: a Newtonian reflector with a magnifying power of 2000, and an ingenious movement which allows the eye to remain at rest, while the instrument sweeps the sky from horizon to zenith.

'For if we are to work together on this, you must have the same advantages as I. You should not have to manage with inferior tools,' he says.

Breaking off from the task he has set himself, of examining all the stars in Flamsteed's catalogue, her brother now joins her in searching for nebulae. It is then that the limitations of his own instrument become apparent—for the 'small' twenty-foot is not suitable for the task in hand. This is accordingly given to Caroline, to look for double stars; while William, needing a more powerful telescope still, begins at once to build it.

For him, to think of something is to suppose it done. The inevitable delay between thought and execution drives him, at times, almost to distraction. Impossibility. He does not seem to know the meaning of the word. For him, there are only problems which have yet to be solved. The formidable energy he had brought to bear on rehearsing choirs and composing part-songs, he now directs solely at mastering the heavens. With Lina by his side, he says, there is nothing he cannot do. That she appears to share his enthusiasm is gratifying, but hardly surprising.

The strange thing is, she finds she is becoming as obsessed with the stars as he is.

Because after all the sadness of leaving beloved Bath—of abandoning her music and everything else she had come to love—she discovers, somewhat to her surprise, that her life is not entirely barren of interest. In fact it is burgeoning: with people, incidents, discoveries... Now, on fine nights, she can hardly wait to get out there—into the dark garden, under the wheeling stars. Seeing her breath coming in cloudy bursts upon the wintry air; feeling her eyes streaming with tears from the cold. She does not care about the cold. She is alive, exhilarated by her great endeavour. Tonight she may find another Nebula, not previously found. 'Messier has it not,' she will write. She will sweep the sky from horizon to zenith, and then in azimuth. Nothing will escape her. Diligent *Hausfrau* that she is, she is beginning to know the sky as well as she knows the kitchen floor, across which, every day, she sweeps her broom...

This, then, becomes the order of their days: after a night spent sweeping for comets (or double stars, or whatever is currently under scrutiny) they rise late, and breakfast on cold meat and small beer. The afternoon—or what remains of it—is spent writing letters (William) or cataloguing the previous night's observations (Caroline) before an early dinner of soup, or a boiled fowl. When the weather is fine and there is no Moon, they spend all night observing, from nine or ten until four or five in the morning. While William mans the telescope, Caroline remains nearby, to write down everything as he tells it to her.

O, the bitter cold of those Datchet winters, when, sitting at the open window of her study on the upper floor, or—latterly—in the hut William has had built for the purpose at the foot of the apparatus, she grows so chilled that she can no longer feel her hands and feet. There are times when the thermometer falls to 10 degrees below freezing or less; the ink freezes in her inkwell, and her fingers refuse to write. On her desk sits Flamsteed's Atlas, and a clock set to Sidereal time. When her brother calls out his observations, she writes down the Declination and the Right Ascension, and other circumstances. Sometimes, her fingers smudge the record, so that she is obliged to copy it all out again the next day; or the guttering candle leaves splashes of wax upon the page. Then there are the times when a mistake creeps in, not through her fault, but through that of a blundering assistant (they have been training Mr Orpen's boy, but he has not proved a quick learner).

With so much against them, it is a wonder they achieve anything at all.

Nor are these procedures without more serious hazards. Such is William's impatience to get on with the work, that he begins his series of sweeps with the newly completed 'large' twenty-foot telescope when that instrument is still unfinished—balancing precariously on a cross-beam high above the ground as he makes his observations, and shouting each new calculation down to his sister. She is on tenterhooks lest he should fall; and indeed on one occasion he narrowly avoids being dashed to pieces, when the scaffolding collapses in a high wind, just after he has descended from his perch.

Added to the dangers of falling, or of beams forty feet long and six inches thick crashing down upon one's head, are others—not as likely to be fatal to life and limb, but unpleasant enough. Working in darkness and—as often as not—in haste, increases the risk of tripping over the telescope's supporting spars. She has lost count of the bruises she has acquired on her legs. With such huge instruments, which are constantly being moved into different positions, it is all too easy to bang one's head on protruding bits of apparatus. Professore Piazzi, visiting from his observatory in Palermo, had broken his shins falling over the rack-bar, poor man. Mr Orpen's boy had got a lump as big as an egg on his forehead, from walking into a brass handle in the dark.

One night it has snowed heavily, but William is adamant they should continue in spite of this. For there is no time to lose, he says. Between them, they have already increased the numbers of known nebulae twenty-fold; they must not weaken now. It is ten o'clock at night when they begin—the clouds having lifted to reveal a few faint stars, glimmering high up in the ink-black heavens. William has already climbed up to the front of the telescope, and is making some adjustment to it. Something is not quite right with the lateral positioning of the apparatus, he informs her. This has to be shifted by hand.

It falls to Caroline to do this.

At either side of the telescope's wooden framework are posts, furnished with great iron hooks—such as butchers use for hanging their meat—and to which the guy-ropes tethering the structure are attached.

'Make haste!' she hears her brother cry, from twenty feet above her head.

But as she runs to obey this injunction, she slips on a patch of melting snow and falls, impaling her leg on one of the hooks six inches above the knee.

The shock of it is so great that she does not at first cry out. Blood spurts from the wound and falls in a great arc across the snow.

She cannot help but think of *Schneewittchen*:

die Haut so weiß wie Schnee, Lippen so rot wie Blut, und Haare so schwarz wie Ebenholz...

Again, William shouts:

'Lina! What are you up to?'

'I am hooked!' she manages to reply, half-fainting from the pain of it.

A moment later, he has scrambled down from his perch and is at her side.

'My God, Lina—what have you done?'

Between them, he and one of the workman succeed in disengaging her, although a good piece of her flesh is left behind. The workman's wife is summoned to help, but she is no use at all, poor silly girl, coming over all faint at the sight of the blood. In the end, the patient has to be her own surgeon, by applying aquabaseda, and binding up the injured leg with a handkerchief.

Had she been a soldier on the field of battle, Dr Lind says afterwards, she would have been entitled to six weeks' nursing for such a wound.

Near-fatal accidents aside, their life at Datchet goes on quietly enough, with only the occasional visit from their neighbours at Windsor—King George and his wife—to break the pleasant monotony of their days. The royal couple have formed the habit of dropping by to see what their astronomer is up to—which is only fair, given that they pay for his upkeep, not to mention that of his sister.

The first time it happens, Caroline is taken unawares.

'There is a carriage outside in the lane,' she calls to William.

He seems unperturbed.

'Oh, yes. His Majesty said he might call by. I said I would show him around the instruments, you know…'

The visit passes off successfully, with their royal guest loud in his acclamation for all the innovations that he sees, and William doing what he loves, which is talking about telescopes. Caroline is too overcome with embarrassment at the deplorable state the house is in, with buckets all over the floor to catch the rain, and the sitting room thick with soot from a smoking chimney, to enjoy herself. While her brother and his fellow enthusiast lose themselves in the pleasures of scientific exposition, she does her best to entertain Queen Charlotte. That lady seems as ill-at-ease as herself—once or twice smothering a yawn, or feeding sugar-plums to her little Black page, as the men talk on. As the King's consort, she has little or no say in how he chooses to amuse himself, Caroline supposes. But it seems that Her Majesty, whether bored or not, must have noticed the disruption the unexpected visit had caused. For on subsequent occasions, a footman arrives half an hour before, with a basket of provisions and a little note, announcing that their majesties are to call.

The early summer of 1783 brings another visit, from a visitor as unlooked-for as the Royal Personages had been.

Caroline is in the garden, picking raspberries for a Summer Pudding. She is wearing her oldest dress (the blue one; now so faded it is almost white). Her hands are covered in crimson stains—her lips, too, she supposes, from eating those that fall. All around is the hot, dry smell of mown grass, and the buzzing of bees. William... She does not know where William is, at that moment. She is alone, suffice it to say, and thinking of nothing very much. The notes she must copy up before supper. The letter she must write to Alexander, who has announced his—surely foolish—intention of getting married. How hot the Sun is on the back of her neck...

Suddenly there is the creak of the garden gate. She hears her name pronounced. It cannot be... and yet, evidently, it *is*. She whirls round, so hastily that a spray of brambles leaves a deep scratch on her arm.

'I hope I find you well?' says Edward Pigott. 'I am afraid I took the liberty of calling... since I was at Windsor, you know, and it is so very near...'

'Mr Pigott.'

Having said his name, she is at a loss as to how to continue. She feels her face colour up with blood, hateful sensation. If he had not been standing between her and the house, she would have run away.

Fortunately, he is master of the situation.

'I am delighted to find you alone, for I have a particular favour to ask of you.' He stands for a moment, as if choosing his words carefully. She had forgotten how handsome he is; although there is something about him—an air of abandonment, or slight neglect—which speaks of some inner turmoil... 'Is your brother at home?' he says at last.

Of course. It will be for William that he has come.

'I will go and see,' she replies.

But as she is suiting the action to the word, he puts out a hand and—extraordinary sensation—touches her upon the arm, just below the rolled-up sleeve.

'You have hurt yourself,' he says.

She glances down at her arm, which is indeed beaded with blood, and at his fingers resting there.

'It is nothing,' she says.

'I am afraid there has been a misunderstanding between your brother and myself... that is, between your brother and my friend Mr Goodricke.'

She forces herself to meet his gaze. Impossible to lie to him. 'I believe my brother may have said something about it…'

He gives a faint smile. 'I do not doubt it.'

She had never seen William so angry. 'That insolent puppy!' he had cried. 'He has the temerity to accuse me of trying to claim his precious stars as my own. As if he were another Newton, with discoveries worth stealing. Whereas the truth is, he is a Nobody. Who had heard of him, before Pigott found him?'

The trouble, as far as she can tell, has arisen over variable stars—which, to the best of her knowledge, Mr Pigott had first mentioned to William and herself five years before, in Bath. Now it seems as if Mr Pigott's friend Mr Goodricke has announced the discovery as his own. He has presented a paper on the variable star Algol to the Royal Society—or rather it has been presented on his behalf, for he is deaf and dumb. The week before this paper was read, William, who had been alerted to the possibility that Algol was variable by Dr Maskelyne, had also presented a paper on the subject. There was nothing wrong with that, of course—it was just that the timing was a little unfortunate.

It had caused some ill feeling—not least on William's side. ('The arrogance!' he had cried. 'To suppose that I should want to pre-empt his paltry discovery… which, by the by, is not his discovery at all, but Pigott's. It is all most irregular, I find.')

A consciousness that his own behaviour was not above reproach had perhaps fuelled William's anger—he, who has always been the mildest of men.

'I am sure that my brother bears you no ill-will, Mr Pigott. Nor Mr Goodricke, neither,' she adds quickly. 'Rest assured it is quite forgot.'

'Nevertheless,' he smiles. 'I wonder if you would do me the favour of telling him that I am here—and that I have come to ask his pardon, on my own account, and that of my poor friend? For you must understand, Miss Herschel…' Here, a softer light comes into his eyes. 'Mr Goodricke is very young. He is not versed in the ways of the world, as we older ones are.'

'I will tell my brother that you are here,' she says stiffly.

"Older ones"! She is not so old that her feelings cannot be hurt; nor is Mr Goodricke so young that he cannot learn manners.

Something of her wounded pride must have been apparent, for he says swiftly

'That was ill-expressed. I did not mean to offend you. I sometimes forget,' he adds with a rueful smile, 'that I am talking not only to a fellow-astronomer but to a woman...'

This, though doubtless well-intentioned, does not improve things.

'It is not I but my brother you have offended,' she replies hotly. 'That Mr Goodricke has offended, I mean. For William has no quarrel with *you*, Mr Pigott...'

He bows his head, seemingly cast down by her words.

'I am sorry if your brother is angry with Mr Goodricke.'

'My brother is a generous man, Sir.' To her horror, she feels her eyes start to fill with tears. She blinks them away. 'He does not bear grudges—especially against those, like your friend, whom he has cause to respect as fellow men of science. But to be accused of... of *appropriating* another's researches for his own... that, Sir, he should not have had to bear.'

Until that moment, she has kept her voice steady; now it cracks slightly. She turns her face away, so that he should not see her confusion.

He is silent a moment.

He is angry, she thinks, almost hating the unknown young man who has caused her to use such sharp words to one whose good opinion she values so dearly.

But then he smiles, and it is as if the Sun has come out from behind a cloud.

'Your indignation does you credit, Miss Herschel,' he says. 'I envy your brother in many things—not least in having such a champion. But I can assure you, Mr Herschel's reputation remains unscathed. He is still the Discoverer of Georgium Sidus, and my friend is but a novice...'

Again, his expression grows fond, as if craving indulgence for a favourite child.

'But lacking, it would appear, the humility becoming to a novice,' she cannot stop herself replying.

It has always been her greatest weakness: the desire to have the last word.

Edward Pigott, however, does not seem to take what she says amiss.

'You are right, of course,' he says, his eyes bright with amusement. 'Mr Goodricke is not one to efface himself—at least, where astronomical matters are concerned. In person, you know, he is the Epitome of reserve. For he cannot speak. It may be,' he goes on, still in the same whimsical tone, 'that his very silence in company makes him the more determined to assert his presence in other ways… But my dear Miss Herschel, I am concerned for your hurt.' The look of tender regard he gives her would have melted a heart far less disposed towards softness where he is concerned than her own. 'Can we not find some salve to apply to it?'

It takes her a moment to realise it is her arm he means.

'O no! It is quite all right…' It is with a feeling almost of relief that she sees William, coming toward them down the path. 'Here is my brother. He will be so pleased that you are here. For his feelings towards *you*, Mr Pigott, have never altered, to the best of my knowledge…'

And indeed William could not have been more delighted to see his friend. For he could never stay angry at anyone for long—it is one of his many amiable qualities.

'Why, Pigott—are you here?' he cries, enfolding his brother astronomer in his arms. 'You could not have come at a better time. For we have much to talk about. Tell me…' His face assumes a mischievous look. 'Have you found any more comets, lately? For I must tell you, Lina and I are not to be beaten in this.'

'I had not the least idea of doing so,' says Edward Pigott.

Quarrels over variable stars notwithstanding, that evening turns out to be one of the pleasantest of her life. For Pigott must stay for dinner, of course he must, William says, brooking no argument. Lina will be most upset if he does not. There is half a cold goose, and a piece of gammon besides. And claret—his Majesty had sent over a case only the other day. He would be glad to have Pigott's opinion of it. After dinner, when it gets dark, they will take a look through the new twenty-foot (a great improvement on the old one, to his mind), at any stars, variable or otherwise, their good friend has a mind to...

Mr Pigott, perhaps to make up for his earlier thoughtlessness (for no woman likes to be told that she is old) is the soul of tact. He makes them laugh with tales of the wonderful hot-air balloon he had seen on his last visit to Paris: 'For you know the French are determined to beat us in this, since'—with a bow to William—'they cannot compete with our discoveries in the astronomical realm...' He praises her cooking—'O, how this reminds me of our delightful Bath dinners!'—and admires the improvements she has made in the parlour, which, for once, is not smelling of damp, but of the night-scented stocks she has planted under the window.

She is on the point of leaving them to their conversation, for there is still the washing-up to do, when William says, 'Come Lina—leave all that. I am sure you can do it in the morning. Why not give us a song? Pigott here will be disappointed if you do not, for he has always been an admirer of yours...'

She protests that she is not in voice—has not practised for ever so long—and that, in any case, the instrument is not in tune...

Needless to say, her brother pays attention to none of this.

'Just one song, Lina. For I am sure I hear you warbling about the place often enough, when you think no one is by...'

'Please,' says Edward Pigott. 'I should so like to hear you sing once more. For you know I have never forgotten your beautiful performance in *Messiah*.'

'A capital idea!' cries William, taking his seat at the harpsichord. 'Here is the very piece...' He opens it at once, and begins to play.

So it is that she reprises the part she had first sung five years before, when it had felt as if everything—fame, fortune, even love—lay all before her, to choose, or not to choose...

I know that my Redeemer liveth
and that he shall stand at the latter day
upon the earth...

The tremulous beauty of the melody—'as if an angel had begun to weep' William had once said—fills the room, so that for the duration of the piece, nothing else seems to exist. Neither pain; nor grief, or disappointment; nor envy, nor any other pettiness of spirit. All are forgotten, in the sheer rapture of Being, of which her voice (not, after all, as rusty as she had feared) is merely the conduit.

And though worms destroy this body,
yet in my flesh shall I see God...

She had not looked at their guest while she was singing, afraid it might cause her voice to falter; now, in the moment's silence after the last chords have died away, she steals a glance at him, and is startled to see that his face is wet with tears.

VIII

It is more than a year before she sees Edward Pigott again. Not that he is ever out of her thoughts for very long. For months after their meeting in the garden at Datchet, she dreams of him, sleeping and waking. The moment when she first heard his voice, as she stood there, among the raspberry-canes: *Miss Herschel...* The moment when she first saw him. The moment—of all the moments, the most precious to her—when he touched her arm: *I am concerned for your hurt...* All these she returns to, in hours of idleness, like priceless treasures to be looked at, then carefully hidden away from envious eyes.

She hears tell of him occasionally from William, of course—since the two men are in the habit of corresponding. But of late, there have been fewer letters.

'Pigott spends all his time in York, these days—hunting out variable stars,' says William, with a shrug.

If Edward Pigott has not the time to spare for his oldest friends, the gesture seems to say, it is no concern of *his*.

And of course they are as busy as ever with searching for nebulae. Caroline's self-appointed task—encouraged by William—is to familiarise herself as much as possible with those that are listed in Messier's Catalogue. Only thus will she be able to distinguish unknown objects—that is, comets—from those already identified. Until the middle of June, she had been making good progress, but the weather since then has been dreadful—foggy by day (in July!) and cloudy by night. It is as if her own prevailing melancholy has transferred itself to the atmospheric conditions. 'The night being indifferent,' she writes on 6th August 'I look'd for some of Mess. Nebulae, and saw 81 & 82; but could not see 97; nor that near Delta Ursae Majoris. Cloudy.'

Cloudy it remains, for the next six weeks. The fruit trees in her garden grow mouldy with blight. Even the Moon looks sickly: its hue a dull red, like a pewter plate thrust in the fire, instead of its usual silver-gilt colour.

It is a relief when, towards the end of this spell of dull days, a violent storm breaks through the oppressive atmosphere. She watches it from her bedroom window. It seems as if the whole firmament is on fire. Great peals of thunder rattle the tiles upon the roof, and the rain falls without ceasing for three hours. In the morning, when she goes to inspect the damage in her garden, she sees that one of the great elms in the pasture beyond has been struck by lightning, its trunk split from top to bottom, as neatly as if with an axe.

When she does meet Edward Pigott again, it is because of variable stars... at least, that is what takes William to London. Her own reason for following him to the metropolis is somewhat more mundane. For there is to be a meeting of the Royal Society—the first of the new year—which William is to attend, to hear Mr Goodricke's paper on Beta Lyrae read. He (William) is to spend the night with Mr Aubert at Deptford, where the latter has promised his guest a tour of his Observatory. As well as a Bird transit, and a Dollond reflector, he has just acquired a fine new clock by Mr Arnold.

Knowing Alexander Aubert's interest in such matters, William is determined to take with him his latest findings on double stars. Of course the notebook containing the observations cannot be found (when can anything ever be found, in that Wilderness of papers which lies upon his desk?)... So that in all the to-do of searching it out, it is not until she goes back into the house, after seeing him off, that Caroline notices that her brother has left his travelling-bag behind. This contains, amongst other necessaries, his flannel waistcoat—a sure guard against the ague, which has racked him for two winters past, and against which he has been known to rub himself all over with a raw onion. In this inclement weather—it has been snowing heavily—such a prophylactic cannot be done without.

She makes up her mind at once: she must follow him to London. If she leaves at once, she will still be in time for the two o'-clock coach from the Crown. On previous visits, she has been offered a bed for the night by Mr Aubert's friends, Mr and Mrs Gibson, who have a charming new house near Deptford High

Street. Since Mr Aubert himself is a bachelor, with male servants, it is only within his power to accommodate gentlemen, he has explained.

Once seated in the lumbering coach (for the roads are icy and treacherous, and progress necessarily slow), Caroline feels the pleased excitement of one taking a holiday from duty. In truth, she ought to be spending the day in more domestic pursuits—there is a shirt of William's which needs the sleeves setting-in, and a piece of brawn to be soaked for tomorrow's dinner. But, as they journey through the snowy fields, which sparkle in the low winter sun as if they have been scattered with handfuls of diamonds, she feels her heart lift, and a feeling—almost—of happiness pierce her.

Will *he* be there? she wonders. She supposes it will be so. For if his friend's paper is to be read, then it stands to reason that he will be amongst the listeners. Perhaps he will speak to her, or smile at her, at least. She loves to see him smile... She pushes the thought away. It does not do to have such thoughts. In a few weeks' time, she will be five-and-thirty: much too old for lovesick fancies.

In the years that have passed since her first meeting with Edward Pigott, she has often had cause to reflect upon why things have turned out as they have. For. although she knows only too well that he cannot love her for her looks, she had once thought that he might care for her in spite of them. It was not such a foolish notion. Were they not united in their passion for the stars? For music, too; and poetry. Nor was it solely their mutual delight in intellectual pursuits which had persuaded her, for a time, that Edward Pigott might have found it in himself to care for her...

Of course she is older than he is—a fact she had discovered by chance when they were talking of his having witnessed the Transit of Venus. That had been in 1769, when he was sixteen, he said. She had been nineteen at the time, although she did not say so. But she wonders now if perhaps the discrepancy in their ages (although how could he have *known*, unless William had told him?) might have mattered to him...

Either that, or he simply did not regard her in that light. As a friend—yes; as a partner in scientific endeavour—certainly. But not as a woman; not as a lover; or a prospective bride.

Night after night, she had lain awake, turning these things over in her mind.

'Why does he not love me? Why?' she had wept in her extremity. Did she not love him enough for two? The cruelty of it was almost more than she could bear.

And yet she has had no choice but to bear it.

Month, after month, she had watched her blood appear—mocking her with her barrenness; her failure to attract a mate. She would die barren, she realised, during one of these terrible, sleepless nights. No man would ever love her, because she was un-loveable. A freakish thing, like poor, mutilated Farinelli, with his angel's voice. Disdaining, as she had, the claims of marriage and children for those of Science and Art, she had denied her natural function...

Now she is paying for her presumption. That the man she loves does not—cannot—bring himself to love her is a bitter draught to swallow.

It is dark by the time they reach the Strand, and lamps blaze in all the great houses along the street. Snow has started to fall once more; its spiralling flakes catch the light which streams from the tall un-curtained windows. There are more people about than might have been expected, in such weather—peering in the windows of jewellers' shops, and waving their arms to hail passing chairs. The sight brings back memories of her first—or rather second—visit to London, with Mrs Colnbrook. What an Infant she was! Not that she is a great deal more practised now in the ways of the world than she was then...

She could have journeyed on forever, looking at the lights, the crowds, the falling snow—but all at once, it seems, they are arrived, in front of Somerset House. She feels a flutter of nervous apprehension at the prospect of—at last—setting foot inside that august Institution. She hopes her appearance there will not cause too much consternation amongst the Society's Fellows—for whom the presence of a woman beneath that roof will be, to say the least, irregular. She hopes, too, that William will not be angry with her for making such a commotion about a waistcoat. Having nursed him through several bad bouts of illness, she knows her anxiety to be well-founded, however.

The meeting is already in session when she enters the building, whose imposing portals fill her with a sense of her own insignificance. For is this not the Forum where all the great Minds of the Age meet? That she—a mere Nobody—now finds herself amongst them, makes her tremble at her own temerity.

She had intended to leave William's bag with the Porter, and to send a note announcing her presence by the same factotum; but the great echoing marble hall is empty, and so she has no choice but to climb the stairs, to where the double doors to the meeting room stand open.

From within, comes the sound of a voice, which she recognises as Sir Henry Englefield's. Setting down the bag, which has suddenly grown heavy, she creeps closer.

At once, her attention is arrested by a name she knows:

'...at ten o'clock it was not so bright as Gamma Lyrae, but rather brighter than Theta and Xi Herculis. Mr Edward Pigott thought it nearly equal to Gamma Lyrae...'

She catches her breath. He *is* here—she is sure of it! Noiselessly, she moves closer still, until she is standing in the doorway.

The sight which meets her awe-struck gaze is not, in itself, awesome: just rows and rows of seated gentlemen—perhaps two hundred in all—their attention directed towards the speaker upon the platform. Some of these, she sees, with an agitated sense of the incongruity of her own presence, are familiar to her. Mr Blagden is there; Dr Maskelyne; Mr Aubert; and of course her brother. Others—the majority—she does not know. Some are young, with the dandyish carelessness in their dress which even young men of Science affect; others are old, and decidedly lacking in any sense of Fashion.

All, whether familiar or unfamiliar, young or old, fashionable or not, pay her not the slightest bit of attention—intent as they are on what is being said. She is grateful for this, for to have been noticed by such a crowd would have been terrifying. There are times when being small and unremarkable as to looks has its advantages.

Across that sea of sombre brown, blue, black and grey (interspersed with an occasional splash of brighter colour—a rust-red coat, or a saffron-yellow), Sir Henry's voice rises and falls, its measured tones chronicling varying magnitudes and weather conditions.

He mentions another name she knows:

'As Beta Lyrae is a quadruple star, Number Three of Mr Herschel's Fifth Class of Double Stars, I was desirous to see if any of the small stars near it would be affected by its different changes...'

In the same instant, she sees Edward Pigott at last—sitting in the front row, in a dark green coat of elegant cut, his lightly powdered hair tied with a black velvet ribbon. As she watches, he touches the shoulder of the young man in blue sitting beside him, who turns his head at this summons. A smiling look passes between them.

The smile is still on Edward Pigott's face as he glances round at the room behind, perhaps to take account of how his friend's paper is being received. At once she wants to shrink back out of sight behind the door, but by then he has seen her. His smile fades momentarily, giving way to a look of faint surprise; then grows bright once more. He nods at her politely, before turning back towards the speaker. For Sir Henry, it appears, is drawing to a conclusion. Sensing this, his audience stirs slightly, flexing limbs grown stiff from enforced immobility, and preparing to reward both reader and Originator of the paper with well-deserved applause.

Had she not been distracted by his—Edward's—presence, she would have been listening with avid attention; as it is, she is barely able to comprehend a word—even though some of it concerns her brother's comparison of Hevelius's catalogue with Flamsteed's, with which she had herself assisted.

By this time, William has also seen her. *His* look is unequivocally one of astonishment. As Sir Henry ends, and the applause begins, he leaves his seat and hurries over to her.

'Why, Lina, what brings you here? There is nothing wrong at home, I hope?'

With a feeling that she has perhaps been over-hasty in her decision to follow him to London, she explains her presence there.

'You dear goose! What a lot of trouble you have had for no reason! I am sure Aubert would have lent me a suit of clothes,' he says.

A little put-out by this reception, she is about to remind him of the flannel waistcoat, when he cuts across her.

'Ah, Pigott! I must congratulate you. A most interesting paper,' he says.

Edward Pigott inclines his head.

'Thank you. But it is my friend Mr Goodricke who deserves your praise more than I...'

'Indeed,' says William Herschel stiffly. 'Then please convey it to him.'

'You may do so yourself,' is the reply. 'For I know he is anxious to renew his acquaintance with you—and to pay his respects to Miss Herschel, too,' he adds, looking at Caroline.

And indeed, coming towards them through the crowd of learned gentlemen, most of whom seem intent on grasping him by the hand, or clapping him upon the back, is the handsome youth at whom Edward Pigott had smiled.

'There you are!' the latter cries. 'Come—here is Mr Herschel, full of kind things to say about your paper. But first you must meet Miss Herschel—my very dear good friend...'

'Your servant, Sir.'

She drops a curtsey. The young man—Mr Goodricke—bows.

'If you speak slowly and clearly, and direct your remarks towards him, Mr Goodricke will be perfectly able to understand you,' murmurs Edward Pigott in her ear.

'I must congratulate you, Sir, on your excellent paper,' she says to John Goodricke accordingly.

He bows again. Then he draws notebook and pencil from his pocket, scribbles something, and hands it to her.

Miss Herschel is too kind, she reads. *But I am but a novice in these matters*.

Remembering her sharp words to Edward Pigott the summer before last, she feels her colour rise. Could it be that her angry reproof had been conveyed to its object?

But his gaze is innocent of any mischief. The large, light eyes regard her calmly. The silent lips curve in a charming smile.

'We are all novices, are we not, where Astronomy is concerned?'

He acknowledges the remark with a slight inclination of the head.

'But I must present you to my brother,' she says, with a smile that embraces both the young deaf-mute and his friend.

For William has turned away, and is now deep in conversation with a red-faced gentleman of self-important bearing, whose name she does not know.

She touches her brother upon the sleeve.

'William, here is Mr Goodricke who wants a word with you...'

The sentence is barely out of her mouth when she wishes it back again. How difficult it is in such circumstances not to give offence!

Her face grows hot with blushes.

'I mean...' she begins; but Edward Pigott comes to her rescue.

'Mr Goodricke would, I am sure, be honoured by a word from Mr Herschel,' he says. 'That is, if my father has quite finished expounding his theories on the respective merits of reflecting and refracting telescopes,' he adds *sotto voce*.

Caroline cannot refrain from staring. So the red-faced gentleman who has been talking to her brother with such an air of self-satisfaction is Edward Pigott's father! It is hard to detect the slightest resemblance between them. She supposes Mr Pigott the younger must get his good looks from his mother, to say nothing of his amiable disposition... It strikes her that, whilst he has often spoken of that lady with the warmest affection, he seldom mentions his father—and then only with a kind of sarcastic raillery, not indicative of tender feeling.

Loving Edward as she does, she cannot believe that the fault could lie with him. A reason for the Melancholy which she has detected at moments when he thought himself unobserved, now suggests itself. With such a father, who can be surprised at the son's being given to low spirits?

The object of these private reflections seems in excellent spirits at that moment, however—smiling delightedly as he propels his friend forward, to where the eminent astronomer is standing.

'Mr Goodricke,' he says distinctly, 'is a great admirer of yours.'

At this prompting, John Goodricke holds out his hand, and, after a barely perceptible instant, William Herschel takes it.

'I was interested in what you said about dark spots as a possible cause of Beta Lyrae's variations,' he says. 'For I find myself much occupied at present with the question of dark spots upon the Sun…'

She is afraid that the poor young man will make nothing of this, for it is said with William's customary rapidity. But Mr Goodricke appears to catch at least the drift of it, for he nods, and scribbles something in his notebook.

Having read the note, William nods vigorously in his turn.

'Yes, yes,' he says. 'I will send you the paper forthwith. For it may be that some of its observations will have a bearing on your researches into variable stars…'

'I see that you, too, are to be congratulated, Miss Herschel,' says Edward Pigott in an undertone.

'I do not understand you, Sir.'

He smiles.

'You have effected a *rapprochement* between my hot-headed young colleague here and your esteemed brother—and for that I am eternally in your debt. For to be friends with two people who have fallen out is not an enviable role… especially when both are of—let us say—a *fiery* disposition.'

'They are astronomers, Sir. Fire is their element.'

'And air, too, one must suppose. But tell me, Miss Herschel, how is it that you have come to grace these gloomy halls with your presence? Are ladies at last to be admitted to the ranks of Fellows of the Royal Society? I, for one, would welcome such an innovation—if only because it might help to civilize what can sometimes seem like a very *uncivilized* Beargarden…'

'No, no.'

Briefly, she explains about the forgotten bag, and—in a low voice which will not reach William's ears—the flannel waistcoat.

'I see that I am doubly indebted to you,' Edward Pigott says. 'Not only have you brought together my two dearest friends, but you have preserved one of them from almost certain death through exposure to the elements.'

Laughing, she is about to protest at this absurdity—if only to have the pleasure of hearing him tease her some more. But at that moment, his attention is caught by something across the room. A look, or a gesture, from his friend, perhaps…

'Forgive me, but I must go. Mr Goodricke and I are invited to dinner with Sir Joseph Banks, and it is already past four.' A look of faint embarrassment crosses his features. 'I do not know if Mr Herschel and yourself are also to be of the party?'

'We have other arrangements, Sir.'

'In that case, I must bid you goodbye, for the present.'

He presses her hand—a private signal of farewell; then makes his bow—a public one. As he and his young companion move towards the door, their progress is slowed by the same polite ritual, enacted with all those that are encountered along the way.

But in the end they are gone.

She feels her own singularity then—a woman, in a crowd of men. In Edward Pigott's company, she had not felt herself out of place… Where on earth is William? Surely he cannot have gone, and left her behind? If he is capable of forgetting his luggage, she knows he is also perfectly capable of forgetting his sister.

At last she sees him, still talking to Mr Pigott the elder. It is only then that she thinks to wonder that the latter's son had neglected to introduce her to him.

'Ah, Lina, there you are,' says William. 'I was just saying to Mr Pigott here that we have had a fair turn-out today, in spite of the weather…'

'A turn-out including members of the fair sex, too,' says Nathaniel Pigott, with a wink. 'You did not say, Herschel, that you was to bring a young lady…'

'My sister, Sir,' says William.

Even after so many years in England, he is still ill-at-ease with English humour.

''Servant, Madam,' says the elder Mr Pigott carelessly. 'Now, Herschel—about that telescope you was to build for me…'

But just then, William, too, appears to be reminded of something.

'Come, Lina. Mr Aubert has his carriage waiting. I must bid you goodbye, Sir,' he says to the importunate Mr Pigott. 'I am afraid in all this snow it will take us at least an hour to get to Deptford.'

IX

From Datchet, with its fogs and damps, they move—first to Old Windsor, then (when the landlady there turns out to be a scheming wretch) to Slough. Not the most beautiful of names, and not the most beautiful of places. Still, the house—square-built of brick, with a sound roof and weather-tight windows—is an improvement on draught-ridden Datchet. For William, it is the fulfilment of all his aspirations, to have a garden large enough, not only for the twenty-foot telescope, but for the forty-foot he is in the process of building. To this end, he has been granted £2,000 from the King's private purse—a sum which, though it sounds considerable, is not (Caroline feels) especially generous. Since the estimated cost of the telescope is £1,395, with an annual running cost of £150, and mirrors costing £500 apiece, the sum offered (and accepted) does not, after all, seem excessive.

But although she had not liked Datchet, there are times, in the months that follow, when she finds herself looking back on the peaceful solitude they had enjoyed there with something like regret. For now begins a time of constant racket and upset, with upwards of thirty workmen digging holes for the foundations of the new telescope, and felling trees for the construction of the scaffold which is to bear its weight. All day long, there is a sawing of wood and a hammering of metal, with the wash-house turned into a foundry for the making of tools. Nor do the workmen—loud, uncouth hobbledehoys that they are—show any restraint as regards shouting, singing and whistling, seeming to think it a great joke when she begs them to stop.

After a night spent hunting for nebulae, how are she and William to get any sleep at all, with such a Bedlam going on around them from dawn till dusk?

For if the twenty-foot had seemed a huge structure, with the scaffolding which supported it reaching higher than the roof, it is dwarfed in every respect by the gigantic forty-foot. This—a vast tent-shaped construction of wooden struts and ladders, supported on circular brick foundations capped with Portland stone—towers above house, garden and surrounding countryside, so that, both while it is being built and after, it becomes the focus of much local curiosity.

Is it a church tower they are building? enquires one village wag. No, says another, it is more like a gallows—or an engine of war...

Certainly, there is something military about the structure, especially once the great tube of the telescope has been hauled into place. This is made out of a single sheet of rolled iron, first shaped by being bent around a circular wooden frame, then joined together without rivets—a process similar to the one for making stove-pipes, or the funnels of ships.

If the denizens of Slough had been jocular in their speculations as to the nature of the contraption before, now they grow positively ribald.

'That's a bloody big 'un, and no mistake,' is a typical remark, directed over the garden wall. 'Don't reckon as I've ever seen a bigger...'

As for the workmen—their filthiness knows no bounds.

'Why do you s'pose it is, Jack,' one says to another, as Caroline is passing on her way to the workshops, 'that the gu-v'nor'—he means William—'is so set on having a forty-foot one, when he's already got a twenty-foot? Most men 'ud be glad of a ten-inch one...'

'Or a nine-inch.'

'Nine inches 'ud satisfy *me*,' leers the first one, as—face flaming—she sweeps by.

Brutes. What do any of them understand of what she and William are trying to achieve, or of the sacrifices they have made? What do any of them care for the stars, or for the vastness of Space? All they care for is gratifying their base appetites.

Although (she has to admit) without the workmen, their great Endeavour would have taken rather longer to accomplish—if it could have been accomplished at all. Building a scaffold fifty feet high would have been taxing enough—to say nothing of making the enormous tube. As for the mirrors which the tube is to contain, these are still more difficult—requiring as they do, the most perfect technique in the casting, grinding and polishing.

No, they could not have managed without the workmen.

In the barn set aside for the purpose has been set up a kind of altar, on whose convex surface the mirror—some four feet in diameter—has been placed, and held fast in a twelve-sided frame. Twelve men—the acolytes of this strange rite—grasp the twelve handles protruding from the framework's sides—each of which is numbered in accordance with the numbers each man wears upon his smock, both for ease of giving orders ('to the left, Number Three; to the right, Number Seven') and to protect the men's clothes from splashes of the chemicals with which the huge mirror is coated. It is then moved slowly on the mould, for several hours and in varying directions, in order to produce the parabolic shape so necessary to the astronomer's art.

Her brother himself oversees the process, for his years of polishing mirrors by hand have given him an instinctive feel for the curvature required, and he always knows when to change from the 'glory' stroke—in which the polisher directs his stroke outwards like the spokes of a wheel—to the 'eccentric' stroke—which, by avoiding the middle, helps to achieve the shape and finish needed.

Nor is this the end of the procedure, for William is obliged to install the mirror, which weighs almost 2200 lbs, in order to test it—a laborious and potentially hazardous business in itself. But the mirror's finish has to be perfect before it will be of use to him—and so it must be lifted up on pulleys, and lowered into place, and adjusted, and inspected, on several successive occasions, before he is able to pronounce himself satisfied at last.

'For you know, Lina, it will give us almost double the light of the instruments I have made so far,' he says to her one night, at the end of one such exhausting series of trials. 'I will see such sights with it as I know not what…'

She murmurs her appreciation of this fact, as both stand gazing up at the Colossus, whose black framework seems, from this angle, to blot out the sky.

It is not until some weeks after that she herself ventures to try the instrument, whose viewing-chair is reached by climbing a ladder above the spectators' platform. Even at this height—only half-way up the structure, she does not dare to look down, although William assures her it is quite safe. Unlike the earlier models, the viewing platform of the forty-foot is at the front, not at the side—also an advantage with regard to light-gathering, says William.

That night the great tube is directed at Sirius. When the star enters the field of the telescope, she is almost dazzled by its size and brilliance. So bright is it, in fact, that it is impossible to perceive anything else around it. Only after she has been gazing for twenty minutes or so, is it possible to make out stars of lesser magnitude.

'Did I not tell you, Lina?' her brother says happily, when she reports this finding. 'We shall have more light than we known what to do with…'

But in fact it is not long before the disadvantages of the forty-foot telescope become apparent. With so large an expanse of metal comprising its mirror, the instrument takes a long time to adjust to changes in air temperature. By the time it has done so, the night is often half over. And it is cumbersome to move. Too often, one spends much of the time intended for observing in tedious mechanical arrangements. With the twenty-foot, one could be ready in less than ten minutes.

It is as well, Caroline thinks, that William—to say nothing of his Royal Patron—knew nothing of this when he began his ambitious Enterprise.

The building of the forty-foot is far from complete when, at the King's request (that is to say, at his *command*), William has to go to Germany. He is to present one of the smaller telescopes he has been commissioned to make for his Majesty to the university at Göttingen, on the latter's behalf. Alexander is to accompany him; there will be time for a visit to the family in Hannover afterwards. Alexander duly arrives from Bath, bringing his wife with him. She is to stay with Caroline at Slough—to keep her company, it has been decided. Although the truth of it is, her company drives Caroline to distraction. Such an empty-headed, gossiping creature she is, caring nothing for books—which make her head ache, she says—nor for music or any other thing. Nor is she—vain, silly girl!—much help when it comes to the rough work around the house, for it spoils her hands, she says.

Of work there is a great deal, as ever. In order to keep track of it, Caroline writes it all down. Cataloguing has by now become something of a Mania with her, so that everything, from small to great, finds its way into her records. Thus in those first three weeks that her brothers are away, her journal shows that she has spent her time as follows:

> listing all the Nebulae which have been discovered so far—both in Flamsteed's time and latterly, by herself and William;
>
> cleaning all the brass-work for the seven- and ten-foot telescopes;
>
> sewing [her brown dress needs a new collar];
>
> shopping with Mrs Herschel [which at least keeps *her* happy];
>
> showing Dr and Mrs Kelly, and Mr Gordon [a natural son of the Duke of G.] around the instruments;
>
> putting all the Philosophical Letters in order;
>
> paying the Smith and the Gardener [who calls her a stingy so-and-so because she will not pay him for the days he is not wanted];
>
> calculating all their recent sweeps, with reference to Flamsteed's Catalogue;
>
> entertaining Dr and Mrs Maskelyne [now *she* is a sensible woman. Not too delicate in her ways to pick up a needle, nor a duster, neither];

visiting [with the Maskelynes and Dr Shepherd] the Marquis of Huntly;

ruling pages for the Register of Sweeps [a very time-consuming business];

putting up Mrs Alberts and the Papendiek family for the night [a great inconvenience. People are constantly inviting themselves to stay, as if the very fact of there being a Telescope on the premises makes the house an Hotel];

ruling paper [again] and cutting out ruffles for shirts;

sweeping for comets from 11 p m until 1 o'clock;

paying a bill for timber [sweeping having proved impossible that night because it was cloudy];

showing visitors [again] around the instruments. These include Prince Charles, the Queen's brother, the Duke of Saxe Gotha and the Duke of Montague...

and so on and so forth. She has not the patience to write down all the rest. If it had not been for what happened on the 1st August, she would have consigned these dull pages to the fire.

But on that—as it turns out—fateful day, the entry reads as follows:

I have calculated 100 nebulae today, and this evening I saw an object which I believe will prove to morrow night to be a Comet.

It does indeed prove to be a comet. From that moment on, her life will follow a different trajectory.

It is a beautiful evening. She has wandered in the garden after supper, to watch the light fade, and the first stars appear. Around her, rises the scent of honeysuckle, and of new-mown grass, from the surrounding meadows. Moths flit through the twilight—one grazing her face with its wings: a spectral kiss. The sky deepens from rose to violet, and from violet to black. Soon she will ascend to her rooftop, and set up the telescope. But still she lingers. How pleasant it is to dawdle here, in the cool of the garden, with no claims upon her time but those she makes herself. Much as she enjoys her brother's company, it is good, this once, to have her thoughts at her own disposal...

If there have ever been occasions when she has wished for another kind of life, now is not one of them. To be alone, on such a night (Mrs H. having gone to bed early, with one of her headaches), is all she desires.

The realization that, in that moment, she is entirely happy, makes her smile.

Humming softly to herself—an aria from *Die Entführung aus dem Serail*—she crosses the courtyard to her own dear Observatory Cottage, and climbs the stairs. On such a clear night, she hopes to spend a good four hours sweeping. 'Minding the heavens' is her phrase for it. With luck—and diligence—she might net several as-yet unrecorded nebulae, to show to William on his return.

The telescope—designed expressly for her by William—is not one of his larger constructions, but a Newtonian reflector with a focal length of two feet, mounted on pivots in a box-frame, so that it can be raised and lowered with ease. Though small, it possesses great light-gathering power, with a mirror 4.2 inches in diameter, similar to that of the seven-foot reflector, with which William had first sighted the planet Uranus. The sweeper's magnification—X24—is comparatively low, but its observational field is large, enabling the observer—herself—to see unknown objects within a wide context of more familiar surrounding stars.

It is thus perfect for hunting comets.

Still humming, she sits down on the stool which—placed exactly at the right height within the wooden stand—brings her eye to the precise spot for viewing. Then she waits, the music running on in her head, as her eyes gets used to the dark. For seeing, as William never tires of saying, is something one has to practise. The eye is a precise and delicate instrument; it cannot be hurried. Ten minutes accordingly pass. To her dark-adapted gaze, the sky seems a vast inverted bowl, filled up with stars. She knows this to be an illusion; Space is not fixed, as the Ancients believed, but limitless. A bottomless well, into which we are all falling...

She adjusts the angle of the telescope, by winding the brass handle designed for the purpose. She locates the Pole Star; moves across towards Boötes, and Coronae Borealis; then down to the horizon, and Coma Berenices...

Schauen Sie, Carolina!

...then back across to Ursa Major, with all its familiar stars. There they are: Alkaid, Mizar, Alioth, Megrez, Phad, Merak, Dubhe... And... something else. Is there? She looks. Blinks. Looks again. It cannot be... can it? She takes her eye from the glass, and rubs at it furiously. A speck, a piece of dust, must have confused her. But when she reapplies her eye to the instrument, the Shape is still there.

Quite unmistakable. Like that of a burning torch, flung across the sky...

Transfixed by what she sees, she finds she is unable to move; in fact hardly able to breathe, in case her breathing should cause the apparatus to tremble. Although it is not the Sweeper that trembles, but the observer—despite the fact that the night is far from cold.

Bright Star. How bright it is! She feels she could look at it forever. This, then, she thinks, is what her existence so far has been *for*.

She does not know how long she sits there, watching it—her Stranger, her Visitor—as it moves steadily across the sky, on its way to what distant realm? She cannot say. Only that (so she has been assured, and so she believes), there are other realms, apart from this one.

Worlds beyond this world. The thought induces a kind of terror.

Shaking herself out of the strange paralysis the sight has induced, she reaches for her notebook, to record the co-ordinates of the as-yet unidentified Object. She will check them tomorrow.

If, as seems likely, it proves to be what she thinks it is, she will write directly to the Society.

Yet still she sits, her eye to the glass, unable to tear herself away. My Star, she thinks, her eyes filling suddenly with tears, so that the comet—so bright, so irrefutably *there*—blurs into a formless haze of trembling light.

She writes at once to Dr Blagden at the Royal Society with her news:

> Slough, 2d Augt, 1786
>
> Sir,
>
> In consequence of the friendship which I know to exist between you and my brother I venture to trouble you in his absence with the following imperfect account of a Comet.
>
> The employment of writing down the observations, when my Brother uses the 20 feet reflector, does not often allow me time to look at the heavens, but as he is now on a visit to Germany I have taken the opportunity to sweep in the neighbourhood of the Sun, in search of Comets; and last night the 1st of Aug.t about 10 o'clock, I found an object very much resembling in colour and brightness the 27 Nebula of the Conaissance des temps, with the difference however of being round. I suspected it to be a comet; but a haziness coming on, it was not possible intirely to satisfy myself as to its motion till this evening...

To her letter to Mr Aubert, she appends a drawing she has made of the comet's location, in relation to certain nearby stars:

> In Fig.1, I observed the nebulous Spot at the centre. A bright red, but small Star upwards, another very faint white Star following... The only Stars I can see with the naked eye, which might be of service to point out the place of the Comet; are 53 & 54 Ursa maj. of which it is ab.t an equal dist. with the 14 15 & 16 Coma Ber. and makes an obtuse angle with them...

She also drafts a letter to Mr Pigott—for are they not fellow comet-hunters?

> Knowing, as I do, your interest in such matters, I thought it might please you to know that I have discovered a Comet…

But in the end, she does not send it, for she does not have his address in Belgium.

Dr Blagden and Mr Aubert are both most appreciative of her discovery; the latter, in fact, is positively fulsome in his praise—although, admittedly, as much of this is directed towards her brother as herself:

> I wish you joy most sincerely for the discovery. I am more pleased than you can well conceive that you have made it and I think that your wonderfully clever and wonderfully amiable Brother, upon the news of it, shed a tear of joy.

Although he is gracious enough to conclude

> You have immortalized your name.

She knows this to be absurd—for has not William immortalised it already? And yet she cannot help but take pleasure in the remark.

Dr Blagden has taken the liberty, he says, of informing the gentlemen of the Royal Society of Miss Herschel's comet. He has mentioned it in letters to Paris and Munich, and is sure that there will be a great deal of interest in the phenomenon. Even so, she is unprepared for quite how much interest there is.

On 6th August, the President and Secretary of the Royal Society, together with Lord Palmerston, arrive in Slough, with the express purpose of viewing the comet through Miss Herschel's telescope. Also of the party is Miss Burney, whom Caroline thinks very pretty and smart, if a little sharp in her manner.

'La, Miss Herschel, how pleased you must be!' she says, when she has taken her turn at the instrument. 'For this is the first Lady's Comet, is it not? I am sure I was very desirous to see it for that reason alone...'

Caroline is not sure what to make of this remark, and so merely bows, with what she hopes is a dignified air. A Lady's Comet, indeed! She is not aware that there is more than one kind... unless this is an example of the author of *Cecilia*'s famous wit.

Further letters of congratulation arrive by every post; for the first time she can recall, there are more for herself than for her brother.

The day she hears the news is a day like any other. William has just returned from Germany, to a household still in some disarray as a result of her discovery. For she has been so taken up with answering letters, and receiving visitors—not to mention sweeping for comets—that she has had no time to prepare her usual celebratory dinner on his return; nor is the house any less untidy, or the garden any less of a confusion of wooden spars and piles of bricks, and other essentials of the builder's trade, than before he left.

But if William is at all put out by this dereliction of duty on his sister's part, he gives no sign of it. No one, in fact, could have been more delighted than he appears to be at her sudden fame, nor at the reason for it.

'Well done, Lina! You see, I was right, was I not, when I said that we should make an astronomer of you?'

'I was lucky, that is all. It so happened that I was looking at the right place in the sky at the right time...'

'Luck is but a small part of it,' her brother replies. 'For if your many hours of observing the wonders of the heavens had not taught you what to look for, then your being in the 'right place' as you put it, would have counted for nothing...'

Now he whistles to himself—a favourite air from *Semele*—as he sorts through the mass of correspondence which has accumulated during his absence. She is hovering nearby—for if there are bills to be paid amongst them (and she knows he has been ordering materials for his telescope-making) she will have to see to them without delay. Sighing a little to herself—for it is hard, after so many weeks of basking in glory, to have to concern herself again with such dull matters—she is gazing out of the window, when she is brought up suddenly by a sharp exclamation from her brother.

In his hand is a letter. She knows from his expression that the news it contains cannot be good.

Demon Star

✸✸✸✸✸✸✸✸✸✸

X

Groningen, 1768

All the sounds he ever hears are in his first four years.

First there is her voice—his mother's—crooning to him, in such tender accents. *Mijn liefde. Mijn darling. Mijn engel. Mijn klein zoon.* Then another voice—louder; amused: his father's. 'Speak English, won't you? We don't want him growing up a little Dutchman.' All the words are there, whether he understands them or no. All the sounds, too. His mother's breath—a gentle sighing, that is like the wind stirring the branches, on the fine warm days when his cot is taken outside, to be placed beneath the apple tree, where the petals fall softly, so softly, upon his face.

His mother says, 'Look, he's smiling,' and his father replies, 'He doesn't know how.'

There is the sound of the birds singing in the trees. His mother says their names. *Robin. Merel. Sanglijster. Koekoek.* The clouds moving overhead, soundlessly, all the while.

Later, when he moves from the cot to a bed of his own, there are other sounds. The click-clack of his mother's embroidered slippers on the black-and-white tiled floor. Her silk dress rustling. The snuffling of the little dog that follows at her heels. There is the sound of her laughter, when Rikki sits up and begs for sweets, or rolls over and plays dead. And at bedtime, the murmur of her voice, going on over his head in the darkness...

Sheherazade, innig verblijd dat hare vertelligen met zooveel aandacht en goedkeuring door haren heer en gebieder werden aangehoord, maakte zich, zoodra de nacht was ingevallen, gereed de beloofde geschiedenis van Noureddin en de schoone Perzische slavin te beginnen...

Try as he might to stay awake, he is always asleep before she reaches the end of the story.

Greta, the maid, laughs even more than his mother does—but hers is a different kind of laughter. It comes out of her chest in a great gasp—*Ha*—followed by another, and another, until the tears stand in her eyes. She has other sounds, too. A wheezing in her chest that is like that of Rikki, the dog, only louder and wetter. It gives a bubbling note to her voice. *Goede jongen. Slaap goed. Schreeuw niet*. She has smells, too, Greta: a warm, doughy smell like fresh yeast; a smell of underarms. The smell of the hard, red soap with which she scrubs her hands. Sometimes, a smell of beer, or *brandewijn*.

His mother's smell is lighter, more delicate; flowery. A jasmine scent. It is his favourite smell, apart from cinnamon biscuits. But the sounds are what he longs for, now. He had not realised how many there were, until they were gone.

Footsteps on the wet road outside. A church bell chiming. The rattle of a cart over the cobblestones. Dogs barking. The shrieking of a fishwife in the market: *Vissen! Verse vissen!* A girl singing.

Adieu dansen, springhen en snaren gheluyt
Adieu trommel, trompet en fluyt...

Doors slamming. A man shouting. A woman weeping...

Was that the last thing he heard—the sound of his mother's tears? He doesn't now recall. He does remember his father's voice, from that time: gruffer, now, with no laughter in it. 'The doctor says he will live. But...' He does not hear the rest of the sentence. Waking, after his long dark dream, in which he runs and runs along endless corridors of a strange house, he finds himself in an altered world.

He remembers opening his eyes, to see the clouds moving across the sky, beyond the tall windows. How quiet it is! He thinks it must be Sunday, it is so quiet. But if it is Sunday, then why are no church bells ringing? This strikes him as strange. When they see he is awake, they come to him—his parents, and Greta. Greta's face is all red and blubbered with tears. His mother's too. Why are they crying? The little dog is held up for him to see. He smiles, and his mother cries again, silently.

He opens his mouth to tell them it is all right—his head no longer hurts—but when he says the words, no sound comes out. He sees his father turn away, to hide his own tears.

On the branch outside the window sits a bird. Its throat trembles with song, until it seems as if it must burst—but of the song itself, there emerges not a single note.

By this time, there is Henry. Henry's face is squashed and red, and his hair sticks out in tufts. His mother holds Henry up for him to see. She is smiling, now, although there are tears in her eyes. '*Kijk, Johannes*,' she is saying, although he has to guess the words from the shape her lips make. '*Haar is Henricus, jouw broeder.*'

It is only later that he learns that Henry has come to stay. Now he is opening and shutting his mouth, and waving his fists around. He smells bad, too. Greta comes to take him away. Mama seems glad that he is gone. She closes her eyes a moment, then opens them again. She holds out her hand. '*Kom*,' she says. He sees her lips say it. He climbs up on the bed, and crawls across the wide white space to where she lies. Her face is almost as white as the pillow. She holds out her arms. '*Mein leifde*,' she says.

It is as if she has spoken inside his head.

She sees, then, that he understands. '*Mein darling*.' She kisses his eyes. Her smell is warm, sweet, milky. He keeps his eyes closed, drinking in the sweetness. He will stay here with her forever. There will be no need for Henry.

He has a bigger bed, now, with blue and gold curtains around it. It faces the window. When Greta comes to draw the curtains, he shakes his head. No. After that the curtains are always left open, as are the shutters on the window. Above the tops of the houses you can see the sky, which is filled up with stars. He knows how to count now—*een, twee, drie*—but there are so many stars you fall asleep long before you can count them all.

He is learning to read, too; Mama is showing him how. She points to the picture, then to the letter that is underneath. A for *appel*, B for *bal*. He has a ball, with red-and-blue stripes, but he prefers his spinning top. It goes round and round so fast it looks as if it is standing still. Sometimes his father takes him to the park, if it is fine, and he spins his top on the fountain's smooth stone lip, or chases his hoop up and down the gravel paths for hours. Henry comes too, although he is no good at spinning tops. If he runs too fast, he falls over. Then his face grows red, and his mouth opens in a silent howl.

If Mama is feeling well enough, she will walk with them as far as the pond and back. But there is a new baby now—a sister called Harriet—and Mama is often too tired for walking. He likes Harriet: she is small and pretty. She smiles at him, every time he leans over her cot. He gives her his ball, but her hands are too little to hold it. When she is bigger, she will come with him to the park.

After his sister Mary is born, his mother is very ill. She lies in bed for days and days. He is the only one she can bear to have near her, because he makes no noise. He sits beside her, holding her hand, or stroking her forehead with a cloth soaked in rose-water and vinegar. When she needs anything to be fetched, or Greta to take away her tray, she writes it down, and he carries the message for her.

He can read now, and write his name. He can point to the spot on the globe in his father's study where Groningen is to be found. He knows the names of the constellations: Andromeda; Cassiopeia; Orion; Ursa Major; Lyra. Perseus is his favourite. His father has a book with a picture of Perseus slaying the Medusa. He can read the story for himself when he is able, his father says.

He does so not very long after, making out the words as best he can—although parts of the story are hard to understand. How can a shower of gold (he pictures golden guilders) cause a woman to have a baby? Was that how he and Henry and their sisters had come about? The part in which Perseus and his mother Danaë had been locked in a box and thrown into the sea by

Perseus's grandfather, terrifies him. Could such a thing happen to him? He very much hopes not. Also frightening is the part in which Perseus, armed with his sword and shield of polished bronze, enters the cave of the sleeping Gorgons.

Lying wide-eyed in the darkness of his room, he can almost see the writhing of the snakes that grow from the monsters' heads, can almost hear (although he cannot hear) their hissing—*Versssse vissssen*— as Medusa opens her terrible eyes…

They are to go to England, to his grandfather's house. He is to go to school. His school is in Edinburgh—a long way from York, where his grandfather lives. In truth, he would prefer to stay at his grandfather's house, with his mother and Henry and the girls, but his father says no. He must go to school and learn how to converse with others. It is not enough that he knows how to read lips; in Edinburgh they will teach him how to talk with his fingers. He will learn Greek and Latin, too; and Mathematics. When he comes home for the holidays, he will have a horse of his own to ride. His grandfather has picked it out from his own stables.

He is a little afraid of his grandfather, because of his fierce blue eyes. Grandmama is nicer; she gives him sugar plums. She had been a great beauty in her day, his mother says. He thinks her beautiful still, with the diamond rings glittering like stars on her small soft hands, and the smell she has—of lavender water, and the powder she wears to make her face white. His grandmother never grows angry with him, because he cannot hear. She never shouts, so that her face grows red, the way his grandfather does. Instead, she speaks to him slowly, so that he can follow what is being said. She lets him hold the skeins of coloured wool, with which she makes her pictures of gentlemen hunting stags, and ladies with greyhounds. She shows him how to lay out a game of Patience.

'Dearest child,' she says, stroking his hair. 'Come and sit by me. We will be quiet together. My poor, sweet, beautiful boy…'

His grandfather likes to hunt more than anything in the world. He has planted fine woods on his estates for the purpose. An ancestor of his grandfather's was a bishop, who had been sent to the Tower for being a supporter of the Nine Days' Queen. She had had her head cut off, but the bishop had been pardoned, on account of his extreme age and piety. That was a lucky escape, his grandfather says. Another ancestor had fought on the King's side during the Civil War. He had ended up in the Tower as well, but had got away, disguised as a butcher.

'That, too, was a lucky escape,' says his grandfather, ruffling John's hair with his hard hand. His grandfather's name is John, too. He lived in Rotterdam and Copenhagen, when he was in the King's service. That was a fine time, he says. When John is older, he will tell him about his adventures; they are not for young ears. Now he is an old man, John's grandfather says, he is happy to do nothing but cultivate his garden. He grows the finest apples in the north of England.

After the deer parks and orchards of Bramham and Ribston, Edinburgh is cold and grey and forbidding. One half of the city is tumbledown, narrow old houses perched on top of a cliff; the other half is still being built. Everywhere you look, there are fine new buildings going up. It isn't safe to walk the streets after dark, for fear of falling into a gaping hole.

His school is in the older part of the city, near the university. It is run by Mr Braidwood. It is he who is teaching them the system of signs—some of which he has devised himself—which is to take the place of speech. Words are spelled out in gestures—some universal, some not. 'My...name... is... John' involves a mixture of pointing at the subject (oneself) and spelling out the letters upon one's fingers.

It is laborious at first; later, one grew quicker at it—so that it becomes as quick as writing; as quick as speech, in fact.

A universal method of communication, Mr Braidwood says. *Vox Oculis Subjecta* is written over the door of the academy. It is on the edge of the Meadows, below Arthur's Seat. The local people call it Dummie Hoos. 'Hoos' is the Scottish for house. 'Dummie' is what he is, because he cannot speak. But since, for the first time, he is with others like himself, he finds he does not care what people call him. Towards the end of his time at Braidwood's, he forms the habit, at nightfall, of climbing the Salisbury Crags, which lie behind the school, in order to look at the stars. The skies here are very clear, and dark—when it is not raining.

The year before he leaves, Dr Johnson visits the academy. With his great swollen nose, loose-lipped mouth and eyes so small they appear to disappear into his head, he is the ugliest man that any of them have ever seen. Nor are his looks improved by his clothes, which are slovenly in the extreme—AS IF, Sandys says to John, HE HAD DRESSED HIMSELF IN THE DARK. Sandys then mimes the said activity, indicating darkness with hands held in front of his face. HIS WIG IS TOO SMALL, agrees Roberts—his gestures mimicking the putting-on of the unfortunate article—IT LOOKS AS IF HE HAS SINGED IT...

But the small blue eyes beneath the singed wig have a shrewd expression, as they roam the ranks of boys, drawn up at this early hour in his honour. He himself has been deaf for many years, on account of the scrofula, he tells them. But he has not allowed this to interfere with his studies. Indeed, he likes to think that he owes his great love of reading—and the knowledge that comes with such study—to the single fact of his deafness.

When told that some of the boys could speak, he asks, can they pronounce any *long* words? Mr Braidwood says that they can. The great Compiler accordingly writes one of his *sesquipedalia verba* upon the slate, which is pronounced by the scholars. He declares himself satisfied: they are prodigies all, he opines. He has a kind word for each of the young gentlemen—even those who have mocked him (a circumstance of which he appears not entirely oblivious).

To John he says merely: 'I am told you are a mathematician, Sir...'

John nods, half-afraid he might be called upon to expand on this.

But Dr Johnson only smiles and shakes his head.

'Mathematics is a fine calling, but it is not as fine as Poetry,' he says. 'For Mathematics speaks to the Mind, whereas Poetry speaks to the Soul—a distinction you may come to appreciate, by and by...'

Then he moves on, down the line of boys, with Mr Braidwood at his elbow, pausing to ask a question of one, and make an observation to another. He does not mind in the least spending time in this way, he is observed to say to his learned colleague—indeed it is a pleasure to him. For he himself had been a boy once, and is not so old that he has forgotten it entirely. Had not Shakespeare been a boy, too—and Milton, and Homer? Inky schoolboys all, but no less worthy of regard, for all that…

Harefield is amongst those who have earned the good Doctor's praise; because Harefield can speak. On the boys' walks into the city, it is he who acts as go-between in the purchase of lemonade or tobacco or any other necessary. Harefield was deafened by a blow upon the ear when he was six, and so recalls the rudiments of language. Others—like Coombs and Sholto—have learned the trick of speaking through mimicking the motions of lips, and then humming. It is not hard to do, they assure John.

He himself has never got the hang of speech—perhaps because his only remembered words are Dutch. Now, if he imagines the way that words might sound, it is always his mother's face that he sees; the shapes her lips made—*kom, Johannes*—in calling him to her side. He recalls the vibration—like that of a trapped bee—he had once felt, on touching her throat, as she was speaking or laughing.

He supposes she must have sung to him, when he was an infant, although he has no recollection of it. He has tried singing, too, but has produced nothing but a toneless buzzing. Mr Braidwood had caught him at it one day, and told him he need not persist. The voice is subject to the eye—had he not already proved it to his satisfaction? The language of signs is a superior method of communication to that of speech, because it requires the mind to be engaged. No mere flapping of lips could ever come near it.

He has no need of sound—that much is true. For him there is a music in motion; in colour; in touch; in taste, and smell. A symphony is to be *seen* as much as heard in the way the branches of the ash tree outside his window move when the wind rushes through them; the deep notes of the organ are *visible* to him in the darkening shades of a stormy sky. The good Doctor had exhorted them to read Shakespeare, and so he had done so: 'this brave o'er-hanging firmament, this majestical roof fretted with golden fire…' That was a kind of music, was it not? It spoke to the eyes, but resonated in the heart.

Now, when he gazes at the stars from the summit of Arthur's Seat—wrapped in his warmest cloak, for the nights here are very cold—it is that 'majestical roof' that he sees. A structure so vast only the Great Architect could have built it—yet so delicate, in its jewelled complexity, that the finest goldsmith or worker in ivory could never match its perfection.

How they sparkle, the stars—flashing not only gold, but red, blue, green! If he lives to be a hundred, he will never tire of looking at them. They are silent, too. People spoke of the 'music of the spheres', but that was just a figure of speech.

He is sorry to leave Edinburgh, but he is to go to another school. This is not a house for dummies, but for the sons of gentlemen, which is what he is. Within hours of his arrival at Warrington, however, he has been laid out on the floor. His nose is bleeding. Someone had stuck out a foot as he was passing. A face had leered into his, its expression mimicking his own—or what might have been said to be his own. He has never stared, or lolled his tongue, or rolled his eyes in such a way. But being dumb, he knows, is tantamount to being an idiot. This, at least, is Fitzsimmons's view. Fitzsimmons does not care for dummies. He is very plain on that score. His father is an earl—or rather, it is put about (by Fitzsimmons himself, perhaps) that his father is an earl. Fitzsimmons's father has, in point of fact, never been seen.

Fitzsimmons's friends are Cardew and Poynter. Cardew is rumoured to have a mistress in Manchester. His father has estates in the West Indies. He has been accustomed from a young age, he says, to having a nigger to kick. In the absence of the nigger, Goodricke will do very well. Poynter is a dull and stupid fellow. If it were not for the unquestioning manner in which he carries out Fitzsimmons's orders, it might have been possible to feel some sympathy for Poynter.

Certainly Poynter is a dunce when it comes to Composition, since he cannot string two sentences together. History, Geography, Chronology and Latin prove equally beyond his wits. In every class but one, he is obliged to sit at the front, with the other dullards. Only in Dr Enfield's class, is the order which prevails elsewhere turned on its head, with the slow-witted and indolent lounging at the back of the room, and those intent on learning compelled to sit on the front benches.

John himself sits at the front, although he is not dull; merely deaf. From that vantage-point, he can follow what is being said by the master as swiftly, for the most part, as the majority of his fellows, who are not in the habit of paying close attention. Only when the tutor turns his back on the class to write upon the board, does John lose the thread of what he is saying; and even then, the good gentleman is usually careful to repeat it, for John's benefit.

Poor man! Had all his pupils been as obedient—or indeed as silent—as John, his life might have been a great deal easier. As it is, he seldom manages to keep order, let alone to impart anything in the way of knowledge to his recalcitrant flock. There he sits, turning the pages of his chosen text, in an effort to find the passage he wishes them to construe, while confusion reigns around him, with paper darts flying as thick as hail, and the less fortunate scholars having their papers torn from their hands for the manufacture of the same.

All semblance of deference abandoned, Fitzsimmons and his crew loll with their feet on the desks, replying with insolent looks and sneering asides when any attempt is made by the tutor to quell them. 'Gentlemen—please!' is his all-too-oft-repeated refrain. 'I pray you, young gentlemen—desist!' But his pleas fall on deaf ears—deafer, certainly, than John's, since they are deaf to reason, and not merely to sound.

Only the sudden arrival of the headmaster—or some other tutor, appalled at the hubbub—brings the riot to an end. Then all motion ceases—with one boy frozen in the act of tweaking his neighbour's ear; another whisking his feet down off the desk and falling to his studies with an innocent air; a third, with the facetious remark he has been about to deliver drying on his lips, standing smartly to attention at the appearance of this august Power. Then and only then (John supposes), does the silence in the room correspond to the silence which is his natural state.

For indeed stillness and silence are the same, where he is concerned. The tumult of flying books and violent gestures so often to be found in Dr Enfield's classes has for him the same quality of disturbance as it does for any member of that community in possession of all his five senses—it is just that he sees, rather than hears it.

The Parson's Cant, the Lawyer's Sophistry,
Lord's Quibble, Critick's Jest; all end in thee...

Dr Enfield had set it as a riddle for the class to decipher. John had got it at once, of course, as his tutor had known he would.

'*You* are not to answer, Mr Goodricke. For you have the advantage over the rest of us in this respect...'

Dr Enfield has made a study of speech, as well as silence—the one better enabling him to know the other, he says. Elocution is in fact his forte. For that reason, perhaps, his words are easier to read than those of most of the other masters. He has no comprehension of signs, so that conversation is limited, on the part of his pupil, to the written word. But this is as John himself prefers it: his signs are reserved for those—his mother, Henry, Harriet—who know how to interpret them. In the wider world, which means Warrington, they can only expose him to ridicule.

Through the good offices of Dr Enfield, he is now proficient in the classical authors. Neither the masculine sonorities of Virgil nor the sweeter resonances of Horace hold any terrors for him; for three years running he has carried off the Latin prize. Mathematics—also taught by Dr Enfield—is his passion, however. It is not long before the pupil outstrips the master in this capacity for—as Dr Enfield says, with a rueful air—he had only taken on the post to oblige the Academy, which could not afford a replacement for Mr Walker.

XI

York, 1779

When John goes home at the end of term, Cousin Edward is there, with his father. They have lately come from France, where the Pigotts, father and son, have been engaged in surveying the country between Louvain and Caen. Cousin Edward wears an elegant suit of snuff-coloured velvet. His hair is lightly powdered and his cravat tied in the latest fashion. He looks like a Frenchman, Grandfather says. It is also remarked that he has yet to find himself a wife.

'O, but he must not marry yet,' his father—Cousin Nathaniel—says with a wink. 'He is too valuable to me as an assistant just now.'

Later, says Cousin Nathaniel (warming to his theme over a good dinner), when all their affairs are settled and Edward is a man of property, then—ah, then!—he might marry with impunity. To which Edward himself says nothing, but merely looks at his plate, as if he wished it—and his father—at the bottom of the sea.

Cousin Nathaniel has returned 'like the Prodigal'—as he puts it—to pursue a matter of property. Now that old Fairfax is dead, Gilling Castle is in the hands of a woman—'and a very weak-minded one, at that'. It is well known that Cousin Anne Fairfax is in thrall to her confessor. A more devious priest you could not hope to find. If someone who had the family's interests at heart did not step in, the wretch would whisk the whole lot—Gilling, its lands and rents—from under their noses, and hand it over to Rome.

Not that he, Nathaniel Pigott, could be accused of being remiss when it comes to matters of conscience. He hopes he can hold his head up with the best of them in that respect. Five children—three of 'em living—all baptized in the True Faith. But when it is a matter of leaving one's heirs without a shilling to bless themselves with—well, he, for one, knows where his duty lies.

Cousin Anne Fairfax has been much laid up of late, with the low spirits that so afflict her. Having the care and expense of managing such an estate is too much for a woman, that is the truth of it. She should not be burdened with it any longer, if he has his way. What is wanted is a man's good sense. Once he is in charge, that sly priest will be sent packing. He, Nathaniel Pigott, will do it all; Lady Anne—poor spiritless soul—need not lift a finger.

In return, Cousin Nathaniel says, he will want nothing but a modest annuity—enough to cover his costs, and to recompense him for his time and trouble. As to the eventual disposal of the estate: he has ideas about that, too. A woman in Cousin Anne Fairfax's feeble state of health should not expect to marry. Better, by far, if Gilling were to pass to a more vigorous branch of the family—of which the Pigotts, with two surviving sons and a blooming daughter, are the obvious example.

'My father is determined to have Gilling for himself,' says Cousin Edward, with a smile that has no mirth in it. 'He wants it for his posterity, he says—he means myself and Charles Gregory, I collect—and yet I suspect that it will be sold long before we come to inherit, to pay my father's creditors. You are not to suppose,' Cousin Edward goes on, with the same queer half-smile, 'that it is gaming I mean, or drabs, or horses—of any of the more usual addictions to which my father is prone, and which has eaten up all his money so far, necessitating the sale of our estates in Gloucestershire, of which you may have heard tell…'

Again, the mirthless smile contorts Edward's handsome features, so that for a moment it seems as if he is about to weep.

'It is a harder mistress than any of these to whom my father is in thrall. It is she who has consumed house, lands, and money, and has stolen every waking hour since he first beheld her fair, false face. O do not ask her name,' says he, with a whimsical look. 'She has as many names as there are stars in the sky. She is Medusa, Andromeda, Berenice, Mira, Cassiopeia. She is Virgin and she is Whore (by this I mean only the Goddess of Love, you know; you must indulge the figure). She is Seven Sisters—each more beautiful than the last—and she is one: the Pole Star, around whose refulgence my father endlessly revolves.

You will see from this,' says Edward, 'that my father and I are "out" with one another at present. He calls me an unnatural son, because I do not see eye to eye with him on this (I mean Gilling, of course—not the stars). He accuses me'—here, the smile, which has been tending that way, resolves itself into a frown—'of wanting to snatch the bread from my little brother's mouth, and of denying my sister her marriage portion through my obduracy. You shake your head, Cousin John; you smile, and say to yourself that this is just poor Edward's foolish fancy. No loving father (you object) could accuse his son of such wickedness, nor rail (as my father rails) that he will not be thwarted in this, and that he will cut me off without a penny. But there, good cousin, you do me an injustice,' says Edward, shaking his head in turn. 'For ours is not a family much given to rationality, and my father is the least rational among us. His moons and stars have so bewitched him, that he has a care for little else...

Come,' he adds, with a changed face, 'let us talk no more of such things. I have not yet shown you the new reflecting telescope which Mr Short has made for me. It is my delight—for you see, I am as mad as my father in this. He has infected me with his dangerous enthusiasms, and I fear that there is no hope for me, while a star remains unmapped in the firmament.'

Two years have passed since that conversation—which, in truth, was several conversations, for Cousin Edward's mind ran very much on this theme, and he—John—could only make out parts of it at any given time. For although his cousin generally remembered to look straight at him when he was speaking, it was an effort to follow everything that was said. For the hearing, conversation may be carried on with only half a mind—the rest being caught up in something else entirely; for one such as he, it required a degree of concentration of which the former could have no conception.

Fortunately, his powers of concentration are considerable, as is his memory. Though he is sure that Edward has forgotten his outburst by now, *he* has not.

Nor has he forgotten his first sight of the night sky through the reflecting telescope, whose magnification was almost a hundred times greater than that of the naked eye. It was, he thinks now, the defining moment of his life: that warm Summer's night, the heavens had opened, and tumbled their treasures into his lap. He had never seen stars so brilliant, or so large. Their glitter made his heart contract. It had been Perseus—his old love—on whom the glass had been trained. After a few moments, he had taken his eye from the eye-piece and looked up, to view the constellation unaided.

Perseus's shape was quite plain. There was his prancing leg and upraised arm; there, the hand that grasped the Medusa's hair—all stitched in diamonds on the sky's black velvet. As he watched, a shower of stars burst from the hero's head.

He must have gasped, or made some involuntary start, for he felt a touch upon his arm, and met the other's joyful gaze.

'The Perseids,' his cousin said, mouthing the words so that he understood. 'It is the season for them.' And then, before he could turn his attention back to the miraculous glass, 'I have so wanted to show this to you. Is it not beautiful, the realm of light?'

In Glamorganshire, Edward tells him, his father has erected an observatory. 'You must certainly come and see it,' he says, his quarrel with his father apparently forgotten. 'It is to be the latest of its kind. My father insists upon nothing less.'

In the event, the observatory was broken up less than two years later, and its contents brought to York, so there was no opportunity to see it. By then, John himself was returned to York, having finished his studies. He received a letter from Edward, full of his latest observations of Mercury, which he claimed to have sighted closer to the Sun than anyone else had ever done with any instrument. 'I have indeed the advantage of a very keen eye,' he wrote.

> The observations were taken with the Bird quadrant; altitudes noted with the Sisson transit—a very fine instrument, in my opinion. By the by, we are to be at York once more this summer—my father having leased a house at Bootham Bar, the better to pursue his Gilling claim,

which, as you may have heard, has reached a delicate stage...

'We are either to be paupers, or as rich as Croesus—it changes with every wind that blows,' says Edward, when they meet again, a few weeks after this. 'My role, it appears, is principally to guard my sister's virtue against the fortune hunters who are certain to lay siege to her, once the case is settled and we are rich once more...'

Eight years younger than her brother, Mathurina Pigott seems a female version of him—with the same fine dark eyes, the same soft brown hair, and—it appears—the same amiable disposition. She has been seven years with the Good Sisters at Louvain, Edward says—'during which time she has learned singing, and dancing, and sewing, and all the other things which become a young lady'; now, it seems, their father has determined she should be married.

John thinks he has never seen so exquisite a creature.

In her grey silk gown, she seems a Being too refined and delicate for their dull Yorkshire existence. Her skin is like that of the white peaches on the wall of his grandfather's kitchen garden, he thinks. She does not speak to him—at first he supposes it is because he has done something to displease her. Then he discovers, from Edward, that she is afraid he will not understand her.

'For, you know, her English is no more than passable. She has spoken only French these past seven years...'

John is all too aware that the fact of his deafness creates an awkwardness with some people. Supposing him stupid as well as deaf, they prefer to communicate with him through an intermediary, or not to communicate with him at all. He does not want Mathurina to think him stupid, and so he makes efforts to polish his French, the better to surprise her.

His chance comes in the garden at Bramham, where she is walking with his sister Harriet. He sees them descending the steps by the Grand Cascade, and hurries to meet them. When he hands Mathurina the letter, she glances at him with a question in her eyes.

He smiles, as if to say, 'Read it. Then you will know everything.'

She raises an eyebrow, and half turns away, to screen the pages, over which he had laboured so assiduously, from view.

Chère Mademoiselle, he has written. *Il faut que je vous présente mes compliments...*

It seems an age before she turns to face him again. A small smile plays around her lips.

'Dear sir,' she says, in her beautifully imperfect English. 'I am very happy to walk wiz you in *ze jardin* at half past two.'

Of that walk he retains only impressions: the feel of her hand, resting on the crook of his arm; her profile—O, how charming a profile!—shaded by the fine straw of her hat.

Since no conversation is possible, they content themselves with looks and smiles.

As they step from the shade of the arbour into full sunlight, a cloud of fritillaries flies up from the gravel walk, in a flash of white and orange wings.

At once, he makes the sign for 'butterfly'—which is also the sign for an angel.

She smiles—Angel that she is—and imitates the gesture.

Once the Pigotts are established in York, the two families see each other almost daily. From the Goodrickes' town house near the Minster it is a few minutes' walk to Bootham Bar, where construction of the new observatory is proceeding apace. This edifice consists of two octagonal rooms one above the other—both about 14 feet in diameter, with windows in one, and a slit in the roof for the transit. The famous Dolland achromatic takes pride of place, and, fixed to a pillar, the Bird quadrant.

'My father says it is better than Greenwich,' says Edward, pointing out these features to his cousin.

For his own observations, John has relied, hitherto, on more modest instruments: a telescope made from spectacle lenses, and a pair of Levina's old opera glasses. Now—as Edward puts it—he will have the 'run' of the observatory—which if not as fine as the Astronomer Royal's premises, is certainly not to be sneezed at.

Edward is in good spirits, for he has discovered a comet, just the day before. Comets have been very much in the news of late—following the discovery of a fine specimen by the famous Dr Herschel. Of course Dr Herschel's 'comet' turns out not to be a comet at all, but a new planet. When news of this reaches him from the Royal Society, Edward—who knows the Herschels well (for the sister is something of an astronomer, too, he says)—writes at once to the great man to congratulate him.

That same winter—1781—they receive news that the British forces, under Lord Cornwallis, have surrendered at Yorktown. A black day for England, John's grandfather says. Those damned Yankees have been aided and abetted by the French, whom everyone knows love nothing so much as to annoy their neighbours across the Channel. A knavish crew. He for one cannot understand why anyone should want to do business with a Frenchman. They are as slippery as eels—or frogs, if it comes to that. *Les Grenouilles*. 'Ha, ha! That's a good one!' He repeats the witticism, his enjoyment increasing with every repetition, to anyone who will listen.

John would have paid no attention—it is, he supposes, easier for him than for most—if he had not been afraid that old Sir John's remarks might reach the ears of his cousin.

And indeed, those of his cousin's sister.

The sight of her white-peach skin, flushing bright, then growing pale again, makes him tremble. A single glance, from her almond eyes, pierces him with desire... Until now, he has not minded his deafness; now, the knowledge that he will never hear her voice—*M'sieur*—is a torment to him.

'She must marry within two years, or she must return to the Good Sisters at Brussels,' says Edward. 'That is my father's wish. Two of his sisters—I mean sisters in the temporal, not the spiritual sense, you understand—are nuns already. Mathurina will be carrying on the family tradition.'

Incapable as he is of saying what he feels—which is that it seems to him a remarkably stupid and heartless 'tradition'—John's expression must have conveyed his feelings plainly enough, for Edward goes on:

'Pray do not look so affronted, Cousin. It is what we Catholics do, if we have children to spare—which my father assuredly does. We put them to good use, petitioning on our behalf to *Le Bon Dieu*. You seem surprised, Cousin (for John had shaken his head in disbelief). But I assure you, it is the same in all the best families. And do not forget that my sister has two years at her disposal. If she cannot get a husband in that time, she is not the young woman I know her to be. Make no mistake; under that *très correcte* exterior, there exists a fiery spirit…"

Since their walk in the garden at Bramham, he has seen her several times more—regrettably, always in company. *He* calls by to see Edward and *she* is on her way out, accompanied by her mother and Mrs Hoare. Or she is busy with her sewing and can spare no time for a tête-à-tête. On those rare occasions when he is asked to stay to dinner, he will be sitting at one end of the table, she at the other. There is no opportunity to exchange more than a few nods and smiles.

'She is well guarded, *ma soeur*,' says Edward. 'You will not see her walking about the town with other young Misses, making sheep's eyes at the officers. She is much too valuable to my father for that.' He places a heavy emphasis on the word 'valuable'—the whole sentence being pronounced with a sneering expression.

Edward and his father are 'out' with one another again. It seems there is nothing Edward can do to please his irascible parent. Even in matters astronomical, Nathaniel prefers to discuss his findings with John these days—bellowing his observations into the young man's face, with much raising of the eyebrows and gesticulating with the hands, the better to express his meaning.

'Shouting makes no difference to him, Father, for he cannot hear,' Edward protests—but to little effect. Nathaniel remains convinced that the only way to convey what he wants to say is at the top of his lungs.

'I am, I fear, a sad disappointment to my father,' says Edward with his sideways smile. 'He considers me a dilettante. A popinjay. If—forgive me, I quote verbatim—"even the poor mute" can do better than I when it comes to astronomical discoveries, then what use am I? My education—I beg pardon—my "long and *expensive*" education has been for naught. I am a booby, a Nothing. I am, in short, no son of his,' concludes Edward with a burst of diabolic laughter.

As to the reason for the quarrel, he remains vague. 'It is always money, money, money, with my father,' is all he will say.

In the hall at Bootham Bar, Mathurina lays a hand upon John's arm. 'I am very cross with you, Mr Goodricke,' she says, with a beguiling pout. 'You 'ave not written me any more pretty letters.'

He is all contrition.

'O do not make a sad face on my account,' she goes on, with a little toss of the head. All her speeches are accompanied thus with gestures, so that her meaning is easier to comprehend than that of most others. Or maybe he pays less attention to most others. 'I am sure you do not care a fig whose feelings you hurt…'

She seems about to leave him, but he detains her with an imploring look. A hand placed upon his heart.

'That is all very well,' she says. She seems mollified, however. 'Perhaps I should give you another chance…' On her lips it appears as *anuzzer*.

He nods. Greatly daring, he takes her hand. She allows him to hold it for no more than a moment; perhaps two.

'When you 'ave finished your *observing*, you may come and meet me in the garden, under the rose arbour,' she says. Then, her smile changing at once to a look of faint exasperation, '*Oui, Maman, j'arrive!*'

She meets his eyes as she turns away to obey her mother's summons, and hers sparkle with mischief—brighter than any star, he thinks, comprehending the figure for the first time. A blush lies across her cheek, mantling its even tint—like that of a rose, he sees. For the first time in his life, he feels the impulse to attempt poetry. The variable hearts of women suddenly seem to him a subject as worthy of study as the variable habits of stars. 'Having a mind to observe the variable stars in Cygnus,' he writes in his journal that night 'abt. midnight I looked for all the stars between Gamma and Eta Cygni in order to find the Nova of 1600…'

It is past four o'clock before he goes to bed. Even if the sky had been cloudy, which it was not, he could not have slept a wink, thinking of all that had passed between them that afternoon... In the rose arbour, she had let him hold her hand. Although she appeared outwardly calm, her agitation betrayed itself in the rise and fall of her small white bosom, beneath the fine lace *fichu*. They gazed for a long time into one another's eyes. Hers were—and are—the most beautiful he had ever seen, in a lifetime of observing the faces of others, and these expressive orbs in particular, with greater attentiveness than most people.

In Mathurina's eyes, he thinks (his rapture keeping him awake, as the sky outside his window grows steadily lighter) are incorporated the best elements of dark and bright. More beautiful still—to him—than their colour and brilliance, is the perfect sympathy they seem to convey. It is as if her Soul looks out of them. Everything he desires in another being is in that look; there is no need for words...

How long they remained looking at each other he cannot say. An hour, perhaps? Or only a minute? When they are together, Time means nothing.

She spoke at last, and it was with some reluctance that he shifted his gaze from her eyes' twin stars to her lips—only to find himself enraptured anew...

For if her eyes reveal her Soul, her lips, with their curving symmetries, express her Self. She has a way of thrusting her lips forward in a kind of pretty pout, as she pronounces each word, which stirs him profoundly. It is, he supposes, the result of her schooling in the French language—for he has observed the same voluptuous movements of the lips in other French speakers; although none of these, it has to be said, has affected him in quite the same way...

'I 'ave to go,' she said, but the reluctance with which she spoke gave the lie to it.

He shook his head: she must not go so soon; but she insisted.

''Ave you forgot *ze* time?'

He had, indeed, forgotten the time; wished it consigned to the Devil, in fact. It was Time which had brought their blissful encounter to an end; Time which would take her away from him at last. Cruel, envious adversary!

He must, he sees, make terms with Time. 'Being desirous to have a Clock,' he writes in the journal he began that summer,

> I made choice of Mr Hartley to make one for me. He has now finished it and it is put in my room—in the middle, between my two windows and opposite to the fire, but not near it, my room being of great length...

He has moved, by this time, from his aunt's house in Ogleforth, to the Treasurer's House. His apartment is on the second floor. From its windows, the pinnacles at the east end of the Minster are clearly visible—ideal objects with which to time the variations of astronomical bodies. He can now compare his findings with Pigott's, made from the observatory in Bootham Bar. 'The going of my clock is to be estimated by the vanishing of any star behind the Minster,' he writes.

> The way to compare my Clock with Mr Pigott's Clock is by the last stroke of the Minster Clock—thus—I must mark the time of my Clock at the last stroke of the Minster at 12 o C & Mr Pigott must do the same with his. We must hear at almost the same moment...

Such beautiful synchronicity offers a means of restoring what he does not have; of regulating what might otherwise have remained beyond his control. Although he is careful to correct any false impression given by the last sentence:

> Some faithful person, upon whom I can depend, always tells me every stroke of the Minster & when he tells me the last—I always mark the Clock.

He sends to Mr Dollond's for two eye glasses, one with a magnification of X80 and another of X160, but they do not answer his expectations. His new telescope proves more satisfactory, however. He shows it to Mathurina, when she calls at the house later that day. It is a week or so after their meeting in the garden.

He is engaged in taking a sighting thought the cross-wires of the instrument when she creeps up behind him and claps her hands over his eyes.

'What is the matter? Are you not you pleased to see me?' she says, observing his momentary confusion.

He hastens to reassure her, although his heart is hammering like an over-wound clock.

'What are you doing? May I look?'

Without waiting for a reply, she slips between him and the telescope. Mounted as it is on its stand, it is too high for her, and so he adjusts it accordingly. She puts her eyes to the glass, but soon loses patience, for there is, of course, nothing to see, beyond the spires of the Minster and the clouds passing slowly behind them.

She turns, and he catches the scent of her hair—a sharp intense smell, like that of new-mown hay, he thinks.

'Tell me,' she says, when she is facing him once more. 'What is it you desire so much to see?'

There can of course be only one answer, and he gives it, indicating the object of his affections.

YOU.

'O, you naughty boy, you know that is not what I meant,' she says. Her smile says otherwise, however. '*Alors*. Here I am,' she continues. 'But you know that I cannot stay. I must take some jellies to Mrs Kemp, who suffers with the putrid throat.'

She clasps her own white throat, with a pathetic air, to indicate the nature of the affliction.

He takes the notebook with its silver pencil from his pocket. *Let her wait*, he writes. *Stay here with me*.

'*Ah! que tu es méchant!*' She shakes a finger at him. 'You know I am much too old for you…'

There is, in fact, three years between them. He shakes his head to show that it is of no consequence.

'Besides,' she adds, with a mischievous look, 'my father would never allow it.'

This is nearer the mark, and he frowns.

He thinks me not good enough for you, because I am deaf...

At once she looks contrite. 'You must not think that,' she says. *Sink zat*. Her inability to pronounce 'th' is delightful to him. 'My father regards you like a son, I am sure of it...'

But he is glad not to have a son like me, he cannot resist replying.

There is no denying it. His own grandfather can hardly bear the sight of him, these days. Flawed as he is, he offers a constant reminder of the heir the old man might have had. One whose ears would ring from the report of the gun, as his quarry came down; and who could roar out a jest, or an oath, in the merry-making afterwards.

She is turning away, her face downcast, when he catches her by the wrist, and draws her to him. She allows him to hold her for a moment; then she pulls away.

'*Faites attention*,' she says. 'My mother will be here directly.'

But he has something more he wishes to say:

I care nothing for what others think of me, he writes. *All I care for is what you think of me...*

When she has read the note, Mathurina smiles.

'Ah, now *zat* would be telling,' she says.

'At noon'—he writes in his journal later that day— 'I saw Venus through the transit telescope in Mr Pigott's observatory—it was then in her inferior conjunction. It appeared thus,' here he is obliged to draw a diagram. 'It was all at 7 degrees and a half higher than the sun. Her brightness is very remarkable.'

XII

His clock has stopped. He manages to make it run again, but while he is away in London, it stops once more. Hartley says it is caused by his not pulling the string down hard enough. This is on account of not being able to hear the mechanism, he surmises; he now takes pains to make sure it is done correctly. Without an accurate timepiece, his observations would be impossible. 'Having now a mind to make my Clock run sidereal time, because I can then compare it with Mr P's clock, which also runs sidereal time, I altered the Pendulum,' he writes.

London he finds a much finer city than York. With its grand new houses fronted with white stucco, and its beautiful churches, whose spires seem made, not of stone but of spun sugar, like extravagant examples of the confectioner's art, it appears to him like something from a dream. Its streets are much dirtier than those of York, however. That such architectural magnificence—Pall-Mall, St James's—can co-exist with such filth seems inconceivable; yet there it is. Now it is high summer, the place stinks like a midden, with flies swarming thickly around the heaps of ordure—horse dung, dog dung, and worse—which are strewn all around. It is nothing to see a man conversing with a friend, turn in mid-sentence, and unbutton himself, to release a frothing stream upon the wall; or a woman hoist her skirts above a gutter already brimming with excrement, rotting fruit, dead cats and other discarded matter.

Even the Shambles at its worst is not as bad as this.

There is also the prevailing danger that some violence might be met with. The night they arrived, a man had his throat cut a mere hundred yards away from the gate of the George Inn. By the time they took him away, the body had been stripped of all but its small-clothes.

'A disgraceful thing,' Edward says, as they take a glass of brandy-and-water before retiring. 'If a man cannot walk the streets of the capital city in safety, then what has the world come to?"

They breakfast early on cold beef and small beer, and then set off on foot to Greenwich, to see Dr Maskelyne. It is a relief when they leave the noise and dirt of the Old Kent Road for the pleasant lanes of New Cross and Deptford. By the time they reach Blackheath, the country is quite wild. It is not safe after dark, says Edward, for the footpads are notorious in these parts. In broad daylight, however, it is a pretty scene: the village with its church spire rising above it, in the midst of a green moor, reminds John of his own dear Yorkshire. Reaching Greenwich, he is astonished at how fine the buildings are—particularly the Observatory, which commands a view of the park, and the Royal Naval Hospital behind it. It seems a subject fit for Canaletto.

'Ah yes,' says Maskelyne, when this is remarked upon. 'Even though we are surrounded by such pleasant country, we are not such rustics as all that! But I confess I am heartily glad to be out of the stink of London. Here, one has all one needs for perfect felicity."

He insists on showing the two gentlemen around his house, with its small, but well-appointed rooms: 'Wonderfully convenient, you know, for my needs are small... indeed, I employ but three servants—Bessie, who does the cooking and rough work, William for the boots and silver, and Joseph, who helps me with the instruments...'

Later, after some hours spent in astronomical talk—the Astronomer Royal favouring them, amongst other things, with an account of the famous experiment to determine the weight of the Earth he had conducted at Mount Schiehallion in Perthshire some years before—they visit the Observatory. Here, they make the acquaintance of the young man already referred to.

'He is very quick in apprehension, is Joseph,' says Dr Maskelyne, his face beaming with an almost paternal pride. 'When I took him on, he had not so much as laid eyes on an achromatic telescope, nor considered the stars to be anything other than lights in the sky. Now astronomy is meat and drink to him, is it not, Joseph?' he cries to the silent youth in his suit of fustian, who is presently setting up the large Transit for his master's guests to try. Joseph ducks his head with an awkward smile—as tongue-tied in his way as I am in mine, thinks John.

'So here it is: the *pièce de résistance*,' says Maskelyne, when the telescope is ready. 'Come, Mr Pigott. Will you be the first to try it?'

'Not I,' replies Edward. 'I cede that honour to my young kinsman here—for we are cousins, you know, on our fathers' side. It is Mr Goodricke who is to do great things. I am the mere factotum...'

'You do yourself an injustice, I am sure,' says Maskelyne; but he steps aside, making vigorous signs to John that he should approach the instrument. He does so. But when he puts his eye to the glass, all is darkness.

'It is perhaps a little cloudy,' says Maskelyne, seeing him frown.

He tries again, adjusting the focus a little. This time, it is clearer. Now there is nothing between him and the heavens, laid bare with all their nebulae. Just now it is the gold and blue double stars of Gamma Andromeda he beholds—the brightness of one intensifying that of the other, so that they appear as one enormous star, marvellously brilliant... *this majestical roof, fretted with golden fire*... He draws a breath and lets it out.

Reluctant to surrender the vision, but knowing that Edward is impatient for his turn, he steps away from the Transit.

A fine instrument, he writes on his pad, for Maskelyne.

'I am glad you like it,' says that gentleman, with many smiles and gesticulations. 'I have others, of course—but this is the largest...' His gesture is that of a man boasting of the prodigious size of the fish he has just caught. 'Indeed, the room was constructed to hold it.'

A magnificent room, writes John.

It is octagonal in form, with eight tall windows. The height from floor to ceiling must be thirty feet. Set into the walnut panels on each side are clocks, solar and sidereal. The great telescope itself is on wheels, so that it can be moved from one window to another.

'I do not think you will find a finer room in England,' replies Maskelyne. 'Though of course, I am partial. Have you see St Paul's yet? No? You must certainly go, whilst you are here. His *second* greatest building, in my view,' he adds, smiling at his own witticism. 'Its dome is much admired...'

His hands describe it.

'But I say, we too have a dome, here at Greenwich—only it is invisible, being that of the firmament above our heads. Come, Mr Pigott, if you are finished star-gazing, I will show you my collection of astrolabes. We have time before dinner—for it is only a fowl and some boiled mutton, you know. We manage very simply here...'

'*Simple*, his life may be,' observes Edward later that night, when they have returned—by chaise, this time—to the George Inn. 'But it is at least free from the cares to which those of us without an income are subject. What I would not give for such a "simple" life—aye, and such a stipend from the public purse, too! To have a house of my own, and the money to indulge my whims...'

Here, he falls into a reverie, gazing at the fire, which has burned low. There is but another shovelful of coals left in the bucket. When they have finished their grog, they will go to bed, exhausted after the excitements of the day—for, although neither would be the first to admit it, both find London tiring. Edward, however, seems reluctant to bring their colloquy to an end—although it is he who must supply the larger part of it. Now he shivers slightly, as if a goose has walked across his grave.

'How strange if I were to end up like Maskelyne,' he says. 'A fusty old bachelor, with only my *instruments* for company...'

On his birthday, John is surprised to receive a visit from his mother and sisters. Mathurina is with them, looking quite bewitching in pale pink figured silk.

'O, the dear girl has become quite part of the family since you went away,' says Levina, seeing his eyes go to her. 'Have you not, my dear? She is teaching Harriet to read French, and Mary to do *petit-point*... Even Lizzie here has been less of a rattle since Mathurina took her in hand. Quite what we will do when she is married, I do not know.'

Mathurina raises her eyebrows at this, and gives a tiny, almost imperceptible, shake of the head.

'You need not look so coy, my dear,' says Levina, intercepting this look. 'John does not mind what we say—do you, my son? We can say anything in front of John.'

Bored with such talk, Elizabeth, a stout blonde child of six, now contrives to upset her chair. She is not hurt in the least, but the ensuing commotion is more than her mother's nerves can stand.

'Lizzie, you are to leave off crying at once. A great girl like you—for shame!'

'Come, Lizzie.' Mathurina holds out her hand to her young cousin. 'We will take a turn around the garden, you and I. John may come too, if he wishes,' she adds, as if the idea has just occurred to her.

Released from the tedium of the grown-ups' conversation, Elizabeth runs happily up and down the gravel paths of the knot garden, whilst her elders follow, at a more sedate pace.

Mathurina slips her arm through John's. He presses her hand. It is enough that she is here beside him. And yet... He withdraws her hand from his arm, and scribbles something on his pad.

Tell me you are not to be married.

'I am not to be married,' she says.

It is Edward who first proposes that they should direct their attention towards variable stars—a topic on which he (Edward) has been corresponding for some months with Dr Herschel. It is Edward, too, who suggests the star Beta-Persei, otherwise called Algol, as a promising subject for observation.

'For I know you have been much preoccupied with the Wonderful Star, of late...'—by this he meant Mira, named thus by Fabricius—'but I think you will find the Demon Star as full of wonders, if not more so...'

When looked at, Algol does indeed prove an interesting study. Its variations of magnitude seem to follow a set pattern. Whether this is caused by dark spots upon the surface of the Star itself, or the fact that its light is regularly eclipsed by another Star, passing in front of it, he (John) cannot say. But he will certainly make it his business to find out...

Early in November, he draws up his own chart of stars, using Bayer's system of Greek letters to denote varying degrees of brightness, and also drawing on the notation Edward has devised.

This is as follows:

o	not Visible
y	scarce Visible
x	seen with some difficulty
*	tolerably bright
*	still brighter
**	very bright

Algol, by this reckoning, is of the second magnitude, John notes on 4th November. On the 7th, he observes it again, and finds it the same as before. He cannot help but feel a little disappointed. Perhaps, after all, there is nothing remarkable about it? Then, on November 12th, comes a startling change:

> This night I looked at Beta-Persei & was much surprised to find its brightness altered. It now appears at abt. the 4th magnitude. It was hardly distinguishable from Rho Persei—I reckoned it as nearly equal to it in brightness...

The following night both he and Edward look for it, and find it again of the second magnitude. Thus it remains, for the next fifteen nights. On December 28th comes another change:

> At 5 I looked at Algol. It was much less bright than when I saw it two or three days ago. It appeard to be of the 4th magnitude. It was abt. the same brightness and colour as Delta & Gamma Persei—rather a little brighter than Rho Persei—not quite as bright as Beta Trianguli & Epsilon & Zeta Persei & no brighter than Beta Arietis. I must however confess that it was rather hardly distinguishable from Rho Persei, they sometimes appearing of the same brightness & sometimes the Rho seemed to be brighter. Mr E.

> Pigott nearly agrees with me & am very glad he has now confirmed it as my last observn. on the change of this star was hardly credible on act. of the quickness of the change...

For the next few nights he forgets to eat, and barely sleeps, so intent is he on charting the variations of the heavenly body the Ancients called the 'devil star' on account of its unreliable nature. 'Winking demon' was another of its names. For the first time, he understands why. Just when you thought you had it in your sights, it slipped away again, out of reach. Now bright, now faint, now flashing bright once more. If he did not know better, he would say it was playing hide-and-seek.

> The singular Phaenomenon of Algol's variation on the 28th inst. & on the 12th of Novr. last, I think, can't be accounted for in any other manner than that of supposing it to have suffered an Eclipse (if I may say so) by the interposition of a Planet revolving round it. This variation is evidently difft. from Omicron Ceti & other variable stars—Mr E. Pigott having sent me a note to desire an extract of my observn. on the 12th of Novr. last, gives the same opinion—thinks the imaginary planet must be abt. half the size of Algol at least. Further observn. will set this Phaenomenon in a clearer light...

The old year reaches its close with a spell of exceptionally cold days, followed by clear, frosty nights—perfect for observing. He needs his warmest cloak, for he is often out until the small hours, checking and re-checking his findings, both with the glass and with the naked eye. He knows, as he waits for his eyes to become dark-adapted, that what he is looking at is the past. For are not the stars he looks at now the self-same stars that the Pharoahs saw; and after them the Babylonians, and the Greeks? Gazing upon them, as he is gazing now, Eudoxus had devised his system of crystal spheres, and Hipparchus had compiled his Catalogue.

As he lies there, his breath making clouds in the frosty air, he seems to see the great chain of his predecessors stretching away behind him. There is Eudoxus, and Aratus, who named the constellations; and Ptolemy and Al-Sufi, who catalogued the fixed stars in them. Copernicus, who discovered that the Earth moved around the Sun and not (as had been thought before) the other way about, is followed by Tycho Brahe, with his theory of planetary motion. Then there is Kepler, whose great discovery was that the planets move, not in circles, but in ellipses. Galileo, inventor of the modern telescope (although it was a Dutchman, Lippershey, who first patented the 'far-seeing device') had dealt a blow to the notion that the universe is immutable. Huygens—another Dutchman—formulated the laws of motion, which were later to be developed by Newton. It was this, as much as their shared interest in gravity, which had made possible the dazzling calculations of Halley. Now, in his own time, a new planet has swum into view, and stars, once thought to be fixed, are found to be variable...

Searching the sky for what he knows to be there—for is it not an open book to him, its constellations the hieroglyphs of a language now familiar?—he is reminded of his schoolboy self, all those years before, on the heights of Arthur's Seat, gazing at the stars in the hope that one day he might decipher their secrets. That day is certainly nearer; although he would not presume to say that he understands more than a fraction of what is there. Edward has been studying the skies for a decade and more, and yet considers himself a mere novice. Had not the great Newton described himself as a child, playing upon the sea-shore and diverting himself by picking up this pretty pebble or that, whilst the great ocean of truth lay all undiscovered? *His* 'ocean' is the sky, and his shells and pebbles stars and planets—of which Algol is only the latest. Childish or not, he will never forget the delight he felt in finding it.

It was, of course, Perseus who led him to the discovery; Perseus the destroyer, and warrior prince of his childhood imagination. It was Perseus's hand that had slain the Gorgon, and which now carried her severed head across the sky for all eternity. The eye that winked from that head was his star, his Algol. *Al-Ghul*—the Ghoul—as the Arabs called it. Night after night, it grew bright, then dim, then bright again. Changeable orb.

All through January he watches it, noting the variations in its brightness. On 14th, his observations are hourly—sometimes half-hourly, beginning at seven, and continuing until half past nine, when cloud obscures the view. This clears by midnight, and he goes on for the rest of that night, until the sky is light. From these observations, he concludes that the duration of the supposed eclipse is seven hours, and that for the star's brightness to change from the second to the fourth magnitude takes a mere three-and-a-half hours. 'Singular indeed,' he writes. 'If the period of Algol's variation is regular—this will prove it has a planet revolvg round him…'

Edward concurs with him in this. He himself saw the star a little before six o'clock, he says, and thought it less bright than usual, although rather brighter than Beta Arietis. He—Edward—has drawn up a table, indicating which days this (supposed) planet might be seen from the Earth, were its revolutions, as calculated, to last between twenty-three and forty-six days.

It is remarkable how closely their respective observations seem to agree.

Although, to tell the truth, each confides in the other so much, that it is often difficult to determine where the findings of one leave off and those of the other begin. They are twin souls, says Edward—'two seeming bodies, but one heart', as the poet says. 'Though he speaks of women, in that instance,' he adds, with an arch look. 'But the sentiment is the same…'

Like Edward, John has made a chart to compare the star's brightness with that of others of similar size and colour. On 19th January he observes Algol to be

> a good deal less bright than Alpha Persei & Alpha Andromeda [although] much brighter than Beta Arietis & Gamma Pegasi [indeed] rather brighter than Alpha Pegasi [in short] either between Gamma Pegasi & Alpha Andromeda [or] Beta Arietis & Alpha Persei; [remarking that] all these stars are the same colour as Algol

> [adding]

> I did not like to compare with Gamma & Beta Andromeda & Alpha Arietis because they are of difft. colours—but as far as I can judge Algol is not as bright as them—they are a good deal larger than Algol—Alpha Andromeda and Algol are of the whiter light and consequently brilliant…

On 31st January, he observes 'the star at 5 & 6 PM, 11 PM, 12 AM, 1 AM and 2 AM,' concluding that 'its period is 17 days.'

Still he is not satisfied. All through February and March he works, often long into the night, comparing relative magnitudes and calculating durations. If he could only establish the pattern of Beta Persei's changes, he would be closer to discovering what causes them…

On 18th March, there is an eclipse of the Moon. He and Edward are to observe it together—that is, in their respective observatories; his being no more than the front parlour, whence he had given orders for his clock to be removed, the better to time the stages of the phenomenon.

Even though he has observed the radiant Orb through the telescope many times before, it is with the same feeling of wonder as on that very first occasion that he beholds it now—its mountains quite distinct, its edge not sharply defined but soft, and luminescent. Ghostly, he thinks, with a pleasurable shiver. To see it thus is to experience, in a way impossible with the naked eye, the fact of its *moving* through Space and Time—as he himself, in common with the rest of humanity, is also moving…

> *With how sad steps, O Moone, thou climb'st the skies*
> *How silently, and with how wanne a face…*

He would not call himself expert in matters of poetry, but he feels that the long-dead Soldier-Poet has described the phenomenon very exactly.

Thomas, his servant, is at his side as always, awaiting instruction. As darkness begins to creep across the Moon's face, John—observing now with the naked eye—checks his clock, scribbles a note, '11 PM—Eclipse now commencing' and hands it to him. Thomas knows for whom it is intended—since this is now a matter of custom—and leaves the room at once.

Twenty minutes pass, and the darkness is now almost total. At that moment, John becomes aware that his servant must have returned, for a figure now stands beside him. He puts out his hand for the note, which will confirm that his cousin's observations and his own have begun simultaneously—but encounters only air. As he turns, in surprise, the figure darts at him, and kisses him full on the mouth.

His heart stops. Starts again. It feels as if he is bathed from head to foot in fire.

Mathurina. Even in darkness, he knows her smell; the scent of her skin, her hair... He reaches for her—holds her a moment—but she squirms out of his arms. He feels the soft exhalation of her laughter on his cheek.

Then her shadowy figure flits to the far side of the room, and wraps itself in one of the long velvet curtains that hang on either side of the window—thinking, no doubt, to surprise him once more.

But his eyes are used to the dark. He will find her again. In the meantime, he has his observations to finish, '11.30—Eclipse now complete,' he writes.

In the soft blackness which now surrounds them, she is no more than a vague shape, a concentration of shadow. Cloaked by that obscurity, she can be his at last... For it is not a shadow, but a living woman, he takes in his arms. Now it is his turn to kiss her. He feels her gasp with the pleasurable shock of it. In that darkness, she is as silent as he is; for even if she had spoken, he would not have known it. Speech, in any case, is unnecessary; theirs is a grammar of touch. Their lips are not for speaking, but for kissing; their hands communicate nothing but the urgency of desire.

One kiss. Then she is gone. As the Moon moves out from behind the Earth's shadow, she slips from his embrace like a will o'the wisp. Before that cold bright light can reveal her face, as Cupid's had been revealed to Psyche, she flees from the room, leaving only the faint ghost of her perfume on the air.

He is trembling all over. Moonlight floods in, and he stands there, like a madman, bathing in its glare. He will die if he cannot have her.

Next day, when he calls at the house, on the pretext of comparing his notes on the eclipse with Edward's, he learns that Mathurina has left early that morning, to visit their aunt at Louvain, where the good lady has been taken dangerously ill. 'Of course she has given all her money to the Church,' says Edward. 'So Mathurina can hope for nothing, if she dies. But she insists on going, in spite of this. My sister—surprisingly, you might think, considering her patrimony—has a good heart.'

If he had had the power of speech at that moment, he would have cried out that she was an angel. Perhaps it is as well that he does not. He contents himself with a curt nod, which expresses nothing of the agony he is feeling. To be without her for a month or more... It is more than flesh and blood can stand.

Fortunately, he has his stars to console him.

> This night I discovered that Iota Cancri was double & also that the 1st ad Phi Cancri, he writes on April 3rd. The former has a star of the 8th Mag. near it at 22" dist. The large star is of the 4th Magd...

On April 19th:

> I discovered three double stars.

They are not listed in Herschel's catalogue, and so he sends all three, together with those he had found on 3rd and 4th April, to the eminent astronomer, so that he might amend his records accordingly.

Double stars. Privately, he chooses the brightest, and names it for her; its twin is himself, endlessly circling around her.

Still her visit drags on and on; although her aunt does not die, she does not get better, either. These details he gets from Edward, since he has no way of communicating with Mathurina directly. To have asked for a letter to be enclosed in one of

Edward's would have been to draw attention to what must remain, for the time being at least, a matter between themselves alone.

Since he is denied the comfort of letter-writing, he tries his hand at verse, but can get no further than the first line;

Bright star! Queen of the firmament!

How did other men manage? he wonders. Scribbling ream upon ream of verses as if it were no effort at all. She had lent him Mr Gray's *Poems*, but he could not get on with them, finding it melancholy stuff. Since he has no skill at Art, he must confine himself to Science—where at least he knows what he is about.

He has a new telescope—an Equatorial by Ramsden—which Dr Shepherd had procured for him; a second-hand instrument, but in excellent condition. It will make all the difference to his researches, he feels sure. It being a fine morning, he decides to walk round with the note himself, inviting Edward to come and view the instrument in situ; on arriving at the house in Bootham Bar, however, he finds his cousin surrounded by a Chaos of half-packed trunks and boxes.

'Ah, Cousin John. I was just about to send…' In his agitation, he speaks too fast, and it is some moments before John can make head or tail of what he is saying. 'I am to go… of course it is my father's doing… it seems my aunt is at last… my sister cannot manage alone…'

The mention of Mathurina compels his attention. He makes a sign to Edward to speak more slowly.

'Of course. Forgive me. I am to go to Brussels. My aunt is dying—or may, indeed, now be dead. Since I am the eldest, my father wishes me to represent him.'

This much he has already gathered.

What of your sister? he writes.

'Mathurina? Oh, she is quite well, I believe. Distressed, of course…'

Pray send her my condolences.

'Oh, I will. I will.' Edward seems distracted for a moment. Then he appears to collect himself. 'Come,' he says. 'Let us sit down for a moment. There is something particular I have to say…'

He has written to Maskelyne, it transpires, telling him of their discoveries concerning Algol. He has asked him to communicate the same to Herschel—which Maskelyne has done. Now London is abuzz with the news.

'You are to write at once describing what we have learned so far, so that it can be read at the Royal Society. Sir Joseph Banks himself has requested it.'

I would rather you did so.

'My dear fellow, I shall be away. And besides, it is your discovery…'

Ours.

Edward's eyes grow suddenly very bright. He looks away for a moment, as if not quite in command of himself.

'You are good to say so; but I am quite clear on the matter. Beta Persei is yours. My observations served merely to confirm those you had made already.'

Very well. I will write.

'Good. Send it to Dr Shepherd in the first instance. He will make sure it is received in the right quarter.' Edward smiles. 'Now I must respectfully request your absence, dear Cousin. If we sit talking here any longer, I shall miss the packet to Ostend.'

XIII

Setting aside his lingering doubts as to the propriety of doing so—for surely Edward ought at least to have been joint-signatory of such a letter?—he accordingly writes to Dr Shepherd at Cambridge, with a digest of his observations on Algol. To this end, he has ordered his notes and corrected them, so that the whole account reads more smoothly and elegantly, but they are in substance the same as those he has made over successive nights between 12th November (fateful date!) and 3rd May.

York, May 12, 1783

Sir,

I take the liberty to transmit to you the following account of a very singular variation in Algol or Beta Persei, which you will oblige me by presenting to the Royal Society, if you think it deserving that notice. All that has been hitherto known concerning the variation of this star, as far as I can find out after the most diligent researches, is comprised in the following passage in DU HAMEL'S Historia Regiae Scientiarum Academiae, liber IV, Sect. 6 caput VIII de rebus Astronomicis, ann. 1695, p. 362. "*Id quoque testatur D. MONTANARI stellam lucidiorem Medusae, diversis annis, variae esse magnitudinis: nullam pene in ea mutationem potuit advertere D. MARALDI annis 1692 et 1693; sed anno 1694 aucta est et imminuta infigniter, modo quarti, modo tertii, modo secundi ordinis stella apparuit.*" This, however curious, is only a very vague and general information; but the following observations, lately made, exhibit a regular and periodical variation in that star, of a nature hitherto, I believe, unnoticed...

The Latin sonorities and polished phrases serve only to ornament what is in fact quite straightforward. In his journal (where he had no need of such elegant devices) he had put it much more directly:

> Comparing all my observations on Algol it appears that it changes from the 2nd to the 4th magnd. in abt. 3 hours & a half & from thence to the 2nd again in the same space of time, so that the whole duration of this remarkable variation is 7 hours & this variation recurs regularly & periodically every two days & twenty hours & three quarters.

There. In a nutshell. Quite beautiful in its simplicity. And he (despite his polite disclaimers) had been the first to see it. He is eighteen years old, and there is nothing of which he is not capable.

If the letter itself is less assured in tone than the journal, it is in part because of its author's awareness of the scrupulous standards expected by his learned audience, and in part because he is as yet uncertain why the phenomenon he has described occurs as it does.

> If it were not perhaps too early to hazard even a conjecture on the causes of this variation, I should imagine it could hardly be accounted for otherwise than by the interposition of a large body revolving around Algol, or some kind of motion of its own, whereby part of its body, covered with spots or such like matter, is periodically turned towards the earth…

Three days after the letter is sent, he receives a reply from Dr Shepherd, saying that his paper is to be read to the honourable members of the Society that very night, he himself having concluded that the research described within it would be of considerable interest to the same.

He can hardly wait to communicate the news to Edward.

York, May 17, 1783

Sir,

My paper—A Series of Observations on, and a Discovery of, the Period of the Variation of the Light of the bright Star in the Head of Medusa, called Algol—was delivered two nights ago to the Royal Society by the Rev. Anthony Shepherd D.D., F.R.S. and Plumian Professor at Cambridge.

I understand from Dr Shepherd that the paper was well received.

I need hardly say how gratified I am to have received such an honour; nor how sensible I am of your part in procuring it for me.

My compliments to Miss Pigott; and my sympathies to you both in your sad loss.

I am, Sir,
Your most obedt humble servt,
John Goodricke

It is another month before Edward's business in Belgium is concluded—his late aunt's affairs having proved unexpectedly complicated. When the two friends meet again, it is with the warmest emotion on both sides: each clasps the other close, as if he were a long-lost brother.

'My dear cousin. How I have missed our talks,' says Edward, seeming much moved.

With Mathurina, the reunion is necessarily more restrained; although John cannot suppress a feeling of disappointment at her coolness. She seems hardly to remember him.

'*M'sieur.*'

In her appearance, too, he perceives a change: it is as if she had grown smaller and paler; a less substantial being altogether than the wanton he had clasped in his arms the night of the Moon's eclipse. Her three months' sojourn in her native land has restored the air of metropolitan smartness he recalls from their first meeting. She seems brittle, doll-like in her pale perfection.

Beside her, he feels like a provincial clod; a hobble-de-hoy; a dummie.

'My brother says that I am to congratulate you, *M'sieur*...' His confusion must be obvious, for she goes on, 'You have discovered a star, he tells me.'

He nods, foolishly. To his horror, he feels a blush beginning. Mingled with his embarrassment is pleasure, at the thought that his name has been mentioned between them.

A few further phrases, banal in nature, pass between them. He trusts she is in good health? (he writes). Excellent health, she replies. She hopes his mother and sisters are well also? Never better, he informs her. Then she is gone, with a cold little bow, and a smile scarcely deserving of the name.

It is as if his beautiful, passionate, Mathurina had never existed; as if her place had been usurped by this simpering stranger.

An explanation is not long in coming—delivered, almost casually, by her brother. She is to be married, he says, to a certain Comte de Valois—'or is it de Valery? No matter. He is rich, that is the important thing—at least where my father is concerned. He has a fine estate in Touraine and his pedigree is irreproachable. The fact that he is sixty and as ugly as sin is of no consequence... Why, you look askance, Cousin. Surely you do not wish my sister to end her days in a convent? For that, you know, will be her fate otherwise.'

Not for the first time, he is glad of his mute condition, which prevents him from giving vent to the violence of his feelings. That he should lose her to another was bad enough; but that his rival should be an old man, with an old man's stinking breath and wizened frame, is insupportable. The thought of it turns his stomach: her youth and freshness, forced to submit to that loathsome decay.

As soon as he can he seeks her out. She is in the sitting-room she has made her own—a refuge, she said once, with a mischievous look, from her mother's low moods and her father's ebullient ones. She has furnished it in palest yellow: even the lilies in the Chinese vases are of the same shade as the silk which covers the walls, and the stiff brocade curtains. Here she sits placidly sewing, with her little dog at her feet. She glances up as the servant announces him, with what seems to him an affected smile.

As soon as they are alone, he thrusts the note into her hand.

I have heard your news.

She raises an eyebrow. 'Indeed? You wish to offer your *félicitations*, no doubt...'

He makes no reply, but stands glaring at the carpet, on which there is a design of yellow ribbons, twined about baskets of roses.

She puts aside her sewing at last, and pats the space beside her on the sofa. He sits down with an ill grace, and she takes his hands in hers, forcing him to look at her.

'You are angry,' she says. 'But you must see that I have no choice in the matter.'

He starts to write something, but his hand is unsteady. He tries again.

That is why I am angry.

'Do not be,' she replies, with a softer look.

I love you he starts to write—but she stays his hand before he can finish writing.

'You must not say such things,' she says. 'You must not even think them. Now you must go. *Adieu, petit cousin...*'

He sees from her face that they are no longer alone. He glances round. Her mother appears in the doorway, a look of profound suffering upon her face.

'Mathurine, où es tu? J'ai mal à la tête. Ah! que je souffre...'

She breaks off when she sees him, with a look of surprise.

'Cousin John has been helping to tidy my silks,' says Mathurine, holding up a handful of brilliantly coloured skeins. 'Bad Frou-frou made such a tangle, did you not, you naughty thing?'

She gathers the little dog to her and kisses it with a fervour John thinks excessive. He takes his leave of both ladies. Bowing low over Mathurina's hand, he is glad to feel her tremble. Perhaps after all she is not made of stone. In her hand is the crumpled piece of paper, torn from his pad, on which he has written his ill-starred declaration.

Throughout June and July, he is engaged in a series of observations of the constellation Cygnus—its great cruciform shape being clearly discernible across the sky.

> Mr E. Pigott having told me that the Nova in Collo Cygni is now visible, I looked for it tonight at 11h with an Eye tube magnifg. 8 times...

He finds the star, but thinks it no brighter than before. Over the next five nights he observes it, using a plan of his own he has devised to show the stars in the area, but the results are just as disappointing.

Compounding his frustration is the summer cold from which he is suffering, which makes his nose stream and his eyes weep constantly. Dr Braithwaite prescribes sea air, and rest. He complies with the first stipulation, if not the last—moving the seat of his observations to Scarborough. Each night, after spending the days muffled up by the fire with his feet in hot mustard-water, he gets up, puts on his cloak and sets out along the promenade, to continue his pursuit of the elusive Swan.

Hateful bird! It was thus Zeus had appeared to Leda—a manifestation as monstrous, in its own way, as that of the golden shower which had so puzzled him as a child. This, if anything, is worse, because more readily comprehended. In picturing the outrage, it is Mathurina's face he gives to the terrified girl—her white limbs which writhe beneath the vast white beating wings of her assailant...

It had not struck him until now how many of the ancient tales revolved around some no less bestial act. The constellations are a record of such horrors: Europa's rape immortalised in the brutal horns of Taurus; Ursa Major representing the terrible fate of Callisto.

Shivering in the light wind which blows from the ink-black sea, he trains his instruments (carried there for the purpose by the faithful Thomas) on skies of exceptional clarity and darkness. Still he sees nothing. Perhaps there is nothing to see. Nova Collo Cygni obstinately refuses to give up her secrets.

Back in York at the end of July, he sends an exasperated note to Edward:

> Observations of Nova Collo Cygni so far entirely fruitless. I can discern no difference between its present appear-

> ance and that of the star I have called b in my own plan of the area, which is derived from observations made this time last year.

Edward's reply is equally terse:

> Novo Collo not visible this time last year. Can't say if it is or is not the star you refer to.

John's response makes his irritation plain:

> According to my plan, b (which you call Novo Collo) did appear in June last year. If it did not, then I have been wasting my time.

A reply comes by return:

> That is not for me to say.

He almost throws it in the fire, but restrains himself, and waves the servant away.

'Sir,' he writes—when he is master of his temper once more—

> Since we cannot agree on this—and given that you have been observing the star (call it what you will) for far longer than I have—I must respectfully decline to observe it further. Yrs etc.

Next morning, a packet arrives which, on being opened, discloses copies of all the charts his fellow astronomer has made for the preceding twelvemonth. It is undisputable: within them, he finds no trace of the elusive b.

He is composing a retraction of all that he has said, when Edward stands in the doorway.

'My dear Cousin. Let us not fight over trifles.'

I am a fool.

'That is not so. Come, give me your hand…'

I wish all this could be blotted out of the record.

'To what end, pray? Being men of science, we should take a sanguine views of such differences of opinion.'

You are generous, as ever. But the fault was mine.

'Dear fellow. You—as ever—are too hard on yourself.' Edward's gaze is fond. 'Let us leave off star-gazing for the present and walk over to the stables. I want your opinion on a pretty little Bay I am thinking of buying. My father, who is in a generous mood—perhaps not unconnected with the thought of the benefits he hopes to enjoy when my sister is married to her French count—insists that a gentleman (that is myself) must be *well-mounted*.'

On September 10th there is another eclipse of the Moon; he observes it for several hours, as it slowly turns from white to red, until it is the ominous dark colour of a fresh bruise. The weather is bitingly cold; the air tears at his lungs, with every breath he takes, and he can feel the tears standing in his eyes. He wipes them away with the back of his hand. *She is gone*, is all he can think. *I will never see her again, never*. The Moon is as red as blood, now. He takes his repeater from his pocket and begins to count the minutes. One. Two. Three. His breath comes and goes in great clouds of white.

The frost sparkles on the ground like fallen stars. *Never*, he thinks. *Never*.

Try as he might, he cannot erase the memory of the last time they met—when she had stolen upon him all unawares, and they had kissed and kissed, until they had no breath left for kissing. He aches for her. Night after night, he lies sleepless, in sheets disordered by his tossing and turning. In the morning, those sheets are soiled with the evidence of his misspent passion. The image of the way she looked the last time he saw her is with him always, waking and sleeping.

He had risen early, a little after sunrise, to stand in the street as her carriage went by, bound for Dover. There had been a glimpse—no more—of the pale oval of her face, framed by the fur trim of her travelling cloak; then she was gone. Had she seen him? He cannot say. Her lips were pinched, as if to repress their trembling; her eyes downcast. Those eyes—beautiful in shape and colour—look out of her brother's face, too; a constant reminder, if any were needed, of all that he has lost.

That had been his last *sight* of her. His last *meeting* had been even less satisfying, to his mind. It was at Ribston, where his mother had arranged a dinner—by way of recompense perhaps, for having failed to secure her cousin's child a husband nearer at hand.

'For I had hoped, you know, that you would make your home in Yorkshire. France is so very far away,' said Levina, with a sad shake of the head. 'I fear we will never see you.'

He had looked at Mathurina then, to gauge her reaction to this. But before she could reply, her father, flushed with the wine he had drunk and—no doubt—with pleasure at the bargain he had struck, answered for her:

'Why, Madam, France is not so very far away. I consider myself as at home there as I do here. My elder son would undoubtedly say the same, would you not, Edward?'

'Undoubtedly, Father,' said Edward, with the barest suggestion of a raised eyebrow.

'So you see, we are to have no such words as "never" and "far away". I am sure M. Le Comte will be only too happy to bring his bride for a visit shortly.'

'Which is why he has sent his secretary to collect her,' murmured Edward, so softly that only John could make out the words.

He burns with fever; his head as light and swollen as a bladder filled with air. He has been sick for some days now; he cannot say how many. His water is as yellow as stewed tea, and he shivers all over. His hands cannot hold the instruments steady. If he is no better tomorrow, they will bleed him. This, though painful, is better than the vile intrusion of the leeches. Those fat black bodies growing gradually fatter... His throat closes with nausea at the thought. He has been spitting up bile all morning; a foul slime now lies in the bottom of the bowl.

If he cannot have her, he does not want to go on living.

Perhaps it was the Moon that had sent him mad, that night in March. 'Mad as a March hare' they said, didn't they? When he was a child his grandfather had said it of old Mr Bartholomew, who kept bantams in his front parlour and set a place for his dogs at table—because, he said, animals had souls. He had asked his grandfather to repeat the interesting phrase.

What is a march-hair (he had written) *and why is it mad?*

'Now look what you've done, Sir!' (That was his mother). 'Putting ideas in the child's head...'

But the old man had been unrepentant, as ever:

'Whatever ideas he does or does not have in that head of his are of no account, for they cannot get out again. But even were he able to express the opinion he has heard me deliver, it would not signify. Old Bartholomew is mad, that is the fact of it. The boy will hear worse things, before he is much older...'

Which was true enough. Dummie was one of them. Idiot. Clod-pate. Dolt. Deafness and stupidity being so closely associated in the vulgar mind. Madness, though—that was a different kind of affliction altogether. One day you were in your right senses; the next day, not. He had built a world that was as ordered as the heavens; a thing of reason; calculation; harmony. Now Love had undone him—reducing all he had worked so hard to achieve to Chaos and darkness.

Throughout October he is observing Alpha Cassiopeiae.

> It is now nearly equal & sometimes brighter than Gamma Cassiopeiae & certainly brighter than Beta Cassiopeiae...

It was the Cassiopeian stars he used in his observations of Algol, and so it is of the utmost importance that his account of their respective brightnesses should be as accurate as possible. 'I think I cannot err,' he writes, with something of his old circumspection— 'unless I observed them last year under unfavourable circumstances & without any caution as to the weather which as far as I can trust my memory was not the case.'

What does it matter, any of it? She is gone, and he will never see her again. He will die a virgin, driven mad with lust—which, it is well known, acts like a canker in the blood, poisoning the thoughts and corrupting the flesh. Febrile dreams oppress him nightly. Her white body twisting in his arms like a landed fish. Her mermaid's hair falling over his face, long seaweed strands getting in his mouth and blinding his eyes…

In his wilder moments, he dreams of going in search of her—of rescuing her from the clutches of her husband. He will spit in the rascal's face and call him Libertine. Let him ask for satisfaction—it shall not be denied him! There will be the customary meeting of Seconds, followed by an assignation at dawn, from which he will be obliged to flee, having laid his adversary low with a single shot. She will be waiting for him, wrapped in a cloak of sables, in a closed carriage at the end of the lane. They will wander the world together, exiled from society by their unruly passion…

Even as he consoles himself with such thoughts, he knows them for what they are: stories out of the Gothic romances of Mr Walpole, for which his sister Harriet has lately conceived a passion.

XIV

Over the next few weeks, he and Edward continue to exchange notes on their observations, but there has been a noticeable diminution in the numbers of these, since their inglorious falling-out over the Swan. Now John is observing the constellation again, but with no greater success than before. On October 25th he writes: 'Looked at the Nova in Collo Cygni. It was hardly visible...' On November 12th: 'The night being fine, I looked for the Nova in Collo Cygni, but could not see it at all...' Then, in the midst of these dull researches, on November 20th comes an excited note from Edward: 'Have discovered a comet in the Whale's head between Alpha and Gamma Ceti...'

When he takes his own instrument—a fine new Night Glass, with a very large aperture capable of magnifying up to twenty times—he sees it quite distinctly.

> I looked for it tonight abt 7h & at 11h it visibly changed its place, being more northwards—from this motion it evidently appears that this was indeed a Comet...

He is glad for Edward, who has made no new discoveries of late. For himself, he is weary of stars and their brightening and fading. They are fickle creatures, with no heart to them. One might as well give up one's waking hours to studying lumps of ice. Rocks. Bones. Or any other inanimate Thing. But when he conveys as much to Edward, the other looks at him strangely.

'Are you quite well, Cousin? I have never known you to speak so slightingly of our profession before. What is the *point* of astronomy, you ask me? You will be asking me next what is the *point* of living...'

In truth, he is not well.

The weather has been exceptionally cold—9 degrees, by his Dollond thermometer—and he is plagued with a sore throat, which soon turns to a cough, and will not go away. On 30th December, he is so ill that he cannot leave his bed. His mother sends jellies, and a box of dried quinces from his grandfather's orchard, but a heavy snowfall next day makes the roads impassable between York and Ribston (where the family are presently staying) so he sees the New Year in alone. Racked with coughs and shivering with fever, he can do nothing but wallow in his sweat-soaked sheets, and torment himself with thoughts of what might have been. If he had only stood up for himself like a man, he might have won her. If he had spoken out... But he could never have spoken out, because he cannot speak—that is the fact of it.

On 12th January, he is well enough to get up. He orders a fire to be lit in the drawing-room and sends out for beefsteak; he has grown sick of soup. As he is sitting down to enjoy the first good breakfast he has had in almost a month, the servant comes in with a letter. He knows the hand before he breaks the seal.

'*Cher Monsieur,*' he reads—and then can read no more. For a moment, he is overcome with faintness. What if something has happened to her? But no (he reasons)—for she would not then be writing. He unfolds the letter once more. A sweet scent—unfamiliar and expensive—rises from its pages.

Azay-le-Rideau
1e Janvier 1784

Cher Monsieur,

J'espère que vous êtes maintenant en bonne santé. Mon frère m'a dit, il y a quelques semaines, que vous étiez malade. Mon pauvre cousin, que je suis inquiète pour vous! Pour ma part, je vais très bien, comme toujours.

Je vous envoie mes meilleurs sentiments, petit cousin, et j'espére que vous ne m'oublierez pas.

Mathurine de Valois

Trembling with delight, he reads the words once more—and then again, until he has got them by heart. *Je suis inquiète de vous*... He is sorry to have caused her anxiety—and yet delighted to have been the subject of such tender concern. Edward—dear Edward—has evidently told her of his illness and so she has written… All his fears in that instant melt away. *J'espére que vous ne m'oublierez pas*… Forget her! How could she imagine that he could ever forget her? She is engraved upon his heart as the stars are upon the sky; indelibly, eternally.

He kisses the name she has signed, although it is that of another. In a transport of joy, he seizes pen and paper, and begins composing a reply—*Chère Madame*—before realising that such a reply is impossible. Even if her husband (bearer of that hated name—which he must love, since it is now her name) is not in the habit of reading his wife's correspondence, the arrival of a letter from England—and one in a strange hand—will, at the very least, excite remark.

His hastily scrawled phrases lie upon the page like so much chaff.

> *Je me souviens de notre dernier rendez-vous…*

Ridiculous to contemplate sending such a letter. She cannot seriously expect him to reply.

In the end, his response is limited to a—casually framed—request that Edward, when he should next write, would convey his—John's—respectful greetings to Madame de Valois on his (John's) behalf. Edward says that he will do so. 'For she lives for letters from home, poor girl,' he says, unwittingly twisting the knife in his friend's heart. 'She is so very dull at Azay-le-Rideau that any word is like balm to her spirits. I sent news of you in my last, as a matter of fact,' he adds. 'For I know Mathurina regards you almost as a brother…' Another twist of the knife.

By January 19th, he has resumed his studies with a new vigour, all his sickly misgivings of the past few weeks forgotten.

> Algol varied to-night & I have made 6 good observations on it, from which I have determined the time of its least magnitude or greatest diminution of light to be 6h—48'. Appt. time true I believe to 10 minutes, if not less…

With a revival of his old confidence he adds:

> Last month I sent another Memoir to the Royal Society, in which I have determined the Period of Algol's changes to be 2d—20h—49'- 3", true to ten seconds & have also added a few other remarks...

His thoughts are never far from France—that, to him, mysterious country, remote as any star, which now holds all that is most dear to him. An advertisement in the London Chronicle, to which Edward has alerted him, mentions the recent discovery, by a gentleman of that country, of a new comet.

> I looked for it tonight & immediately found it in the Tail of the Northern Fish with about 355 Degrees of Right Ascension & 5 Degrees North Declinn. Its nucleus was very bright & about half a minute in diameter...

He wonders if Mathurina might also have seen the comet—for is she not also in France?

> By comparing my observation with that of the Compte Cassini Jany 24th last, I think that the Comets light is decreasing & that it is coming from the Sun. It is a very fine Comet...

He pictures her watching it from the window of some old grey château, her little dog in her arms. Would she think of him as she gazed at it? He dares to hope that she might. For a young woman versed, as she is, in the rudiments of astronomy (she would not have been her father's daughter otherwise) the appearance of a comet will be worthy, at least, of remark. Will her husband share her enthusiasm? It seems doubtful, from what he knows of the man—a cold fish, he supposes, whose passions are doubtless confined to the intricacies of his family tree. Although national pride alone might spur the gentleman's interest in his countryman's discovery...

It remains cold: on February 12th, his thermometer registers 12 degrees when he consults it at 7 a m. He orders the stove to be lit in his observing-rooms, and still his fingers are almost too cold to manipulate the instruments. But it feels good to be working again. On days like this, he will immerse himself completely in the problem in hand, eschewing all society, and stopping only for the brief period it takes to consume a slice of cold mutton and a mug of beer. Hours pass, and he takes no notice of their passing, brought to consciousness of the time only when the room around him grows too dark for him to see clearly what he is doing, and he is obliged to send for candles.

He is absorbed in his charts of Alpha Cassiopeia—studies set aside during his illness and now resumed—and so does not observe Edward's approach until the latter touches him on the shoulder.

'My dear fellow.' Edward seems unusually agitated, and his eyes are bright with emotion. 'I wanted to be the first to congratulate you. It is wonderful news.'

Then, seeing John's puzzled frown: 'You mean you have not yet heard? Dear Cousin, you are recognized at last! I had it from Maskelyne this morning. Here...'—thrusting the letter he is holding into the other's hands—'Read it for yourself.'

He does so, but for some unaccountable reason, the words will not keep still—dancing around in front of his eyes as if possessed of a life of their own.

'Sir,' he reads at last. 'It is with the greatest pleasure that I communicate to you the following, on behalf of my esteemed Fellows at the Royal Society...'

All the breath seems to leave his body. He reads the words again, although the intelligence they convey is scarcely credible to him. He has been awarded the Copley Medal for his work on variable stars—specifically for his discovery of the variability of Beta Persei, also called Algol. Wide-eyed with the shock of it, he looks again at Edward, who nods his smiling confirmation of the fact.

'You are commanded to appear at the Society's chambers in London a month hence,' he says. 'They will present you with the medal then.'

Suddenly, Edward's arms are around him. He feels the brief press of a smooth-shaven cheek against his own.

'I could not be happier,' Edward says, drawing back so that they both stand face to face, 'if it were myself who had received the honour.' He draws a handkerchief from his sleeve and dabs at his eyes. 'I shall accompany you to London,' he goes on, when he has mastered his emotions once more. 'It will be a great thing to see. A youth not yet twenty years old, receiving the accolades of distinguished men of science twice his years...'

They arrive in London in mid-March, although the presentation is not until 1st of April—an unfortunate choice of day, he remarks to Edward.

For is it not All Fools' Day? Perhaps it is a joke, and they do not mean to give me the medal at all...

At which Edward laughs, and shakes his head.

'A very grave joke, if it is to make fools of the whole of the Royal Society,' he says.

It is John's wish to spend a few weeks in the capital, in order to improve himself in the different branches of his chosen field. Of the two cities, there is no doubt in his mind that he prefers York, but there are times when it could not but seem a shade provincial. And London is of course the centre of the universe—not least in astronomy. Dr Maskelyne will receive them; and Sir Joseph Banks is to hold a reception for them at his fine house in Soho Square.

'For you are launched in Society at last, Cousin,' says Edward with a smile. 'You must take care that it does not go to your head.'

It is too late, for I am quite eaten up with Pride...

In truth, he is enjoying the attention. At the Duke of Cumberland's ball, he finds himself at the centre of a bevy of smiling beauties, in gowns cut so low they expose a good half of each creamy bosom; he does not know where to put his eyes.

'You are the talk of all the drawing-rooms,' says Edward wryly. 'Watch out—or one of these good matrons will snap you up for her daughter...'

It is one of those moments when he is glad that his deafness absolves him from replying.

There is another moment, at another party, when he is similarly taken aback, by a remark not in fact addressed to him.

'Is he not handsome?' a young lady in blue whispers to a young lady in pink.

'Hush, Arabella.'

'O, he cannot hear us,' is the reply. 'For he is deaf as a post, they say.' She throws the object of her interest a melting look, which he affects to ignore. 'I should like to bite his lips—they are so very like ripe cherries…'

'Arabella, *dearest*…'

'He has large hands and feet. Do you suppose it is true what they say about men with large feet? I should like to find out, should not you?'

'*Arabella*!'

It is an effort to restrain his blushes. Although afterwards, he wonders what she had meant about his feet…

His astronomical researches prove less fruitful than his forays into Society, for the atmosphere is not clear enough to see. A permanent fog lies over the city, it seemed, cloaking everything in uncertainty. He looks for Nova Hydra on several successive nights, and finds it much diminished, since his last observations in January. He is not sure whether this is a true variation, or merely the result of the bad air.

On April 1st, he is present to hear Dr Shepherd read his paper on Algol to the Royal Society; he cannot, of course, read it himself. It is a continuation of the work he had submitted the previous May, and develops some of the ideas contained in the earlier paper. His subsequent researches have enabled him to determine with even greater accuracy the periodicity of Algol's variation.

'All error cannot as yet be excluded,' reads Anthony Shepherd, with the distinctness born of years of preaching. 'But I think that the period is now, by the following calculation, ascertained to within ten or fifteen seconds.'

Dr Shepherd then turns to the chart, which stands on the easel behind him, and on which the Mean Times of Algol's least brightness are listed. As he does so, there is a general stirring in the ranks of learned Fellows, as some lean forward, the better to read what is written there, while others fumble with spectacles or pince-nez, to the same purpose. Only John himself does not move, for he already knows what the chart says. Instead, he keeps his gaze fixed on the moving lips of the speaker, as the latter proceeds slowly down the list of calculations, pausing between each one, to make sure that his audience is following.

'Between January 14th at 25 minutes past 9 and October 25th at 39 minutes past 6, there was an interval of 99 revolutions, each of 2 days 20 hours, 49 minutes and 14 seconds...'

For a few moments, John allows his gaze to roam around the magnificent chamber in which they are sitting, with its marble pillars and plaster ceiling decorated in the Greek fashion, and its tall windows casting a cold light on those assembled there. Some are known to him, if only through their fame; others are not. But he feels, as he sits there, in the place of honour below the rostrum, that he has found his home at last...

He catches Edward's eye, and the other smiles. *My brother*, he thinks, wishing it could be so. But that can never be. Where is she at that moment, the woman who should by rights have been his bride? There have been no more letters; only a stiff little message, relayed to him by Edward, that Mme de Valois was quite well, and begged to be remembered to him.

'It appears to me now, that the duration of the variation is about eight hours.' Dr Shepherd turns once more to the paper he is holding. 'But as it is difficult to hit exactly the beginning and end of the variation, this may occasion different observers to differ in this respect...'

He notices Dr Herschel, sitting a few seats to his right, in front of the podium—and sees that the other has seen him. After what seems a moment's hesitation, the great astronomer and discoverer of Georgium Sidus favours him with a stiff little bow, which he returns. The ill-feeling which had arisen between them over the reading of his paper on Algol last May has not, it appears, been entirely dispelled—although of the two he was the injured party. He recalls how angry he had been when Pigott told him of Herschel's clumsy attempt to pre-empt his discovery, by reading his own notes on Algol's changes to an informal group of learned gentlemen gathered for that purpose at the Crown Inn.

It had been most unethical behaviour, and he had written to Herschel to tell him so. Perhaps it was fortunate that Pigott had persuaded him not to send the letter. Instead, Pigott had offered to write himself—for Herschel was an old friend—to ascertain the truth of the matter...

Now Dr Shepherd has reached the section of his paper which deals with Flamsteed's observations on Algol, made some eighty years before his own. He has summarised both his own findings and those of his distinguished predecessor, the late Astronomer Royal.

'Presuming, therefore, on the justness of Flamstead's observation of January 1696, I compared it with one of mine, viz: October 25th at 6 hours and 39 minutes...'

Around the chamber, the rows of learned gentlemen are nodding their approval at this thoroughness of approach.

An abstract follows of the observations he has made between August and November 1783 of the variations in Algol's brightness. He has tried to make it as succinct as possible—not wanting to weary his fellow scientists unduly. Now he glances around the chamber, and is relieved to see that—although one or two have their eyes closed, the better to hear what is being said, presumably—none of them is actually asleep.

At length an end is reached. Around him, people start to applaud. Although he cannot hear it, he feels the atmospheric disturbance created by all those pairs of colliding palms. For him, sound has an equivalent in movement, and not a single pair of hands in the room is still.

Dr Shepherd makes a brief, deprecatory gesture, as if to disallow his share in the applause; then bows towards John.

As one man, the company rises to its feet, still clapping, but directing its looks and smiles in his direction. He feels Edward take his arm, urging him to stand up. He does so, his face suffused with blushes, and makes his bow with as much grace as he can muster. Still the applause goes on. He has never known the like of it. The last time he had been so singled out—in Dr Enfield's class, when he had taken the Mathematics prize, the prize for

Latin and Greek and the prize for Logic—he had been pelted with ink-darts, and there had been a particularly nasty encounter with Fitzsimmons and his crew in the corridor afterwards.

Generous hands guide him towards the podium, where Sir Joseph is waiting to hand him the coveted medal. Sudden panic overwhelms him. He has nothing prepared. What is he to say? As the applause subsides (some of the older Fellows having turned an unhealthy purple with the exertion) he scribbles a note, and hands it to Edward.

'Gentlemen, you do me too much honour,' Edward reads to the assembled company. 'I can only offer my heartfelt thanks, on my own behalf and…' Here he breaks off, smiles, and shakes his head. '…on behalf of my esteemed colleague, Mr Edward Piggott—without whom my poor researches would never have seen the light of day.'

Afterwards, they enjoy a fine dinner of beefsteaks, followed by a wonderful dish of stewed venison, washed down with several bottles of claret. He has never drunk so much in his life; whenever he looks, his glass is always full, and all the toasts are to him—'Our Prodigy'—and to Astronomy, 'that jealous mistress without whom… &c &c.' He remembers laughing a good deal, although at what he could not say. Later, he and Edward, accompanied by Englefield, go on to the Playhouse in Drury Lane, the rest of the company having staggered off into the night. Mrs Siddons is playing Lady Macbeth, but it is impossible to make out much about it; he retains only an impression of sweeping gestures; an anguished look; a brandished dagger.

At some point he must have fallen asleep, for the next thing he knows, Edward is shaking him, and the theatre is half-empty. At Mrs Briggs' in Little White Lion Street, they have a supper of oysters and champagne, which Englefield says is a great restorative. Soon after this, Englefield leaves them; when John asks where he has gone, Edward shrugs, and says he is satisfying a call of Nature. It must have been a very violent purge, for Englefield is gone half an hour, and returns very red in the face and laughing. As he sits down, calling for more champagne to be brought, he whispers something to Edward, looking at John.

Edward frowns and shakes his head. 'No,' he says. 'He is not...'

What he is not—if indeed it is he himself that is being talked of—he cannot make out, it having been said so rapidly. Not sober, not in his right senses, not like other men? All these are true enough. Englefield, he sees, has neglected to button himself—his John Thomas protrudes through his breeches like an angry red snout. There is no way of telling him that does not involve the further impoliteness of pointing. For some reason this makes him laugh. He knows—because he has been told—that his laughter sounds like that of any man. There is, after all, nothing the matter with his voice-box; it is merely the connexion between it and his brain that is at fault.

It is surprising, he thinks sleepily, that his tongue has not atrophied, after so many years of disuse...

In the street the cold air is like a slap in the face. He staggers, and would have fallen face-first on the greasy cobblestones, if Edward had not caught him. 'Steady, old fellow...' He feels, rather than hears, the admonition—its soft whoosh of syllables warm against his cheek.

Against a wall, a man is tupping his doxy—white buttocks heaving in a fury of agitation. This strikes him as very funny. He begins to laugh, thinking, *I laugh like any man*—which makes him laugh the more. His stomach hurts with the exertion. Tears course down his cheeks unchecked.

He feels Edward grasp his arm, drawing him out of harm's way, as ever. *Dear Edward*, he thinks. *Dear, dear Edward*... His thoughts from that point on are a jumble. Edward's face, bending over him... His eyes—so like her eyes—gazing into his with a look of mingled reproach and pity...

No, that is later. First there is the staggering journey home. He remembers being violently sick in the street—all the food and drink he has consumed over the course of the evening spewing out of him, to spatter the pavement in a stinking mess. His tears flow once more—an involuntary emission. Then he is lying on his back, looking up at the stars, which have emerged on purpose to greet him. He names them all. Ursa Major. Draco. Camelopardalis. Cepheus. Lacerta. Andromeda... Ah, Andromeda, his poor abandoned beloved. Chained to her rock, while the monster draws ever closer... And where is he, her Perseus? Drunk in a gutter in Seven Dials, with his coat covered in filth and his breeches torn. He has failed her, he has failed her...

He feels the hot tears fall down. His weeping, had he but known it, sounding like that of any other man.

In the morning he wakes with foul breath, and a head like a bubble of glass. His medal is on the mantelpiece, where someone—Edward, presumably—has placed it. There is a letter propped beside it. He breaks the seal. It is his mother's hand.

'My dear Son,' he reads. 'It grieves me to be the bearer of such tidings, but I must ask you to come home at once. Your father has been struck down with an apoplexy. The doctor fears he will not survive a fortnight...'

Edward returns at that moment from his walk.

'Such a glorious day, my dear fellow! I have never seen Rotten Row so thronged with people. The whole of Society must have been taking the air...' Something of his friend's heaviness of spirits must have become apparent, for he goes on with a smile, 'Come! You must not sit moping here. Exercise is the only cure for over-indulgence...'

John hands him the letter.

He reads it swiftly, and a look of contrition comes over his features.

'John—I am so sorry. Your father is a good man.' Which mine is not, he might have added, but does not. 'We must start at once for Yorkshire.'

In vain does his friend endeavour to persuade him to remain in London, where the Season is only just beginning.

'Dear Cousin. There is nothing to keep me here, if you are gone. For it was for you I came—to witness your triumph. The rest is nothing but foppery and parties.'

XV

In the event, it takes his father three months to die. After the seizure which had laid him low, he had rallied a little—so that he was able to rise from his bed for a few hours at a time, to sit in a sunny patch of the garden at Lendal, or—supported by two serving-men—to shuffle the length of the terrace and back again. But of his former enthusiasms he takes not the smallest bit of notice. On the table in his study, his books and maps lie gathering dust. Abandoned, too, is his egg-collection and shells; the curving Scimitar in its japanned sheath; the dragon's foetus in its jar; and all the other curiosities amassed during his years in the foreign service.

Now he sits, dumbstruck—as dumb as I am, thinks John—in his high-backed chair, his gaze dull, as if everything were of equal indifference to him. When a spoon is brought to his lips, he opens his mouth to receive it. When some of the pap runs down his chin, he makes no move to wipe it away.

'O, what shall I do?' cries Levina, wringing her hands. 'Your Father is become an Infant again. I have borne seven children—two of them now in their graves—but this I never thought to have to bear…'

'Hush, Mama.' This is Harriet. 'Do not distress yourself so.' Harriet is seventeen and has inherited their father's seriousness of disposition. 'You know that Grandpapa will look after us, even if Papa cannot.'

This, though undoubtedly true, is tactless, and brings on a fresh storm of tears. Sometimes, thinks John, there is an advantage in being silent.

Later, he talks with Harriet in the garden. She is adept at the signs; Henry has never mastered them, and his mother has forgotten half she knew.

WILL FATHER DIE?

I DON'T KNOW. MAYBE.

YOU WILL BE HEAD OF THE FAMILY.

You forget Grandfather.

He touches his forehead with his fingertips, then opens his hand, as if consigning the idea of the old man to the air.

Grandfather is old.

Grandfather will live forever—if only to prevent me from inheriting.

Harriet is thoughtful a while, digesting this. She does not disagree with what he says, however. Then her face clears, and she turns to him again, a mischievous smile animating her features, so that she is almost pretty. Harriet should smile more often, he thinks, conscious that she has little occasion to. It is a dull life for a young girl. Still, she might marry soon...

Are you in love?

He smiles at her eager face. He should try and do more for her. Bring her out. If Mathurina had been there, she would have known just how to bring Harriet out... He brushes away the thought.

I am in love...

He sees her eyes widen with pleasure; a smile beginning on her lips.

...with the stars.

He sees her face fall.

You are teasing me.

He thinks for a moment she is going to walk away.

No. Wait. You are right. I am in love.

Harriet's eyes grow round behind her spectacles.

Who is she? Tell me.

I cannot. It is a secret.

She smiles, delighted by this.

Is she beautiful?

Her bunched fingertips touch her chin, then sprang open, miming the astonishing refulgence of a face.

Very beautiful.

Do I know her?

He hesitates only a second.

No. Now no more questions.

At that moment Elizabeth runs up, her dress all dirty from playing in the flowerbeds. Mary follows at a more sedate pace, already a young lady, at thirteen.

PROMISE YOU WILL SAY NOTHING TO MOTHER.

I PROMISE.

'What are you doing, flickering your fingers like that?' demands Elizabeth. 'Is it a game? Can I do it?'

'When you are older,' says Harriet. She directs a look at her brother that is full of meaning. 'I will teach you.'

YOU MUST TEACH HER NOW, OR SHE WILL NEVER LEARN.

'Very well. Pay attention, Lizzie.' Harriet points at herself. 'This means "I".' She crosses her hands over her heart. 'This means "love".' She points to her sister. 'This means "you".'

'I... love... you!' shouts Elizabeth, suiting the actions to the words.

'You must not shout,' says Mary. 'You know Grandpapa said we are to be quiet and good for Papa's sake.'

'John is always quiet,' says Elizabeth thoughtfully. 'That means he must be very good indeed. I should not like to be as good as John.'

'There is no danger of that,' replies Mary.

In his haste to leave London, he had neglected to pack his instruments; these are sent on later, by the carrier. Now, aside from his obligations in the sick-room, his evenings are passed in idleness, with nothing to distract him but his nightly promenades around the garden or—since he does not play cards—the few books in his father's library not devoted to the complexities of jurisprudence or the legal systems of Ancient Rome.

Wandering in the garden one fine June night—the Dragon is high in the sky, and Arcturus wonderfully brilliant—he steps out from behind a hornbeam hedge right into Sir John's path, to the discomfiture of both parties. His grandfather gives a start, and perhaps gives vent to an oath, although it is too dark for John to be certain. Since there is no help for it, they fall into step for a while, pacing the gravel paths that meander between the clipped hedges in a silence John is inclined to classify as awkward, although he is more used to silence than most.

Simply, his presence—and its particular silence—makes Sir John uncomfortable. His grandson has known it, almost from the start. When, in spite of the best doctors money could buy—to say nothing of the best schooling—he had wilfully refused to learn to speak, John knew himself a disappointment in the old man's eyes. He suspects that, even if he had mastered that subtle art, it would not have advanced him much in his grandfather's affections.

The superstitious horror which a whole man feels for a cripple is, in fine, what bluff Sir John—Envoy Extraordinary to the court of Stockholm, MP for Ripon and Privy Councillor to the King—feels for him. That his deafness had been the result of illness and not some inherited disorder in the blood makes not a whit of difference. Besides which, there exists no natural sympathy between himself and the old man. Henry has always been Sir John's favourite. Both love horses, gambling, shooting, and dogs. The pursuit of learning—of Science in particular—is something for which both evince an aristocratic disdain, as if there were something not quite gentlemanly about it.

When informed by his daughter-in-law, upon her son's arrival from London, that the latter had been awarded 'a very fine medal by a very learned Society,' Sir John's reply was terse: 'A medal? For star-gazing? What earthly use is that?'

Now, as they reach the bottom of the long double flight of steps, which leads up to the terrace, John is surprised to feel the old man take his arm. They mount the steps in time, Sir John holding fast to his companion, as if suddenly afraid of falling. As they reach the top, he seems to be breathing with some difficulty. Afraid that he might have been taken ill, John turns towards him. In the light that falls through the open doors of the Drawing Room, he sees that his grandfather's eyes are dim with tears, and his lips are trembling.

He thinks, *It is as hard for him to lose a son as it is for me to lose a father*, but the knowledge seems only to fix them in their mutual isolation.

It is not that night but another, some weeks later, that his father dies—an event foreshadowed by a change in the weather. Now, a strange opalescent haze hangs in the atmosphere, obscuring the stars and imparting a reddish look—like that of dried blood—to Sun and Moon alike. Though it is the middle of Summer, there is not a trace of sunshine to be seen—only a dry, sulphurous fog that stings the eyes, and the back of the throat. According to Maskelyne—from whom he has received a letter, commending his paper on Algol—it is the same all over Europe, with pestilential air blighting the crops, and sending the dogs mad. M. Lalande had given a paper in Paris on the probable causes of the phenomenon—which some attributed to comets, or to Sun-spots, although neither cause had been conclusively settled. In the meantime, the foggy weather continues, as if Summer had changed to Autumn, and day to night.

So it is on the night in question, with a dull red moon casting a baleful light on everything below. From where he sits, he can see it—round as a copper penny in the sky. It is late—around three—and he has been keeping vigil all night, having sent his mother away to rest for a few hours. The candles are burning low, and a sickly yellow glare lies over the scene, which seems, to his fancy, to exist at some distance from himself, like a painted tableau. There lies the wasted figure in the bed, in his stained nightshirt and the tasselled cap that has slipped sideways, to incongruous effect, revealing the scant grey locks. There is the slumbering nurse in her chair, and there the black-clad figure—himself—seated on the stool beside the sufferer, whose eyes never stray from his face, although they do not seem to see him.

When the moment comes, he holds his father's hand, to calm him, and signals to the nurse to fetch his mother. But by the time she returns, it is over. *A stopped machine*, he thinks, looking at what remains of his father. All that he had been is gone, leaving only an absence.

At this melancholy sight, his mother can do nothing but weep, and fling herself upon the poor Shell that lies there, as if her tears might infuse it with life once more. It is he who closes his father's eyes, shutting up forever their mild blue gaze; he who sends for Dr Harker, in order that the time of death might be certified; and who gives instructions for the body to be washed and the jaw bound up, before his siblings are summoned. They must not see their father as he has seen him; there is a respect due to the dead—and besides, it might frighten Lizzie.

When all that has to be done has been done, he gives the servant a note to be taken at once to Sir John, at Ribston:

York
9th July 1784

Sir,

It is my painful duty to inform you of your son's, and my revered father's, demise, at a quarter after three this morning.

I am, Sir,

Your most obednt humble servant,
John Goodricke

As heir presumptive, he sits at Sir John's right hand during the funeral service; although the old man barely looks at him, sitting stiff-backed as the obsequies are read, and rising abruptly to his feet at the end of them. It is Henry's arm he takes as he quits the chapel; John being left to follow with his mother (his grandmother having taken to her bed; she cannot abide funerals, she says). All through the service, Levina has not left off crying. Now she clings to her eldest son's arm, as if without its support she might succumb to the overwhelming tide of her grief. Bringing up the rear of their sad procession are the girls—like their mother dressed all in black, with black veils over their faces. This last strikes him as having something extravagant—if not actually Papistical—about it. Not that he cares on his own account, but his father had been a plain man, who disliked all forms of ritual.

Although he cannot deny it makes a striking picture: the black-clad figures all in a row, against the heavy dark oak of the pews on which they sit. A pale light falls from the chapel's high windows, illuminating pale hands and paler faces. At the back of the crowd—which includes members of most of the principle families of the region—he catches a glimpse of Edward, in a fine suit of black velvet. He is, it turns out, the sole representative of his family.

'For you know,' he explains, with that mixture of amusement and disdain which has become habitual with him where this subject is concerned, 'my father cannot set foot inside a Protestant church. Not even for a near cousin, which your father indubitably was. He is quite inflexible on that score. Why, his immortal soul might be in peril… I, of course—being beyond redemption already, as he sees it—can be spared for the purpose quite readily…'

Seeing from the other's face that he has perhaps gone too far with this sally, he adds: 'Forgive me. I have grown so used to speaking my mind where my father's idiosyncrasies are concerned that I forget myself. Cousin Henry was the best of men, and no doubt the best of parents. Your loss is therefore greater than I can ever imagine, given that my father is neither of these things… But come,' he goes on, when—the bier with its sad cargo having been removed to its last resting-place in the family vault—they stand once more in the Great Hall at Ribston. 'At least you have this to console you. You will be Sir John ere long, unless I am much mistaken. Your grandfather cannot last much longer, surely? Then you will be master of all this, and more…'

You are premature with your congratulations, he writes. *My grandfather is in excellent health.*

'Now I have offended you,' says Edward, with a rueful look. 'And for that I am truly sorry. All I meant was that, when the time comes, you will be a man of means. Free to do as you please. Instead of a pauper, at the beck and call of an irascible tyrant. Like others I could mention, but -' He sketches a bow—'out of deference to the solemnity of the occasion, will not.'

He hopes for a letter from Mathurina, but none comes. Has the news of his father's demise been conveyed to her, he ventures at last to ask Edward.

The latter is all contrition. 'My dear fellow. It quite slipped my mind. She asked me to convey her sincerest sympathies to you—and to your poor mother, of course—on your sad loss. The fact is, she has not been well, else she would have written herself.'

When pressed for further details, he merely shrugs.

'She… I hardly know how to express this, without indelicacy. She was *enceinte*, you understand. Now she is no longer in that condition. A blessing, one must conclude, given what one is able to surmise about the unfortunate union into which my sister has entered.'

The joy he feels at the news that she is safe and well is almost outweighed by other, more shameful feelings: relief that her womb no longer groaned under the weight of another's offspring being uppermost.

'I cannot agree with my good friend Herschel on this,' says Edward, interrupting these reflections. (They are engaged in looking over Flamsteed's catalogue of stars, with a view to discovering any inaccuracies.) 'In my view, there are several errors to be found.'

I am of your mind, writes John, his hand trembling a little. *There are some errors.*

'We are in harmony, then—as ever.' Edward smiles. 'When I hear tell of my poor, sad sister—or of any number of other unfortunates who have had cause to regret the married state—I am glad that I am not of their number. For in truth, dearest Cousin,' he continues with some emotion, 'I would not change the perfect accord which exists between us for anything else in the world.'

Throughout August, John continues the laborious task of comparing his own observations of Capricorn, Aquarius and Lyra with their representations in Flamsteed's *Atlas*.

To Herschel he writes:

York
7th August 1784

Sir,

The Perusal of your paper on the proper motion of the Sun & Solar System published in the last volume of Philosop. Transns. gave me great pleasure especially as the Theory of the Solar motion perfectly coincides with my sentiments. I have however upon comparing Flamstead's Catalogue with that of Ptolemy, Tycho, Herelius &c., as also with Flamstead's observns. in the 2d vol. of his Historiae celestis, where he often marks the magnitudes of stars when observed, discovered several errors in that part of it which relates to the changes of the stars & take the liberty to send to you the following corrections...

He reads over what he has put. Does it sound a shade presumptuous? Perhaps he should mention that he is not alone in his reservations.

Mr Edwd. Pigott in a letter he wrote to me lately has the following remarks in 29 Persei & 70—80 & 81 Herculis & he desires me to communicate them to you. I will here transcribe part of his letter...

Edward, he reassures himself, is a friend of Herschel's.

If I meet with any other thing worth remarking, he concludes, I shall take the first opportunity to communicate them to you...

Perhaps after all it was tactlessly phrased; he does not have Edward's smoothness of expression. Herschel, at any rate, seems to take the matter amiss. The tone of his reply is distinctly cool. He is of course John's senior by more than twenty years, as well as the discoverer of Georgium Sidus. The younger man's remarks must seem like an impertinence, indicative merely of the arrogance of youth, in drawing attention to the mistakes of his elders.

Such was not his intention. He writes again:

York,
2nd September 1784

Sir,

As you seem not to have perfectly understood the meaning of my Letter, I have taken the liberty to write to you again & to set the matter in a clearer light. I hope the following explanation of that letter will give you satisfac-

> tion & make it appear that I have not misapprehended your paper…

That strikes the right note, he thinks.

> I beg leave to mention here that I did not mean to lay the errors to your account but to Flamstead's…

Flamsteed, being dead, could not object. 'Be assured of my perfect esteem,' he ends, with the barest suggestion of a flourish. 'I remain, Sir, your most obedient & very humble Servt, John Goodricke…'

September is given over to the study of Lyra. On 10th of that month he writes:

> I thought Beta Lyra was much less than usual. It was much less than Gamma Lyra & was less than a star of the 4th magnitude.

By 30th he concludes,

> that it varies during the space of about 36 or 40 hours & its Period is 6d—10h—+—just.

With his customary cautiousness, he adds:

> If, however, it shd happen otherwise, then I have been deceived by the weather & the fallacy of sight & will no more trust to such exceeding small variations…

In his heart, he knows it is not so. For they have enjoyed an unbroken series of beautiful days, as is often the case in early Autumn. *Air clear*, he writes, in an observation made on September 12th.

This is at Edward's request; the latter suspecting that Eta Antinoi, in the neck of the Eagle, might also be variable, and desiring his young colleague's opinion on the matter. Did Goodricke know the tale? his friend wonders. The Star in question had been named by the Emperor Hadrian, in honour of his beloved—the beautiful youth, Antinous, after the latter had died saving him (the Emperor) from drowning...

He did not know the story, but he is happy to observe the Star. As to his eyes, he thinks—they are as keen as ever.

From where he lies, flat on his back on the lawn of his father's house in Lendal, he can make out the pale yellow and blue twin Stars which together comprise Beta Lyrae, with the aid of nothing but a pocket-glass. There it stands, the Lyre, as if it has been flung there only that instant by the Muses, as a token of mourning for Calliope's lost son. Although he, reunited with his beloved, is surely happy at last... Yellow and blue twinkles the double star, growing brighter or dimmer as its companion revolves around it.

So, too, had Orpheus grown bright when his Eurydice was near; darkening unto death when her brightness was removed, and she was carried off to the lightless realms of Hades. Even then, he had refused to accept that she was gone, braving those gloomy halls to win her back again. The attempt had ended in disaster: the rescuer overcome, in that last instant, by the cries of the one he sought to redeem. *Look at me. Why don't you look at me*? Turning, and in that shocked moment, seeing the realisation of all she had lost flare in her eyes as she slipped back, out of his reach forever.

He has heard nothing from Mathurina for more than half a year; has not set eyes on her for a twelvemonth. Yet still she haunts his thoughts. Bright moments rise up out of nowhere to unman him. There was the time in the rose arbour—her face like a rose itself—when she had let him hold her hand. The time she had slipped her arm through his as he escorted her home along High Petergate, her little feet in their clumsy pattens slipping and sliding on the icy cobbles, so that she was obliged to cling tighter and tighter to keep from falling... How happy he had been—and how careless of that felicity!

He thinks of the way she looked at their last meeting, her dear face frozen into a pale mask of itself, like one under sentence of death. And in truth, was it not a kind of death—to be exiled, as she was, from all those she loved, and from those that loved her?

Unlike Orpheus, he cannot fetch her back. Nor, to add to his torment, is he able to confess what is in his heart to the one best able to hear it—brother of his Inamorata and dearest friend. He wonders if Edward has ever been in love. If he has, he has never said so. Perhaps, unknown to John, there is a Beloved somewhere. Or perhaps he cares nothing for such matters, preferring the study of heavenly bodies to that of corporeal ones...

His observations of Hydra and Delta Cephei proceed at a slow pace. On 20th October he writes:

> 2 Hydra appeared as a Star of the 4th or 5th Magnd. 1 Hydra of the 6th or 7th & 3 Hydra of the 7th—they were rather low...

Adding disconsolately

> I have some doubts whether I have hit upon the right stars.

His usual practice would be to compare his findings with Edward's; but the latter has been less assiduous of late, where his astronomical studies are concerned. At their last meeting, he had seemed distracted and out of sorts, leafing through John's scrupulously compiled charts as if he could hardly be bothered to give them the time of day.

'To tell the truth, I am not myself today, dear Cousin,' he says, tossing the papers aside with a barely concealed yawn. 'My father complains that I have no proper object in life—this, from a man who has no object but that of indulging his own desires!—and that I must find myself a profession, since he can no longer keep me.'

You already have a profession.

'I suppose you mean Astronomy.' Edward smiles. 'But, you know, that will never amount to anything where I am concerned.

I am a mere *dabbler* in the realm of stars. My father long ago concluded as much—and so, I am afraid, must I...'

You are saying these things to tease me.

'O no. I am quite in earnest.' Edward's smile takes on a melancholy tinge. 'I am thirty years old. I have been star-gazing since I was breeched. What do I have to show for all those years?'

You do not need me to tell you all the discoveries you have made.

'Trifles. A comet or two. That is nothing, compared to Herschel and his planets...'

Why do you not mention variable stars?

'Because the discovery was not mine, but yours. I merely brought the subject to your attention... Ah, you are scribbling a refutation, I see. But you know it to be so. Pray, do not think I resent it. Nothing could be further from the truth. Indeed, if my life *has* an object, it is the furtherance of your career—my own having proved such a sad disappointment.'

XVI

He looks up, one day, to see his sister Harriet, standing in the doorway. It is immediately apparent that something is wrong.

How do you do, Hat?

His pet-name for her. He mimes the putting-on of the said article.

Harriet's face remains stony. Slowly, she draws her index finger across her chin.

Liar.

For a moment he stands there, dumbfounded.

What have I done?

She glares at him.

Don't pretend you don't know.

His incomprehension must have been obvious, for her shoulders droop suddenly.

Why did you not tell me about you and Mathurina?

He gives a start; then recovers himself.

There is nothing to tell.

Her eyes flash.

Then why does she write to you?

She takes the letter from her reticule and thrusts it towards him.

He sees at once that it is *her* hand—and that the name written on the outside is his own.

Where did you get this?

He cannot suppress a smile.

It was enclosed in a letter, addressed to me.

Her fingers sketch the act of writing.

I am not a complete fool...

She knocks the side of her forehead with her fist, shaking her head angrily.

I never said you were.

Is she your mistress?

He stares at her, horrified that she should be familiar with such a term.

No! I swear…

She seems unimpressed by his vehemence, however.

I would not have told, you know.

I know. I'm sorry.

His fist makes small circles upon his breast.

I will leave you to read your letter.

No. Please stay.

For a moment his sister seems undecided; then, with a show of indifference, she sits down upon the window-seat, and remains there, her hands folded in her lap, until he has finished reading.

Azay-le-Rideau

18e Octobre 1784

Dear Cousin,

I am sure you are surprise I write in English—but you see I have practise for some time. I hope you are well, dear Cousin—and I ask you forgive this letter is sent in such a way. When my little Harriet writes to me the first time, it seems such an agreeable idea to write back to her—and also to you. For you know that my husband regards every letter which is sent from this place. A letter to my little cousin Harriet he will not regard in the same manner as he regards a letter to you.

Dearest John. May I not call you by that, to me, so dear a name? For it has been dear to me for so long… Can it be that you still think of me, a little? You must know, dear one, that I remember everything. My life would be a torture without memories—especially those, dearest John, which are of you…

I remain, my dear friend, your most affect. cousin,

Mathurina de Valois

P.S. If you like to write to me again, you can send it with Harriet's next. Sweet child, she of course suspects nothing…

He touches Harriet's shoulder. She turns to face him.

WRITE YOUR REPLY. I WILL WAIT.

I DO NOT WISH TO REPLY.

'Oh, but you must!' she cries. 'I cannot bear it if you do not. That she should be made unhappy, because of me... No, I could not bear it.'

On 24th October he is observing Delta Cephei.

> This star now appears brighter than yesterday, he writes. It seemed nearly between Zeta & Epsilon Cephei but rather nearer Zeta—somewhat brighter than Gamma Lacertae & somewhat less than Eta & Iota Cephei...

Brightness, he knows, is a relative matter, which can be affected by a range of considerations: air quality, weather conditions; the state of the observer's eyesight—even the observer's state of mind. Just now, things seem very bright to him indeed.

After brightness, darkness is not slow to follow. In December, he receives news of a death which cannot but touch him profoundly. This is that of Dr Johnson. He recalls the occasion, when he himself was but a child, of that august gentleman's visit to Dummie Hoos. Even then, the Great Cham had seemed old—a quaint figure in a bob-wig and a dirty yellow coat with snuff stains down the front, who had catechized the boys remorselessly on their knowledge of the poets. 'For you know that a man must have poetry as well as bread if he is to live,' he had informed them. 'Poetry is the art of uniting pleasure with truth, by calling imagination to the help of reason.'

To his ten year-old mind, the notion that poetry might be as sustaining as bread—or indeed, currant buns—had seemed whimsical, if not actually nonsensical. Now he sees that, of the two, poetry might be the more essential.

In January he sits for his portrait in pastels at the fashionable salon of Mr Scouler. The artist—a saturnine individual in a plum-coloured coat—stares at him intently for a good quarter of an hour before putting chalk to paper, positioning John beside a table, on which is placed a large globe, showing the constellations. His face, by the artist's direction, is half-turned towards it, his gaze looking out of the picture, while his finger marks a place in an open volume of astronomical diagrams. The one he indicates is one he had drawn himself, showing the light curve of the variable star Beta Persei, also called Algol. He has a new coat for the sitting: blue velvet, faced with scarlet, with a row of large diamond buttons down the front. His hair is powdered in the latest fashion. He is not sure about the expression the painter has given him, which seems to him to be too severe, but Edward reassures him.

'You look every inch the Man of Science,' he says. 'And men of science do not smile. Ours is a serious calling. That coat becomes you,' adds Edward, with an impish look. 'Why, if I were a woman, I would fall in love with you myself.'

They are in London to hear Englefield read John's letter to him on Lyra, to the members of the Royal Society—having travelled down the previous week from York, in conditions so appalling that it is a miracle they ever reached the capital at all. At Doncaster, the roads were so icy and full of mud that it seemed the coach must become stuck fast in the mire. Crossing Markham Moor, the skies had opened—a relentless downpour which soon turned to sleet, and then to snow—so that by the time they reached the inn at Carlton the horses were exhausted, and the entire party, inside the coach and out, was frozen to the bone from the rigours of battling the tempest.

'This is what comes of living in such a remote and comfortless spot as ours,' Edward had complained, as they sat shivering over a meagre fire in the White Horse's one good bedroom. 'You do not see our learned colleagues making the journey to York to hear their papers read. It is all London, London, with them...'

Now, however, Edward is all smiles, bowing and nodding to those with whom he is acquainted in the crowd, as he steers John to the place of honour at the front. 'A full house,' he says. 'They are all agog to hear what new discoveries have been made. For though we are provincials, still we have the edge over these London astronomers, do we not?'

John makes no reply, for he does not have his writing materials readily to hand; and besides, he is impatient for the reading to begin. To have his words broadcast in this way by another is, he reflects, the same principle as the Aeolian harp, which remains dumb until the wind sweeps by and releases its music. If he, in this instance, is the silent lyre, then Englefield, with his ruddy face and twinkling eyes, makes a very creditable Aeolus—or perhaps Boreas is nearer the mark, given the state of the weather...

When all have taken their seats, Englefield rises from his, and ascends to the lectern, his stout figure decked for the occasion in a russet-coloured coat of fashionable cut. After a short interval to allow his audience to settle, he begins, moving swiftly over the preliminaries—'Sir—&c, &c...' to the heart of the matter:

'On the 10th of September 1784, whilst my attention was directed towards that part of the heavens where Beta Lyrae was situated, I was surprised to find this star much less bright than usual, whereupon I suspected that it might be a variable star...'

There follows a slow nodding of heads, as the initial speculations put forward in the paper are digested. Then silence—visible to John as an utter stillness—descends once more upon the room.

He lets his attention drift.

That morning a letter from Harriet had come, enclosing another, from Mathurina. 'Dearest,' she had written. 'I have receive your letter with much pleasure. You cannot know how joyful it makes me to know that there exists so dear a friend in the world...'

O God, how he longs for her! To know that she feels as he does is almost worse, he cannot help but feel, than to suppose her indifferent.

> When we last met, you wrote to me a certain word (you will recall the one, I am sure) which at that time I have forbade you to write. Now I have it in front of me, that so precious piece of paper, and kiss the word—and with it, the One who wrote it...

He forces himself to pay attention once more.

'I have often perceived that the relative brightness of stars is affected not only by the different states of the air, but also by their change of position occasioned by the Earth's diurnal motion, and that particularly in stars of great altitude...'

Why had she not spoken out earlier? If he had known that she returned his feelings, he might have found the courage to go to her father, and beg him to look kindly upon their union. Although it would not have been an easy conversation. Whatever grudging respect the old astronomer felt for the achievements of his young colleague would surely have been cancelled out by the single fact of the latter's deafness. Let his daughter marry any kind of man but that; he would not allow her to become a breeder of mutes...

Cousin Nathaniel is sitting across the aisle from where he and Edward sit, his hands clasped upon his belly in an attitude of profound self-satisfaction. From time to time, he nods his head approvingly, as Englefield reads, as if he were entirely familiar with all that the paper contains—and indeed, might have written it himself, if he had had but time.

Englefield is continuing, at his usual leisurely pace, through the long list of observations John has made of Lyra's changes between September and January. Though these had been of absorbing interest to him at the time, he can hardly expect the same degree of interest from the rest of the company; although none betray obvious signs of weariness. No yawns, or scratched heads, or ostentatious gazing out of windows, disturb the prevailing tranquillity. And yet he wishes he had thought to make his notes a little shorter.

At last it is over. He feels Edward touch his arm, and he rises to his feet, to take his bow. Amongst those applauding, he notices Herschel; the latter returns his gaze with a cool nod. He had taken care to make a respectful reference to Herschel's catalogue in his paper. Following their *contre-temps* of a few months before, his relations with the great man have been somewhat strained—which is a pity, for he has always been an admirer.

His sister—Miss Herschel—is, according to Edward, also something of a Prodigy. It was she, Edward had once confessed, who had first made him see the potential of variable stars as a subject of study. An extraordinary woman. Diminutive as a child, and yet with a strength of will to rival that of any man. Why, she thought nothing of sitting up all night with her telescope, and then rising—after no more than two or three hours' sleep—to make breakfast for the household. She was no mean cook, neither. To say nothing of her prodigious musical gifts...

When taxed as to the exact nature of his interest in the lady (for perhaps, after all, John thought, his friend's heart was not entirely unsusceptible to feeling) Edward had blushed; then laughed.

'My dear fellow, you are quite mistaken. My feelings for Miss Caroline are no more than those of a brother for a favourite sister, even though she is *not* my sister... exactly like yours for Mathurina, I collect...'

Now, as he moves away from the platform through a crowd of applauding Fellows, he notices that Edward is no longer at his side, but is talking to someone across the room—a woman. From Edward's description of her, and the fact that William Herschel is also of the party, he guesses this to be the famous Miss Herschel. At the same moment, he sees Edward glance over at him, as if he is the subject of their conversation, and—catching his eye—make signs at him to join them.

As he does so, he sees Edward say something to Herschel's sister, at which she nods, before turning towards the newcomer—himself—with a smile. Speaking with the precise enunciation he has observed in those (his Beloved amongst them) for whom English is not their native tongue, she congratulates him upon the success of his paper.

He takes out his notebook and writes his thanks, hoping that the conversation will not be long, for in truth he finds it taxing to have to read lips for more than a few minutes. With Edward, and others of his intimate circle—One in particular—he finds it less tiring, but only because he is able to rely, not only on seeing the words spoken, but on looks, gestures, smiles, and touches, which provide clues as to their interpretation. With strangers, he finds himself at sea, with no familiar landmarks in sight.

Fortunately, Caroline Herschel seems to divine this, and keeps her remarks admirably brief... Which is a pity, because—knowing her interest in the subject—he would, under other circumstances, have liked to solicit her views on variable stars.

But just then he sees her touch her brother upon the arm. She must have said something to him also, for he turns from talking to Cousin Nathaniel, and holds out his hand. Words of congratulation follow. He is not sure exactly what is said, but he gets the gist of it—enough to know that it is Sun-spots which have been mentioned. Herschel, he knows, has written a paper on the subject. He accordingly scribbles a note, requesting a copy.

As he is handing this to Herschel, he sees Edward say something to Miss Herschel, which seems to please her, for she blushes and smiles. For a moment, she is almost pretty. Her eyes sparkle, and a little dimple comes and goes in her cheek.

It occurs to him, as he watches them together, that—whatever Edward himself might believe about the nature of the connexion—there is nothing sisterly in Caroline Herschel's feelings towards his friend.

His observations on Delta Cephei, which have been virtually suspended for the first three months of the year on account of bad weather, are now resumed. On 11th March, his Ramsden thermometer records a temperature of 26°—a degree of cold uncommon for the season. '*Chérie*,' he writes to Mathurina, *'J'espère que tu n'as pas eu froid ce matin. Ici, le temps est glacial. La neige ne fond pas et recouvre les champs depuis de semaines maintenant. Il me semble que le printemps n'arrivera jamais...'*

An image of her little hands, quite blue with cold, flashes across his mind. If only she were here, he could warm her hands in his. Breathe his breath into her, like the Prince in the fairytale, restoring La Belle au Bois Dormant to life with a kiss...

Since observing for more than the briefest period is out of the question, he contents himself with going over his old notes, huddling as close to the fire as he can get without bursting into flames himself. Still he cannot get warm. The head-cold which has dogged him all winter responds neither to his mother's prescription of brown soup and eels in aspic, nor to Edward's more robust regime of a brisk walk 'to heat the blood', followed by hot whisky-and-water. In truth, the only thing which would have restored his spirits was the arrival of another letter from his darling. '*Écris-moi souvent*,' he had written; but had as yet received no reply.

'You are mopish, I see,' Edward remarks, on finding his friend still in his nightshirt at twelve o'clock. 'Come. I have the very thing to rouse you from your torpor. A new treble object telescope by Watkins is just arrived in my father's observatory. Get dressed, and we will try it out together.'

It is too cloudy.

He is cross, and sick at heart. Confound Edward for his infernal good humour!

Edward reads the note, and smiles.

'It is not as cloudy as all that. You are low-spirited, that is all.'

At once he feels ashamed of his ill-temper. Flinging off the frowsty bedclothes, he strips off his nightshirt and makes signs to Edward to wait. The shaving-water his servant had brought earlier that morning has gone cold; but it will have to do. He makes a cursory attempt at washing, and dries himself on his dirty shirt. Fresh linen lies across the back of the chair on which Edward has seated himself while these ablutions are being carried out. He turns, his skin already prickling with goose-flesh, and reaches out his hand for the clean shirt. As he does so, he meets his friend's eyes, and is startled by the expression he reads there. If he had not known better, he would have said it was a look of yearning. As if Edward had lost the dearest thing he owned…

A moment later, everything is as it was before. Edward hands him the shirt. He puts it on, and pulls on his breeches after.

A letter comes at last.

Azay-le-Rideau
8e Avril, 1785

My Dear,

I hope you are very well and that the bad weather is now disappeared. I have not write for so long because Monsieur de Valois—thus it is that she refers to her husband—permits me no time to myself alone. Always he watches me—if I pick up a book, he demands to know what is it that I read? If I write a letter, he must see to whom it is I write.

No one comes to the house anymore, unless he wishes it. There was a young priest—my only friend—to whom I confessed everything. (O do not be afraid, dearest; our secret is safe with the good Father. He says he will pray for us and that Le Bon Dieu will forgive us.) Now poor Father Jerome is sent away. M. de Valois insists I speak only to his own Confessor.

O my Friend, if you knew what things I must endure for your sake! Even these words I must write, by candlelight, while Monsieur snores in the next room…

Her letter leaves him profoundly uneasy. Not that he cares for his own sake, but the consequences, if they are discovered, might be terrible for her… After agonising for a day and a night, he comes to a decision. There can be no more letters. When Harriet, as is now her custom, appears later that day, and holds out her hand for a letter, he shakes his head.

IS IT NOT FINISHED?

IT IS NOT WRITTEN AT ALL.

He motions her to sit down.

WHERE IS YOUR LETTER?

Frowning, she takes it from her pocket.

I WANT YOU TO WRITE THIS AT THE END OF IT.

He hands her the note he has drafted on waking.

My brother, Mr John Goodricke, respectfully asks to be remembered to you. He hopes that you are taking <u>particular care</u> in the cold weather we have been having. <u>He fears</u>

for your safety. The night air can be dangerous, he asks me to remind you.

Harriet stares at him.

YOU WANT ME TO WRITE THIS?

He nods.

I CANNOT WRITE MYSELF. IT IS TOO GREAT A RISK.

YOU WILL BREAK HER HEART.

But she picks up the pen and begins to copy out what he has written. When she has finished writing, she dusts the letter with sand, and seals the packet with a blob of scarlet wax.

'It is done,' she says. 'And I am very sorry for it.'

XVII

As April moves into May, the cloud which seems to have hung over Yorkshire for almost half a year suddenly lifts, and he gets his clear skies at last. On 24th April, he remarks: *air very clear, and observation good.* Sprawled on his back in the garden at Lendal, a little after ten o'clock that night, he lets his thoughts roam where they will... Above him rises the great dark canopy of the night sky, with its intricate patterning of light. Such aureoles, such sunbursts of light! As if some prodigal deity has flung down handfuls of precious stones—diamonds, rubies, emeralds, sapphires, pearls...

He is reminded of his grandmother's rings, with which, as a child he liked to play. 'A ring for every child,' Lady Mary said. 'Outlasting the child, in some cases.' Turning the rings this way and that, so that their stones should catch the light. 'These, at least, do not die. A consolation, one might say...'

> April 24th, at 10h. a little brighter than 7 Lacertae; considerably less than Delta Cephei.
>
> At 12h. scarce at all altered, but if any thing it is a little increased...

As he focuses the glass on one star or another, it feels as if he were lying at the bottom of a vortex. At its outer rim are the constellations, whirling in their stately dance; at its still point is a solitary pair of eyes—his own—and a solitary heart.

> April 25 at 10h. and 11 h. little less than that of Delta Cephei, and considerably brighter than 7 Lacertae.
>
> April 26, at 10h. and 11h. less than 7 Lacertae, something brighter than Epsilon and brighter than Xi Cephei...

If he cannot forget her, he can at least ensure he has as little time as possible for thinking about her, by devoting every waking hour to work.

A consolation, one might say.

By the end of June, he is satisfied enough with the observations he and Edward have made to write to Maskelyne. Mindful of the offence he had given to Herschel through his tactlessness, he begins with a polite preamble:

> York, June 28, 1785
>
> Sir,
>
> The improvements which of late years have been introduced into astronomy, should be attributed not only to the diligence and accuracy wherewith astronomers prosecute their observations and discoveries, but in part also to your exertions, and especially to that kind encouragement which you have, on many occasions, afforded those who make this science their chief study; and I am happy to have this opportunity of acknowledging myself one of those who are much indebted to you in this respect.

Civilities having been got out of the way, it is down to business:

> Under these impressions I thought I could not do better than to address to you the following account of a periodical variation in the star Delta Cephei, which I lately discovered...

He then goes on to list the results of his hundred nights' observation, opining modestly that

> They may probably lead to some better knowledge of the fixed stars, especially of their condition and their remarkable changes.

Maskelyne acknowledges the paper with no less warmth than before, but indicates in his reply that an opportunity to read it to the Society might not be forthcoming for several weeks, there being such as backlog of learned papers to get through. And indeed, with new theories of the origins of the Earth and the philosophy of history being formulated by the week, to say nothing of new inventions—and this incessant craze for ballooning!—it is a wonder they have time for the stars at all...

He, at least, has time. On July 31st, he and Edward conduct a series of observations of Jupiter, and of its first satellite in particular:

> When the Satell. was very faint & only seen by intervals, a thin cloud covered Jupiter. The Observation seemed to be tolerably good but the above circumstance & the Watch I used render it rather a little doubtfull. My Watch being with Mr Arnold

—frequent exposure to the damp night air having done its workings no good, Arnold said.

> I used Mr E. Pigotts Watch but the minute & second hand did not agree, however I took as much care as possible...

Later the same night, at Edward's suggestion, they climb the three hundred steps of the Minster's Tower, to get a closer look at the object in question. The view from the top (which he had previously seen only in daylight) is remarkable: the sky a mass of stars over the dark city, in which a few points of light—candlelight, firelight—glimmer like blurred reflections of those heavenly bodies.

As if overcome by the emotion of the moment, Edward spreads his arms wide and shouts something; it is too dark to make out what. They remain there for an hour or so, sweeping the sky with their night-glasses, so that the stars seem to fly in and out of focus—now dim, now bright. There is Zeta Auriga, with its orange and blue twin stars denoting the arm of the Charioteer; there Draco—the Dragon—and Perseus, the dragonslayer. Algol is very brilliant tonight... As he watches, he sees the demon star wink at him.

On the way down, a gust of wind blows the candle out, and they have to grope their way in the dark, with only what little light is to be had through the Tower's slit windows to guide their footsteps upon the winding stair.

Next morning there is a letter, addressed to him at his lodgings.

> Sir, it says. I had not thought you cruel—and yet you must be, to treat me so very unkind. Why do you not write? You say it is dangerous. Yet all the danger is mine. If I do not fear it, why should you? Can it be that you are a coward? I had thought you at least a gentleman…

It is not signed, but he knows the hand so well that any signature would have been superfluous.

To his sister's next letter, a postscript is appended, at his direction:

> My brother, Mr J. Goodricke, craves your pardon for any offence he might have given you. He hopes that you will understand how much it pains him to have caused you distress. He assures me that he would rather die than lose the esteem you once felt for him. He knows himself undeserving of that esteem, and yet without it, his life is worth nothing…

Harriet purses her lips as she comes to this last sentence.

DO YOU WANT ME TO WRITE THIS?

YES.

She makes no reply for a moment or two.

WHAT IF HER HUSBAND READS IT?

Her fingers touch the place where a wedding-ring should be; then mime the reading of a letter.

HE WILL NOT READ IT. IT IS A LETTER FROM HER COUSIN. HER FEMALE COUSIN…

She gives him a long look.

EVEN SO, IT WOULD NOT DO FOR HIM TO READ IT.

On 17th September—his birthday—another letter comes.

Azay-le-Rideau
Septembre 10e, 1785

Dearest,

You will see that I have decided to forgive you! I do not think you mean to be unkind. Also, you need trouble little Harriet no longer, for there is an address—quite safe—that you may write to (she supplies it). M. de Valois will discover nothing.

Write to me soon, sweet boy, for I live only for your letters…

Your affectionate Cousin and true Friend,
Mathurine de Valois

Soon they have gone beyond civilities. '*Ma chérie*,' he writes. '*Je voudrais baiser ta bouche, et tes belles yeux*…' or is it *beaux*? It matters not. '*My Beloved One*,' she soon replies. '*I would kiss your charming hand. Send me your picture, Sweetheart, or I die*…'

He has never been happier in his life. His mornings are spent in writing to his Beloved; his nights in observing the moons of Jupiter, with his Beloved's brother.

Quand je regard les étoiles, il me semble que je regard ton visage.

In his mind's eye he sees her face, with its beguiling mixture of darkness—those eyes!—and brightness.

Belle Etoile! Que je t'aime! Il m'est insupportable d'être séparé de toi…

She will, he trusts, forgive him his execrable French, just as he will forgive (a thousand times!) her faltering English. He hopes she will also forgive his attempts at poetry.

Andromeda! Turn not thine eyes to me
Lest—fair captive—they slay me with their darts…

A schooling in mathematics has left him ill-equipped for the language of love. He wishes now that he had paid more attention to Dr Johnson's advice on poetry.

In October, he resumes his observations of Beta Lyrae, spending long hours flat on his back in the dark garden, as the constellations wheel overhead. Here is Beta Orionis, its cold blue radiance counterpointed by the ruby-red of Alpha Orionis—the one marking the hand, the other the foot of the great Hunter, eternally in quest of his prey. Here is Taurus, with Aldebaran its glinting eye; and over there, rising, Sirius—dimmed by the murky horizon below its supreme brilliance; above it, the Heavenly Twins...

Twin stars. Twin souls. Fixed forever in mutual sympathy.

It will soon be a year since she had first written to him. He wonders how he had lived until then. His life was a dull thing, with no spark of joy to light it. Now it is illuminated by her love. She is everything to him; Sun, Moon, Stars—he would give them all, for a single glance, a touch of her lips, a smile. What are stars and planets, and all the rest of that glittering trash, when he has a living woman to adore?

Edward is in London at the end of November to hear John's paper read; he himself cannot be spared—his mother requiring him to escort her and his sisters to Bath. They are to spend Christmas there with Aunt Henrietta, with whom his sister Harriet has always been a favourite and who, his mother devotedly hopes, might one day 'do something' for her. 'For it is hard on poor little Harriet,' Levina says, 'having no one to take her into Society, now that your father is gone.' His mother's eyes, well-washed these past few months, now grow watery again. 'How she will ever find a husband I do not know.'

John suspects that their visit to Bath has more to do with his mother's desire for distraction, after the long dull months of her first year of widowhood, than it has to do with Harriet's need, or otherwise, for a husband. Nor is it the Season; Bath is almost as cheerless, in the late Autumn weather, as York—albeit with a greater number of evening parties. Still, their arrival there seems to have brightened his mother's spirits a little. Aunt Henrietta's house is in the Crescent—a gratifying enough circumstance as far as Levina is concerned. It is but a short walk from there to the Upper Rooms, where the more respectable of Bath's denizens are in regular attendance for cards, and conversation of the more refined sort.

His younger sisters are no less easily pleased. Mary professes herself delighted with the shops in Milsom Street, and Lizzie with the public gardens, where, when the weather is fine, she is allowed to roam. As to Harriet: she is, she says, perfectly indifferent to her situation—whether it is here or there is all the same to her, as long as Mama is happy... The perfect confidence which had existed between her and her elder brother has given way to a certain wariness. Increasingly, it seems to John, his sister avoids being alone with him; and the intimacy they had once enjoyed—secure in their private language—is no more.

Only once does Harriet refer to the events of the past year, in which she had been so reluctant a participant.

DOES SHE STILL WRITE TO YOU?

He nods.

SHE NO LONGER WRITES TO ME.

Before he can reply—although what would he have said, his Beloved's neglect of his sister being so much on his own account?—Elizabeth runs into the room, talking of iced puddings, and there is no further opportunity to renew the subject.

While he is still in Bath, a letter comes from Edward which puzzles him extremely. After a lengthy account of the kind reception with which John's paper had met—'Maskelyne asked me most particularly to convey to you his grateful admiration &c, &c'—there comes a postscript:

> Do not be surprised to find me back in York when you return, for a Circumstance has arisen which makes my presence here imperative. Be assured that my family are all in excellent health; as to the state of our mental faculties, that is another matter...

Arriving back in York, he loses no time in going round to Bootham Bar. On the way there he meets Edward, who has stepped out with the same purpose as himself, it seems. The two friends embrace.

'Let us repair at once to Nancy's.' This is their preferred coffee-house. 'For it is Bedlam at home. My mother does nothing but weep and sigh, and weep again. My father rails incessantly against the ill fortune which has brought him such a daughter. My sister...'

John stops dead. His consternation must have been obvious, for Edward says

'Of course. You do not know. My sister is returned from France. She has left her husband and will not go back to him, she says. The whole family is in an uproar... Why, what is the matter, dear Cousin? I see that I have shocked you. O do not be afraid. She will be made to see reason, of that you can be certain...'

He stands there, in utter confusion—unable to move or think—the indifferent crowd passing on either side, until Edward takes his arm to move him out of the way of an approaching cart.

Why had she not written to tell him of her intention? Perhaps there had not been time...

'John...' Edward's face has a frightened look. 'What is the matter? Are you sick?'

Sick. That is the word for him. Love-sick, and sick at heart.

I have a headache, he manages to write at last. *It is nothing. I shall be well again directly.*

All he wants is to be by himself. But Edward will not hear of letting him walk home unescorted.

'To think that I troubled you with the absurdities of my family—the members of which, I must say, are all as mad as each other—when you are far from well,' he reproaches himself, when they are once more in John's rooms. He studies his friend's face for a moment. 'You are terribly pale. May I not send for Dr Harker?'

I told you. It is nothing. He forces a smile. *Go to your sister. I am sure she needs your help more than I.*

'Poor Mathurina! She has been unlucky twice over, I fear. Unlucky in her husband and...' Edward pulls a wry face. '...unlucky in her parents, although it pains me to say so.'

When he is alone once more, he leaps to his feet and begins to pace up and down the room, in a frenzy of agitation. He must see her—but how? Impossible now to run after Edward; and, in any case, she will not be alone—had not her brother said as much? *It is Bedlam at home*... No, he must find another way... He must write; that is the first thing. Seizing pen and paper, he sets himself immediately to the task... But the words will not come. What had been easy and fluent is now clogged with difficulty. *Chérie*... no, that will not do. *Chère Madame, J'espère que*... equally impossible. For it may be that her letters will not be read by her eyes alone, in her father's house.

At last, after consigning several spoiled drafts to the fire, he settles on a form of words as terse as it is serviceable:

Treasurer's House
January 12th 1786

Madam,

I must request the honour of an interview with you at your earliest convenience.

I am, Madam,
Your Devoted Servt & Affect. Cousin,
John Goodricke

The ink is scarcely dry when he rings for Thomas, instructing him to take the message at once, and impressing upon him that it must be delivered into no one else's hands but the lady's. Then he sits down to wait, in an agony of impatience.

He can settle to nothing; reading is impossible. His instruments lie scattered on the table like so many neglected toys. Which is what they are, he supposes: playthings, to while away an idle hour. Mere foolishness—that is what his life has been. He has frittered it away on worthless puzzles.

At last Thomas returns; he almost snatches the letter from his hand, such is his eagerness to read the reply. But a glance tells him it was not worth the waiting:

Madame de Valois begs to be excused, but she is not receiving visitors at present.

That is all. He controls himself with an effort, not wishing Thomas to see him weep.

How the day passed he could not afterwards have said. He supposes he must have eaten something at some time—for there is the evidence of plate and cup: the former with its freight of a partly-eaten cutlet of veal; the latter drained of whatever it had contained, although he has no memory of eating or drinking. For a period of time—hours, perhaps—he sits at his table, looking through his notes (looking *at* them might have been a better way of putting it, since of their contents he retains not one whit). The observations he had made of Delta Cephei and Eta Antinoi, which had once seemed the most fascinating thing in his life, now strike him as meaningless scribbles.

Did it matter, really, whether a star grew brighter or did not?

He must have fallen asleep in his chair, for when he opens his eyes, it is with the sense that time has passed, and that something about the room is not as it was. It has grown dark, and the fire has died down, so that it is only by its inconstant glimmer that he makes out the figure that stands there. It is a boy; a youth, rather, in clothes that hang too large upon his slight frame. Perhaps a messenger...

With that thought, he is out of his chair; but then something about the other's appearance checks him. Is there not a familiar look to that slender shape—and to the pale face which regards him from under the tricorn hat, with an expression at once amused and tender? His face must have betrayed his amazement, for he sees the other smile. Then the stranger—who is not, after all, a stranger—sweeps off the hat in one swift movement, so that all her beautiful hair comes tumbling down.

How it was she came to be there, at that hour, and how exactly she managed to elude the vigilance of her gaolers—'for that is, *enfin*, what they have become, my parents'—is not something she conveys to him then. Nor does she tell him of the flight from France which had preceded it. The details of this—the enlisting of the aid of a sympathetic servant, and the bribing of another, in order to effect her escape from her husband's house—he is only to learn of later. For the moment, all that matters is the moment—the fact that they are together.

Even if she had been inclined to speak of all that she had suffered, he would not have understood her—for the meagre light afforded by the glowing embers of the fire is barely enough to see by, and certainly insufficient for the reading of lips, or notes. But there is enough light to see all that they want to see, during the hours which pass—which are not, in any case, devoted to merely looking. In the absence of sight, as well as sound, the remaining senses come at last into their own.

Touch: his arms around her; his mouth against hers; the feel of her body, her skin, her hair...

Smell: the intoxicating odour of that hair and skin, and so much else besides. New-mown hay, wild roses, and a sharper, animal smell, undisguised by the artificial tang of musk and tuberose.

Taste: amalgamating elements of both touch and smell, in the salt-taste of a kiss (indistinguishable as it is from the sensation); the smell of warm flesh and spilled wine mingling with the honey taste of her, salt and sweet together...

He kisses her eyes; her lips; her breasts. The warmth of her skin is another revelation. It is not an ivory doll which lies in his arms, but a creature of flesh and blood—animate, sensual, real. He holds her close against him. When he reaches his moment of dissolution—that sweet death—he cries out, feeling the sound in his throat although he cannot hear it. In the midst of these transports, he feels her clutch him. How strong she is! That one so slight and delicate-looking should possess such strength is a source of wonder to him. Wondrous. She is altogether that.

He feels as he did on beholding the stars for the first time: new-made, new-born—as if sight were meant for nothing else but this. As if he had been blind, until that moment...

Now it is as if the rest of his senses have caught up with sight. This is what touch (smell, taste) is *for*.

He presses his ear to her heart, and it is as if he can hear it beating.

Is it hours or only minutes later, that he feels her stir? They are lying half-asleep, clasped in one another's arms, on his unmade bed, the only light (now the fire is dead) that of the Moon. There had been no time to draw the curtains, and now it floods in, unearthly luminescence, painting her body with silver.

Her body. O her body… its sharp little breasts, its narrow waist, which he can span with his two hands, almost. Her soft belly, as smooth as alabaster. Her slender arms. Her legs, with their tapering thighs, that open to him so sweetly…

He takes her in his arms once more. But she is already drawing away. She kisses his mouth, with the air of one taking leave.

He will not have it so. She must not go. He holds her close, and since he is the stronger he prevails.

Her answer is not to resist. She lies in his arms like an inert thing.

His ardour is cooled at once by this mute refusal. He lets her go, and she rises from the bed to find her clothes, left where they had been cast off in the first frenzy of passion.

He watches her dress. When she is once more in her borrowed shape, she takes up pen and paper from the desk, and by the Moon's blanched light, begins to write.

I will come tomorrow at the same time, he reads.

He kisses the writing, then turns—but the writer is gone.

Some moments later, he watches her from the window, a tiny figure, in the black shadow of the Minster.

Lyra is overhead, its stars quite distinct; he can make them out plainly: Beta, Delta, Epsilon, Zeta…

He thinks, she has come back to me, my Eurydice.

XVIII

He sleeps late, and is still undressed, his hair dishevelled and his robe untied, when the servant brings the note. It is from Edward. At the sight of that familiar hand, he feels a blush spread across his body. Can it be that Edward knows? He trembles at the thought of it. Not that he is afraid of his cousin—the mildest of men; nor does he feel any shame on his own account. But that *she* might be exposed to recrimination, or worse, because of what they had done... A memory of their entwined limbs, and of the way she had felt under his hands, overcomes him. He must have emitted an involuntary groan, for the servant looks at him strangely. Recovering himself, he makes a sign for the man to wait. He unfolds the note. When he has read it, he breathes more easily. There is nothing to indicate knowledge, or suspicion, in those few phrases.

> Should you care to step round for an hour, I have something of interest to show you. Come to the observatory at 12h...

The only thing at all unusual is in the post-script:

> Do not call at the house, for they are all at sixes and sevens.

He has no intention of doing so. After what had happened—if indeed it had happened, and was not some febrile dream—he would have difficulty enough keeping his countenance in front of Edward. How he would manage an encounter with Edward's father he could not imagine.

Impossible that it should not show on his face, the rapture he is feeling. The thought that she is *his*—that he now possesses her, in body as well as soul (for had they not already pledged themselves to one another?)—makes him tremble with happiness. His eyes, in the looking-glass, hold an afterglow of that delight.

I will come again tomorrow at the same time...

How is he to get through the tedious hours of daylight, until he can hold her in his arms again?

Edward is not in the Observatory when he gets there, a few minutes before his time, and so he waits, amusing himself by sifting through the charts of observations which are spread out upon the table, many of which correspond to those he himself has made. And indeed under an entry headed June 20th 1782, he sees his own name:

> Mean Transit—7h 43′ 22.08″—Mercury—by Mr J. Goodricke: lost in Brightness tho still B...

Out of the corner of his eye, he sees a flicker of movement, and glances up.

But instead of his expected friend, it is a female Shape he sees—dressed all in grey, and with its face veiled... Shrouded as she is, he would have known her anywhere. He goes to embrace her, but before he can do so, she turns away. For a moment she stands there, head bowed, like some Attic figure of mourning. Then she lifts the veil. On her pale cheek is the mark of a fading bruise.

He feels an access of rage—an impulse to rush at once for the door, and find whoever has perpetrated such an outrage. But she restrains him.

'No. It will do no good.'

He seizes a pencil and scrawls in the margin of an astrological chart:

Who has done this?

Mathurina shrugs.

'My husband, or my father—it matters not. They are as bad as each other.'

I will kill any man that lays a hand on you again.

This brings a faint smile to her lips.

'You are very bold, Cousin. But it will do no good, I tell you. My father wishes that I return to my husband, and return I must…'

I will not let you.

Another smile; but when he takes her hand and begins to kiss it, she pulls away.

'No. You must not. My brother will be here directly."

Does he know…?

She shakes her head before he has finished writing.

'He knows we are friends, that is all. I have begged him to bring you to me. For I am not allowed visitors,' she adds with a bitter smile.

I cannot bear to see you so unhappy.

Her expression softens. 'I know. That is the only thing which keeps me from despair… Ah, here is Edward,' she says, as the latter enters.

Come to me tonight.

'I will try,' she murmurs, veiling her face once more.

My poor dear sister,' Edward drops a kiss on the top of Mathurina's head. 'I know your visit will have been of some comfort to her,' he says to John. 'Is it not so, Mattie?'

She nods; then says something to her brother.

'He is gone out,' is the reply. 'We are safe for another hour, at least, for he will have his dinner at the Fox & Hounds.'

Mathurina must have said something else, for Edward embraces her, then accompanies her to the door.

'My sister will take a turn in the garden for half an hour, while my father is away,' he says to John. 'The poor child has been confined to her room for almost the whole of the past fortnight. My father is determined to break her will by any means he can…'

Is there nothing which can be done to help her?

A pained look crosses Edward's face.

'I cannot say. They are both as stubborn as each other, my father and sister. The question is—which one of them will give way first?'

It is midnight before she arrives; although he has been expecting her for hours, jumping up in a nervous flutter when he fancied he saw her shadow at the door, and emptying one glass after another, even though he has no need of such intoxicants, if *she* is near... When she enters the room at last, he takes her in his arms, and—after covering her face with kisses—draws her to the bed. There, by the light of the fresh candles he has ordered to be placed there, he undresses her—drawing off her breeches, as she lies there laughing; and pulling her shirt over her head, to reveal the beauties beneath. In that golden light, she seems a precious Image carved from marble—Goddess, or Nymph—except that her flesh is warm. He bends to kiss the smooth globes of her breasts, feeling as he does so, the beating of her heart, and the motion of each breath, as it comes and goes. He kisses the mouth that draws the breath, and feels the breath quicken to a sigh...

On the table by the bed are the verses he has copied out. As they lie there, sated after their pleasures, he reaches for them, to show them to her.

If ever any beauty I did see
Which I desir'd, and got, 'twas but a dreame of thee...

The good Doctor had been right: there *was* a use for poetry...

She smiles as she reads the words.

'This is pretty. Did you write it?'

He is tempted to say yes. But he shakes his head.

'I do not know poetry,' she says with a rueful air. 'The nuns did not encourage it.'

She is leaning propped up on one elbow, her back half turned towards him. Enchanted by this new view of her, with its sinuous curves, he reaches for her again, but she pushes him away.

'Later. First you must teach me. For we cannot converse with pen and paper forever...'

He looks at her, not understanding what she means.

Mathurina smiles.

'You must show me how to talk with hands, the way you do. In silence,' she says.

So begins a time of bliss, whose joys are made all the sharper by the need for secrecy. During the day, he can see her only occasionally: by arrangement with Edward, to whom she conveys her desire for 'a little walk with John', to relieve the long dull hours of her incarceration. 'For I am to see no one but the Priest, until I regain my senses,' she says to her lover, in what he supposes must be an echo of her father's words.

HAVE YOU LOST YOUR SENSES, THEN?

He brings his fingertips together, as if holding something precious, then draws them apart, as if to reveal its absence.

MY FATHER THINKS SO.

She holds her hands so that the palms face outward; then twists her wrists, so that her palms face down. A gesture of contempt.

I HATE HIM.

'What are you doing?' asks Edward, joining them in the garden. 'It looks as if you are warding off a swarm of bees…'

'John has been showing me how to talk in his language,' replies Mathurina. 'Since he is so good as to write to me in mine, I thought it the least I could do. See? It is the cleverest thing. This is Love'—she crosses her hands upon her breast—'this Hate'—she makes the gesture she had made a moment before. 'This means Happy…' She taps one palm against the other, in silent applause. 'This means Sad…' Her hand moves downwards across her face, as if wiping away all joyful emotion.

'You are fortunate,' her brother tells her. 'John has never taught *me* his language, in all these years.'

One night she arrives breathless, as if she has been running. Her eyes are shining.

COME, she says. I WANT TO GO DANCING.

From the bundle she is carrying beneath her arm, she pulls out a dress, and a wig. Then she begins stripping off her boys' apparel.

HELP ME UNDO THIS, WILL YOU?

He is happy to oblige. But when he tries to take her in his arms, she pushes him away.

THERE IS NO TIME FOR THAT, NOW…

When she has taken off all but her chemise, she draws the dress over her head, and makes signs to him to fasten it. With the curled white wig concealing her own dark hair, and twin spots of rouge on her cheeks, she is suddenly a stranger to him.

QUICK!

She makes urgent gestures to him to rise and dress (for he has undressed in expectation of her coming). Only his finest clothes will do: his new blue coat, white breeches, and lace-trimmed shirt, and the wig he has not worn since his last appearance at the Royal Society, preferring as he does, his own hair.

WE MUST DISGUISE OURSELVES. THEN WE WILL BE SAFE...

THIS IS LUNACY. His wig will not sit straight. Confound the thing!

LOVE IS LUNACY, she says, holding out, as a final flourish, the mask he is to put on.

She turns him this way and that, surveying him with evident approval. She tweaks a stray thread from his sleeve, and unbuttons another button on his waistcoat.

YOU LOOK VERY HANDSOME. She spreads out the skirts of her gown, which is of silver-tissue—like spun moonlight—and faces him. AND I?

YOU LOOK LIKE A PRINCESS.

Although privately he prefers her as she is when they are naked together, her hair all tangled and her face flushed after love-making.

As they descend the stairs, he sees that she is still wearing her clumsy boys' shoes. When he points this out to her, she laughs.

ALL THE BETTER FOR WALKING.

It would not do to spoil her satin slippers in the mire.

She will not say where they are going, but flits ahead, like a wraith, her black cloak swirling around her. A few flakes of snow have begun to fall, and now settle for an instant on the hood she has drawn over her head, appearing, against its velvet, like tiny stars.

In Blake Street, there is a crush of carriages. As each draws up in front of the Assembly Rooms, the doors swing open to release a flood of light—together with a bevy of servants, bearing umbrellas, to shield each new arrival from the worst of the storm. Blazing torches, carried by the footmen, cast a sinister glare upon the scene, so that its throngs of cloaked and masked figures seem, to John's eye, to be part of some antique rite, with the familiar city transformed, by the whirling snow, into a ghostly simulacrum of itself.

As Mathurina goes to ascend the steps, he puts out a hand to restrain her. She turns at once to face him, her eyes alight with mischief behind the black velvet mask.

WHAT ARE YOU DOING?

I TOLD YOU. I WANT TO DANCE.

Before he can protest further (for the last time he danced was so long ago that he has forgotten how), she eludes his grasp, darting up the steps as lightly as if she were made of air, not flesh, so that he has no choice but to follow. He surrenders his cloak, as she has done, to the servant at the door.

Inside, all is confusion, with figures in dominos and masks mingling with more fantastic forms: a dancing bear, a Turkish Sultan, a Roman general, a Harlequin. As he catches up with Mathurina on the stairs leading to the upper floor, a pair of revellers identically clad in short white tunics, their limbs and faces painted gold, run past them, holding hands. Castor and Pollux, he surmises. On the staircase are other figures from antiquity or myth. Cato converses with the Emperor of China; while a buxom Phyllis links arms with Romeo, as her Corydon pays court to his Juliet.

At the top of the stairs, Mathurina holds out her hand to him.

'Come on. The music is starting,' she says, putting on her dancing shoes.

In the ballroom, the floor has been freshly chalked, and the great chandeliers blaze with a multitude of candles. A scent of warm flesh, perfume, and hot wax assails him. On a little dais at the far end, a group of musicians are assembled: two violins, two oboes, and a bassoon. In the centre of the room, fifty or so couples are already drawn up, awaiting the signal to begin.

She must have seen the alarm in his eyes, for she draws closer, so that their faces are almost touching.

'Just do exactly as I do,' she says.

A footman is passing with a tray of glasses filled with champagne. John seizes one and tosses it back, the wine going at once to his head. Now he is ready for anything...

They take their places—just in time, it seems. For, as if at a given signal, the row of gentlemen to which he has attached himself bows, as one man, while the ladies facing them curtsey, simultaneously. Each line begins a series of slow advances and retreats—small rocking steps, forward and back, forward and back—drawing near to the opposite line of dancers, and then withdrawing. John watches Mathurina's lips. *One*-and-two-and-*one*-and-two-and... Nor is it merely a matter of counting steps; there is a *posture* to be held—with the body turning this way and that; the hands extended in graceful attitudes, as if displaying a new suit of clothes...

On the second repetition of this figure, the dancers join hands, and trace a stately half-circle upon the floor. The figure is completed by the same movement in reverse—a serpentine shape, in which each partner orbits around the other.

In his anxiety that he might stumble, or make a fool of himself by moving when no one else is, he at first walks his way through the measure, rather than dancing it. But after a few moments, it all begins to come back to him, and his awkwardness vanishes. For is there not something of mathematics in it: a sequence of movements, joined to other movements, in perfect synchronicity?

It is—he supposes from the slow pace of it—a *menuet*. Out of the corner of his eye, he sees the chief violinist beating time with his bow, as the rest of the musicians puff and saw their way through the piece.

His faltering steps grow more confident.

Another circling shape is described—this time involving two couples, not one. These touch hands, before passing first in front, and then behind their diametric opposite; and then repeat the figure once more in mirror-image.

As he dances—Mathurina encouraging him with little nods and smiles, and secret looks, to tell him when a change of direction is imminent—it seems to him that he has always known how to do this. It is as natural as breathing. Circle and return. Circle and return.

It is the figure traced across the heavens by his Demon Star and its companion.

As the dance comes to an end—concluding, as it had began, with a stately bow and an even more extravagant curtsey—he catches Mathurina's eye, and she smiles at him. How beautiful she is, with the heightened colour the exercise has given her—her breasts rising and falling under their filmy covering, her eyes sparkling with the audacity of the adventure.

Another tray of glasses goes by; he takes two, and hands one to her. This time, she seems as glad of the refreshment as he is.

The room is full now, with a mixture of the fashionably dressed, and the fantastically costumed. He thinks he recognises one or two, beneath the black masks, Turkish headdresses, and pasteboard armour, and feels a twinge of unease. It would not do for anyone they know to see them together... They will have one more dance, then go. They have tried their luck enough for one night, he thinks.

But before they can take up their positions again, he sees her face change—its look of smiling triumph replaced by one of alarm. Something is the matter—but what?

At once he is at her side, his look asking the question.

By way of answer, she taps the middle and index finger of one hand upon those of the other.

MY FATHER.

He steals a glance in the direction she is looking, and sees at once the danger they are in.

Cousin Nathaniel stands in the doorway, in conversation with another gentleman, who is dressed as a cardinal, in scarlet gown and hat. He himself is in the guise of some mediaeval seer—Paracelsus, John guesses—in a fur-trimmed gown of antique design, covered with Kabbalistic symbols. His mask takes the form of a black beak, like that of a plague doctor.

One thing is obvious: they cannot hope to pass him, without attracting his notice. And yet to stay where they are any longer risks certain exposure...

With as much *sang froid* as he can muster, John guides his partner to one side of the room, which is flanked with pillars, that make an annex, on either side. As they reach the safety of one of these, the music must have struck up again, for the dancers begin a new measure—their movements, he fervently prays, further screening himself and his companion from view.

But this can only be, at best, a temporary refuge.

He squeezes Mathurina's hand, and is rewarded with a tremulous smile. But under the velvet mask, her face is terribly pale... An idea strikes him.

ACT AS IF YOU ARE FEELING FAINT.

He has to repeat the signs more slowly, before she understands. Almost before he has time to react, she staggers and falls against him. He catches her; then, with something of an effort (for she is heavier than she looks), lifts her up, and carries her towards the door, the lines of dancers parting to let them through.

Descending the stairs affords him some anxiety, in case he should drop her; but he manages it without mishap. In the hall, a footman fetches their cloaks, while another runs for *sal volatile*. A third summons a carriage from somewhere. Throughout, his fair companion plays her part to the hilt: letting her head fall limp until the smelling-salts are held to her nose; and allowing herself be carried to the waiting vehicle by nobody else but her lover (although, in truth, his arms are in need of a rest by now), with every appearance of one recovering from a swoon.

Only when they are safely back in his chambers, does she drop her play-acting at last, flinging herself into his arms with an access of laughter that contains a good deal of its opposite—so that it is impossible to tell, as he holds her, whether she is shaking with mirth or sorrow.

Throughout February, it continues cold, with overcast skies and freezing fog preventing all but the most rudimentary observation. Towards the end of the month, the air is clear enough for him to resume his interrupted studies, although these prove inconclusive. On 24th he writes:

> Variable in Hydra not visible with an Opera Glass.

He resolves to track its progress, nonetheless. The star in question, which is to be found in the serpent's tail, is as bright as Mira, with, he suspects, the same periodicity as that star. But he will have to wait for better weather to put his theory to the test… In the meantime, his days are occupied in going through his old journals and notes, checking and cross-checking his findings, and comparing them, where possible, with Edward's.

His nights are spent otherwise. It is hard to believe that one could feel such pleasure, and not die from it, he thinks. When he says as much to Mathurina, as they lie entwined in one another's arms, she laughs at him.

SILLY BOY. Gently, her fingers knock against his brow. ARE YOU AFRAID I WILL KILL YOU?

She touches her neck, then points the finger at him, transforming it suddenly into a blade.

WHAT A BEAUTIFUL DEATH.

He draws her down to him, still laughing, and silences her mockery with a kiss.

His brother Henry has come home, although Hilary term has not yet ended. He has been told his presence is not required at the university, while his gambling debts remain unpaid. There is also the matter of a certain young person—daughter of a local pastry-cook—whom he appears to have got with child. It is all most inconvenient, with a year of his studies still to go…

'Grandfather is being confoundedly awkward about the whole affair,' complains Henry to his sibling, as he divests himself of gloves, hat and cloak, and consigns the whole dripping pile to John's servant. 'He says he won't pay my batells—and without that, you know, the House will not have me back…'

John shrugs.

WHAT DO YOU EXPECT ME TO DO ABOUT IT?

'Talk to the old man, confound it!'

John smiles.

'I mean, write to him. Persuade him.'

HE DOES NOT LISTEN TO ME.

'You are his heir…'

HE WOULD VERY MUCH PREFER THAT I WERE NOT.

'Even so,' says Henry. 'You might put in a word for me. Since you will not have to make a living, and I shall. Although how I am to do it, with nothing but a small annuity to look forward to from Mama, I cannot imagine...'

He rides out to Bramham the next day, with the letter in his pocket, having spent a good deal of the previous evening composing it. Whether it will do his brother's cause any good, he is inclined to doubt; if his grandfather decides to relent, it will be because of his habitual indulgence towards his favourite grandchild, rather than on account of anything John can say in Henry's defence.

As he rides, his thoughts return, as they do in all such moments of idleness, to Mathurina. How beautiful she had looked, the last time they met, as she bent over the bed to kiss him goodbye. Half-drunk with sleep, he had tried to draw her down to him again, but she had pushed him away.

I MUST GO.

STAY A WHILE.

I CANNOT. THEY WILL MISS ME.

WHEN WILL YOU COME AGAIN?

She had smiled, then, arching her eyebrows, in that coquettish way she had.

SOON.

Then she was gone. Tonight, he thinks. Perhaps she will come tonight...

The roads are claggy after last night's rain, and his horse's shoes are soon thick with mud—which it likes not at all, fastidious beast, and which makes their progress the slower. At Tadcaster, the river has burst its banks, and the flooded water-meadows on either side shine like cloudy mirrors. In the midst of this inundation, the willows along the banks seem to embrace their own reflections, their green-flecked branches sweeping low over the still water, like Naiads' tresses... Though he is not looking forward to his interview with Sir John with anything like pleasure, he feels his heart lift at the sight. Surely Spring is come at last? He has been too long mewed up in the city; it is good to breathe a purer air.

Reaching Bramham, he reins in his horse at the brow of the hill, and allows himself a moment to enjoy the scene. Built almost a hundred years before, out of honey-coloured stone, the house, with its graceful double flight of steps echoing the symmetry of its twin colonnades, is the focal point of that gently rolling landscape. Although relatively modest in scale, it is, to his mind, all that a house should be: of classical proportions, yet simple in execution; a gentleman's residence, not some pompous mausoleum... It is a place he can readily imagine living some day—altogether more agreeable than the chilly magnificence of Ribston Hall, which his great-grandfather had built, but where the present Sir John seldom chooses to reside. Instead, the old man is increasingly to be found at Bramham, which was his wife's dowry, and whose woods and fields are his delight—stuffed as they are with birds for shooting, and stags for hunting; even in the winter months, there is plenty of fishing to be had.

John's happiest memories are of the gardens, where, as a boy, he had roamed for hours. The little temples, which dot the grounds, were his refuge; and the chain of artificial lakes, which together make up Bramham's celebrated Cascade, were his mirror—and his first guide to the starry heavens. How often had he lain, on a summer's night, sprawled on his stomach on the stone rim of one of these still pools, as the stars appeared, one by one, in the dark water? Lost in contemplation of the glittering shapes below him, he would lose track of time—recalled to himself only by a touch upon his shoulder from the servant, or younger brother, sent to look for him.

He has another reason to love Bramham, for it was there that he first saw *her*, soon after her arrival from her French convent—was it really four years ago? He remembers his first sight of her, in her grey silk gown, and the way she had looked at him from under her lashes, then looked away... The One who was to eclipse all the stars with her light, and for whose sake he would gladly give up everything—even this inheritance.

Dismounting in the stable-yard, he gives his horse into the charge of a loitering groom, with instructions to brush the worst of the mud from its coat. In the hall, as he waits for his grandfather's summons, he attempts to perform the same office for himself. But he is conscious, as he is ushered into the old man's presence a few moments later, that he cuts a somewhat dishevelled figure.

Sir John is in the Smoking Room, where it is his habit to pass most mornings—or at least, those too wet for any kind of exercise. He does not look up when his grandson walks in, but carries on reading the letter John has brought. At length he casts this aside, with a frown.

'Well, Sirrah...'

John bows.

'You are come on your brother's account, I collect?'

John inclines his head.

'You might as well have saved yourself the trouble. Henry must learn that not everything can be solved with money...'

This last is delivered with a slow deliberateness—not, John suspects, out of consideration for himself, but because his grandfather intends it as his last word on the subject.

John hesitates. The old man is not in the habit of being contradicted. But he has come for no other purpose than to do just that. He takes out pen and paper, and scribbles a reply.

I do not disagree with you, Sir. But I would ask you to exercise forbearance. Henry is very young.

His grandfather's eyebrows have shot up as the note is being written, and remain in that position as he reads it.

'Do you think, Sir, I need reminding of that?' A wintry smile softens his features for an instant. 'He is young—I grant you that. But he is not so young that he does not know how to get some doxy with child...'

I would like to request a small advance on next year's allowance. To be sent to the young woman in anticipation of her confinement...

'You will bankrupt us all, Sir!' But Sir John's expression, as he speaks, is one of veiled amusement. 'Do you propose, then, that your brother's bastard shall be brought up a gentleman?'

I would hope, Sir, that an innocent child might not be made to suffer for what he cannot help.

If the old man perceives the implied rebuke, he does not show it. But he seems suddenly weary of skirmishing.

'Tell Henry,' he says, 'that I will pay his bills—aye, and pay off his mistress, too. Tell him, while you are about it, that he is a young dog—and that I will not put up with his tricks any longer...'

I am grateful, Sir.

'You are a better brother than he deserves,' says Sir John. 'At least there is no danger that *you* will disgrace yourself, as he has done.'

XIX

It is dark when at last he reaches his chambers, for he has returned by way of the house in Lendal, to tell his brother of the success of his enterprise. Henry, though pleased enough at the outcome, is surly at the thought that he must curb his profligate ways.

'I suppose I am to exist on bread-and-water from now on,' he says.

IT WILL DO YOU NO HARM, FOR YOU ARE GETTING FAT.

Henry does not seem to see the joke.

'It is all very well for you to laugh,' he says . 'You do not have to exist on four hundred a year…'

In the arrangements that have been made for his mistress, the pastrycook's daughter, he shows not the slightest bit of interest.

'I do not believe for a moment the child is mine. You know what these woman are…'

I AM GLAD TO SAY THAT I DO NOT.

'I was forgetting.' His younger brother gives a sour smile. 'You care only for your precious stars…'

It occurs to him, riding back through the quiet streets of the old city, that Henry's sojourn in Oxford has not improved him.

Reaching his chambers, he calls at once for candles, and for the fire to be lit, for it is cold as the tomb. Having dined with his grandfather at the latter's request, he wants nothing further. A glass of wine, perhaps… It is then that Thomas gives him the letter.

Mr Pigott's man had brought it that morning, he says. Thomas had told him he need not wait for a reply, since the master was not expected back before nightfall. He (Thomas) hopes that was the right thing to say…

Barely able to contain his impatience, John dismisses the servant, and tears the letter open. He has not seen his Beloved since the small hours of that morning, when she left his bed (O, sweet memory!) to return to her own. Perhaps this is to name the hour that she will come? He can hardly wait. Even these few hours that have passed since they last met have been too many...

But when he reads the letter, it is as if a cold hand clutched his heart. It cannot be... As if stupefied, he stares at the scrap of paper.

> We are discovered. My father's anger knows no limits. If you love me, come at once...

As the horror of it overwhelms him, he groans aloud, the cry tearing his throat in a painful spasm. At once Thomas is at the door, his eyes wide with alarm, but John pushes him aside. He must go to her—now. He must take her away from that house, and from that ogre, her father. He curses himself for his folly, in not having done so before.

Thomas is saying something. Thomas is holding him back. He has no time for this. He flings the servant off, and runs from the room.

Outside, it is raining again, but he pays it no heed. All he can think of is that he must see her. If he can just see her, everything will be all right...

By the time he reaches the house in Bootham Bar, he is drenched to the skin. His hair hangs in dripping strands, and his teeth are chattering. He seizes the door-knocker and lets it fall—again, again, again. But there is no reply. The house, he sees, is dark. They must all be in bed. But he will wake them soon enough... He raises the knocker once more—but before he can bring it crashing down, the door swings open, so that he loses his balance and falls sprawling across the sill.

A man wearing only his nightshirt stands there, looking at him with an expression of consternation. He knows him by sight as one of the servants. He pushes past him into the house. Let any man stop him who would. They will not keep him from her. Climbing the stairs at a run, he flings open the door of the first room that he comes to, which is the drawing-room. It is empty, which is not in itself surprising. What is strange is the room's shrouded aspect: chairs, tables and mirrors all draped in dust-sheets, and the carpet rolled up.

With a sick feeling at his heart, he turns to the servant, who has followed him upstairs.

'They are gone, Sir,' the man explains, mouthing the words, and gesticulating. 'To Belgium, early this morning…'

He will not believe it. He shoves the staring fool aside, and climbs the stairs once more, opening doors as he comes to them—all of which offer further proof of the same story. Packing cases stand all about, with piles of books and clothes spilling out of them. These—evidence of an all-too hasty departure—convince him at last. At the door of the last room—hers—he breaks down and weeps, his chest shuddering with sobs. For the room, bare and cheerless as it is, with all its furnishings stripped away, still retains some faint traces of its former occupant—not least her scent: flowery, sweet.

On the floor, in a patch of moonlight, lies a satin slipper, forgotten in the urgency of that cruel flight. He picks it up and kisses it, poor relic of his lost darling. The thought that she might have believed herself abandoned by him, when she needed him most, makes him weep again.

Thomas fetches him home, and persuades him to go to bed, although he does not sleep at all that night. He will never sleep again. All he can think of is now frightened she must have been, and how friendless—with father and mother conspiring to defeat her, and even the brother she trusted betraying her in the end…

O, why did I ever let her go? he moans silently, soaking the pillow with his hot tears.

In the morning there is a letter, in Edward's hand. He breaks the seal, with trembling fingers. The address is that of an inn fifty miles distant. It strikes him that they will not reach Dover before the evening of the following day. He might still catch them, if he sets out immediately… But then he reads the letter, and realises the futility of such a venture:

Cousin,

My sister has acquainted me with the facts of her Friendship with you—which she assures me has nothing of Dishonour about it. My Father, believing otherwise, is determined that she should be returned to M. le Comte

> with the utmost dispatch, in order to avoid any further taint of disgrace to the family name.
>
> Poor Mathurine is quite undone by all this, as you may readily imagine…

Tears well in his eyes at this. He makes himself read on.

> …but she is adamant that she would rather die than live as De Valois's wife again. She has proposed a plan, which I have agreed to assist her in carrying out. She will seek refuge with the Good Sisters at Brussels, where they will care for her as one of their own…

He reads and re-reads the fatal sentences. With each re-reading, it becomes clearer to him how truly lost she is to him now. Even married to that detested man, she would not be as far out of reach as she will be behind the convent's walls. It is a kind of death. Crueller, even than death—to know she still exists, away from him.

There is one final sentence:

> My sister sends you her affectionate regards, and begs that you will not think too unkindly of her…

If the characters had been inscribed upon his skin, with red-hot irons, they could not have caused him greater anguish.

How long he sits there, with the letter in his hand, he does not know. Only that when Thomas, concern written upon his face, comes in to ask him what he requires by way of dinner, he is still in his dressing-gown.

The rest of the day is a blank.

He supposes he must, at some point, have got dressed and eaten his dinner and sat down at his table again—for that is where Harriet finds him, with a blank page in front of him and a pen he seems intent on destroying in his hand. (Was he intending to write a reply to that fateful letter? He cannot say.)

Her face, when she comes in, tells him she has already heard the news.

I AM SO SORRY.

He nods, but does not reply.

WHAT WILL YOU DO? WILL YOU GO AFTER HER?

IT WOULD BE OF NO USE.

He hands her Edward's letter.

As she reads, her face expresses the emotions—sadness, indignation—he knows he, too, should be feeling; but he cannot feel them. All his capacity for feeling is gone—shrivelled up in the blast of his despair.

She raises her eyes at last. 'But this is terrible. For her to be... *imprisoned* in such a place. You cannot allow it.'

WHAT CHOICE DO I HAVE? SHE HAS DECIDED, OF HER OWN FREE WILL...

Harriet stares at him. 'She has no free will. She must obey her husband—or her father.'

SHE HAS CHOSEN TO OBEY NEITHER.

She is weeping, now.

'I thought you loved her.'

I WOULD TO GOD I HAD NEVER LAID EYES UPON HER.

He cannot stop himself remembering an earlier conversation:

I LOVE YOU.

HOW MUCH DO YOU LOVE ME?

VERY MUCH.

MORE THAN YOUR LIFE?

OF COURSE MORE THAN MY LIFE. MORE THAN SUN, MOON, STARS...

He had thought to make her laugh; now he sees that she is crying.

'I'm sorry,' she says, wiping away tears with the back of her hand. 'It is just that I cannot bear to think of leaving you.'

YOU DO NOT HAVE TO.

'O, but I do,' she says. 'Don't you see? There is no hope for us.'

YOU MUST DIVORCE HIM, AND MARRY ME.

She shakes her head. 'I cannot. The Church does not permit it.'

THEN LIVE WITH ME AS MY WIFE.

She smiles. 'Sweet boy. You do not know what you are saying.'

When Grandfather dies, I will be Sir John, of Ribston Hall...

'Do you think Society does not have its rules, too?'

I care nothing for Society. I care only for you.

The conversation had given way, at this point, to a more active demonstration of his words—their time together being, as ever, short. Now he wonders if she had been trying to prepare him for this.

All that night he tosses and turns, in feverish dreams of her. The feel of her body under his hands, the slippery heat of her, the taste of her kisses, the smell of her hair—all these are a torment to him. It is as if a demon—a succubus—lay with him all night long, whispering poisoned words into his ears, and goading him with lewd images, until he wants to scream aloud. He cannot bear it, he *will* not bear it... To have known such bliss, and to have it snatched away like this, is agony. To know that she—the cause of his distress—is suffering, too, in all likelihood, is no consolation.

Plagued by such thoughts, he lies awake until it starts to get light; then falls into a heavy slumber. When he wakes once more it is broad day, and his limbs feel as if he had undergone a beating. His head aches, and his throat has a scratchy feel. He drags himself out of bed, and it is as if he had aged a hundred years. He forces himself to wash and dress, and swallows the bread and cheese Thomas brings for him. Then he puts on his cloak—he will not stay another minute in this hateful room. Here, where he has experienced his moments of greatest happiness, now holds only the ashes of despair.

Where he is going, he does not know. If things had been otherwise, he would, in all probability, have walked over to see Edward; but there would be no more of that. Even the thought of his friend is painful to him.

He does not think he can face his mother just now.

Not that Harriet would have said anything—but he knows Levina is certain to raise the subject. She is not much given to restraint, where her emotions are concerned. And she had loved Mathurina... They had all loved Mathurina.

So he lets his footsteps take him where they will, with no sense of purpose to guide them. As he steps out into the great yard of the Minster, they are ringing the bells for Matins—he can feel the vibration of it, shaking the air around him. He remembers something Edward once said about its being possible to measure sound, in waves. It was like a pebble, he had said, dropped into a pond, and sending out ripple after ripple, in ever-widening circles. Indeed, he had conducted one such experiment, using church bells, in Brussels...

He does not want to think of Edward, or Brussels.

Shaking his head, as if to dislodge water from his ears, he walks on, pushing his way through the crowds of the devout, that flock towards the Minster's great doors, until he reaches a less populous quarter. Here, in the maze of crooked streets surrounding the marketplace, he wanders in circles, careless of the filth which cakes the slippery stones beneath his feet, and which, mingled with the blood of the slaughtered beasts whose carcasses are laid out on trestles along the street, soon speckles his stockings and breeches.

As he walks, the thought pulses like a drum: *she is gone, she is gone forever*... Shut up behind the walls of her convent, where neither he nor any man would ever see her...How he hates that canting faith of hers! It is nothing but superstition. He passes the house of a woman who, two hundred years before, had been pressed to death beneath a heavy oak door, because of her religion. Those who had done that to her—piling stones and iron bars upon her, and then adding their own weight to the load—were nothing but barbarians; but to give up one's life for such a cause is, to his mind, no less barbaric.

How *could* she have chosen God, over him? He, who had made her his goddess... He steps on a loose paving-stone, which sends a jet of cold, filthy water up the back of his leg. His eyes filling suddenly with tears at the stupid futility of it all, he curses his ill-luck under his breath, and stumbles on.

There is nowhere that does not remind him of her; no street which does not contain her slender ghost, slipping just out of reach as he turns to look... Here it was that they had met that day in the Spring. She had been buying gloves in Piccadilly, she said—the latest kind, brought from Paris. Lilac kid. Were they not pretty? He had taken her arm, to guide her across the street, and given a halfpenny to the crossing-sweeper... This is the house—closed up now, and dark—of her relative, poor mad Lady Anne, who had shut herself up in Gilling Castle with her priest... There is the bridge where he and Mathurina had dawdled, on another afternoon, to watch the lighter-men unloading bales of wool.

Now, as he leans his arms upon its stone balustrade, and looks down at the water which flows so swiftly beneath its arches, he thinks how easy it would be to surrender to those dark depths. One leap, and it would all be over...

Only the thought of how cold it would be prevents him.

The north wind has blown away the clouds, which have covered the city like a pall these past few weeks. It will be a fine, clear night—perfect for observing.

It occurs to him that he has neglected his studies of late. Hydra awaits him.

He accordingly wraps himself in his cloak and, after no more than a few bites of supper (for he has little appetite these days), makes his way to the garden, where Thomas is already setting up the instruments. Dear, faithful Thomas! How much he has relied on his good nature! Without him, all his labours of the past few years would have come to nothing. When all is to his satisfaction, he dismisses the servant with a nod. There is no need for both of them to lose their sleep... not that he himself sleeps very much at all, these days. Since he *cannot* sleep, it stands to reason that he should make as much use as possible of the hours previously allocated to that unfruitful pursuit.

The stars are very bright, tonight; he has seldom seen them brighter. He consults his watch: it is half-past eleven. He looks first for Alphard—'the solitary one' as the Arabs called it—because it is the brightest of the chain of stars which make up Hydra's coils; then moves across to Montanari's variable star, just below the foot of the Crow. He calculates its magnitude, and makes a note in his journal.

He had spent a hundred nights—more—observing Algol, and Lyra. If it takes twice that he will unravel the mysteries of Hydra.

He spreads out his cloak upon the ground, and lies down, letting his eyes adapt to the darkness. Above him the familiar constellations wheel and turn. There is the Crow, and there is the Serpent; there the Centaur, and there Hercules, with his club... He compares the variable in Hydra with Xi Herculis, and makes another note.

As he lies there, it seems to him that his whole life revolves in front of him, with the stars. There is his childhood, very pale and distant, a mere speck in that black vastness; and there (only a little brighter) the moment of his fame. How brief is a man's life, compared to the immensity which lies before him! It is like a comet, flashing across the sky, and gone in an instant. Although even the stars are not eternal. Are they, too, not subject to change? Variable bodies, dimming and brightening in time...

He looks at his repeater, and is surprised to see that an hour has passed. He makes a note in his journal, although his fingers, clumsy with the cold, refuse to write at first.

Now—at twenty minutes to one—the stars are enormous; great wheels of fire, endlessly revolving in endless space... His thoughts turn—quite calmly and without rancour—to Mathurina. How paltry it seems, the love they had shared, in the face of this vast indifference!

That morning a letter had come; he had known the hand at once. He had almost thrown it in the fire, unopened. What could she possibly have to say? Nothing he would want to hear, that much was certain...

The address was that of the convent at Louvain.

'*Dear Friend*,' she had written.

> It is now two days since I am living with the Sisters, and there has not been an hour that I have not thought of you. Since that terrible night when my Father—alerted by a servant whom he had set to watch me—caught me as I was returning to our house after visiting you, my only resolve

was that he should never hear your name upon my lips. No matter how much he raged and threatened, I would not give you away.

So you see, dear one, that even though I am full of sadness that we will never meet again in this world, I know at least that I did not betray you.

Dearest friend, this is to me some consolation for all that I have sacrificed: my mother, father, brothers (although dear, kind Edward has sworn that he will visit me when he can); and you, Beloved One. But you must see that I have no choice in this—for to return to that monster, my husband, would be more terrible to me than death. Here, at least, with the Good Sisters, I will be safe. Even if it means (dear one) that I shall never see your face again.

Sweet boy, do not be angry with me! I know how much I have hurt you, and for that I ask your pardon. But if you knew how many tears I have wept for you, you would not be angry for long. Pity me, rather, for all that I have lost, in leaving the world as I must…

She had signed herself, not in her married name, but as she would now be known: Marie-Mathieu.

He had thrown the letter on the table. Whether he would answer it or not he could not say. Even if he did so, would she be permitted to receive it? She is as lost to him now as if she were on the far side of the Moon; even the furthest star is more accessible to him than she is…

He becomes aware that someone is shaking him. It is Thomas, come to rouse him. Above them, the sky is getting light. Had he fallen asleep then? He gets to his feet with difficulty; a strange drowsiness possesses him. It feels as if all the blood in his veins has turned to ice.

XX

In the morning when he goes to rise, he cannot rise. When he draws a breath, it is as if he has swallowed knives, or a fistful of hot coals. His body is drenched in sweat, and his limbs are aching. When Thomas comes to wake him, he can no longer remember the other's name.

It is as if he has entered a fiery land—lightless as Hell, and just as hot. A realm of voices, murmuring in his ear. He cannot hear what it is that they are saying, but he feels their breath, hot on his cheek. Noxious beings—demons—conspire to torment him. With their mutter, mutter, mutter all the livelong day, and their nods and smiles. O, he knows all about their smiles! Here is one, with his head on one side, the very image of a sage and worthy citizen. Physician. That is what he calls himself, is it not? But a demon underneath it, for all that... Yes! It can only be the Devil who looks out of his eyes (such little, cruel eyes they are, too): Old Nick, the Dark Gentleman, Satan or Lucifer (light-bringer and prince of darkness in one) is Master of *this* vessel. Weak as it is—corpulent, foul-breathed, lice-ridden (his wig is alive with the creatures)—still it knows how to wield its power. It can burn—piling logs upon the fire, so that the room seems a veritable Inferno—or it can freeze, throwing up the windows, until it becomes a Universe of Ice. It can bleed, drawing off fountains off the red stuff with its little silver knife, and it can Physic and Purge, till nothing is left but a husk.

He is that husk; a broken thing; a bundle of sticks. Fit for nothing but burning...

Here is another demon: his name is Fitzsimmons. He has the face of an Angel, but his heart is black as ice. He appears—at the turn of the stair, at the end of a corridor—as if materializing out of the Aether. When he comes, he brings pain with him—a twisted wrist, a jab beneath the ribs, a dead-leg—but what he brings above all is fear. *I will have you*, says his look. *Do not think you can escape me*... Fitzsimmons, though cruel, is beautiful; other visitors are not. There is the hanged man he once saw on the gibbet at Knavesmire, his eyes picked out by crows... or the drunken woman he ran into one night in Coppergate, her nose a rotting hole above another, filled with teeth... He is visited, too, by the vengeful shade of Margaret Clitheroe, in her bloodied weeds. *Why did you not save me*? she moans (it is as if he can hear her moan). Shaking her dripping locks at him, as if he alone were to blame for what was done to her. *When they beat me and spat upon me, I called for you. When they piled the stones upon my breast, I cried your name. O, why did you not come, when I needed you?*

Then the demons are gone, and it is just his mother who sits by the bed, her eyes red with weeping. In the cold light of morning, he sees that she has grown old. His beautiful mother, holding up her little dog for him to kiss. *Kijk, Johannes! Haar is Rikki!* How pretty she was that day, in her blue dress trimmed with lace, and her pearl earrings... Now her hair is gone quite grey, and there are lines between her eyes that were not there before... He opens his eyes again and his mother is gone. But Harriet is there. When she sees that he is awake, she smiles at him—although she, too, has been crying—and takes his hand in hers. The feel of that hand—its moist palm and soft, warm fingers—is the same as on the day they went to see the ducks. She was only a baby, then. He was to hold her hand and not let go, they said. When she saw the fluffy yellow ducklings, she tried to pull away, and go to where they were—but he would not let her, knowing she could not swim...

HE SAYS, HAT, DO YOU REMEMBER THE DUCKS? but she does not seem to understand him.

His life seems to go by in a series of images, as swiftly as if a hand dealt a pack of cards. Here is his scarlet spinning top, going round and round and round... Here is his picture book, with the Medusa's face, frozen in the mirror of Perseus's brazen shield. Here is his Orrery, also made of brass, with the planets turning around the Sun. Here is the Sun itself, casting its golden light upon a face, and a pair of dark eyes, that smile into his own...

He wakes, then, with a cry of anguish, to think of all he has lost.

He dreams he is giving a speech to a room full of people. He is wearing his best blue coat with the diamond buttons. Sun streams in through the windows, shining on marble pillars and painted ceiling. And there they all are, row upon row, the astronomers—Herschel and Messier, and Maskelyne, and Banks—all of them waiting to hear what he has to say. He has a great deal to say. He will astonish them all. Because no one has seen what he has seen, in all his nights of observing the Demon Star, or knows half as much as he does about its changeable ways. But when he opens his mouth to speak, no sound emerges. The looks on the faces of those assembled turn from surprise to derision. He tries again: still his tongue refuses to utter a word.

Then he remembers... He cries out. Someone (Edward? No, not Edward. Edward has gone away) comes to him. Strong arms hold him. A cup of water is brought to his lips. He sleeps again.

When he wakes, another Apparition is there: a mewling, simpering thing in white bands and a black gown. This is called Parson; he would have charge of his Immortal Soul, if he would let him. Parson points to the place in the prayer-book where it says Repent. He repents of nothing. If what they did was a sin, then he will gladly pay the price for it. Burn. If burning is the price. Freeze. Bleed. Die for her a thousand times, his body broken on the rack, if that is what it takes, if that is what it takes... Mutter, mutter, mutter. Will they *never* leave him alone? How he longs for the days of his silence. Now all is gone to babble and confusion.

Silence. He longs for silence. Darkness, too. Because darkness is never dark, when there are stars... Quick. Draw back the curtains. Let him see them once more: the Hunter, the Virgin, the Lion, the Serpent, the Bear. How clear and large they are tonight! How bright they burn! Durable fires. Soon, they will enfold him in their glittering web... If only he were not so hot. So thirsty...

With finger and thumb, he touches the corner of his mouth: the sign for 'water'. But the room is empty. There is no one there to see or understand. The Moon's light floods in. Cold cold cold. He shivers in sheets that have turned to skeins of ice. His throat is on fire. Will no one bring him water?

It is then that he sees that he is not, after all, alone. For she is there: his Beloved. In a gown the silvery colour of the moonlight on the wall, she stands before him. She touches his lips with her fingers—so smooth, so cool—and at once his thirst disappears.

SLEEP NOW.

She closes her fingers together on either side of her face, to signify the closing of eyes—and he does so.

Luminous Particles

✹✹✹✹✹✹✹✹✹✹

XXI

Louvain, 1786

All though that terrible journey, Mathurina is silent and withdrawn, her tears and protestations having given way to a sullen lethargy. She speaks only when spoken to (and to their father not at all), and refuses to eat, turning her face away when the food is placed in front of her, as if its sight and smell were disgusting to her. It seems as if she has lost the will to continue; her gaze being turned not outward, to the fields and villages through which they are passing, but inward, to the one realm where she is still unfettered. She no longer weeps; but once or twice Edward thinks he sees her lips move, as if in silent colloquy with some unseen person.

When they stop for the night at Ferry Bridge, she goes straight up to her room without touching a morsel of the cold fowl the landlord has set out, although their mother implores her to take something. 'Let her go fasting to bed, if she wishes it,' says their father, tearing off a good-sized portion for himself. 'Perhaps that will bring her to her senses.' Later the same night, as Edward lies sleepless on his narrow pallet, he hears the sound of weeping coming from next door. But when he goes to investigate, he finds Mathurina's door locked, and the key taken away; his father evidently having decided to take no chances with his wayward child.

Next morning, after an indifferent breakfast in the inn's fusty little parlour, he is sitting down to write a letter to Goodricke—for he has a bad conscience about having left York in such haste—when his mother and sister join him; the latter very pale, and with dark shadows under her eyes that show she has not slept.

Anne-Mathurine is trying to coax her daughter to eat. 'Try at least a little of this coffee... it is not so very bad. *Un petit morceau du pain...*'

Just then comes an ill-tempered shout from upstairs. Their father requires his breakfast without delay.

'I suppose you think me a whore, too,' Mathurina says, when their mother has gone to answer this peremptory summons.

'You do me an injustice,' Edward replies. 'I take no account of Father's intemperate moods.'

'But you have conspired with him to return me to my husband.'

'I am sorry if you think so. You must know that I have only your best interests at heart...'

She makes a face at that.

'Surely,' he persists, 'however bad it is in your husband's house, it cannot be as bad as the way you have been treated since you returned to York?'

'Ah, as to that...'

There comes the sound of their parents' voices on the stairs: their mother's gentle murmur overlaid by their father's hectoring tones.

'Step outside with me for a moment,' Mathurina says in an undertone. 'For there is something you must know...'

'How now, Madam?' says their father. 'I trust we are to have no more foolish sulks from you. Why, where do you suppose you are going?' he goes on, seeing that she is walking towards the door. 'The coach will be leaving directly.'

'My sister is faint, Sir, and in need of air,' replies Edward with the smoothness he finds it politic to use in dealing with his father. 'We will not be five minutes.'

Then, as they stand there in the muddy stable-yard, she tells him why it is she can never return to her husband.

'For you must know that I have given myself to another,' she says, with that defiant tilt of the head he knows all too well. 'And I will die rather than renounce him.'

'Who is it that you mean? Is there someone in France?'

She stares at him a moment.

'I cannot believe you have not guessed it already,' she replies, 'since you and he are such friends. Why, only the day before yesterday, you were star-gazing together...'

Now it is his turn to stare. What is she saying?

'You cannot mean John G...'

'Shh. Yes.'

She glances nervously over her shoulder, although there is nobody about, except for a gaggle of stable-boys, more interested in pelting a rat with stones, than in anything their betters might have to say.

He feels light-headed; sick. A blow to the stomach could not have been worse. He struggles to compose himself.

'How long has this been going on?'

She smiles.

'We loved each other from the moment we saw each other.'

It was not exactly what he meant, but he bows his head in acknowledgment of the words. He does not think he can trust himself to speak.

'I have been his mistress these past three months,' she adds flatly.

For a moment he almost hates her—although she cannot know (*must* not know) how much her confession hurts him.

It is then that she tells him of her plan.

They reach Dover early next morning, and their father goes at once to secure a passage. For there is no time to be lost, he says, if they are to embark on the next tide. A boat is found—it turns out that the captain is a friend of his. This puts Nathaniel Pigott in a high good humour, and the two men retire to Captain George's cabin, with a bottle of Port, to drink a toast to fellowship. Thus it is that Edward and Mathurina are thrown once more in one another's company—their mother and younger brother becoming seasick almost before the white cliffs have been left behind. To escape the stench of it, and the groans of those similarly afflicted, brother and sister go up on deck. Here, above that noxious 'tween-decks fug, is a different world: the air thick with flying spume, and stinging their eyes with its salt; the boards beneath their feet heaving alarmingly, with every swell.

Mathurina prefers it, she says, to being confined in close quarters. 'Here at least one can breathe freely,' she cries. She seems impervious to the squalls of rain which strike them in the face with every gust; seems rather to enjoy the sensation of being outside in such inclement weather.

'For you cannot know what my life has been until this moment,' she says. 'To have been thus imprisoned, harried, tormented…'

From high above their heads, come the shouts of the sailors, clambering about in the shrouds, and the crying of seagulls, borne back across the expanse of iron-coloured waves, which lie between them and France.

'I am very sorry for you,' he says.

'Then help me do what I wish to do...'

When she had broached the subject to him, in the dirty yard at the inn, two days before, he had thought her mad; or, if not mad, then possessed by a foolish whim. Now he sees that she will not be shaken from her purpose.

So precipitous had been their departure from York, that there had been no time to prepare their uncle and his wife for their arrival in Louvain, beyond a hasty letter, sent ahead from Calais. M. Beriot, their mother's brother, therefore receives them with some consternation, fearing serious illness or sudden death; nor is he much reassured when the truth of the matter is made known to him. The house at the Rue des Chats—one of those streets of tall, grey, shuttered houses, built around a century before, of which the old town is composed—is not large enough to accommodate them all without discomfort, and Nathaniel Pigott at once sets about finding another; for, he says, once their unfortunate business with M. le Comte is concluded, they can expect to stay upwards of a month in the Low Countries. The

Transit of Mercury is to take place on 3rd May—an event he, for one, is determined not to miss.

It strikes Edward that, even where the reputation of a daughter is at stake, his father does not forbear to put his own interests first.

That Mathurina is watched at all times makes the furtherance of their plan difficult enough; that she is lodged with her cousins, in a room on the upper floor, and is not allowed to leave it without permission, makes things altogether worse. But there is little time to lose, if they are to contrive her escape; M. de Valois has been written to, and it will only be a matter of days before he arrives to claim her...

At dinner two nights later, Edward tries to catch his sister's eye, not having had any communication with her since their arrival. But she keeps her gaze fixed resolutely upon her plate, on which the food remains untouched. He is conscious of a rising exasperation with her for her intransigence, mingled with a dread of what is to come. Is it not enough that she has thrown the whole house into disarray with her reckless behaviour? Must she compound the fault by refusing to show the least sign of repentance? Tears would have been better than this mulish, white-faced silence, which only serves to increase their father's irascibility.

Not that Mathurina cares a straw for that. 'I will never speak to my father again, for as long as I live,' she says. 'He has treated me no better than a Slave, to be bought and sold in the market-place; indeed, he has used me worse. For a Slave, at least, can marry whom he wishes, but I must be made the whore of an old man...'

Until that moment, he had not realised that her hatred of their father exceeded even his own.

Nathaniel's voice is all that he hears that night, as the rest of them sit silent and preoccupied—his mother, brother and sister, and himself on one side of the table, his cousins, Heloise and Augustine, and their mother on the other. His uncle Beriot sits at the far end of the table from his brother-in-law, and is the only one who attempts to reply to the latter's remarks.

'A fine soup, this, brother.'

'Catherine has always known how to make a good soup.'

'A great skill, in a wife. One could scarcely ask for more. Unless it were obedience...'

M. Beriot's nod seems neither to disagree nor entirely to concur.

'What does the Bible tell us? "A virtuous woman's price is above rubies"...'

'I have always found it to be so,' murmurs their uncle.

Their aunt says nothing, merely signalling to the maid to bring the next course.

'Ah!' cries Nathaniel Pigott, evidently in high good humour. '*Gigot d'agneau aux asperges*. I cannot remember when I last ate so well. Truly, brother, you are fortunate in your cook...'

At the end of that interminable meal, of which he tastes not a single bite, Edward rises to follow his father and the rest of the men to the smoking parlour. As he passes his sister's chair, she slips a piece of paper into his hand.

Tomorrow, it reads. *I shall say I am ill, with women's pains. You must accompany me to the Apothecary's.*

He shoots her a glance, but her face is unreadable beneath the demure lace cap.

He touches her shoulder.

'Tomorrow,' he says softly.

Situated in the oldest part of the city, the Beguinhof is a collection of crooked old houses, built of soft red brick, around a courtyard garden. Here, women in flight from perils of all kinds can take refuge, temporarily, or forever. In the past, Edward had sometimes had occasion to ride past it, and had glanced up to see the white face of one of the inmates peering out from behind high barred windows. Idly speculating about the sad histories of those that dwelt there, it had never struck him that his own sister's might one day be numbered amongst them...

It is still early when the coach sets them down outside the gates, at his instruction. The street with its tall narrow houses is quiet; deserted. Even so, he cannot stop himself from glancing over his shoulder, to reassure himself they are not pursued.

It had been Mathurina's idea to leave before the household was stirring. Only their cousins had been roused from their beds—a necessary audience to Mathurina's story. For she would die if she did not get some relief, she had cried. She had not slept a wink—her pains were so bad. Nothing less than the strongest sleeping-draught would do to relieve them. Edward would take her to the Apothecary's (she went on to insist). They would return directly. There was no reason in the world to waken Father and Mother...

'It is very hard to leave without saying goodbye to Maman,' says his sister now, as the heavy carriage moves slowly through the silent streets. 'But if I were to see her, I should lose my resolve.' She gives a grim little smile. 'I cannot afford to do that.'

Resolute or not, she is weeping bitterly by the time they come to knock upon the great barred gate. He holds her close, and strokes her hair, cursing himself for his own weakness. If he had only had the courage to stand up to their father... But he had not had the courage. He is nothing but a fop; a wastrel, condemned to spend his life humouring the foibles of a tyrant.

At length a shutter opens, and a face looks out. In a trembling voice, Edward states their names, and business. The shutter closes again. It seems an age before a smaller door, within the gate, swings open to admit his sister. She clings to him then, still weeping, for both know he cannot follow.

Nathaniel Pigott is momentarily reduced to speechlessness by the news of his daughter's defection. He goes white, then red—a sign that his anger is about to erupt, which it does the next instant.

'God damn her!' are his first words. 'She has made fools of us all. Sitting there as meek as a mouse, when all the while... It is not to be borne. It is not! As for *you*'—his rage now being directed at his elder son—'do not think that I do not know how you and she have conspired against me.'

That his daughter had not only gone against his wishes, but had, a second time, undermined his authority in the eyes of his son-in-law, only serves to increase his bitterness.

'Better that she had died at my hands, than that she should live, to bring shame upon our family! O why, merciful God, did I not strike her down where she stood, instead of letting her live, the whore, to blacken our name still further through her ingratitude?'

'Sir, you do yourself no honour, to speak of your own child in such a way...'

But his son's words only make the old man fly into a worse passion.

'Get out of my sight!' he cries. 'You infernal puppy! You shrinking violet! How do you dare to talk to me of honour?'

If it had not been for his mother's intervening at that moment, things might have got uglier still. Goaded to the limits of endurance, Edward comes as close as he ever had to striking his father. Only the anguished look on Anne-Mathurine's face prevents him. That her tears are all on her son's account, even though she would doubtless receive her own share of her husband's ill-temper, makes him feel even more ashamed of his own spinelessness. What a life she had led.

He leaves the room, without another word.

'That's right,' comes his father's voice after him. 'Take yourself off! You are no son of mine from this day. You need not think there will be anything in it for *you*, when at last I am called to my Maker. No! As of now, I have but one child: my one true heir, Charles Gregory. All the rest are as dead to me. Dead!' the old man shouts, shaking his fist at his son's retreating back.

He has been almost two months in Louvain when the letter comes. It is post-marked a week earlier. Afterwards, he wonders how he could have been living all that time unawares—eating and sleeping and going about his business—with no notion that the worst thing to have happened in his life had happened... He does not recognise the hand, but seeing that it is sent from York, he seizes the letter with alacrity. For there has been no reply to the three he had written, and—knowing what he knows now—he guesses that his friend is angry with him. Perhaps this will explain the silence...

But when he reads the words, they make no sense. He reads them again, but their meaning still eludes him. He flings the letter away, as if it were an evil thing. It lies there on the table. He picks it up again.

It cannot be true—it cannot. And yet he knows that it must be true...

His eyes fill with tears.

York, April 20th 1786

Sir,

I am enjoined to write to you by my mother, Mrs Henry Goodricke, although I hardly know how to begin.

My dear brother, John Goodricke, is dead—of a fever brought on by a chill he contracted while observing, some weeks ago. He had been in poor health, & in low spirits, this past month & more—since your departure, & that of another member of your family, to Belgium (a circumstance which will not, perhaps, surprise you).

My mother & I never ceased to beg him to take better care of himself; but as you—who knew him so well—will doubtless attest, he was not one who could easily be ruled by any will but his own.

As a consequence, I have lost a brother who was dearer to me than myself; & you have lost a friend, & a true companion in your endeavours. The World is the poorer for it.

Forgive this ill-expressed & halting letter—as painful, I fear, for you to receive as it is for me to write.

I am, Sir,

Your affect. Cousin & Friend,
Harriet Goodricke

It seems the act of a cruel and capricious Deity, to have taken away, in the space of barely a month, the two he loved best in the world: the one sequestered behind the convent's high walls, so that she is as if dead to him; the other, dead in actuality.

Bad as he knows himself to be, he had not thought himself deserving of such a punishment.

'O forgive me, forgive me,' he weeps, unsure whether he is asking pardon of the living or the dead.

His first impulse when he hears the news is to return straightaway to England. His father will not hear of it, of course. Ever since he had been thwarted in his intention of returning his daughter to her rightful spouse, he has been in a towering rage. As the weeks go by, and Mathurina shows no signs of repenting of her folly, her father's mood grows blacker. He is a man who hates to be crossed in anything—and this deliberate flouting of his will is a treachery he cannot forgive. To Edward he says barely a word, and when he does speak, it is with the most violent ill-temper. As for Mathurina—he has forbidden her name to be spoken in his presence.

Ingrate. Unnatural daughter.

Preoccupied as he is with these grievances, Nathaniel has little time for trivialities. The death of his cousin's eldest child is regrettable, of course—but one can hardly count it a very grave loss, under the circumstances. A blessing, rather—given that the poor mute had so little worth living for. Had it been one of his own children, he would have said just the same.

So: there will be no going back—for the funeral, or any other reason.

Hateful as his father's sentiments are to him, Edward knows that there is a grain of truth in what the old man says. For nothing can change what has happened, however devoutly he wishes it could be so. Therefore he remains where he is, in Louvain—comforting himself with the thought that at least he can be near his sister.

It had fallen to him to tell her the news of Goodricke's death, since she has had no other visitors. Their mother might have visited her, if she were not so entirely under their father's thumb—and *he* has forbidden all contact with his rebellious daughter. Since she is so determined to devote herself to God, he says, he, for one, will not stop her. Let her waste away in her prison cell, ungrateful child that she is. He will have no more to do with her.

Charles Gregory is no less vehement in his refusal to accompany Edward to the Beguinhof, on the grounds that seeing Mathurina in such surroundings would 'give him the horrors'.

And so it is he alone—her co-conspirator and author, at least in part, of her fate—who deals her the final blow.

She knows, even before he speaks, that something is wrong; he can see it in her eyes. He tries to speak; but no words come.

'What is it?' she says at last.

When he tells her, his voice breaking into sobs, she says nothing for a long time. Then:

'I knew I should be the death of him,' she says. Her face is as white as her veil.

He puts out a hand to comfort her, but she flinches from his touch.

'Do not come near me,' she says. 'Do you not know that I am death to those that love me?'

She cries out, then: a sound so terrible in its anguish that he feels his heart contract within him.

'My poor John,' she weeps. 'What have I done? O what have I done?'

Hearing the commotion, two of the good sisters come hurrying in, to take her away. But she refuses to go with them, wrenching herself free from their arms, and flinging off the novice's veil to reveal her poor, shorn head.

'Tell my father he has won,' she cries. 'For he has destroyed me, and everything that I held dear.'

Of the months that follow, he retains only the haziest impression. Nor does he care to remember anything of that hellish time. He supposes he must have been ill, or mad; or both. He recalls that he and his father—both barely on speaking terms—had made Observations of the Transit of Mercury. He had written to Maskelyne about it. In the same letter, he had conveyed the news of Goodricke's death; although he supposes that Maskelyne might already have heard it. Maskelyne must, at any rate, have passed the news on to Herschel, for, sometime later, a letter came from Miss Herschel at Slough.

He does not remember what the letter said, nor what he wrote in reply.

His thoughts are a wilderness of winding paths, in which he wanders for hours; of thickets full of briars, in which he finds himself ensnared. There is nowhere to go but back to the beginning, and nothing to feel but the smarts and stings of an undying regret.

He has not even the consolation of visiting his sister at the Beguinhof, for she has gone to the English convent at Brussels. There, the rule is stricter and contact between the novices and the outside world discouraged. Nor are his letters answered. It is as if, having lost the man she loved, his sister no longer wishes for any reminder of the life they once shared.

I must make a new life, in Christ Jesus—since the old one is gone forever she writes, at last.

After that, he, too, stops writing.

XXII

After months of bitter wrangling, the rift with his father happens suddenly.

One morning, Edward comes downstairs to find the house all higgledy-piggledy with boxes and piles of straw. They are going to London, his mother says, with a half-embarrassed glance at her husband. *He*, at that moment, is preoccupied with giving instructions to the servants concerning the proper packing of a telescope.

'It must be wrapped up with care—with *care*, you clumsy dolt! For the great Herschel himself polished the mirror at my request…'

Edward recalls the occasion only too well: it had been another instance of his father's complete lack of scruples. Having written to the famous astronomer (along with half the world) to congratulate him on his discovery of the new planet—a letter as full of flattery as he could make it—Nathaniel Pigott had ended by requesting a favour of him, in typically unctuous style:

> Was I very sure that, if in the least inconvenient, you would, sans ceremonie, refuse it, I would ask a favour of you, which is to repolish for us the speculum of a reflector, which is somewhat tarnished…

Of course (went on this piece of shamelessness), he—Dr Herschel—was under no obligation to perform this service &c—but if he were so inclined, the matter could be easily contrived, as Miss Porter would be travelling to Bath the very next week, and could bring the mirror with her… Thanking him for this favour in advance, he remained &c…

'And to think it didn't cost me a penny!' the old man chuckles to himself, as pleased with himself at the memory of this audacious stroke, as he had been when he had first pulled it off. 'My mirror polished to perfection by the best grinder of mirrors in the country (although he *is* a German). I call that a capital investment!'

On catching sight of his elder son, Mr Pigott's good humour instantly vanishes, however.

'*You*, again!' his look seems to say. 'I cannot think what you are doing here, under my roof, since our relations have, to all intents and purposes, ceased...'

Back in London, Edward takes lodgings in Kensington. These are shabby enough, but they will have to do. Since he must manage on the interest from the small legacy his grandfather has left him, together with what little money his mother is able to spare, he is obliged to cut his coat to suit his cloth. He has never indulged himself overmuch with rich food and fine wine, or the taking of snuff; clothes are another matter... But if there had been a time when a large proportion of his income had been spent on velvet coats, Mechlin ruffles, and silk waistcoats, that time is past. He no longer cares how he looks; the cut of a sleeve or the tying of a cravat is nothing to him, now.

Nor does he miss theatre-going, although at one time he would have made sure of attending all the new plays. Now their extravagant displays of disappointed love or furious jealousy, seem to him like the senseless rantings of lunatics. On occasion, his old comrade Englefield manages to persuade him to come out—once is to see a performance of Mrs Inchbold's *Such Things Are*, at the Haymarket, which, though filled with revolutionary rhetoric (for the lady is a known Jacobin), fails to engage him.

Still less diverting are his—now infrequent—visits to the opera, which had once delighted him so much, both for its onstage spectacles, and for the potential it offered for backstage liaisons. Now he finds the former to be an empty show, of garish costumes and exaggerated expression; whilst his present impecunious state prevents him from being able to enjoy the latter—intimate suppers at Simpson's and the obligatory presents of snuff-boxes and rings, being now beyond his means.

Not that he avoids dissipation altogether; it is just that it takes a less elevated form. For with his instruments still packed away, and the London skies in any case too smoky for good observation, his night-walks are for a different purpose than that of astronomical study. Sometimes, returning to his rooms at one or two in the morning after some base encounter, he catches sight of the stars, and is reminded of how far he has fallen. Those nights spent under the clear dark heavens star-gazing with Goodricke were the happiest of his life. How close he had come to declaring his feelings! Only the fear of seeing the other recoil from him in disgust had kept him silent...

Now the disgust is all on his side, at his own depraved appetites. He is like a man who, drinking to excess, spews to release the poison, before returning at once to the carouse. At such times, beholding himself in the mirror in the ashy light of dawn—his hair dishevelled and his breeches stained with evidence of the night's debauch—he wonders what sort of man he has become.

He avoids contact, as far as possible, with his friends in the scientific world—for what does he have to say to them? He has no new discoveries to tell, or theories to discuss. Astronomy—once his joy—has lost all charms for him.

Of the Herschels he hears only indirectly, through Englefield and Maskelyne (both of whom write to him from time to time). So it is that the fuss over Miss Caroline's latest comet —her second? Or is it her third?—does not escape him. He does, in fact, write to congratulate her; but resists going down to Slough in person. The thought of that cool, *noticing* gaze of hers being turned on him is more than he feels able to bear.

When he *does* visit his old friends again, it is at the behest of his former schoolfellow, Maurice de Grave, who has come from Paris for the express purpose, he says, of seeing the great Herschel in person. That he might have other reasons for wanting to quit his native land in a hurry is something both, by tacit agreement, refrain from dwelling on. Certainly the news from France is disturbing. There have been riots in Paris on account of the high price of bread. Now the Assembly has set itself up in opposition to the King. Their esteemed colleague at the Academie, the astronomer Sylvain Bailly, who had previously only expressed himself with vehemence upon the subject of the moons of Jupiter, had leapt upon a table, in the middle of a crowd of Deputies, to swear his undying allegiance to the People.

Where it will all end is anybody's guess.

Slough is just as he remembers it: a dull little backwater, with nothing to be said for it except that it is Herschel's home. *He* is just the same, too—if a little older and greyer. When the carriage sets them down in the lane—himself and Maurice de Grave—the astronomer is watching from an upstairs window, and calls down to them, quite without ceremony. The Chevalier seems somewhat disconcerted to find the great man so very plain as to dress and speech—although, as he says afterwards, it was ever thus with Genius, even in France. Miss Caroline he pronounces *sympathique*, if completely lacking in style, as clever women so often are.

He, for one, says the Chevalier, believes that women have a place in Science. Had not Mme Lavoisier assisted her husband in his experiments in chemistry? A charming woman, with whom he has often had the pleasure of conversing. Proof, if any were needed that the Weaker Sex need not concern itself solely with trivialities. If they are to play a part in forging a new world, based on Scientific Truth and Rationality (argues M. de Grave), women must throw off their domestic chains and put their shoulders to the wheel of Progress, along with their brothers-in-arms...

Such ideas are the currency of the times—the throwing-off of chains for all classes of people being a recurrent topic in all the salons, where the Rights of Man are much discussed by those who have never felt the lack of them. London is full of Jacobins, loudly proclaiming their adherence to the principles of Reason, Progress, and Liberty—above all, to Liberty. The old ways are to be swept away, and a new order will begin. How exactly this longed-for liberation from the shackles of the past is to be achieved is not explicitly stated; that it will involve some necessary bloodshed—by way of a purgative—to cleanse the body politic of its corruption, is, however, understood.

When the letter comes from York, he knows at once that the news it contains cannot be good. It has been two years since he has had any communication with his father; nor has Nathaniel Pigott chosen to break this silence with more than a cursory note:

> Sir,
>
> Your mother has asked to see you. Come at once, for her days upon this Earth are numbered.

Had it been left to their father, the letter might not have been written at all, Charles Gregory says. As it is, he himself has undertaken to deliver it, and to fetch his brother home in the Fairfax coach.

Anne-Mathurine had never been strong; in recent years, a constitution already prone to low-spiritedness has been further weakened by the self-denying ordinances of religious observance. Instead of the pretty, still-blooming woman she had been a few short years before, she has grown thin and pale, through constant prayer and fasting. When Edward walks into the room, he scarcely recognises her: his dear, sweet-faced mother, grown so worn and broken-down. Even her beautiful hair is almost gone, with only thin strands of grey showing beneath her lace cap.

He cannot restrain his tears at the sight.

She, for her part, can do nothing but exclaim over and over, '*Mon pauvre fils, mon pauvre fils*...'

'She blames herself for what has happened,' Charles Gregory says, later that same night, as both sit by the sleeping woman's bedside. 'She believes that God is angry with her, or he would not have taken Mathurina, and caused Father to drive you away...'

'If anyone deserves to be held to account it is he,' cries Edward. 'He is an unfeeling monster.'

But it is himself he blames, for having left his mother at the mercy of such a brute. He had cared only for his own suffering, never sparing a thought for hers.

'I have been a bad son,' he weeps, when at last his mother surrenders what had been, at best, a tenuous hold on life.

'Promise me,' she had whispered at the end, 'that you will not forsake her, *ma pauvre petite fille*...'

After the funeral, Edward remains in York for some months, finding himself strangely disinclined to leave it. London, with all its tawdry glitter and trash, seems another world. Here, in grey windswept Yorkshire, there is darkness, absence, loss—but also the memory of brightness... Wandering in the garden at the Treasurer's House, he recalls blissful hours spent in his Beloved's company. Here, by the sun-dial, is the very spot where they had set up their telescopes; there, on that stone seat, is where they first discussed their theories about variable stars. How young they were, and how charged with energy and passion! Men of Science, building a new world, in which Truth and Reason would prevail...

Barely ten years have passed since that time, and yet he feels he has aged a century.

In the garden of the house in Bootham Bar, a few nights later, he sees a comet—his first for years. It seems a kind of sign; a good omen, he thinks, for the future. Knowing that at least one Herschel—Miss Caroline, if not her brother—will share his excitement at the discovery, he at once takes up pen and paper:

York, Jan 15th 1793

My Dear Sir

tho you did not give us a call when last summer you went to Scotland; I shall nevertheless have the pleasure of sending you the earliest account of a Comet I saw yesterday evening; at 9 o clock it was nearly between the Stars Q or No 42 and No 46 in Flamstead's Constellation of Andromeda but rather nearer the Q—this afternoon at 5.30h it had nearly the same R.A. as Y Andromeda & was about two Degrees more south than that Star—as it is very visible to the naked eye, being brighter than Stars of the 3d Mag:de—possibly it has already been discovered in the south; if not, I shall later have the pleasure of sending you more exact Obserns—

and am, Sir, your most Obed:t

Edwd Pigott

The comet, which had seemed such a good omen to him, augured less well for others. Had not such phenomena once been thought to predict wars, plagues and the deaths of kings? Not that he himself is superstitious, but there had certainly been an awful appositeness to the timing of this one... Six days after he dispatched his letter—writing also to the Royal Society (for it had been a long time since any findings of his had been drawn to the attention of the learned members there)—the Jacobins decided to cut off the French King's head. Perhaps they had seen the comet as the sign they had been waiting for, to carry out their barbarous deed?

Instead of an Age of Reason, it seems they have entered a realm of nightmare.

It is his sister he fears for most—Brussels being rather too close to Paris for his liking. In Paris, it seems, murder is all the rage. Nuns and priests are amongst those licensed to be summarily executed—hacked to death, like the unfortunate inhabitants of the Paris Abbey; or drowned in the river, like those members of religious houses unlucky enough to fall into the hands of the Revolutionary Army at Nantes. Many have already perished, along with those unfortunate aristocrats who had not yet escaped to England.

Of those that had been prudent, or fortunate, enough to do so, he has had the pleasure of meeting M. Talleyrand—former architect of the Revolution, and now its greatest critic. This is at Mickleham, where Mme de Staël has rented a large house. Here, basking in the pleasant air of the Surrey countryside, are to be found a random collection of noble refugees. M. de Montmorency is often to be seen strolling about the grounds, and M. Jaucort, arm-in-arm with the charming Vicomtesse de Châtre, said to be his mistress. Here, too, will sometimes appear handsome General d'Arblay, often as not engaged in reading poetry to Miss

Burney… or Germaine de Staël herself, declaiming passages from her essay, *The Influence of the Passions on Happiness*, to an admiring audience of counter-revolutionaries.

But for Edward's sister, and other less fortunate souls who now find themselves trapped upon the wrong side of the English Channel, there is no such refuge. He has written to her several times, but has received no reply. He is beginning to fear that the worst has happened.

It is then, when he has almost given up hope, that the letter comes…

If he had hoped to avoid meeting with the representatives of the revolutionary army by putting in at Ostend, instead of at Calais, he is disappointed. The whole coastline, it seems, is swarming with soldiers—no doubt as determined to forestall invasion by counter-revolutionaries, as those on the English side are to avoid being over-run by bloodthirsty Republicans. He is detained for two days while his letters of safe-conduct are examined—which is tedious, but not uncomfortable, the place of detention being a local inn, where the landlord's wife cooks a very good dish of *moules*.

If he has cause for anxiety, it is less on account of the risks he himself is running (for the mood in the country is ugly, and a foreign visitor, however impeccable his credentials, might easily fall foul of a mob of drunken soldiers), and more because he is afraid that he might be too late to carry out his instructions. He is still trying to come to terms with what those instructions are. Although of course it all makes sense—he can see it now. His sister's choosing the life she has chosen, which had seemed at the time to be merely a further demonstration of the perversity of her character, is now revealed as the only course of action she could have followed…

When at last he resumes his interrupted journey, it is through a countryside so blighted by the signs of poverty and neglect, that it is almost unrecognisable from the landscape of his youth. Instead of well-tended pastures full of fat brown cattle, there are fields full of nettles and thistles, with the occasional starved-looking beast seemingly abandoned to its fate. The neat, whitewashed farmhouses, with steep red roofs and painted shutters, have given way to tumbledown shacks. Tiles have fallen from the roofs, paint flaked off, and mould blackens the once-white walls.

Starvation and hardship have left their mark, too, upon the inhabitants of the region. The rosy-faced girls and strapping youths he recalls seeing on their way to and from the milking-parlour or the hay-field, have vanished into thin air, it seems. All that remains in these ravaged communities are the very old, and the very young. Ancient crones, in ragged black, hold out their hands to him for alms as he rides by. Hollow-eyed waifs appear suddenly at the sound of his horse's hoof-beats, to beg for scraps and—when disappointed—to throw stones after the passing stranger.

More terrible even than these signs of want, is the silence which now reigns over the blasted fields and stricken villages. All the busy sounds of daily life—the shouts of market women calling their wares, the happy shrieking of children, and the good-natured quarrelling of farmers closing a bargain, are all gone; nor do the broken-down farms betray the usual signs of habitation. No cocks crow, no dogs bark; no cows low from the byres. No church bells ring out across the mournful fields, to proclaim the Angelus; nor do any clocks strike, to mark the passing of the hours.

Some of the villages through which he passes seem to have been abandoned in a hurry—so that washing still flaps on the line, and the ashes of a fire still smoulder. Others, though apparently inhabited—for a thin line of smoke rises from a chimney, and a scrawny chicken or two scratches in the yard—are strangely quiet, and devoid of people. Sometimes a face looks fearfully from a window, or a child is hastily drawn inside, and a door slammed shut.

It is as if, Edward thinks, some dreadful enchantment had fallen over the country; as if people held their breath, waiting for the spell to be broken.

On the evening of the following day he reaches Brussels. Here, too, everything is silent as the tomb. The bustle and clamour which had once filled the streets is now entirely subdued. Those who had once loitered at street corners, or congregated in local coffee houses, to exchange the news of the day, now hurry home without stopping. Spies and informers haunt all the taverns, it is said. Since to speak out of turn in the wrong company is to put oneself in mortal danger, it follows that it is safer to say nothing at all.

Arriving at the old market square, Edward makes his enquires, and is met with suspicious looks, and incredulous shrugs. No, they do not know the street he mentions. No, they have never heard of the person to whom he refers... Only when he is about to walk away in disgust, vowing to himself that he will find the place if it means tramping the streets all night, does a figure detach itself from the muttering group, with a murmur of '*As-tu de la sonnette?*' He has indeed come provided with 'the chinking stuff'—enough, fortunately, to overcome any reluctance, on the part of his self-appointed guide.

Even so, the latter, an ill-favoured youth of around fifteen, does not stay a moment longer than it takes to point out the house—one of a row of modest but respectable looking dwellings, built above shops—before melting away into the gathering dusk. The sound of Edward's knock seems as loud, in that quiet street, as cannon-fire. No answering sound comes from within; nor any sign of life. He knocks again.

At length, there is the sound of bolts being drawn back. A face looks out. By the light of a guttering candle, Edward makes out the lineaments of a man of about sixty.

'You will wake the whole town with that noise,' the old man says. 'What is it you want so urgently that it means dragging honest people away from their dinners?'

Edward states his name, and purpose.

'I do not know who you are talking about,' is the reply. 'There is no one of that name here...'

'For the love of God,' says Edward, putting his foot in the gap, as the door is closing. 'At least tell me that she is safe and well...'

On his return to London, he finds another letter waiting.

Our Lady's Convent, Winchester
19th July 1793

Dearest Brother

You will by now know that I am in England, whence we arrived last Wednesday fortnight, having sailed from Rotterdam. The English Convent at Brussels is closed up, and will remain so until these terrible troubles are over. I pray you have done what I asked of you—Heaven bless you for your kindness.

As for myself, I want for nothing; the Sisters here have been very good to us. I was sad to hear of our mother's death, but glad to know that she is now with the Blessed Saints in Heaven, where there is no more death, nor sorrow, nor crying, nor any more pain.

I am, dearest Brother,

Ever your affect. Sister and Friend,

Marie-Mathieu

XIII

Bath, 1821

He cannot say what had made him take out the instruments again, after so long. Perhaps it was young Herschel's letter, inviting him to join the new society he is intent on setting up for those with an interest in matters astronomical. The letter arrived two days ago, and still he has not replied. It was a generous offer, from a man whose eminence is deserved on his own account, and not merely because he is the son of so distinguished a father. It is of course a great honour to be asked to join his Society; although Edward cannot help but think, given how little he has contributed to the Science in recent years, that it is filial piety—a gesture of respect towards his father's old friend—rather than professional regard, which is behind John Herschel's invitation.

Unless Herschel Senior himself had suggested it? That, too, is possible…

He feels a momentary pang of guilt at the thought of his old friend—now so sadly stricken in years—reflecting how long it is since he was last at Slough. Can it be ten years? Even then, Herschel had not looked well, and there had been a tremor in his voice, which had not been so before… Theirs is a friendship which has lasted over forty years, and which has been founded as much, he likes to think, on mutual sympathy, as on a shared passion for the stars. For—in his own case, at least—the friendship has outlasted the passion. And whilst no one could deny William Herschel's reputation as one of the greatest astronomers of his age, in truth, his most significant discoveries had been made over thirty years ago, when he was still at Bath.

As for himself, Edward thinks, he does not miss star-gazing. All those nights spent out in the freezing cold, in the faint hope that something extraordinary—a comet; a planet—might appear, is a pastime for a younger man. His health will no longer stand it. Although, if he is being honest, he has to admit that was not the reason he had given up the practice…

On the table in front of him is spread out a mess of papers—the residue of half a century's observations—together with the disconnected parts of some of the instruments with which he has made them. Here is a mirror; there an eye-piece. The tubes for most of the larger telescopes have long ago been dismantled and stacked in the cellar. Only the smaller glasses remain intact. Of these, several are displayed on stands about the room; the rest are stored, with other memorabilia, in the glass cabinet beside his desk, which he now opens. Ah, there it is… He reaches for one of these, which had lain undisturbed—together with the bundle of notebooks with which it had been sent—for (can it be?) thirty years. With its casing of polished wood and brass, it is a lovely thing—though, sadly, no longer of much use, the mirrors being tarnished.

He recalls the day he received the parcel which contained it—several parcels, it was, in fact. His late and much-missed friend John Goodricke's entire archive, together with his finest instrument (the others, he supposes, had not been thought worth keeping). In his journal he had noted the receipt of the documents, which included an Astronomical Journal, whose contents had seemed, at times, a mirror-image of his own:

> a present from the G. Family at York; knowing the value that I set on everything that belonged to my late most worthy and intimate friend…

He guesses it must have been Miss Goodricke's doing; her sisters would not have thought of it, and as for Henry Goodricke, he had never give a fig for his brother's work—it was all horses and hounds with him… Although *de mortuis nil nisi bonum*, the poor man had not reached forty. The Goodrickes were not a family unduly prone to longevity, it seems. For had not Goodricke's father died before his forty-fifth year? Goodricke himself had not reached two-and-twenty.

'No age. No age at all,' murmurs Edward, in the silence of the room.

He holds the telescope to his eye, and squints through it. The face of the stuffed owl on top of the bookshelf looms suddenly large, so that its fierce beak and round dark eyes seem to fill his vision. He studies it for a moment—a fine specimen; he remembers the day he acquired it, from a farmer whose chicks it had been poaching—then reverses the instrument.

Now, what had seemed close, looks very far away...

'In this, the telescope imitates the effect of Time—so that stars which seem small and pale are furthest away, whilst those which appear large and bright are closest to us,' he had said once to Goodricke. '*Ergo*, when we look at the stars, we are looking at the past—for light must traverse Time as well as Space in order to reach us...'

It had been one of their earliest conversations—he still thinks of them as such, even though, strictly speaking, they should have been classed as soliloquies. But where his cousin was concerned, one would have been foolish to suppose that silence signified incomprehension. There was more wit in one of his looks than in an hour of some people's prattle. A raised eyebrow had spoken volumes.

As for his notes—written without haste, in that fine, Mathematician's hand—they were masterpieces of condensed thought; proof, if any were needed, of the workings of the mind behind the silence.

He remembers their first meeting, as if it had taken place yesterday, instead of more than forty years ago.

It was at Ribston Hall, in the Library—not a room, one might have supposed, very much frequented by its owner, old Sir John Goodricke—except perhaps as a repository for his books on bloodstock and the genealogies of noble houses. Nevertheless, it had been there that he had chosen to receive them—no doubt because it was, undeniably, a fine room, with a fine elevated ceiling and four fine windows commanding a view of the park.

They—his father, Sir John, and himself—had stood for a while admiring the view; his father (never one to lose such an opportunity for self-advancement) spouting some nonsense or other about Gilling, and how he meant to reclaim it from 'that confounded priest', as he put it.

Just then, Edward became aware that there was someone else in the room, as a beautiful youth in blue Nankeen rose from the table where he had been sitting—poring over some volumes which were spread out in front of him—to make his bow.

A little taken aback by this apparition, Edward returned the salutation.

'I am afraid I do not have the pleasure of your acquaintance, Sir…'

'O, it is no use talking to him,' said Sir John, without troubling to turn around from his contemplation of his property. 'For he is quite incapable of replying.'

This, he went on to explain, still with his back to the room, was his son's eldest child—a poor mute, who bore his name. 'Deaf from his earliest years. Although there has never been deafness in the Goodricke family,' he added sharply, turning to face them at last.

'Well, Sir,' he bellowed. 'What are you about, hey? No good, I'll be bound…'

By way of answer, his grandson showed him the book he had been perusing: Euclid's *Elements*.

The old man emitted a contemptuous snort.

'Mathematics, is it? It is always mathematics with you. When I was his age,' he remarked to his guests with some satisfaction, 'my taste was more for riding to hounds than for puzzling my brains with such sad stuff…

Embarrassed on the boy's account, Edward met his cousin's eyes—and was startled when—so swiftly that he wondered afterwards if he had imagined it—John Goodricke winked at him.

His cousin had returned only that week from Warrington, where he had been at school; when asked if he was to go to Oxford the following year, he smiled and shook his head. It had perhaps been a thoughtless question, given the poor fellow's affliction; although he seemed to have managed well enough so far—had been, in fact, quite the model pupil, if all Cousin Levina's talk of prizes for Latin and Greek and Mathematics was to be believed… Not that Oxford—or Cambridge, for that matter—was the Be-all and End-all of learning. Well-equipped as these institutions were for the rigours of scientific study—with the richer colleges vying with each other, it was said, in the building of observatories and the setting up of scholarships for astronomical research—university life, in Edward's opinion, was no substitute for the real thing.

He himself had not been to university, but had never felt the lack of it, having enjoyed the society of learned men from his earliest years. Messier, Magellan, Maskelyne—these had been his mentors, and the companions of his youth. When he was just nineteen, he had been presented, with his father, to Prince Charles of Lorraine, and to the Prime Minister of that region, Prince Staremberg. The following year, he and his father and Father Needham had carried out the most detailed cartographic survey ever made of the country between Namur and Brussels.

At the age of nineteen, he had surveyed the mouth of the River Severn—a significant achievement not only in itself, but because the accurate maps he was able to draw up as a result would help prevent the wrecks which, whether resulting from human error or malicious design, were such a feature of that treacherous shore. The accurate measurement of the Newton well was another of his successes—one he owed, in no small part, to the excellence of his new Ramsden barometer.

Nor had he neglected the stars, during these youthful researches. With Herschel, he had observed the moons of Jupiter, at Bath; and—the proudest moment of his life up to that point—had discovered a nebula in Coma Berenices, which even the great Lalande had failed to see.

He does not think he could have spent his time better, had he attended fifty universities.

York, by comparison with Paris or Brussels, could not but seem provincial.

'*There is not a soul to converse with here*,' he wrote to Herschel.

It was scientific conversation he meant—for there was no shortage of the other kind. Conversations about hunting—which interested him not at all; about parties—ditto; about his marital intentions—worst of all.

'Come, Mr Edward—surely you are not going to keep us waiting forever?' Lady Fothergill had cried, shaking her white head at him, so that the jewels on her wrinkled neck scintillated in the light. 'You are breaking the hearts of all the unmarried young ladies in Yorkshire, with your stand-offish ways. Can it be,' simpered the old horror, 'that you think our home-grown misses not fine enough for you? Perhaps'—a dreadful leer—"some Parisian *coquette* has already captured your affections?'

He had protested—No, no, certainly not! All the young ladies he had met so far in York were extremely charming, and the equal (if not indeed superior) in every respect, to the French version—but in his heart he had wanted to murder the interfering crone.

His father had of course been one of the company—a small but *intime* gathering at Fairfax House, of which Cousin Anne Fairfax was the hostess, in name at least. In fact it was his father's party—one of a series intended to introduce the newly-arrived Pigott family to York society, to maximum effect, and minimum cost, to himself.

'Never fear, Madam! My son will make a grandfather of me yet—and an honest woman of some lucky lass!' he had quipped, to general laughter.

Only when the carriage was being brought round afterwards, did he allow his displeasure full rein: 'In two years' time you will be thirty. At your age, I already had two sons and another in pod. Surely it is not beyond your wit'—this with Edward's mother standing by—'to find a girl you can bring yourself to fuck, with a nice little dowry to sweeten the pill?'

Nor had the subject been allowed to rest there. With his father, such matters were never allowed to rest. There had been talk of unnatural sons, betraying their Catholic heritage by refusing to breed; of filial ingratitude, and—a favourite theme—disinheritance. 'For if you will not do your duty as a man,' Nathaniel Pigott had said, with a particular emphasis on the last word, 'then I must look to your brother. He, at least, is not afraid of the female sex...'

This topic had been returned to, with increasing vehemence, in the years that followed—culminating at last in the threatened re-drafting of the will in Charles Gregory's favour. Not that he—Edward—blamed his brother for what had happened.

> My father since these few years has taken the greatest antipathy towards me, which at present is arrived at such a pitch that I have the strongest reasons to be assured that he has disinherited me

Edward wrote to Lady Anne Fairfax.

> Such an injustice can only be rectified by you...

Although she, poor lady, was much too taken up with her prayers and priests to give much thought to the financial troubles of a distant cousin.

It had been another year before the final rift between father and son had taken place, and then it had not been Edward's conduct which had occasioned it, but that of his sister. Having a namby-pamby for a son was bad enough, in Nathaniel Pigott's opinion; but to have been defied by that son in the matter of a daughter's obedience, he would not brook. Let them both go to the D—-l. He would settle his money on his remaining child. He, though just eighteen, was already man enough to know his duty. When Cousin Levina's girl was of age—the pretty one, not the bluestocking—they would arrange a marriage. There would be Pigotts again at Gilling Castle, if he had anything to do with it...

From Louvain, Edward had written again to Lady Anne, begging her to intervene on his behalf—but to no avail. She did only what her Confessor, Father Bolton, advised, and he—doubtless still smarting from the rancorous encounters he had had over the years with Nathaniel Pigott—appeared to have advised caution in the matter of anyone, however unfairly treated, who bore that surname.

> My father's despotism hatred and injustice are beyond conception; my peace and health are destroyed, my mother (the best of women) has been strongly affected and is now dangerously ill...

At the thought of his mother, his throat tightens, and—even after the passage of so many years—he feels the gathering of moisture in his nose and eyes which is the prelude to tears. Poor Maman! She—as much as he himself—had been the innocent victim of his father's intemperance. The cruel loss of both daughter and son in the space of a few months was a blow from which she had never recovered.

'*Mon cher fils*,' had been her last, whispered, words to him, as she lay dying. '*Je t'implore… garde ta soeur auprès de toi… parce qu'elle n'a personne d'autre que toi dans le monde…*'

Well, he had done what he could—although it was not much. But then, there was not much that could be done, that was the truth of it. She—Mathurina—was as headstrong, in her way, as their father. Knowing, as she must have done, the likely consequences of her actions, still she had not held back. The result had been disaster—as much for him, as for anyone…

He draws the silk handkerchief from his sleeve and blows his nose. Then, with a sigh, he continues leafing through the pile of notebooks which lie before him, all out of order as to date and the significance or otherwise of their contents. In truth they should all be burned, and have done with it…

Here is one, headed Louvain, September 1773. He had been twenty—a mere boy. Already a devotee of the astronomical art—poor deluded devil. Here are lists, and more lists, of all his observations that year:

Noms des étoiles qui apparaissent périodiquement
Étoiles doubles
Nebuleuses

Here are descriptions, some illustrated with deft pen drawings (a skill which had stood him in good stead during his brief career as a surveyor) of planets, sun-spots, and the aurora borealis… He picks up another notebook, headed Bath, 1778. His first visit to Herschel—here misspelled 'Herchell' at New King Street.

> The following Observations were made at Mr Herchells, King Street: the instruments made use of were, a Clock with a Second hand, a Quadrant for Equal altitudes, very indifferent, tho sufficient for to get the Noon to 4 or 6 Sec-

onds or Still more exactly; the Tellescope very Good. April the 12th/Em: of Jupiter's Second Sat: by Clock at 7h.48'29" I Observed with the Trib: Ob: Achro: No.3/ the same Observation by Mr Herchell 7.48.36 with an exceedingly good Reflector...

There follow further pages of notes. His stay in Bath had lasted almost a month, on that occasion. Here are lists of variable stars, taken from the *Philosophical Transactions* and Lalande's catalogue; lists of double stars—and a note on the unreliability of Tycho Brahe's observations for purposes of comparison. Here, too, is a detailed account of the situation of certain nebulae not found by Messier...

'But that is very remarkable,' had been Miss Herschel's response, when he told her of his latest findings. 'To have discovered so many previously unknown objects...'

Her face had been alight with the passionate interest she always took in such matters; unless it was his presence which inspired the interest, although it seemed presumptuous—if not unfeeling—to think so.

He had made some reply. It hardly mattered what. Everything he said she received with the same rapt attention.

Certainly he was aware that Herschel's sister—'that funny little German frump', as he had once heard her described—held him in some regard. Of course, as her brother's friend, his place in her affections was already secure, for her admiration—one might say, her *adulation*—of her elder sibling knew no bounds. But—and here Edward has to admit to a degree of discomfort, in respect of his own conduct—there was more to Caroline Herschel's feelings towards him than sisterly affection.

During those three-and-a-half weeks he spent in Bath in the summer of 1778, he had seen Miss Herschel, and her brother, almost every day. They had spent much of that time star-gazing, for Herschel had by this time set up the first of his twenty-foot telescopes. His conversations with Caroline Herschel, during these late-night sessions, had necessarily been limited to astronomical matters. But the terseness of these exchanges did not preclude other—silent—forms of communication; looks, sighs, brief moments when shoulders brushed, or hands touched across the instruments...

After he got to know John Goodricke, he became more attuned to different kinds of silence—but even then, he was experienced enough to recognise that it could denote intimacy, or the wish for it.

Only a fool or an insensitive clod could have failed to notice the way Miss Herschel blushed when he walked into the room, or the little adjustments she had made, as to dress and hair, after their first meeting, which seemed intended to show her to best advantage. One day, a drab dress would have been enlivened by a new lace fichu; another would see a red ribbon tied into her curls.

These and other little vanities might have passed unnoticed however, if their wearer's behaviour had not betrayed evidence of a similar alteration: the inability to speak more than a few coherent sentences when he was in the room being one of them; a tendency to secret smiles and glances, when she thought no one was looking, being another.

Herschel of course, was oblivious to all this—although even he was driven to remark on the vast improvement in dear Lina's cooking, and to say that they must certainly invite their good friend Pigott again, if this was the effect his presence had on their domestic economy. Why, Lina could conjure a feast out of nothing, it seemed! Scraps and leavings that even a dog would disdain were turned, by her expert hand, into dishes fit for a king...

Edward, who suspected that considerably more than scraps and leavings had gone into the making of their dinner on that occasion, could not forbear from glancing at his hostess. The mixture of affectionate regard and amusement he saw upon her face struck him as entirely admirable, as did the slight widening of the eyes with which she met his look—an injunction to silence, that seemed to seal their complicity.

For an instant, the woman she was looked out from behind the demure mask, and enjoyed—albeit tenderly—the joke at her brother's expense. Then she recollected herself, and who she was with; coloured faintly, and rose to clear the plates.

Sitting over his wine, as Herschel expounded some theory or other about the varying magnitudes of stars, it struck him—not for the first time—that Miss Herschel was in love with him. It was not a thought from which he derived much pleasure.

But what was he to do? It was not his fault that he could not love her. He knew only too well that such things cannot be compelled.

He thinks of the night he had gone to hear her sing, at the Assembly Rooms in Bath; even then, he had deliberated with himself beforehand as to whether or not his attendance might be misconstrued. But then, Herschel had been so insistent: *Of course you must come! We shall expect you*... And he had always been a lover of music.

So he had gone, and Miss Herschel had sung—he had been surprised and pleased to discover how good she was. Indeed, her whole demeanour that night had been a revelation. From the shy little mouse, with hardly a word to say for herself, she seemed transformed into a creature of another kind... a lark, or a nightingale, he remembers thinking. Then, too, there was the way she looked that night—quite the picture of elegance, he recalls, in her black silk gown.

But it was when she began to sing, that she seemed most altered—as if the beauty of the music had transferred itself to her face and form. Radiant. That was the word for her. Like a star that was once eclipsed, and now shines brighter and brighter. Although it was not the music alone, he knew, which had brought that glow to her cheeks, and that smile to her eyes...

Then there had been that time at the ball, a few nights later, when he had asked her to dance. He had had little choice in the matter, as it happened, for to have failed to ask her would have been a cruelty of a different kind.

So they had danced—she was a good dancer and as light as a feather, he remembers—and he had returned her to her brothers with a heavy heart. *Do not look at me like that, with your eyes full of stars*, he had wanted to tell her. *For I cannot love you.*

But that was something that could never be said.

No, if he has reason for self-reproach, as far as his colleague's sister is concerned, it is not because he had been unable to return her feelings, but that, being all too aware of them, he had been unable to spare her the pain of his presence, on occasion. But to have done so, would have been to deny himself the pleasure, not only of Herschel's company, but of her own.

If he could not offer her love, he could offer her friendship; but that was both too little, and too much.

He had called at New King Street on one occasion, a week or so after the ball, to return a paper he had borrowed from Herschel. They had been star-gazing the night before, and indeed, the one before that—the weather having been unusually mild for April. The door was answered by Miss Herschel, who was dressed as if for going out, with a large basket over her arm, suitable for marketing.

'Mr Pigott.' Her face had brightened at the sight of him; then as swiftly grown subdued. 'I will call my brother. He is in his study, I believe...'

'I pray you, do not trouble him. I have merely come to return this.'

He handed her the volume of *Philosophical Transactions*.

'But you are to join us later, are you not?' she said, then blushed.

He pretended not to see the blush.

'O indeed. I would not miss an evening's star-gazing for the world...'

'The evening will be fine, I think.'

I *sink*. He suppressed a smile at her quaint pronunciation.

'Let us hope so. We had excellent views of Beta Cygni the night before last.'

'Yes.'

'But you were about to go out—I am keeping you,' he said.

'It is of no consequence. Only...' She looked abashed. 'Some items I must fetch from the Apothecary's...'

'May I go with you? It is on my way,' he added, seeing that she was about to demur.

'O...' Her eyes grew very bright. 'Thank you,' she said.

Then she said nothing more until they reached the intersection with Charles Street.

'I have been thinking…'—*sinking*— 'about variable stars,' she said at last.

'Indeed?'

What a strange little creature she was, he thought. By turns so shy, and so self-assured.

'I suppose there are many such? I mean, apart from those already noted…'

'Very many, I believe. I do not think they have all been examined yet.'

They had skirted Queen Square, and now found themselves in Milsom Street. Here, the numbers of people going in and out of shops were greater, and they were obliged to weave their way between them.

'They have been catalogued, I suppose?'

'By Maraldi and Montanari.' He took her arm, to draw her out of harm's way, as a curricle, driven at reckless speed by its owner—some spoilt young blade—dashed by. 'Bayer also lists them.'

'But no complete list has been compiled as yet?'

They had ascended the street, passing hat shops, and haberdasher's shops, and Mollond's the pastrycook, and now arrived in front of the Apothecary's. The red and green bottles, with which it advertised its business, gleamed, from its shadowy interior, like little moons.

'Not to my knowledge.'

'Then,' she said, smiling up at him. 'I must lose no time in compiling one.'

He could not have been more astonished when she proved as good as her word. On his next visit to Bath, a year later, she had presented him with a complete catalogue of all the known variable stars—including, of course, those that he himself had discovered.

If he had been in any doubt that she was in love with him before that moment, he no longer doubted it from then on.

Variable stars. Had that been the moment for her—as it was for him, three years later—when she knew that everything had changed forever? The end of the fixed universe—and with it, of all certainty…

At the time, he had had no idea how far-reaching his findings were to be. Not that he was the first to observe that some stars are fixed, whilst others vary. Tycho Brahe had observed this, two centuries before—although, admittedly, it had taken him a while to recognise what it was that he had seen. But then, people see what they want, or expect, to see. When the evidence of their eyes contradicts not only what they expect, but the principles upon which the whole of existence is based, it can take some getting used to…

Because once you introduce the notion of change, it affects everything.

Of course, when he began it, he had no notion of any of this. It was just a task he had set himself; an intellectual game. That the game would end up taking over not only his life, but the lives of those he loved most: the Herschels, brother and sister; his own sister, Mathurina; and the man they both loved above all others—was something he could not, in that bright careless dawn, have predicted.

XXIV

Notebooks, and more notebooks…

Here are pages of observations, made over several years, and from various locations: Bath, London, Glamorganshire, Paris, and York. *Ideas leading to Inventions or Discoveries for the Time measurer at sea*; ideas for the construction of a more powerful telescope; and for measuring the mountains of the Moon. Lists (always lists!) of catalogues of fixed stars—Flamsteed's, Bradley's—and lists of magnitudes of stars, fixed and variable.

Here is a note on Herschel's Comet—or what was thought to be a comet; it proved, in fact, to be something far more singular:

> Herchell's Comet [again that quaint misspelling!] is at an immense distance far beyond Saturn, and possibly may be a 7th Planet…

That entry is headed York, August 17th 1781; on 3rd November of that year he had written:

> Examined the stars in the Swans head & neck for near an hour, with one of Dollonds Opera Glass's… Seeked for the Nova near the head, of 1670, but saw no stars equal to the Alpha or Epsilon that could possibly be it.

On November 14th:

> At 9 o'clock p.m., I discovered a Comet near the neck of the Swan…

He had immediately sent a note round to Goodricke. On the few occasions they had conversed (if conversation was the right word for a dialogue conducted almost entirely in writing), his cousin had displayed more than a passing interest in such matters. The stars, he confessed, had been a subject of fascination to him since he was a child. Sadly, he had no instrument worth the name to carry out his observations—a pair of Opera Glasses and a construction of his own devising made from spectacle lenses, having sufficed until now…

Touched by the younger man's evident enthusiasm, Edward had offered him the loan of one of his own telescopes. 'For, you know, in our house we have many—my father never having stinted himself in astronomical matters…'

You are fortunate, then, had been the dry response.

Edward looked at his cousin. Was there something ever-so-slightly mocking about that glance?

'I assure you," he said stiffly, 'I am only too aware of my good fortune. Indeed, my father never ceases to remind me of it.'

The youth was watching his lips as he spoke—a strangely voluptuous experience; now, he looked up, and met Edward's eyes. Was there contrition in those pale blue orbs, or did Edward imagine it?

I meant only that you are fortunate in having not only an intimate knowledge of the heavens, but the instruments to further that knowledge.

It was gracefully put, and Edward inclined his head in acknowledgement of the fact.

'Astronomy has many pleasures—not least that of solitary observation. But there are times, in science as in life, when one longs for a companionable spirit. I cannot test my theories alone, for then they are mere speculation, not corroborated fact. If you are willing, there is much we might explore together…'

Already, the boy was scribbling a reply.

I can think of nothing I should like more.

'That is settled, then,' said Edward.

So it began: the almost daily meetings; the—often hourly—exchanges of notes, comparing this set of observations or that. The varying magnitudes of stars were what occupied them, mostly; each as determined as the other to familiarise himself with all that the heavens might contain, by process of slow, painstaking, effort. If a comet might have been said to have brought them together, there was nothing comet-like about the relationship which ensued. The brief flaring of passion, leading swiftly to oblivion—a trajectory with which Edward was all too familiar—did not describe his association with John Goodricke. No. On his side, at least, it burned with a steadier flame. Constant as the fixed stars.

If there were variations in its magnitude, these were the result of circumstance. The fact that the Beloved was entirely unaware that he *was* beloved, being the most intractable of these.

The frustrations of this state of affairs were compensated for, in no small degree, by the unrestricted access to the Beloved's time and attention he was privileged to have, as a consequence of the studies on which both were now engaged. For no sooner had he proposed the topic—a logical development from his comparison of Montanari's and Maraldi's respective catalogues of variable stars—than his young companion had seized upon it with alacrity. The variable stars in Cygnus—the very same ones Miss Herschel had identified, three years before, in Bath—were their first joint venture in observing; by Christmas 1782, a new star had swum into view.

On 28th December, Edward wrote:

> Algol... at 5h p.m.... this Star being discovered to be Variable, by Montanary and Maraldi, I began, on 23rd October, to examine it... & have continued ever since when was not otherwise engaged—on the 12th Novemr Mr J Goodricke told me he had found it the preceding night, only of the 3d Magde:

—here, he inserted the extract from Goodricke's journal, in which the latter had set out his findings. Their synchronicity with his own had moved him deeply, when he first saw it.

As if their two minds, working in harmony, had become one mind...

> every night since I have been very attentive in examining it, and saw no alteration, not even on 23d, 24th & 26th but this night found it about the 3d or 4th Magde: having the same brightness and colour as Delta Persei, rather less bright than Gamma Persei & Beta Trianguli; also of the

> same brightness as Rho Medusa tho of a whiter colour; & less bright than Epsilon Persei—it seem'd to vary, sometimes appearing rather brighter and sometimes rather less bright than Rho Medusa…

'I believe,' he said, scarcely able to contain his excitement, 'we are on to something.'

As he spoke, Goodricke had observed him with that charming attention, of which, even after their acquaintance had ripened into friendship, he could never tire. The way the other's gaze followed the movements of his lips had the feel of a caress (although he knew it was not). The slight shifting of that gaze upwards to meet his own, when he had finished speaking, felt more intimate than a kiss…

Not that he ever dared to hope for an answering response in the pale blue eyes, which now regarded him so levelly. Once or twice he thought he detected something—a considering look—as if the other guessed his thoughts, but knew not how to address them. But such moments were rare, and, by their nature, fleeting. A shadow of a doubt; an unanswered, and unanswerable, question. Nor did Edward—used as he was to disguising his feelings—permit himself to express such thoughts very often.

Only when he was certain—Goodricke's back being turned—that no one but himself would hear, did he allow his passion free rein.

'I love you. You are dearer to me than life itself,' he had said once, thinking himself safe; and then had been startled when Goodricke had turned from the window, smiling—a response occasioned (of course!) not by his imprudent words, but by Mathurina's arrival, at their garden gate…

Mathurina. How blind he had been, not to see what was happening in front of him! All those months that he and Goodricke were so engrossed together had offered the perfect opportunity for his sister and his friend to pursue their affair undetected. Besotted as he was, it had never even occurred to him that either could have had the remotest interest in the other. Was she not three years older than he? A grown woman, with a husband, too; while Goodricke was a mere boy. They had nothing, it seemed to him, in common—except himself. And yet their love had been fulfilled, where his had not…

Blind. He had been blind. Egotistical. Foolish. The variable brilliance of Algol, demon star, had dazzled him, and taken away his reason.

Of course the discovery had properly been his—or (since Algol had previously been identified as variable by Montanari and the rest) the *confirmation* of that discovery had been his; although it was Goodricke's, and not his, observations that decided the matter. His explanation of the phenomenon, too, had turned out to be the correct one; even though, for a time, he had concurred with Goodricke in putting forward an alternative hypothesis.

> Algol, having, on further consideration

—he wrote, on January 2nd 1783 (excitement making him unusually incoherent)—

> stronger reasons to believe that what I wrote to Mr J. Goodricke on 19th Decemr 1782 may possibly happen, induces me to make the following memorandum of it—the opinion I suggested was, that the alteration of Algol's brightness, was maybe occasioned by a Planet, of about half his size, revolving round him, and therefore does sometimes eclipse him partially…

For he was increasingly convinced that the Star's periodic increase and diminution of magnitude were the result of its being eclipsed by another star. He remembers demonstrating the phenomenon with the aid of an orange, and an apple, one night as the two of them sat over their wine at dinner.

'If we suppose *this*'—the orange—'to be the brighter of our two stars, and this'—here, he passed the apple in front of it—'to be the dimmer article, then our observations make perfect sense…'

Until one of us eats the apple, Goodricke had scribbled upon the tablecloth; before suiting the action to the words.

No, there was no doubt that the glory of Algol and variable stars belonged by right to him. Goodricke had been no more than the facilitator of that glory. An able assistant, at best... That, Edward suspected, was Herschel's opinion—although the latter had never gone as far as to say so. Because who knew better than Herschel, his old collaborator, how much time Edward had devoted to variable stars? Three years before, he—Edward—had laid eyes on John Goodricke, he and Herschel, and Caroline Herschel too, for that matter, had been deep into the subject. Indeed, if anyone apart from Edward himself deserved the glory of that discovery (why not call it such?) it was Herschel.

Had not Herschel—some might say prematurely—read a paper on his own observations of Algol's changes to a group of learned gentlemen at the Crown & Anchor, a full two weeks before Goodricke presented his own paper at the Royal Society? This had occasioned some resentment on Goodricke's part (the first and only time Edward had seen his friend betray signs of *amour propre*): 'I cannot believe that he would do such a thing,' he had written, with unusual fierceness. 'Surely the great Herschel, Discoverer of Planets, has no need to purloin another man's research for his greater glory?'

It had been a source of private amusement to Edward (then lately returned from France) to find Goodricke so incensed over the matter. For was not he himself—Goodricke, that is—profiting from another man's research—that is, Edward's? To be fair to Goodricke, he had never ceased to protest against the unfairness of the thing, and to point out their joint responsibility for Algol's discovery. But he was a young man, and young men are susceptible to vanity—especially when, as was certainly the case with Goodricke, they know themselves to be deserving of notice. And so, although he protested at first, he did not let his chagrin at his friend's having been neglected in his favour interfere unduly with his enjoyment of his triumph.

To be introduced all over London as "Mr Goodricke, the astronomer—discoverer of Variable Stars," would have turned the head of even the most modest of men. To shake the hand of Maskelyne, and Messier, and Banks, and know himself their equal—that, too, was an honour not to be taken lightly. For Edward, it was enough to know that his Beloved enjoyed such honours and triumphs—the highest accolades afforded by their profession. That he enjoyed them at Edward's expense made it seem all the sweeter.

The matter had been smoothed over, of course, and the ill-tempered note thrown in the fire—but not before Edward had written to Herschel, on Goodricke's behalf, in order to obtain a fuller account of the unfortunate affair. In his reply, Herschel had not attempted to disguise his hurt feelings. That an old friend should suspect him of plagiarism—it was too much!

> May 20, 1783
> Datchet, near Windsor
>
> Sir,
>
> I have the favour of your letter and will give you the history of my little paper which will certainly clear me of every intention of giving offence with it...

The first indication that he had received of the discovery was from Dr Maskelyne, he said—with an injunction not to mention it to anyone till it was published.

> Accordingly I kept it to myself till I had notice of it from Sir Joseph Banks, without any form of direction to keep it from others...

He had, by this time, made his own observations of the phenomenon (he supplied a detailed account of these).

> Having occasion to go to London on Thursday I drew up my observations on Algol that morning and put them in my pocket, with an intention to show them to my astronomical friends...

On arriving in town around four o'clock, he went immediately to the Crown & Anchor (favourite haunt of the astronomers), where

> Several gentlemen expressed a desire of hearing it, and—accordingly—Sir J Banks read it after dinner…

The note of dignified reproof with which he concluded had conveyed the great astronomer's displeasure all too clearly:

> Thus you see Sir that the paper was read without the least thoughts on my part of any paper of Mr Goodricke's. It was an affair publickly known, so that I might naturally suppose some paper of yours or Mr Goodriks had been communicated upon the subject. My reason for endeavouring immediately to verify the Phonomenon was first of all my love for Astronomy; in the 2d place to pay a proper attention to new facts and to the discoverer of them…

It had almost been the end of their friendship. Fortunately, he had been able to enlist Caroline Herschel's help, in soothing the distinguished astronomer's ruffled pride. He recalls the time they had all met at the Royal Society, at the reading of Goodricke's paper on Beta Lyrae—the last time, as it turned out, that his brilliant young protégé set foot inside those hallowed halls… What might have been an awkward encounter between the elder astronomer and his young rival had been smoothed over, by Miss Herschel's intervention.

Her unexpected appearance in their midst (which had caused angry muttering amongst some of the Fellows) had been entirely auspicious, where he—and Goodricke—were concerned.

Afterwards, the latter had remarked on the lady's good nature, and intelligence.

'I am glad you liked her so much, for I like her very much myself,' he had replied. 'Although I am amazed you were able to discover her character, in so short an acquaintance,' he could not resist adding.

One can discover a great deal from looking at a face, was his friend's reply.

'Then you can never have looked closely enough at mine,' he had been tempted to reply, but did not. Perhaps it was as well that hearts could not always be read in faces.

He thinks of the time they climbed to the top of the Minster tower, stepping out onto the roof in the blaze of starlight. The leads had been slippery underfoot; he had put out his hand to steady his friend's progress, and their hands had inadvertently touched.

Whilst Goodricke had been engaged looking through the telescope, Edward had taken the opportunity to say what was in his heart.

'If you knew how much I care for you, you would have pity on me. For no man can love as I do, and not feel the desire to be loved in return.'

Goodricke had raised his eyes at last, and smiling, gestured towards the glass, as if to invite his friend to take his turn. Edward had done so; and there it was: the Jovian planet and its four Galilean moons, endlessly revolving in its orbit.

'So must I circle around you,' murmured Edward. 'For that is my Destiny. I can no more escape it than Callisto, Io, Europa or Ganymede can escape the pull of yonder great glittering silver orb...'

In a sudden access of freakish spirits, he flung out his arms and cried, 'I embrace my Destiny!'

When he turned back to the glass again, Goodricke was regarding him with a quizzical air.

That night was the nearest he ever came to declaring his love. He wonders now, with hindsight, whether to have done so—rash and foolish as it would have been—might not have served to prevent the catastrophe which followed.

In silent condemnation of the dust and disturbance all this shifting about of papers has brought to the room, the cat, which has been sunning itself upon the windowsill, now leaps upon the table, and, after walking up and down a few times to indicate its displeasure, sits down upon a pile of papers, and regards him gravely with its beautiful, pale green eyes.

‘I know, I know,’ he murmurs, meeting that calm, unblinking gaze. ‘It is dinner time.’

Having achieved what it had set out to do, the animal—a pretty red queen, which he had named Callisto—turns its back on him, and begins, with deft deliberation, to wash its face.

After his beloved Fop had died, he could not have borne to get another dog. A cat could not love in the same way; its affections were governed solely by self-interest. Although he had known a few of his own kind of whom the same could be said.

XXV

He had not known, when first he came to move to Bath, that his wanderings—like those of the unhappy Jew, he sometimes thinks—were almost at an end. For since that time—and with one particular exception—he has not left the city for more than a few days. And whilst it is true that he has not given up his peripatetic habits entirely, having changed his lodgings several times—from St James's Square to Belmont and from thence to Rivers Street—he can certainly, after five-and-twenty years, consider himself an established resident. Not that the city's celebrated amusements mean much to him, these days. He no longer cares for dancing. Card-playing, once his delight, has long ceased to tempt him. He cannot not recall the last time he set foot in the Pump Room, or went to the theatre. His circle of acquaintance grows smaller by the year...

Quite what had prompted him to return, after an absence almost as long, to the city, where, at twenty-five, he had spent a few pleasant weeks, he cannot say. Perhaps it was simply the memory of that happy state—when his heart had been free and his passions engaged only with the Heavens—which drew him back; the echo of those long-ago conversations with Herschel and his sister, in the garden at New King Street. It was this, no doubt, which prompted him to write, as soon as he was settled in his new abode, to notify his friends of his changed address, as well as of his continued interest in matters astronomical:

Bath—St James's Square No. 37
Oct: 22d 1796

My Dear Sir

An <u>old correspondent</u>, with much pleasure takes up again his pen to acquaint you with some Astronomical discoveries he has made: he would have written sooner, but being very desirous of perusing your last paper on the manner of Observing the Mag.des of the Stars, occasioned his waiting until now; that paper is not yet to be had at

> Bath, he therefore will no longer defer writing, as the Stars he is going to mention are approaching the Sun: they have never been examined with any magnifying powers, which may perhaps induce our Eminent Astronomer to inspect them, & which would please greatly the discoverer—

The discoveries in question were his observations on the periodical changes of magnitude in the stars in Coronae Borealis and Sobieski's Shield (the latter named by Hevelius in honour of the King of Poland); he later sent a paper to the Royal Society. It struck him, as he was writing, as a pleasing example of the Synchronism which governed so much of life, that the topic on which he now addressed his old friend was that which had brought them together: the variable brightness of stars.

After a detailed account of his findings, he had concluded with what had now become a joke between them—for Herschel, of course, was famously reluctant to leave Slough. He was too wedded to his books and his comforts—not least those provided by the estimable Mrs Herschel—to risk the dirt and discomfort of the public highway.

> I must now reproach you for not coming to Bath as you had given us to expect and hope you have not entirely set aside that intention...

Nor, he guesses, was it just the unpleasantness of the journey which deterred the great astronomer from returning to his old home. Herschel, Edward surmises, was one of those for whom the past held no interest. Former triumphs, whether musical or astronomical, were not to be revisited; nor need the disappointments and set-backs which preceded them be brought again to mind. The past was dead and buried; all that concerned the thinking man was the Here and Now. It was, Edward thinks, an eminently Rational philosophy; unfortunately, it was one he could not share. For what was his own life but a sequence of variations upon past themes: a turning, and re-turning, to one time, one place, one kindred Soul?

He had acquired a portable Sissons transit from Sir William Musgrave the summer of his arrival in Bath, and it was with this that he resumed his long-interrupted researches into variable stars. Here—unlike London, with its smoke and glare—the skies were dark, and frequently clear, for the county was known for the prevailing mildness of its climate. This proved all the more to be the case once one had quitted Bath itself for the open country.

One afternoon in mid-December—it was that of the Solstice—he had ridden out to Salisbury plain, with his instruments following behind in the cart with the servant. The Sun was setting as they reached the place, which, in that blood-red illumination, seemed all the more imbued with awful power.

Wandering amongst the great stones, which, some said, were the portals of an ancient temple, he reflected on what kind of men they were who had built such an edifice. Stukeley had called them Druids—worshippers of the Sun. For were not these stones a giant sundial, by which the Seasons of that Star might be measured? He and the great Halley had aligned the monument with Magnetic North, alleging that its builders were familiar with the principle. Certainly its circular form suggested the clock, or astrolabe. Although seeing it now—its stones looming blackly against the blazing sky—it was hard not to feel that the place had been designed for some occult purpose, quite apart from the rational investigations of Science.

Nor would its ghosts give up their secrets too readily to one such as himself. For what was he? A Believer, who no longer believed in anything. A Rationalist, whose Reason, long ago, had been overturned by Passion.

The sky turned from scarlet to orange, from orange to rose, and from rose to deepest violet. A Symphony in Colour, he thought, his eyes growing dim with the emotion which the contemplation of Beauty always aroused in him. He gazed until the light was gone, and the first stars were winking palely from the dark blue firmament. A temple; a sundial; a celestial clock—it could be any of these, or none…

A figure moved between the standing stones, and he felt his heart jump. But it was only Silas, come to tell him that the telescope was now set up, and a saucepan of coffee brewed.

So it was that what he sometimes thinks of as his 'posthumous' life began. For was it not a kind of death, to have lost all that gave life meaning?

Since there is no help for it, he must—painfully, slowly—build his life again, from the shards that are left: his stars and comets; his seaweeds (for he is amassing a respectable collection); his friends (but not lovers; he has done with love); his cat; his books; his cellar of fine wines; his notebooks; his letters; his memories of everything he has lost.

His poor sister! It has been five years since he since he last beheld her face. Since her return to Belgium in '98, when it had had been judged safe for the Good Sisters to return to their former home, he has seen her only intermittently—an infrequency at least in part occasioned by the hostilities which have existed, in one form or another, for most of the past twenty years, between England and France. The ostensible purpose of at least one of these visits was astronomical: a series of observations he was making on the physical causes of variable stars. His theory, reached after years of speculation, was that the bodies of the stars themselves were dark and solid, but that it was the luminous particles surrounding them, which caused their brightness to vary.

He was to give a paper in Paris on the subject, the following week.

Such matters could not have been further from his thoughts as he entered that cheerless cell, where Mathurina—now Soeur Marie-Mathieu—sat waiting for him, with all the bright beauty she had once possessed extinguished beneath a shroud of black, and her fiery spirit quenched by her seventeen years' incarceration.

They had begun by speaking of various matters: their father's worsening state of health; and his obdurate refusal, even in the face of Death, to receive his elder son.

'Father was never one to change his mind, once he had reached a decision,' she said.

She had asked after Charles Gregory, marvelling that the brother she had last seen as a young man—'caring for nothing but cards and dancing'—was now a father of four. Of her sister-in-law, she remarked only that it did not surprise her that Mary should have got exactly what she wanted—which was Gilling Castle, and the Fairfax money, as well as all the rest. That Mary, her dead beloved's sister, should have achieved all that she had not, was something she did not have to say.

A silence fell as each considered the subject which was uppermost in both their minds.

She had looked at him for a long moment without speaking. Then:

'Tell me,' she said in a low voice, 'How was my beloved child, when you saw her last?'

Ten years had passed, during which time she had grown from a child into a young woman; still, it was a shock to see how like her mother she had become. The pale oval of her face; her narrow shoulders, and slender waist—above all, the expression in her large dark eyes, all brought Mathurina to mind...

Of her father, there were fewer traces, even though she was now, at seventeen, only a year older than he had been the first time Edward saw him. But that she was her mother's girl—glancing up from her sewing when the Mother Superior ushered him into the room, in just the same quick nervous way—there was no doubt.

Was she happy? he asked her. Did she like school? Did the nuns treat her well? To all of which she answered in the affirmative.

In her modest white frock and cap, she might have been a young nun herself, with an air of submissiveness, which struck him as both touching and sad. It was, he thought, as if all the life had been drilled and catechized out of her.

Only when—despairing of getting any further response from her—apart from these nods and smiles and shyly lowered eyes—he asked her what she liked best of all about school, did she surprise him.

'I am fond of singing,' she said, a smile brightening the soft contours of her face. 'And drawing, and Composition. But most of all, I like Mathematics.'

Ah, then it was that he caught a glimpse of her father…

With hindsight, the year '03 had not been the most propitious time for visiting Paris.

The war, which had been threatening to begin for some months, had now begun. To be travelling in the cause of scientific endeavour was no defence, it appeared. Nor did Edward's French birth and his command of the language save him from being arrested as a spy; in fact it made him more of a suspect, his captors said.

'You expect us to believe, M'sieur, that your reason for visiting France at this time has only to do with the stars?'

The young lieutenant had scarcely been able to conceal his incredulity at the notion.

'There is no other reason.'

'But M'sieur…'

Now it was the turn of the other man to speak—a civilian, by his dress, and older by some years than the young officer. Infinitely more dangerous, too, Edward saw, as the interrogator held him with his cold blue eye. An eye that, ten years back, would have gazed without mercy on any Citizen or Citizeness unfortunate enough to have been brought before the Committee.

His name, he said, was Dupont—a lie, Edward thought. Such a man would have a number of aliases, the better to prosecute his nefarious ends.

'You say you are to give a paper at the Institute in Paris? Why, then, did you not go straight to Paris on your arrival in Calais six days ago?'

He had smiled as he said this, and Edward had felt a twinge of unease. It had not occurred to him until then that he might have been followed.

'That is easily explained.' It would not do to let Dupont—or whatever his name was—see that he was afraid. 'I have a sister in holy orders. She is with the Good Sisters at Brussels…'

Dupont's smile vanished.

'Holy orders, you say? I'll warrant there are some holy traitors amongst that black-clad crew… Priests!' He spat the word out, as if it had a foul taste. 'We had some dealings with priests—aye, and the “good sisters”, too—in the Year Two. Quite a number we sent to perdition—or wherever it is you Believers go—in that year and afterwards...’

Edward had forced himself to keep silent, although he had felt like seizing the villain by the throat. Murdering atheist. It was men like him who had turned France into a charnel-house. Thousands had been slaughtered, for his perverted ideals, and those of his fanatical creed. For all their talk of Virtue and Reason, they had brought nothing but death.

He had been detained three years at Fontainebleau—a strange time, with nothing but his memories for company. He had been allowed writing materials, and so had continued with his paper on luminous particles; but even this could not absorb every waking moment of his time. And so he found himself returning in thought to those few short years in York when Goodricke was alive, and he had been happy... or, if not exactly happy, then at least knowing himself to be alive, with every nerve attuned to the beauty, and brevity, of existence.

What else was being in love, if not that?

The window of his room at the chateau looked out over a strip of grass, with a wall beyond it. Against the wall was a pear-tree, and in Spring, a blackbird had built its nest there. On fine evenings, it liked to sing. He could never hear a blackbird’s song afterwards without thinking of John Goodricke—a curious thing, because Goodricke himself would not have been able to hear it.

When he casts his mind back to that time, it is always a series of pictures that he sees—vignettes, or stage settings, for scenes from his glorious, misspent youth. In these tableaux of dissipation, a smoky light hangs over everything: the ballrooms with their glittering chandeliers, and the women with their fans, and towering headdresses, all intent on watching the play.

A game of Faro: the hands, with their sparkling rings, throwing down the cards.

Dark-red rooms, and dark-green rooms, and rooms papered in yellow ochre. The smell of those rooms! Wax candles (tallow, in the cheaper establishments); perfume; pomade; sweat; spilled wine. Always music playing somewhere—a woman singing (ah, those ethereal sopranos!) or a string quartet, gravely sawing away.

Eyes meeting over the green baize tables. Hands touching, as the cards flash down. Jack, king, queen, in the trembling light that falls from candles in need of trimming.

What it was to be young, twenty years ago, and to have all to play for!

During those three years of his incarceration, he had plenty of time to reflect on the peculiar combination of chance and design which had brought him to this place, and to wonder by what different conjunction of circumstances things might have turned out otherwise.

For it took so very little to change a life. A word could do it; a glance. Even as he sat there, secure in his comfortable cell, with his books about him, a hand was cocking a pistol, or signing a death-warrant. Letters were being written: *I love you; or I do not love you...*

Were these things, as the Ancients believed, determined by the Stars—the happiness or otherwise of lovers, and the peacefulness (or its opposite) of nations, controlled alike by planetary motions—the influence of Venus, or of Mars?

Such ideas were laughed at now, by all but the most credulous and superstitious. But what if there were some truth in the notion, after all? Were there not recurring patterns in the movements of stars and planets which suggested a controlling Intelligence—call it Chance, or Destiny, or what you will?

How little he knew of the workings of the Universe, even now! He had spent his whole life peering at the minutiae of the Solar System, only to find that he did not understand it at all. Was it a Machine—or was it the Mind of God? Was it—as Herschel believed—a vast Laboratory, in which new stars were continually forming out of nebulous gases? Or a garden—to employ another of his distinguished colleague's favourite conceits—in which one might witness the germination, blooming, coming to fruition and withering of stars, as surely as if they had been organisms of the vegetable kingdom?

A laboratory; a garden; an ocean; a desert, perhaps… For there was as yet no proof that any other living thing existed in that wilderness.

Here, in his spacious prison, he toyed with such ideas, for there was little else to occupy his time. As a child, he had interested himself in the *causes* of things. Why is the sky blue? What makes the Sun hot? How is it that we cannot see the Stars during the daytime? Only, when most others put aside such childish questions, to concern themselves with more important matters, he had not.

What makes the stars shine?

That was the question with which he was preoccupied at present.

But there were others:

Why is it so difficult to find one's heart's desire?

—that was another.

Why do Men yearn towards Good, yet so often choose to do Evil?

—that was a third.

Perhaps the ancient Astrologers, with their runes and symbols and star-charts, might have had the answers, he could not say.

He thought, with a kind of terror, 'What is Space but Death?'

A vertiginous emptiness, towards which we all hurtle, in mad headlong flight.

And the Stars… If they were Worlds, as much as this one—then what kind of worlds were they? What freezing cold, beyond any cold found here on Earth; what scorching heat, hotter than that of a million Suns, was to be found there? What clouds of poisonous gases might there be, in place of breathable atmosphere? What mountain ranges, what frozen seas, what deserts—icy or molten—might not constitute their landscapes?

As to the inhabitants of such worlds—if inhabitants there were—it stretched the bounds of Imagination to think of them.

In the more untrammelled of their late-night talks, he and Herschel had often speculated upon the nature and constitution of such Beings. For, said Herschel, it stood to reason, did it not, that in a Universe as vast as this, there must be other Worlds, and other Creatures. He himself believed the Moon to be inhabited.

'Perhaps—and it is not unlikely—the Moon is the planet and the Earth the satellite,' he had said. 'Are we not a larger moon to the Moon, than she is to us?... And what a glorious view of the heavens we should receive from the Moon, were we able to visit it! For my part,' Herschel concluded, with the smile, at once mischievous and childlike, with which he was wont to deliver his more outlandish pronouncements, 'were I to have to choose between the Earth and Moon, I should not hesitate to fix upon the Moon for my habitation.'

At the time, he—Edward—had been inclined to dismiss such notions as romantic folly; now, in the isolation in which he found himself, he was not so sure...

What would they be like, these other-worldly creatures, these Moon-men? Would there ever come a time when one would be able to meet one face to face—as explorers of the New World did their conquered peoples? It was not so very long since Banks, returning from his travels, had brought back Omai, to present him to the King. Might a Moon-dweller, one day, seem no more wonderful than a visiting Tahitian chieftain—albeit come from somewhat further away than a Polynesian isle?

The thought made him smile. An image of this hypothetical luminary, resplendent in a glittering silver robe, as befitted his Lunar origins, rose up before his eyes.

He thought, we are insignificant in the face of all this—the Universe, and all its nebulae. Worlds upon worlds. There is no end to them. Stars being born every second, and dying as rapidly... The vastness of Space. The mind cannot conceive of such Immensity without a shudder.

Herschel had calculated the distance of Uranus from the Sun as more than sixteen times that of Earth. The Universe, said he, was far greater than had been previously suspected. Citing Huygens, he had gone on to speculate that 'it was possible that some of the fixt Stars might be so far from us that their light tho' it travelled ever since the Creation at the inconceivable rate of 12 million of miles per minute, was not yet arrived to us...'

How tiny the Earth was, Edward thought—a speck—in such a sea of emptiness… or rather, not emptiness, but plenitude, since it was swarming with objects of all kinds—stars, comets, nebulae. To know oneself to be surrounded by such a burgeoning of Matter, was at once terrifying and exhilarating—like standing on the edge of a precipice, overlooking an alien landscape. There, in the distance, were the cloud-capped mountains, and shining rivers of this Terra Incognita; below one's feet was the Abyss. One false step, and the viewer—astronomer, poet, call him what you will—would be plunged into endless night. The trick was to keep one's eyes fixed on the horizon…

It did not do to think too much about the Infinite, he concluded.

XXVI

He rings for Silas, and has him bring up the tray; although in truth it is a little early in the day. But he has few vices, now; this one—the pouring of the fine old Tokay, and the consumption of its attendant macaroon biscuits, is not, by any standards, a severe one. Indeed, there would have been times when it would scarcely have been worth the mention, in a catalogue of sins which—whilst by no means of the blackest—were not negligible, either.

'Drinking, gaming, tobacco and whores,' Englefield had once said, 'have been the undoing of me—as they are of most men—although, admittedly, there has been a falling-off in respect of the last-named, of late. Of course *you*, my dear Edward, are much too prudent to have wasted yourself on such things.' Englefield's gaze was fond, but there was a shrewdness in it. '*You* have not indulged in such foolery...'

He had laughed it off at the time, with some remark about how he had been too busy indulging in his own preferred vices—for star-gazing, seaweed collecting and the like—to have had much leisure for anything else. But, as he spoke, he was conscious of not being quite candid with his old friend. How much, he wonders, did Englefield know—or guess—about the clandestine desires which had ruled his life?

And if Harry Englefield *had* known his friend's true nature, would he have shrugged, and made light of it—or would he have recoiled in horror? As well as he knows him—and theirs, too, is a friendship which has lasted many years—Edward is unable to say for certain. For although Englefield—man of Science, *bon viveur*, and all-round good fellow that he was—might very well have winked an eye at any other peccadillo, *this* one, surely, he would not forgive...

Edward has never put their friendship to the test, and so he does not know what Englefield's reaction would have been. He knows enough of the reactions of other men to fear the worst, however... With a shudder, he recalls the pathetic figure he had seen on his last visit to London, a year or so ago. He had been in

Lincoln's Inn on some business connected with the investment of the annuity he received from his late mother, when, out of habit, he found himself taking the old familiar path… It had been a fine morning, and he flattered himself that he cut a fine figure, in his new coat of amaranth-coloured velvet faced with palest blue: a coat for a Spring day, and a stroll in the Fields, if ever there was one.

He had been walking along, his Malacca in his hand, with no real intent in mind except to see and be seen, on what was really an exceptionally beautiful day, with the trees all in leaf, and the birds singing, and a handsome youth in the scarlet uniform of a Grenadier coming towards him… As the young man drew near, Edward could not forbear from glancing in his direction—for were they not two fellow human beings, enjoying the fine weather and the exercise of sheer animal spirits which had brought them both onto the street at the same hour?

So—breaking the rule which he had set himself long ago—he met the fellow's gaze, and was rewarded with a wink. 'Where to so fast, Sweet Lips?' came the murmured enquiry.

He was about to reply, in a similarly light-hearted vein (for nothing would have come of it; it had been years since he had frequented the Swan, or any other establishment of that nature) when a commotion at the far end of the street made them both turn round. A crowd of soldiers, accompanied by a rabble of shrieking drabs, came around the corner, in pursuit of some poor wretch, who had incurred the wrath of one of their number, it appeared. Filthy words were being shouted, and savage blows rained down upon the terrified creature—whether man or woman was impossible to determine at first.

For the face of this individual was garishly painted, and the lips rouged, whilst a beribboned hat sat askew upon thick clusters of curls. Only when this was knocked flying by one particularly vicious slap, was the wearer's true sex revealed—the luxuriant false curls no more than a cover for the cropped head of a frightened boy.

As Edward watched, frozen with horror, the silk petticoat with which the lad had further disguised his true nature was torn away, while another blow caused his nose to bleed—twin scarlet streams mingling with the red-and-white with which he had bedaubed himself, to pitiful effect.

'Dirty Molly! Bum-boy!' screamed a voice in Edward's ear, as a clod of mud, thrown by a yelling harridan, struck the blood-smeared face. It seemed meant for him and so, without waiting to see what further humiliations were to befall his poor fellow creature, he turned and fled. What became of his handsome Grenadier, he did not know. One thing was certain: he would not have wanted to pursue their business further in such dangerous circumstances.

A few clods of mud and a broken nose were not the worst of it; there had been men hanged for less.

Notebooks, always notebooks. He wonders how he ever found the time for living, in between all the writing. Words. His life has been measured out in words. Here are letters—transcripts of those he has written, and copies of those he has received—from every man, woman and child who ever meant anything to him, and great number that have not.

Here is one from his nephew, Charles Gregory's youngest—now sixteen, and named for him:

> Sir,
>
> I am obliged to you for the five shillings. I intend to treat the House to ginger beer and Scotch buns. We are to have a half-holiday for the King's birthday. I am in the upper set for Latin, but I do not care for Cricket.
>
> I remain, Sir,
>
> Your most obedt & huml Servt
>
> Edwd Chas Fairfax

Here is another, from the Royal Astronomer at Greenwich, commending his latest contribution to *Philosophical Transactions*, and offering to send a honeycomb—

> very good for a putrid throat, Mrs Maskelyne says…

Letters from Aubert, Blagden, Banks; Cassini, Englefield (dear friend), and Goodricke:

> My portrait is come from the painter's. I believe he has given me a cast in one eye. Besides which, I appear twenty years older than my age; unless it is to be assumed that Astronomy has aged me...

Here is a letter from Caroline Herschel. Its tremulous note is the more noticeable, with the passage of time:

> I am almost ashamed to write to you because I never think of doing so but when I am in distress. I found last night at 10h 24' Sidereal Time a comet, and do not know what to do with it...

Letters from Lalande, Magellan, and Messier; from his father (these he throws to one side with an expression of disgust), and from Mr Planta, at the Royal Society.

Acres of words, in journals as well as letters, to describe the indescribable: the unknown, unvisited, as-yet-undefined worlds of Science. Here is one dated July 1783, noting the curious character of the weather that Summer, which had imparted an unusual quality to the atmospheric conditions:

> the Sun and the Moon last night appear'd both of the same colour, nearly thus (here he had painted a small red disc) exactly as the juice of cherries... but more transparent...

—an effect that was the result of a volcano erupting in Iceland, although he did not learn of the cause till later.

Here is another entry from October 1792, soon after his return from York:

> Being at Kensington on the above-mentioned date, I saw, at nine o'clock at night, a very singular, luminous arch in the sky, about 4 degrees in breadth, resembling much a bright white cloud... or something like the uncoloured

> northern lights, without flashes, but seemingly of a more substantial texture...

Nor are the nebulous phenomena of the heavens the only matters to have exercised his pen. Here is another entry from his journal, written twenty years earlier:

> Went to the Opera, it is a large and fine house, three Galleries one over an other, besides a number of boxes; the Opera was Artaxerxes, the Musick by Giordani, a Neopolitan; the Actors are Savoi, Ristorini, Millico, Morigi, and Actrisses Grassi, Giordani; I don't like the last; Millico and Savoi charming Voices, especially the first; the decorations extremely fine; I saw Mademoiselle Heinel & Slingsby dance, la premiere a beaucoup de grases; le second dance avec Beaucoup gaitee et de legertee, il est estime; the Orquester (his spelling had left something to be desired) excellent, lead by two harpsichords, no organs, delightfull musick, very well executed; they begin at seven and finish at half an hour after ten; people were not dresst so richly nor so well as Paris; the common people throw peals of oranges on the Stage before the play begins...

He remembers the occasion all too well. He was nineteen, and in love with the all-too charming Millico—as indeed, many of those in the house that evening were, both women and men. He himself had gone three nights in a row to hear the counter-tenor sing, and watch him flash his dark eyes at the front row. On the third night, he had waited at the stage door for almost an hour. Millico had emerged at last, his face scrubbed clean of paint, and his arm around the shoulder of a lovely boy.

As they swept past, the Italian's gaze had lingered for a moment on Edward's face. 'Exquisite,' he had murmured. 'Come again tomorrow, won't you, *bellissimo*?'

But the following night, he had not been singing after all.

'Mr Millico is resting,' said the Stage Manager with a smirk. 'His voice, you know. He can't keep it up for more than three nights in a row'—eliciting a crow of laughter from a passing stage-hand.

Hopeless. When he thinks what his life has been, he doesn't know whether to laugh or weep. The futile affairs on which he squandered his youth seem no more substantial to him now than feverish dreams. He wonders what has become of them all—the actors, soldiers, grooms, and Bishop's sons—who were his partners in crime. Dead or married, most of them, by now, he supposes. The only man who remains real to him is the one he couldn't have—perversity being no small part of his nature, he allows.

For was it not perverse to devote his life to Astronomy—the thing his father loved above all—in the full knowledge that his father did not love him? Unless he had hoped, thereby, to win some of the love his father directed towards the stars, through making the stars his own study...

If so, he had been sadly mistaken.

The crowning perversity—or irony, call it what you will—was that Astronomy had been the path that brought him to John Goodricke. From that time on, he had been caught, like a bird in lime; or—to change the figure for one more astronomical—like a satellite, endlessly orbiting around the greater light of its Planet...

Here is another letter, this one from Maskelyne—dashed off in a tearing hurry, to judge from the slapdash hand. This one concerns his favourite protégée: a Miracle in petticoats, he called her.

> I paid Dr and Miss Herschel a visit 7 weeks ago. She shewed me her 5 feet Newtonian telescope made for her by her brother for sweeping the heavens. It has an aperture of 9 inches, but magnifies only from 25 to 30 times, & takes in a field of 1 49' being designed to shew objects very bright, for the better discovering any new visitor to our system, that is Comets, or any undiscovered nebulae...

If he has suffered, in his way, for love, so had she—although he had been powerless to prevent it. The intimations he had received that her feelings for him exceeded those of mere friendship had not diminished with the passing years. That was the cruel thing about love—it took no account of age, or inclination. One still had the feelings at sixty that one had when one was twenty.

This had impressed itself upon him the last time he and Miss Herschel had met (could it really be five years ago?) in Bath. She had been overseeing her brother Alexander's removal to Hanover. Since his wife's death some years before, Mr Herschel the younger had grown increasingly morose. 'With Clara gone, there is nothing for me here,' was his constant plaint. Now he was determined to return to the city of his fathers, and his sister, with her usual concern for her siblings' comfort, was to help him pack.

That reason and (he supposes) a wish to see her old friend Edward Pigott once more, had brought her to her former home...

It was a shock to see that she had grown old—although what could he have expected, after nearly forty years? He himself was no longer young. Although he flattered himself that he wore his years rather better than some. His hair, though grey, was plentiful still; his teeth were good (he had never smoked a pipe, deplorable habit) and his eyes, although not as keen as they were when he had found his first comet, still functioned well enough without the need for spectacles. He had kept his figure, too—unlike many of his contemporaries, more addicted than he was to the pleasures of the table. Not that he was without his vices (an over-fondness for Ombre being the most admissible) but these, at least, could be pursued without detrimental effect as to face or form.

The years had not been as kind to poor little Miss H. Although she had never been a beauty. And to arrive, as she had, on a day of driving rain—the wettest day so far in what had been the worst summer in living memory—had not improved her looks. A straggle of grey curls was plastered down around her face, her bonnet being quite useless against the downpour. Her cloak, too, was sodden—what had she be thinking, to walk all the way from Margaret's Hill?

She had come alone; her brother was quite done up, she explained. The fatigue of packing up all his worldly goods, together with a lowness of spirits—brought on by the knowledge that he was soon to leave what had been his dear home for many years—had knocked him flat, she said.

Edward paid only the most cursory attention to this; Alexander Herschel's melancholic fits seeming of far less urgency than his sister's half-drowned state.

'My dear Miss Herschel. You are wet through. Your shoes and stockings... You will catch your death.'

She had smiled at this, and for a moment, seemed quite her old self.

'I assure you I shall not. I have endured worse weather than this, star-gazing...'

'I am sure you have.'

But she suffered herself to be divested of her wet things, and to be brought close to the fire, which he soon had blazing.

Her wet stockings must be hung upon the fender, Edward said. They would dry in a twinkling.

'For if we are not old enough friends not to stand upon ceremony,' he added. 'Then I do not know what we are...'

'O, we are certainly old enough,' she agreed, with a certain asperity.

They had talked for a while of inconsequential things—Byron's latest, he seems to recall. She seemed agitated, speaking rather faster than usual, and breaking into nervous laughter, as she told a story about the time the noble lord came to see them at Slough.

'Ah, here is the tea at last,' he said. 'Thank you, Silas. Come, my dear Miss Herschel, sit by me. Now we can be comfortable together, just like old times...'

Which of course sent her into a paroxysm of shyness. For the next few moments, she did not look at him at all, but directed her gaze at the dancing flames; at the steam spiralling from her cup—at anything, in fact, but at his face.

'So,' he said, when the silence seemed as if it would stretch out indefinitely. 'Here we are.'

'Yes.' She sipped her tea.

'It is a long time since you were last in Bath. Can it be five years?'

'I believe so. But it is nearer ten since you were in Slough.'

'Ten years! Surely it cannot be as long as that? Why, it seems but yesterday that we stood in your delightful garden, and picked gooseberries together for a pie...'

She turned to him at last, her smile lighting up her face, so that for a moment he caught a glimpse of the girl she had been.

'That was at least twenty years ago.'

'Well, well.' He had succeeded, at least, in making her laugh. 'It was a very fine pie.'

'The older I get,' she said, with one of the little bursts of candour to which she was given, 'the more I believe that Time means nothing...'

It was his turn to laugh.

'Would that it were so! Then these grey hairs, too, might be "nothing"; these wrinkles vanished away...'

Although in truth he had not as many wrinkles as she; but it would have been ungallant not to pretend otherwise.

'I was not talking of bodies,' she said, and blushed as she said it. 'I know all too well that our poor mortal envelopes decay. But it seems to me...' Here she leaned forward, so that her face was nearer the fire, catching up some of its glow. 'when one considers the stars...'

'Ah! I knew we should get to talking of the stars...'

'...that our notion of what Time *is* must be revised. For their light still burns for us, does it not, though the stars themselves may be long extinguished?'

'I have always taken a certain pleasure,' Edward replied, 'in the thought that the very stars we now examine so minutely through our powerful instruments are the same as those the Ancients saw...'

'The very same—although their light has taken a hundred, or a thousand, years to reach us.' She held his gaze with her own. Her eyes, he saw, were still the same unfaded forget-me-not blue.

'Is there not,' she went on, 'a Paradox in that? For if objects can exist simultaneously a thousand years ago and now, then may we not say that is Time overthrown, or...'

'...collapsed in upon itself, like a folding telescope,' he finished for her.

'I see that you are laughing at me, Sir.'

'Not for the world.'

'No doubt you are one of those that believe Time runs in straight lines, from birth to death, from start to finish, from Alpha to Omega...'

'You do me an injustice, Madam.'

'But I am here to tell you that it is not so. For Time, it seems to me, can run forwards, backwards, and sideways, too. How else to explain the oft remarked-upon sensation that one has been here before? Which I have, in fact,' she added with a smile. 'Since it was but five doors down from this house that my brother and I had the honour of receiving you on your first visit to Bath.'

It had not, in fact, been at Rivers Street that they had met, but he did not correct her. In essence what she said was right: Time runs in circles.

'Added to which,' Miss Herschel went on, in the same whimsical tone she was wont to adopt when discussing matters of great seriousness 'is the fact that Time is not an unbroken chain—though, to be sure, one speaks of a "chain of events"—but a mass, shall we say, of tiny moments, of specks, of *particles*. The same particle of time can pass in the blink of an eye—for the Lover, say...' This time she did not blush. 'But it will seem an Aeon to the mind in torment, or to the prisoner, awaiting his sentence...'

'Time can be both short and long, that is understood. That it can return upon itself, so that one may live a moment, not once, but many times, is another of its properties, I collect...'

She looked at him: a steady gaze, in which there was everything that had passed between them.

'One cannot always choose the moments which return to one,' she replied. 'For they come upon one unawares. The smallest thing—a turn of the head, or a glance—is enough to unlock them, and then it is as if twenty years—or thirty—have fallen away. As if Time is no more,' she added softly, her face once more turned towards the flickering flames.

Caroline's hair, which had hung in wet strands about her face when she first arrived, had now dried into the springy curls and tendrils he recalled from the days of their earliest meeting, so that it seemed to him that, after all, she had not altered so very much.

She noticed his looking at her, and made a wry mouth.

'You are thinking what an old woman I have become,' she said lightly.

'Indeed I am not. I was thinking that you still look like a young girl.'

She shook her head at that. 'Now you are teasing me—and I will not be teased. It is unkind of you, Mr Pigott. You, who were always kind to me in the past...'

He had not been kind and both of them knew it. But that it had not been his intention to hurt her, was also understood between them.

Another silence fell.

'Do you believe,' he said at last, his voice not quite steady, 'that in some shape or form we continue?'

She considered a moment.

'I was brought up to believe it. Although now I am not sure. I trust that we do.'

'Like the stars,' he said, 'whose light goes on shining long after the stars themselves are no more...

'We continue in memory...'

'Or in the memory of stars,' he said.

He draws the ink-well towards him, and taking up a fresh piece of paper, begins to compose a reply to John Herschel, thanking him for his letter of the 8th inst. and professing himself sensible of the honour which has been offered to him, but regretting that he must decline the same on account of his indifferent health. He concludes by asking the younger man to convey his—Edward's—respects to his—John Herschel's—honoured father and mother, whom the writer had often had the pleasure of meeting in happier times at Slough. He reads it through, and signs his name with a flourish. What he has written is true enough: he does not care to travel far these days. His warm study, with its books and its telescopes and its seaweed collection, is world enough for him.

He seals the letter, and addresses it, before throwing it onto the pile already waiting on the silver tray for Silas to take to the post. Thanks to Mr Palmer and his mail-coaches, theirs is the fastest service in England, and he can be sure that John Herschel will be reading his letter by this time tomorrow… The Modern Age! Surely there has been nothing like it in the history of the world? With telescopes through which one could view the surface of the Moon, and steam engines on which one could fly along at over twenty miles an hour, and even talk of a great tunnel under the sea that would connect England and France, it seems they must be living in an Age of Wonders…

He must have dozed off for a few moments, for when he looks up again, the room has grown dark, and the servant is standing in the doorway with a letter in his hand. This he thrusts at his master with his customary brusqueness. Silas has many good qualities, but his manners lack polish.

'This come by the coach,' is all he says.

The postmark is a Belgian one. He tears the letter open with some haste. It was never going to be good news, from that quarter. It is not a long letter: three lines in the Abbess's fine, dry hand. When he has read it, he sits for a long time without moving. So it has come at last. He touches the bell, and when the servant reappears, gives his orders. There is an overnight coach which will see them in London by morning; in Dover by mid-afternoon. Then he will see about finding them a passage to Ostend.

XXVII

He thinks of the last time he saw Mathurina, when he was in Brussels, during the autumn of 1815. The city had been full of soldiers—both those who had survived unscathed the terrible battle with which the region would ever afterwards be associated, and those recuperating from their wounds. There had been some terrible sights, he recalls: men maimed, and blinded, and prematurely aged by the horrors they had seen. And yet, despite—or perhaps because of—the military contingent, there was a hectic gaiety about the place, which had not been so before. The threat of invasion had been lifted, and the once-invincible tyrant safely locked up in his island prison. Rejoicing seemed the order of the day—at least to judge from the numbers of cheerfully drunken men in uniform one saw about the streets; to say nothing of the gaudily dressed ladies, in their silken gowns and beribboned bonnets, all loudly proclaiming their joy at that famous victory.

To his account of the city and its doings, his sister had listened with a patient smile. For whatever interest she had in life outside the convent walls was confined to a single topic.

Thus their conversation (the time allocated to their meeting being short) took the form of a catechism, of sorts:

'Have you seen her?'

'I have.'

'How is she?'

'She is well.'

'Describe her to me. She must have changed a good deal since you last saw her...'

'She has not changed so very much. At least...' He hesitated, wondering how best to convey the news he had to tell. 'Her face is much the same. But... she is with child,' he said. 'That is, she was married a year ago. I only heard it for the first time yesterday, or I should have written to you.'

His sister was silent for so long that he began to wonder if she had heard him.

Then:

'Married, you say?' she said, a slight frown creasing her otherwise unlined forehead.

'Yes.'

'Have you seen him—the husband?'

He nodded. 'He is a soldier, with the Hanoverian Guard.'

Her face cleared. 'A German. That is good. He will take her away—she and the child, when it is born. Let them settle far from here, in Germany.'

With its tall grey walls half-smothered in ivy, and its heavy door barred with iron, the place has always seemed a prison to him—never more so than now. He dismounts from the carriage, telling the man to wait. Silas he has left at a nearby *auberge*, with instructions not to sit up for him; for there is no telling when he will return… His footsteps make a dull sound as he crosses the courtyard, of what had once been the dwelling of some noble family—now long extinct. He climbs the steps. The sound of his knock reverberates in the stillness, as if through the vault of a tomb. He has the sensation, as he stands there, that he is being observed. Eyes look out at him through the barred slits of windows, and a whispering—which might only be the sound of the wind stirring the leaves of the ivy—seems to issue from the very walls.

With this nervous fancy uppermost in his mind, it takes an effort of will not to give a start, as a panel in the upper part of the door slides back, and a white face appears. He states his name and purpose, and after a moment's consideration, the face withdraws, and the shutter is slammed shut. There follows the grating sound of bolts being drawn back, and at length the great door swings open to admit him. At his appearance, the silent Portress at once turns, and walks off, not looking back to see if he is following. With her black robes swirling about her, and her footsteps seeming to make no sound upon the polished stone flags of the floor, she seems a spirit of the place; an uncanny emanation.

As if in a dream, he follows her, through stone arches and along corridors, penetrating deeper and deeper into a world of which, hitherto, he has had but glimpses. Now, like Orpheus, it seems he is to be taken to the heart of this dark kingdom…

This, then, is where his sister has spent her life—more years having been passed within these walls than outside them. He wonders how she could have borne it for so long without going mad. To have been so enclosed—so *confined*—shut off from the light of the Sun and Stars alike, and condemned, always, to silence, seems to him worse than death. A sacrifice made for love, which had ended by denying all that love stood for.

At last they reach a door; his guide stands back, and makes a sign for him to enter. On the bed, lies a shape, covered by a grey blanket. He knows this to be Mathurina, although she is terribly altered. They have taken off her veil, and her shorn white head seems that of an old woman.

Her eyes do not seem to see him at first. Then her lips move.

'Come closer.'

He does not recognise the voice as hers. It seems already that of a dead thing.

'Let me look at you.'

He accordingly draws near the bed, and sits down upon the stool beside it. He takes her hand. It is cold and light as wax. Her lips have a bluish look, and her eyes, seeming to stare not at him, but beyond him, are dark as night.

'Is it really you, brother?'

'Yes, Mathurina…'

'No one has called me by that name for many years.'

'I am sorry.'

'Do not be.' A long pause ensues, during which the wasted figure on the bed appears to be gathering her strength to speak again. At last she does speak: 'How are you, brother?'

'I am well.'

She studies his face for a moment.

'No, you are not well. But it was good of you to come.'

He squeezes her hand by way of reply.

'Still star-gazing?' she says.

'Well…'

'Of course you are. It is your passion. One cannot live without passion…'

'No.'

Both are silent a moment. How thin she is, Edward thinks. It seems impossible that one so frail should still have the strength to talk...

'I will die tonight,' she says, as if she reads his thought. 'You are just in time.' The ghost of a smile touches her lips, and for a moment, her face has something of its former beauty. 'Dear Edward,' she murmurs. 'You, at least, did not fail me...'

He weeps at that, and kisses her bloodless hand. She watches him calmly, as if his grief were of no account, now.

For a while nothing more is said. She closes her eyes, as if she no longer has the strength to look at him. After some time has elapsed, it seems to him that there is a change in her breathing... But when he goes to stand up, to call the waiting nuns to her aid, she clutches his hand with surprising fierceness.

'Wait,' she says, her voice so faint that he has to bring his ear close to her lips in order to hear it. 'There is one more thing I would ask of you...'

She is too weak to raise her head, but she makes signs to him that he should put his hand beneath the pillow, and draw out what is there: a letter.

He does not need to read the inscription to know for whom it is intended.

'I will make sure she receives it,' he tells her, and sees from her eyes that she has understood.

Comet Hunter

✸✸✸✸✸✸✸✸✸✸✸

XXVIII

Hannover, 1848

It is snowing again. She watches it fall—slowly at first; then gathering momentum, until the world beyond the window—all she can *see* of the world—is obliterated in a mass of whirling flakes. Fortunately, the room is warm, with the fire Gerda laid that morning still burning brightly, and so it is not such an effort as all that to imagine herself back in the heat of summer... Turning her gaze from the window with some reluctance, for she has always loved snow, and the intricate patterns of its falling, she picks up her pen once more. On the desk in front of her is the heap of small notebooks, which comprise her Day Book. Of these there are more than thirty, containing the thoughts of more than seventy years. Everything she has felt and suffered is to be found here. Open any of these volumes anywhere, and her words leap out at you: annotating, chronicling, describing. Begin at the end, or begin at the beginning—it is all one: her life, laid out in sequence, for anyone to read.

Except that there is no one, now, but herself to read it...

These, then, are the raw material she will turn into Art; or rather (since she does not presume to dignify her scribblings as such), into a Record of all she has witnessed. Her life as the sister of a remarkable man, and her meetings with other remarkable men. She is not fool enough to suppose that anyone would be interested in what she has to say without that.

Now where was she?

Ah, yes. August 16th, 1786. Sixty-two years have passed since that day, and yet it is as clear in memory as if it were yesterday. William had just arrived back from Germany. Two weeks earlier, she had found her first comet. Her exhilaration at her recent triumph had been mingled with joy at her brother's return—a mood instantly quenched, at the sight of his face, as he read the letter he had just opened...

He had turned as white as milk.

'*Was schmerzt Sie, Wilhelm?*' she had cried, reverting in her agitation to their native tongue, but he had not seemed to hear her.

She touched his shoulder, thinking he must have been taken ill, but he shook her off, with some impatience.

'No, no. I am quite all right. It is Maskelyne's letter.' He let it fall upon the table. 'It appears young Goodricke is dead.'

She stared at him.

'But I saw the Maskelynes only two weeks ago,' was all she could think of to say.

'Maskelyne is quite well,' he said, with some asperity, perhaps thinking she had misunderstood. 'It is Goodricke who is dead, of a fever, some three months past. Maskelyne had it from Edward Pigott...'

She could not suppress a soft cry at that.

'O, the poor thing...'

'Indeed. He was not twenty-two.' William drew a handkerchief from his sleeve and blew his nose sharply. 'The worst of it is, he was elected a Fellow of the Royal Society only two weeks before, Maskelyne says. The letter was about to be sent out. The poor fellow died before he knew of it... O Lina! When I think of our late disagreement, it makes me feel quite sorry that I was so severe with him.'

For after their falling-out over Algol, there had been another—the late John Goodricke not having been one to let well alone, it seemed. A letter had arrived, pointing out some discrepancy in William's calculations on a matter to do with the Sun and the

Solar system—she doesn't remember the exact details. Only that it had made her brother incandescent with rage. 'Listen to this! Such a conceited puppy…' He had read out the offending passages in a sneering tone. 'How dare he suggest that I am in error? It is quite clear that the fault is Flamsteed's, not mine.'

He had taken great pleasure in composing a suitably crushing reply. 'What do you think of this, Lina?

> Sir,
>
> Give me leave to thank you for the favour of your letter, and since you have been so obliging as to point out what appears to you to be errors in my Paper… and favoured me with your corrections I must take the liberty to shew you that either you have misapprehended that paper or have not considered the subject with that attention which I could wish you to bestow upon it…

That will put the arrogant young fool in his place…'

Now he seemed quite cast down.

'He wrote me a handsome apology, you know, Lina. I do not think he meant to offend…' He dashed away a tear from the corner of his eye. 'O, it will be a loss to Astronomy, of that there is no doubt. I will write to Maskleyne directly, to ask him to send commiserations to the family. Although there is only old Sir John left now, you know. I believe the rest are all girls. Unless perhaps there is a younger brother… Well, well. It is a sad business.'

'What of Mr Pigott?' she dared to ask; for her brother seemed sunk in thought, all his papers pushed aside.

'Pigott? He is still in France, I believe.' William sighed and shook his head. 'Yes, it was a sad day for him when he lost his friend, for the two of them would have done great things together…'

As soon as she decently could, she stole away to her own room, to consider how best to express her solicitude.

Sir (she wrote)

Having only lately received the sad news of your friend Mr Goodricke's demise, I hasten to send these condolences, tardy as they might seem, in the hope that...

No, no. That would not do at all.

I have only just had the news of Mr Goodricke's untimely death from my brother, who had it from Dr Maskelyne...

No.

I was so sorry to hear the news about Mr Goodricke. I know what a good friend he was to you, and am only very sorry that my own acquaintance with him was so slight...

No, again no. There was no satisfactory way of saying what was in her heart—which was that she mourned as much for the bereaved, as for the deceased.

Knowing as I do your affection for the late Mr Goodricke, I only wish to convey...

What? Fondest thoughts? No, no. Deepest sympathies. That was better.

...my deepest sympathies for your sad loss.

Sometimes the conventional phrases were the best. It was not a time for too much truth.

She signed the letter, and sealed it. In the end, she made no mention of the comet. To have trumpeted her success, while he was still recovering from such a blow, would have been unfeeling. She wondered where he was at that moment, and if he would ever return to England. For its associations could only now be painful to him... The thought made her own tears flow. Never to see him again! It would be like a death. How would she ever bear it?

Through the open window, as she sat gazing sightlessly out, came the clinking of hammers, and the sound of voices. Those insufferable workmen! She went to pull the casement shut, and a sentence floated up to her:

'Gawd, she was a handful and no mistake. Like two puddings in a copper they was, and just as lively...'

'She's a big girl all right, is our Alice...'

This was intolerable!

'Will you be quiet!' she shouted, and banged the window shut—not, unfortunately, before she had heard the muttered riposte:

'She wants it up 'er, that one, and no mistake. Bloody German bitch...'

And—worse—the other's reply:

'Get a bit funny at her age they do, women...'

Tears sprang to her eyes that had nothing to do with grief.

When she was calm again, she went downstairs, and gave the letter to William, to enclose in his to Dr Maskelyne.

'So you have written to poor Pigott, Lina?' he said, glancing at the inscription. 'That was thoughtful of you.' His voice shook slightly. 'When I think of the pleasant times we have had, talking of variable stars and I know not what, it quite grieves my heart to imagine how cast down he will be... A sad day,' he said, shaking his head again. 'A sad day. If it had been my own son who was dead, Lina, I could not be more sorry.'

Death. She has known a great deal of it. When you have lived as long as she has, it seems as if everyone but yourself is dead, or dying. In truth, she was born to death—its shadowy wings beating over her very cradle, which had held, in its time, those baby brothers and sisters whose demise preceded her own appearance in the world. Apart from these familial deaths, there have been many others—some of people known to her, others (victims of the wars and revolutions which have raged throughout this bloodiest of centuries) of those unknown. Soon—if what she hears of the goings-on in the outside world is true—there will be another Revolution. More deaths. More suffering. And all for what? The overthrow of one Tyranny, and the substitution of another. She very much hopes she will not live to see it...

Of all these deaths, there were three which affected her most nearly—although one was that of a relative stranger, and one that of a woman she did not even like. (The third, of course, was William's. Dear, dear brother! Even after the passage of more than five-and-twenty years, she can barely bring herself to think of it.)

She will not think of it.

She will think, instead, of John Pitt. For it was John Pitt's death, at the end of that fateful summer of 1786, which determined the way the rest of her life would turn out. The day that William returned from Upton with a long face and said, 'I am afraid it is all up with poor Pitt. He cannot last the night, I fear...' was the turning-point; as cataclysmic, in its way, as all the wars and revolutions were in theirs.

Not that she knew it, then—as, setting aside what she was doing (the putting-up of a jugged hare), she at once sat down to write a note to poor Mary. In the few months since she and William had come to Slough, the Pitts had been the most hospitable of neighbours; although in recent weeks, since poor John fell so ill, the invitations to dine at their well-appointed table had fallen off somewhat. Now, as she considered whether soup or calf's-foot jelly would be most appropriate to send (for the soon-to-be-bereaved lady would need to keep her strength up) she might have detected—but did not—a new solicitude in William's voice.

'You would have wept to see her, Lina—for I know you have a feeling heart... Poor Mrs Pitt! She hardly knew which way to turn. "O, what shall I do, when my poor John is gone?" she said, in such a piteous voice that I confess I was very near to weeping myself. "For when he is dead, I shall be quite alone in the world..."'

If Caroline had not been distracted by the task in hand (soup, she decided; and perhaps a morsel of the stewed beef) she might have replied that, if Mary Pitt were to be alone, she would at least be comfortably so. With an income of ten thousand pounds, she need not starve; besides which, she had a stepson to provide for her. Nor would the legacy from her mother, old Mrs Baldwin, be a negligible one...

It was perhaps as well she did not say these things. It did not stop her thinking them, in the weeks and months that followed.

John Pitt duly died; a lavish, but dignified, funeral ensued, followed by the obligatory period of mourning. Mrs Pitt, though not a handsome woman, looked very well in black. Moreover, she was lonely; it was very dull at Upton, now that John was gone, she said. She relied upon her neighbours—dear Dr Herschel and his sister—to enliven what would otherwise have been a sad winter.

She had almost given up hope of hearing from Edward Pigott again, when the letter came. She was alone in the house (her brother being out for a walk with Mrs Pitt and her mother) and so was not obliged to share its contents with him. Even so, recognising the hand, she felt a hot blush of self-consciousness rise along her throat. Only when she had carried the letter away to the privacy of her room, did she feel safe.

Her fingers trembled as she broke the seal.

Louvain, 1st Oct:r 1786

Madam,

I have had the favour of your letter of 16th Aug:t, & beg your pardon for not replying sooner, for I have been indisposed.

The death of Mr Goodricke—an event I shall ever lament—as well as other circumstances relating to my family which I shall not trouble you with—have taken a toll upon my Spirits, & I fear that, were you and I to meet again, you would find me sadly altered.

Those happy days that you and I & your esteemed Brother spent together at King Street, when we spoke of variable stars and much else besides, are vanished without trace, alas; in their place is nothing but despondency. My father is adamant that we are to stay in Belgium until at least the middle of next year; & so I fear that I must remain an Exile from my dear adoptive land until that time.

For where there is no Independence, my dear Miss Herschel, there can be no true Freedom. I say this, not in a spirit of filial ingratitude, you understand, but in self-reproach. I know that you, being the wise and generous-minded Being that you are, will not think the worse of me for it.

When one has enjoyed, as I have, the Society of men such as Mr Goodricke & your honoured brother, Mr Herschel, one cannot help but ponder on the inconsistencies of human nature, whereby one Individual is all heart and Soul & feeling, whilst another—let us say no more—is eaten up with rage & spite.

But you must forgive these ramblings. I have been too much left to my own devices of late, and have grown mopish. The weather has been too cloudy, these past few nights, for star-gazing; and, in truth, I confess I have no appetite for it... Allow me to offer, nonetheless, my felicitations on your wonderful Discovery of a comet, of which Dr Maskelyne has informed me. I always knew you for a fellow lover of Science, dear Miss Herschel, & I trust this Comet of yours will not be the last.

I remain
Ever your Hum:l & Obed:t Servant,
Edw:d Pigott

When she had finished reading, she sat for a while, unable to move or think. A cool grey Autumn light fell through the open window, illuminating everything within the room, which she seemed to see for the first time. There was the bed, with its patchwork quilt, and there the chest, with its jug and basin. The rug was one she had made herself, out of torn-up strips of rag; she had worked at it for hours, and yet she seemed never to have looked at it before...

She looked at her hands, lying idle in her lap. Strange, pale, little creeping things. Like creatures found under a rock at the sea-side. Star-fish, she thought.

Phrases and sentences returned to her from those she had read:

Those happy days... are vanished without trace, alas...

It was almost as if she heard him speak the words.

I must remain in Exile...

Tears gathered in her eyes at that.

'O, what am I to do?' she whispered, knowing there was no answer to the question.

One phrase she read again and again, as if it held some special meaning for her:

Where there is no Independence, there can be no true Freedom...

She knew it to be so; dreaded the day she must put it to the test... How unhappy he was! Surely his words had arisen from the depths of despair? She, who believed herself to have visited such depths, was now forced to reconsider. For was she not a free woman, with a comfortable home, and a loving brother to provide for her? Now that his beloved Friend had gone, poor Edward Pigott had nobody and nothing...

'Why, Lina—what are you doing, sitting here all alone?' cried William, appearing that instant in the doorway. 'I have been calling and calling, but you never heard. Come, get your bonnet, for we are invited to Mrs Pitt's for dinner...'

The King, like all monarchs, disliked spending money. It had pleased him to get his astronomer at such a bargain price. Now (at the urging of the astronomer's friends), his Majesty was being asked for further disbursements. He was not, it appeared, amused. At length, and after a good deal of unseemly haggling, an additional £2,000 was offered, to cover the ballooning costs of manufacturing and running the forty-foot telescope—on the condition that that would be the end of it. £4,000 in total! It was an enormous sum—enough to fund a small war.

By way of sweetening this bitter pill, the King and Queen Charlotte had been invited to Slough, to view the great instrument—then spread out in pieces upon the lawn. Also of the party was the Duke of York, the Princess Royal, Princess Augusta, the Duke of Queensbury, the Archbishop of Canterbury and sundry other lords and ladies. It was, Caroline recalls, a charming occasion, with the garden looking better than might have been hoped in mid-September, and all the ladies in their prettiest dresses—lilac, pale yellow, pink, and white, and silver-grey. They seemed a flock of turtle doves, newly alighted upon the grass.

His Majesty had been in a benign mood, laughing and joking (he was not always so of late, William said, being prone to sudden outbursts of violent temper). He had thought it vastly amusing to lead the Archbishop by the hand through the great tube of the telescope, which lay upon its side on the ground. 'Come, my Lord Bishop,' he had cried, 'I will show you the way to Heaven...'—a witticism which was much enjoyed by the assembled company each time he told it.

He had been in less forgiving mood when presented with William's estimate for what the telescope would cost to finish, and had made his displeasure known. When William had returned from his meeting with Sir Joseph Banks (who was acting as intermediary), he was ashen-faced. 'I do believe his Majesty must have been poorly advised,' was all he would say, 'for he appears to think that I have been profligate with his funds—whereas no one could have been more assiduous than I, Lina, in trying to avoid unnecessary expense...

This was all the more painful to her because she knew herself to be one of the 'expenses'. The request William had made, in a letter outlining running costs, for a small annual stipend—'such as 50 or 60 pounds'—to be paid to his 'good, industrious sister' to recompense her for her work as his assistant (for which he would have had to pay at least £100 to anyone else, he pointed out) had not been well received, either. Such a sum, William argued, would give his sister a modicum of independence, 'so that if anything should happen to me she would not be left un-provided for...' This hinted at mortality; but there was another reason why William hoped to see Caroline securely settled.

At the age of fifty, when most men are becoming grandfathers, her brother was contemplating matrimony for the first time. (In this he had perhaps been encouraged by the example of Dr Maskelyne, who had married late —and happily—only two years before.) One thing had led to another. 'Mrs Pitt' had soon become 'Mary'; then 'Dearest Mary'; then 'My Intended'. An offer was made, and accepted. There was nothing Caroline or anyone else could have done to prevent it.

She had never seen her brother so giddy—alternately elated, and cast down. He, who had never taken account of fine clothes, or rich food, or French wines, or any kind of show, now fretted himself into a passion over the cut of a waistcoat, or whether the ruffles on a shirt had been goffered to his liking. Until now, she had never thought he could remind her of their brother Jacob.

As with all his projects, William had thought to carry all before him, through sheer enthusiasm.

'For Lina, we will be just as we were before,' he said. 'Only, of course, dear Mary will be with us...'

They would keep both households going, he declared—Slough for astronomy, and Upton for the matrimonial home. Caroline would, naturally, preside at Slough, as she had always done. What happier compromise could there be?

Mrs Pitt, on being told of this plan, decided to reconsider her decision.

'She will not have me, Lina,' William said, his voice quavering a little. Caroline noticed that he could not meet her eye. 'She is of the opinion—I cannot say why—that such an arrangement will not work...'

She had, she remembers, allowed a moment to pass before giving her answer. She might have been savouring her power—if she had had any power left to speak of—or merely reflecting on exactly how much she was giving up... She cannot now recall. Only that, when she raised her eyes to his at last, she had seen a flash of anxiety in his look—an awareness, perhaps, that he was not behaving entirely well.

'You need not trouble yourself on my account,' she said. 'For I shall be quite independent at last. Indeed...' Here she managed a laugh, which sounded almost convincing. 'I have long intended to set up my own establishment. To be mistress...' She caught his eye, and was glad to see him look away. 'in my own house.'

'There will be no necessity for that.' Relief made him voluble. 'Of course you must remain at Slough. We—that is, Mrs Pitt and I (Mrs Herschel as she will be)—have a plan to fit up the rooms over the workshops for your especial use… that is, if you are agreeable. For Lina,' he went on, evidently taking her silence for acquiescence, 'you need not fear that things will be different when Mrs Pitt and I are married. That is…

He flushed, perhaps conscious of not having said quite what he meant.

'You and I will go on as we always have, sweeping for comets and the like. For you know you are my Chief Assistant in this.' Now it was his turn to attempt a laugh. 'What His Majesty would say if Miss Herschel were not to be at her post, I hardly dare to think…'

She had smiled, and agreed (for what else could she do?) but in her heart there was only despair. In her journal she wrote:

> the 8th of that month being fixed for my Brother's marriage it may easily be supposed that I must have been fully employed (besides minding the heavens) to prepare everything as well as I could, against the time I was to give up the place of a Housekeeper…

But before that day could arrive, came news of another death: that of Alexander's wife, poor silly little Clara Herschel. She had not liked the girl, who had seemed to her empty-headed in the extreme. The six weeks they had been forced to spend in each other's company could not pass fast enough, where Caroline was concerned. So that when the dreadful intelligence was received—not entirely unexpectedly, for the poor lady had been of a feeble constitution—the grief she felt took her by surprise.

For a week she lay abed, unable to eat or sleep, her body racked with sobs, her eyes so swollen with weeping she could hardly see.

'*Ach*, the poor thing, the poor thing,' was all she would say. 'And to think I was so unkind to her, when she had not a friend in the world…' At which she would commence another bout of weeping.

In vain did William remonstrate with her ('Come, Lina! This is melancholy talk. I am sure you have nothing to reproach yourself with...')—his tone becoming increasingly exasperated as his sister's tears refused to dry themselves.

'I have been unkind. I have been unkind,' she continued to moan. 'And now I must pay the price for my unkindness.'

XXIX

How terrible life is, and how wonderful also! When she thinks of all she has seen and done, she hardly knows where to begin in the telling of it. For everything she has set down—here, in these little books, with their worn leather bindings and their thin pages scarcely bigger than her hand—she has been obliged to leave something out. It is like the tale of Tristram Shandy, which she remembers reading aloud to William as he sat grinding his mirrors in the back-kitchen at Bath all those years ago: if you were really to tell the entire history of a life, you would never leave off writing, yet would still never reach an end. Now, as she sits here, still not dead (and O, sweet Jesus Christus, let her die tonight!) she finds that she has only managed to record such a very little bit of it—of all the things that happened, and all the things that were said.

This is partly, of course, because not everything is equally interesting. With a life such as hers, for example, the only things that anyone else could possibly want to know about are those that concern William. She does not resent it. It is why she has written everything down, for those that come after her to read.

Almost everything, that is.

For there is a blank in her Journals—a Nothing—which lasts for ten years. Or rather, it is not a blank, but an excision; she has chosen to remove what was written, as if it never existed. Of course she remembers what she wrote. It is engraved upon her mind, and heart.

> I will never forgive him. Never. He has annihilated me. Anything else I could have excused but this. The loss of my music; the loss of my home; above all, the loss of the One who was so dear to me—all these I have suffered for his sake. But to have given them up for nothing? To have spent the past ten years of my life working only for him... and then to find it has all been in vain—no, that I cannot forgive.

> The sacrifice of my singing career, in the full knowledge that I might have been independent at last—that I bore without complaint. Our removal from Bath—beloved home—in pursuit of his ambitions, I also endured; although no one but myself knows what it cost to leave there. To discover that He—the only man I ever loved—was to take up residence in that city, was a further blow to a sensibility increasingly inured to such shocks (tho' by that *time*, I had long ago given up the notion that anything might come of our Friendship). But to know that all the while, he—the brother in whom I trusted—was planning to Betray me... that was the cruellest cut of all...

Bitter words. But she had meant every one. For had he not betrayed her, as plainly as if he had turned her out of doors without a penny, after all she had given him? All her hard work, all her devotion; all her time.

Time in which, it does not seem preposterous to suppose, she might have made something of her music (for was she not, after *Messiah*, invited to go to Birmingham for a season, as principal soprano?) Time in which (despite her father's kindly meant but cruel words) she might have married. For, unbeautiful as she knows herself to be, many men—famous men!—admire her. Mary Pitt is not beautiful, and yet she has married the most famous of them all... although the fact that she is rich may have something to do with it.

Unkind. He has made her unkind (she who has had only kind thoughts where he is concerned). She hates herself for such thoughts—such cruel jibes. Mary Pitt she does not hate, only... how *could* he, she wonders. If Mary Pitt were clever, or at least witty, she might have been able to understand it. But to have nothing—no beauty, no brains, no wit—to recommend her... nothing, in fact, beyond her fortune; well, it did not say very much for her brother's discernment (or perhaps it said too much). Unkind. She is becoming bitter, and unkind.

It was that year—the year of her downfall—that she found her second comet, and confirmed the reputation she had already established of being, if not the greatest comet-hunter in history, then certainly the greatest *female* comet-hunter. She would not presume to set herself up besides Sir Edmund Halley and Tycho Brahe. But still it might be said that she had earned the appellation bestowed on her by M. Lalande: 'Madame Carolina Herschel, *astronome célèbre*...' Another of his names for her was '*la savante* miss'; she was content with either. To describe her, as another excitable learned gentleman had, as 'most noble and worthy priestess of the new heavens' was, she felt, going too far. A priestess she was not. But a diligent observer, sweeper, *recorder*—all these she was, and more.

Why, if it had not been for the inconvenient fact that her brother William had already been nominated for a prize by the Assemblée Nationale in Paris—thus ruling her ineligible—she might have been awarded even that accolade... Not that she grudged William his success; she cared nothing for prizes, or any other honour. It was enough to know that those whose opinion she valued most knew what she had done.

Tucked into the back of the journal are the letters. *His* letters to William. She purloined them long ago—for who would miss them? It had been her task to catalogue all the correspondence her brother received in those years from all the eminent men of science in Europe, and America. The undertaking was not a light one. There were hundreds of letters, spanning more than twenty years, from dukes and princes, learned doctors, clergymen and diplomats—many of them dabblers in the astronomical art, if not actual masters in the field. Letters from Sir Joseph Banks and from the Conte de Cassini; from M. de Lalande and Dr Franklin. M. Messier's letters were also there; as were the King of Poland's, M. Boneparte's, and M. Méchain's. Here are to be found the hastily scrawled and sometimes near-illegible notes of Dr Maskelyne, and the scented *billets-doux* of the Princesse de Dachow. Every type of handwriting is represented here: the ornate curlicues of Mr Aubert side-by-side with the bold Gothic downstrokes of Captain Krusenstern.

Letters, so many letters. Surely no one would miss a few?

She unfolds one of them now, its pages grown brittle after so many years; the paper so thin that the words show through from the other side, criss-crossing those on the first sheet in intricate patterns. His graceful slanting hand—how it makes her heart beat faster! Just as it had the first time she read it: William handing it to her over the breakfast table, his mouth full of toast, with 'I call that very handsome, do not you?'

York. June 9th 1781

Sir,

It is with much pleasure that I congratulate you on your two excellent Memoirs printed in the last Phil. Trans., as also on the Starry Comet you discovered. I was at the R.S. when your letter to Dr Maskelyne was read, and a few days afterwards he very obligingly sent me a detailed account of it; since my return here the instruments not being adjusted it has been out of my power to make very accurate Observations; having examined Mon. de Sejours "Essai sur les Cometes", I find none resembling exactly yours; that of 1665 approaches the most as to its vivid light and being well defined, but it was of a much greater diameter and had a tail; others having no tail differ by being either too dim, ill defined or Nebulous...

She skims through the next two pages, which she has read many times before and which she know almost by heart. In them, he gives an account of his paper on Mercury, to be delivered to the Royal Society, as well as some observations on double stars and nebulae. He concludes with a final flurry of dependent clauses, and an invitation which, at the time she first read it, brought her heart into her mouth:

If ever you come this way, I beg you will call on me, and pay a visit to our Observatory, both which will give me much pleasure, as also to hear from you soon, and in case I make any discovery or Observation which I think you may wish to be acquainted with, you may depend on my sending them as soon as possible.

Despite repeated invitations, William had never seen fit to make the journey to York. But then, he could hardly have spared the time, having so many obligations to fulfil—not least those to his Royal Patron...

The signature she has traced so many times with her fingertip (and kissed, too, though she blushes to recall it) that it is fainter than the rest. She touches it now.

I am, Sir, your Obed:t
Humble Servant
Edwd Pigott

It was for his sake, as much as William's, that she devoted herself to the stars. For was it not the one subject they had in common? He had admired her singing, it was true—and spoke warmly of the time he had heard Giardini play in Paris; but it was the stars which made his eyes shine, and his voice quicken with enthusiasm.

Her shyness, too, could be forgotten when they talked of such things.

The fire has burned low; she must get Gerda to bring some more logs, for the room is getting chilly. These days she can never get really warm, although she is wrapped in shawls like a Mummy, and keeps the fire in, even in Summer. Shivering a little, she chafes her hands to restore some semblance of feeling to their bluish extremities. How gnarled and ugly her fingers have become! She was always proud of her hands, for their smallness and whiteness—despite the harsh treatment they suffered over the years. All that washing of shirts, and scrubbing of floors—to say nothing of pounding horse-dung!—had left their mark. All that sewing and ironing, too...

She shuffles the pile of letters again, and draws out another in the dear familiar hand. Astonishing how much character betrays itself, in these loops and swirls, these slanting lines of ascenders and descenders. The date of this one is much later than the others—1799—which was after the discovery of her eighth, and final, comet.

> If Dr and Miss Herschel have not seen a Comet that is now Steering its course through the Great Bear, it will give me much pleasure in having been the first that sent them the information...

Edward Pigott's assumption that both would be equally interested in the news he was sending them, was proof enough of the esteem in which he held her. She had it from his own lips, too, not five days later, when he had called in to see them at Slough, on his way back to Bath.

'A Prodigy,' he had called her. What she—a mere woman—had done, was more than most men dreamed of. Even he, for all the hours he had spent at the observing-glass, had only a single comet to his name...

But she is jumping ahead of herself. It seems that there is no straightforward way to tell the story. Either it is nothing but lists of names, and dates, and discoveries—or little inconsequential things, of no interest to anybody... She begins to think that Dr Sterne had an easy time of it with his 'Tristram'; for there was a hero with precious little to do, and an entire book in which to do it. Whereas she not only has to grapple with the facts of her own existence, but with those appertaining to great men, and famous events. She cannot keep it all in mind at once. She has filled up book after book with her chronicle of all that happened, and still she finds herself far from reaching an end.

Sometimes it seems as if she has spent her whole life writing. She will die writing, she supposes.

Sighing, she folds the letter away (how its pages crackle, as thin as skin!). She puts down her pen. Her hand is tired. Her eyes, too, are tired. Her shoulders ache from bending over the page, and peering at what she has written, and trying to make sense of it all—her long, lost, life. For what, after all is said and done, has she to show for all those years, and all that effort?

It is not a long list.

Eight comets
Two-thousand-five-hundred nebulae (give or take a few)
One catalogue of stars
taken from Mr Flamsteed's Observations contained in the second volume of the Historia Coelestis, and not inserted in the British Catalogue, with an Index to point out every observation in that volume belonging to the stars of the British Catalogue. To which is added, a collection of errata that should be noticed in the same volume.
Two gold medals (one from the King of Prussia)
One honorary Fellowship

It seems both a great deal, and not very much at all.

For what of all the rest that might be said to constitute a life? The children? The grandchildren? The lovers? The husbands? The friends?

'I have loved but I have not been beloved,' she thinks, regarding her ring-less hands.

Although that is not quite true. William had loved her, she supposes; as—she hopes and trusts—does her nephew John. Her adored John. As dear to her as any son of her own would have been. 'My Honoured Aunt,' he calls her—but that is only his fun. In truth she has been more like an elder sister to him, notwithstanding the great difference in their ages. She it was who had romped on the floor with him when he was a little child (not being much bigger than a child herself); had taught him to climb trees, and had made mud-pies with him in the garden.

It was she who had held him up in her arms to the telescope, and pointed out the stars in Orion to him. There was Betelgeuse, and Rigel, and Iota Orionis, at the tip of Orion's sword—could he make it out? When he was bigger, she would show him how to sweep for nebulae. She had told him stories: his favourite was the one about the little boy who rode away on the tail of a comet. She had got the idea from Dr Maskelyne, who had once teased her with the notion that she might be tempted to do the same...

Yes, John would certainly weep for her when she died. Margaret, too—whom she had come to love as a daughter. How happy they had been, the dear young things (though not so young anymore, it had to be said)... With their stars, and their music, and their painting and drawing, and their brood of ten children (all still living, thank God) they had made themselves a veritable Paradise on Earth. For they, it seems, have the *trick* of happiness. You either had it, or you did not; it could not be taught.

She herself does not have it; although she would not have called herself unhappy. She supposes she has been content with very little—although at the time it seemed a sufficiency.

She had reflected a long time before replying to Edward Pigott's letter. The tone of it was so very singular. It was as if he spoke all that was in his heart, never minding to whom he was speaking. As if she were a stranger, whom he would never see again, so that he need not fear her censure; or a friend so intimate that nothing need be explained. She knew she was more to him than a stranger; but she was not sure to what extent she might consider herself his friend. And so she confined herself to a brief note, thanking him for his kind remarks upon her discovery of the comet, and hoping that he was by now quite recovered from the affliction which had troubled him.

No letter came back from him; and indeed she did not expect one. It was in fact almost two years before she heard from him again. This was on the occasion of her second comet; she had dispatched a note of the sighting to Dr Maskelyne, as was her custom—although he complained that it had taken three days to reach him, owing to the slowness of the penny post. This she could not allow. The next time it fell to her to inform the Astronomer Royal of such a discovery, she saddled up a horse and rode the thirty miles from Slough to Greenwich, to wake the astonished Maskelynes with her news...

(She remembers the feel of the night air on her skin. The wind in her hair, and the feel of the horse's flanks moving steadily beneath her. The moon had been almost full, she remembers. The road had seemed as bright as day—a white ribbon, unfolding before her, all the way to London. How fast her heart had been beating, with the audacity of her adventure, and the excitement of the news she had to tell...

She had thrown stones at his window. At length the Astronomer Royal's head, crowned with its nightcap, had appeared.

'Dr Maskelyne! Dr Maskelyne!' she had called.

'My dear Miss Herschel! Is it really you? My love...'—this to his wife—'We have a visitor...')

This time Mr Pigott's letter was addressed, not to her, but—as was only proper—to Dr and Mrs Herschel. Having first offered the writer's congratulations on the occasion of their marriage, it proceeded to tender his apologies for not having written sooner, *for I have been tossed about between England and France like a Shuttlecock*; in England, however, he now intended to stay. *I remain in Westminster for the time being, although I must find some other lodgings as soon as possible, there being no room here to set up the instruments*... Astronomy would therefore have to be abandoned for the present, he said.

There followed a passage which, even now, she cannot read without a glow of pleasure:

> But if I am to give up star-gazing, it gladdens my heart to know that others remain constant in their endeavours. The Discovery of a Comet by Miss Herschel last month has excited the greatest interest in Astronomical circles—so I am informed by Dr Maskelyne—and secures her place in the annals of Science. I have myself (despite having no proper instruments to speak of) spent several nights Observing the Star, which I find to be a very remarkable one...

'There, Lina! That is for you,' William had said, handing her the letter across the breakfast table. 'You have all the gentlemen in Europe at your feet, it seems...'

For there had been letters—no less complimentary—from M. Lalande and M. Méchain and others.

'Do not tease so, William,' Mary said; for her sharper eyes had noticed her sister-in-law's discomfiture. 'I am sure that Miss

Caroline has no need of others' praise to convince her of her worth.'

This was undoubtedly true; although she felt no gratitude towards poor Mary for saying it. Soon after, she had gathered up the letter, and withdrawn from the room, muttering something about having errands to see to.

How intractable she had been in her behaviour towards the new Mrs Herschel! In those first few months, she had refused all that lady's overtures of friendship, and avoided her company, as far as possible. In the end, through sheer force of will—to say nothing of many little acts of kindness—Mary had won her round; she herself had made no effort at all to sweeten the atmosphere. She sees now that this was unkind. At the time, it had seemed entirely justified by events. She had lost so much; and Mary Pitt had gained everything. How could she not have hated her a little?

From that time on, all Edward Pigott's letters to her brother concluded by sending his respects to "Mrs and Miss Herschel"; although it was a long time before there were any more letters addressed exclusively to herself. Nor did she hope for them—for what more could they have said than might be comfortably expressed within pages intended to be read by William? Remarks on stars observed and calculations made; regrets that invitations to visit had not been taken up. Respects to be conveyed...

If she had ever wished for anything more to have been said, she had long ceased to expect it. For whilst earthly happiness was offered to some—her brother's expression as he regarded his wife across the table each morning was evidence of this—it was not offered to everyone. Some had to be content to find satisfaction in other realms; that is to say, in the celestial one.

For Edward Pigott, too, she imagined, there would be a consolation in the heavens for the disappointments he had endured on Earth. That these were not dissimilar to her own she came to realize only gradually. Indeed nothing was ever said. But that the man by whom her heart had been broken had himself suffered that cruel reversal had become clear to her in the years that followed. The fact that he never married only confirmed what she already knew.

> A man of sorrows, and acquainted with grief...

It had been another year—or was it two?—before she saw him again. In that time, the French had decided to cut off the heads of their King and Queen, and the whole of Europe was in an uproar—for Revolution, it must be supposed, was as contagious as the Smallpox, and every Nation dreaded the possibility of succumbing to the Plague. For her own part, she blamed the Americans. Had it not been for their passion for Egalitarianism, the Jacobins would never have got hold of the idea of Revolution in the first place. To say that all men were Equal was plainly an absurdity; all it had done was to spread dissatisfaction, and encourage acts of bloody revenge on their betters by the lower orders.

Several of their friends from the Paris Observatory had been forced to flee for their lives; astronomy being of little account to the Sans Culottes, it seemed.

A letter had come from Edward Pigott, saying that a French Gentleman of his acquaintance—le Chevalier de Grave—who had just arrived from Paris (how precipitously he did not say), proposed calling at Slough, in the hope of seeing Dr Herschel and his wonderful instruments...

> I flatter myself that these few lines will procure him that satisfaction, for which I shall feel much obliged to you

For he added, the Chevalier, although not an astronomer by profession,

> is by no means led by idle curiosity; he is a man of letters & of universal knowledge...

In the event, their visitor did not arrive alone.

'For it seemed to me, you know, that I might as well enjoy the pleasure I have procured for my distinguished friend myself,' said

Mr Pigott with a smile. 'It is so long since I was last at Slough, that I had thought to find great changes—but I see that you, Miss Herschel, are not changed at all…'

She had laughed, and denied it.

'O, Lina is always the same,' William had said, with some complacency. 'Planets may appear and disappear, and comets hurl themselves about, but my sister remains my stay and comfort, through all vicissitudes…'

'You are a fortunate man, Sir. For Constancy seems to me to be the least regarded of virtues—and yet without it, Love would not endure…'

He was smiling as he said this, but there was a sadder expression in his eyes.

'Ah, Love!' cried William, pleased to have been given this opportunity to pay a compliment of his own. 'Where would we poor mortals be without it? And speaking of love, I do not believe you have met my wife…'

'I have not yet had that pleasure,' said Edward Pigott gravely, bending to kiss Mary Herschel's hand.

That night over dinner they had talked once more of variable stars, in which the Chevalier was said to have a great interest. Mr Pigott had been speculating of late as to the causes of such fluctuations of stellar magnitude. It was his opinion that the surface of some stars might consist of luminous particles—or rather, that the body of the stars being composed of dark matter, the variation in their light might be accounted for by the said particles, which forming a kind of fluid…

'I conceived of exactly the same notion with regard to the atmosphere of the Sun,' said William, his mouth full of food. 'Luminous spots. Luminous particles. It is all one…'

Edward bowed.

'It comes as no surprise to find that the discoverer of Georgium Sidus is ahead of me in this…'

'It matters not who saw it first,' said William, who was in expansive mood, having consumed the best part of a bottle of very fine claret. 'All that matters is that we can agree. For you know, my love,' he added, winking at his wife across the table, 'it is not unknown for astronomers to quarrel…'

'Indeed? I would not have thought it,' replied placid Mary Herschel. 'For you are often as pleased when some other gentleman makes a discovery as if you had found it yourself.'

There were times, Caroline thought, when her sister-in-law's excessive good-nature seemed indistinguishable from stupidity.

A bitter thought, she knows. She feels ashamed of having had such thoughts, now... But at the time, it had been hard to bear: the obvious happiness of the married pair, and the tender solicitude they had for one another ('Mary, my love, you will tire your eyes with all that sewing. Come, let us walk in the garden...') was too sharp a contrast to her own unhappiness; her sense of being, if not exactly *de trop*, then at least peripheral.

Much of the bitterness she felt was on *His* account... or rather, since he had no notion of her feelings for him, on her own.

'My dear Miss Herschel,' he said, kissing her hand, as he took his leave on that last occasion. 'I wonder if you understand what a Paragon you are? I do not believe there is another woman like you...'

She had hoped that the passage of time might have softened the pain his presence inevitably brought (although there was pleasure too; how handsome he still was; and how good natured!), but found that it was not so. Now they smiled and murmured polite phrases at one another.

She hoped he would return soon to Slough? She knew her brother and his wife would always be pleased to see him. As indeed she was herself...

He thanked her; but rather thought he would be away some time in Brussels. He had a sister there, a nun; it was a sad story; he would tell it to her sometime. Had things been otherwise, he would have liked nothing better than that she and his sister should have been friends. She—poor Mathurina—had more than a passing interest in the stars (their father being so devoted to astronomy), although it could not compare with Miss Herschel's command of the subject.

XXX

Sweeping, always sweeping... Yes, if she saw herself as anything, it was as a kind of celestial housewife, sweeping the heavens with her telescope, as she would a room full of dust. Her peculiar combination of speed and accuracy—the product of all those nights spent observing in the bitter cold, with only the thought of a pan of hot coffee, brewed over an iron stove, to concentrate her mind—was not easily matched. In 1790 alone, she found two comets—her third in January, and her fourth in April. A fifth followed, in December 1791; a sixth, seventh, and eighth, at two year intervals, after that. These last three had been found with the five-foot sweeper, which William had presented to her as a token of her achievements so far. Its mirror was nine inches in diameter, although its magnification was only X30. But its field was wide—ideal for hunting comets. Its ease of movement—it was mounted upon a spindle—meant she could sweep the heavens from horizon to the zenith in six minutes.

It was, she now sees, a golden age; although at the time, it seemed like mere drudgery: a continuation of the punishing routine she had endured for so many years, first in Hannover; later in Bath. Working hard was second nature to her. And yet there was a kind of satisfaction in it. More than satisfaction. Delight. She would set up her telescope on the flat roof of the stable-block where she had her quarters, and begin sweeping the sky for unfamiliar objects. This she did using a system she had devised herself, which left no part of the heavens un-scrutinised.

On the night of the 14th March 1793, for example, she wrote in her journal:

> I looked at the Moon to see if any luminous spots were visible in the dark part but saw none.

(This was at William's behest, for his mind was still running on luminous particles.)

> I swept for comets from the head of Taurus and left off with y in the foot of Andromeda…

How cold it had been! Though it was Spring, there was still a hint of frost in the air. Her breath, coming in white clouds, had condensed in an icy film upon the glass.

> Then I began to sweep with Beta Cassiopeia perpendicular sweeps from the horizon and upwards of 50 degrees. I left off at 4h common time with y Cygni and k Pegasi…

Each sweep cut a swathe through a thickly planted field of stars, like a scythe cutting through a field of daisies, so many there were. Sometimes it struck her, experienced as she was, as an impossible task. So many there were. She could never hope to count them all.

> At 9h 30′ being dark enough for sweeping I began in the usual manner with looking over the heavens with the naked eye, and immediately saw a comet…

This, it turned out, was to be her last. It was on 14th August 1797—fateful day, for she had made up her mind that very morning that, on William's return from Scotland, she would leave the house at Slough, which had been her home these past ten years, and go into lodgings. It turned out to be a disastrous decision—both for her own happiness and (she realises now) for Astronomy. For from that time, she found no more comets, and her role as the only professional Female Astronomer was fulfilled largely through acting as her brother's Amanuensis.

But (she admits) she was always her own worst enemy. Who else would have thrown away everything most dear to her—not once, but twice in a lifetime?

The way it happened was like this: William having set off for Edinburgh, where he was to spend upwards of a month with Dr Wilson, it had fallen to Caroline, as usual, to oversee the household accounts. This, in spite of the change in circumstances, which had been concomitant upon her brother's marriage, was a task she had not relinquished. Since she had always done it, it followed that she alone knew best how it should be done. It was not a simple matter of joints of beef and hundred-weights of coal to be ordered, such as anybody might have been able to understand, but included—amongst other related matters—the running costs of the Large Telescope.

So that when she noticed a discrepancy—a bill she did not remember paying being marked as 'paid'—she had taken up the matter with Mrs Herschel. With the knowledge she had gained of the perfidious nature of tradesmen she was only too ready to believe that a Fraud had been committed. Painful memories of the failed business venture, which had brought her days in Bath to so ignominious a close (that wretched Lizzie Barker!), compounded the feeling that an injury had been done her...

'But my dear sister,' Mary Herschel had gently remonstrated with her, 'there is no mystery in all this. I have paid Mr Samuel's bill. It arrived last week, when you were out. I thought it best to settle it at once.'

'It was not due until the end of the month.'

'It is of no consequence, surely—a few days here or there? Since bills must be paid,' said Mrs Herschel with a little laugh, 'it seems best to me that they should be paid at once.'

'Mr Samuels has always received payment at the end of the month,' her sister-in-law could not refrain from insisting. 'But if you prefer to pay him at another time, that is of course entirely up to you...'

Something of the other's affronted pride must have become apparent from her stiffness of manner to the astronomer's good lady, for she coloured faintly.

'O, do not let us quarrel over so insignificant a matter as a few shillings paid on one day or another. It shall be as you wish...'

But the damage was done, and the rift, once made, was not easily healed.

Perhaps (Caroline sees now), she did not want it to be healed.

'I would not have it said,' she had replied, with all the *hauteur* she could muster, 'that I have ever interfered in the running of my brother's house. Up till now, I have dealt with the menial tasks which fell to me to do, because I believed myself to be of service. But perhaps,' she had gone on, 'it would be "best", as you say, in future, if I were to surrender all such matters to you.'

Plead and cajole all she might, Mary Herschel was unable to persuade Caroline to change her mind. Yes, she had managed her brother's books for twenty years without occasioning the slightest complaint; and no, she would not be induced to manage those accounts any longer. She knew when she was not wanted. To this new sense of injury was added a determination to remove herself from the source of this, and other, injurious thoughts.

Simply: she would move away from Slough—or if not from the town itself (for there was still her work to be done), at least from the matrimonial home.

How vain and foolish she had been, she thinks, shaking her head. Poor Mary! She had not deserved such treatment.

Yes, her pride was the cause of all her woes, she sees. It had driven her from the comfortable apartment at her brother's house, where she had unlimited access to the instruments and a roof-terrace ideal for star-gazing, to a succession of cramped, damp cottages, to which she was obliged to journey in the dark, when the day's work was over, and which she struggled to afford on her meagre salary. It had turned her from respected Assistant Astronomer into a mere assistant—for how was she to pursue her own researches, under such inauspicious conditions? Instead of being a renowned Discoverer of Nebulae and Hunter of Comets, she became, once more, a diligent Compiler of Catalogues.

The new century arrived, and with it her own half-century. Now the face that looked back at her from the glass, though it had not entirely lost its youthful features, could no longer be called young. Sorrow and disappointment had left their mark upon it. Having long ago transferred the hopes she had once had for fulfilment from her private to her professional life, she now found that even this was not to be relied upon.

No, the year 1800, she sees, flicking through the pages of her Day Book, was not distinguished by any new astronomical discoveries at all. Even William, immersed as he was in the comforts of domestic life, had seemed content to revisit work previously done. In fact, he seemed hardly to have concerned himself with work at all, with the holidays he had taken—two weeks in Bath in February, followed by a fortnight in London in April; then six weeks at the seaside with Mary, and eight year-old John; with another three weeks at Bath in November... The driven individual she remembered from their earlier days, who had done without sleep and forgotten to eat in the thrall of his ruling passion, had turned, it seemed, into a family man.

That same year, she herself had spent some weeks in Bath, fitting up William's new house there. Had she seen Edward Pigott? Her journal makes no mention of it, beyond a passing reference to 'a pleasant hour spent with old friends.'

She had seen him; of course she had seen him; although the new house on Margaret's Hill had been a Chaos of dust and half-unpacked boxes. The sitting-room had been just about fit to be seen, however, and it was there, wearing a new gown of pale grey satin, that she had received him.

He was handsome still; his hair only lightly streaked with grey; his features as expressive of sympathy as she could have wished.

They had talked of this and that; she doesn't now remember what. Only that, as they sat there, drinking tea, with the light airs from the open window stirring the curtains, and a shaft of late afternoon sunlight moving slowly across the wall, she had felt a profound contentment: a sense of being perfectly at ease. This, she thought, was what it must feel like to be an old married couple—with no need to talk, unless one felt like talking; and everything that was to be known about the other known; understood; forgiven.

Her meetings with Edward Pigott were not many, and yet she can picture them all with the same vivid recall. From those few (blessed) weeks in the spring of '78, when she had seen him almost every day, to the handful of times he came to Datchet and Slough, and then again when they met in Bath, it can have amounted to no more than a few dozen hours. Fourteen or fifteen days' worth, at most. It was not long. Two weeks, out of a lifetime of ninety-odd years, constituting all she was to know of love, and of the constancy of the heart's affections.

There were his letters, of course. But since so very few of them had actually been addressed to her—only two or three, in fact; and one of those the letter of commiseration he had written on William's death—she could hardly claim those as proof of any reciprocal devotion. Although, on occasion, as in the letter Edward Pigott had written to her brother after he—Mr Pigott—had been released from his French prison, it had been impossible not to feel that at least some of the writer's warmth of feeling had been intended for her...

She unfolds the letter now, and scans the familiar words, which inspire in her the same mixture of sadness and joy as when she first heard them—read out by William over the tea table:

> Oct: 30th 1806
> Bath—St James's Square No. 35
>
> Dear Sir
>
> The reception of your last gave me the most sincere pleasure, as therein I found how much I had been mistaken in thinking you had lost sight of me & my letter during my detention at Fontainebleau, for indeed I have always look'd on a continuation of our intimacy & esteem as one of the greatest satisfactions of my life...

'The dear fellow!' William had exclaimed. 'To imagine that I should have forgotten him, when, all the time, I have been so anxious on his behalf—have I not, my dear?'—this to Mary, who had merely nodded, being distracted just then by some request of her son's (then lately home from school) to pass the jam.

> you will not by this, I hope, apprehend I am going to engage you in a settled correspondence, be assured I know too well the value of your time to entertain any such idea—

“As if I should mind corresponding with such an old friend, when I am showered with letters from all the world on all manner of foolishness!’

> on your next appearance you will find me in St James’s Square—my residence for life—having taken a very long lease of No. 35 & mean to fit up a Garret Observatory as soon as my Astronomical Instruments are arrived from York…

‘Bless the man! A “Garret Observatory”, indeed!’ laughed William. ‘Does that not strike you as a very affecting picture, Lina? The itinerant Astronomer, come to rest at last in his “Garret Observatory”…’ He wiped his eyes. ‘Dear Pigott. What a very splendid fellow he is! But really, it is unkind of me to laugh, for he has had his troubles, poor Soul… Ah, see how very pleasantly he asks to be remembered to you both: “my kindest remembrances to Mrs and Miss Herschel”—that is for you, my dear, and for you, Lina… Why, Lina, are you off?’ he added, seeing that his sister was putting on her cloak. ‘I had thought we were going to do some work this evening…’

She had made some excuse—she doesn’t remember what—but in truth, she could not bear to listen to any more. Her brother was a remarkable man—generous to a fault; kind and affectionate; but there were times when his insensitivity to any feelings but his own struck her as astounding.

Looking back, it seems unfair that she should have blamed her brother for her disappointments. It was not his fault that her living conditions were uncomfortable; nor that, after quitting his establishment, she found no more comets. All this was of her own making. In those years, she was kept busy enough—compiling her monumental Index to Flamsteed’s Catalogue made sure of that. But she was never again to experience the sharp intense joy of discovery; the moment of realisation that she, and she alone, had seen something previously unseen…

Not that she gave up trying altogether—and for that she had Edward Pigott to thank. Following his release from prison, and his return to England, he resumed the correspondence with her brother suspended during that three years' detention. This—given their mutual predilections—quite often concerned comets. In 1807, for instance, there were two—in February and September:

> A few hours ago, I saw a Comet so very distinctly with the naked eye, that I scarcely think to write anything about it,
> Edward Pigott had written, of the second of these.

She had lost no time in making her own observation of the phenomenon, although the time was past when she could have claimed it as her own. Now, she was content merely to confirm the discoveries of others.

Another letter, about another comet, sent—she sees—some four years later, had the distinction only of having been addressed, not to her brother, but to herself:

> Aug:st 31st 1811
> Bath—15 Belmont
>
> Dear Madam
> in case anything has prevented you Observing the French Comet noted in the Newspapers, my last night's Observation with an Opera Glass may serve to point it out—at all events I am happy, as you see, to seize the opportunity of writing to you & assuring you of my sincere regard & best of wishes
> Edwd Pigott
>
> Aug: 30th at 9h—R.A. 156°, N.D. 37—doubtful to a Degree

Strange that this—affectionate as it was in tone, though scarcely a *billet doux*—should have wrung her heart so.

Her next meeting with Edward Pigott was a few years after this, during that famous 'year without a summer' of 1816. She was in

Bath on Alexander's account, to help him pack for the journey back to Hannover. It was—although neither of them knew it—to be a final parting. For, once his boxes had been dispatched to London by the carrier, and his travelling bags packed, and the two of them had taken the coach to St Katherine's Dock, from whence his ship was to depart, brother and sister would never set eyes on one another again.

Nor did she see Edward Pigott again, after that day.

An hour's talk about the stars on a day of driving rain, which had left her looking like a drowned cat, hardly seemed a fitting conclusion to a passion which had lasted forty years. For she had been soaked through when she arrived; she remembers that he had made her take her wet stockings off, to dry them. Years before, when she was young, she would have died of mortification; as if was, they were both too old for such an impropriety to matter.

Still, she remembers how tongue-tied she was, at seeing him again after a lapse of several years. Age, which had made her less concerned about keeping up appearances, had made her no better at disguising her feelings.

So she had taken refuge in Poetry.

He had been reading *Domestic Pieces*, she recalls: the volume lay open upon the arm of his chair.

'Are you an admirer of the noble lord?' he had said, when he saw the direction of her glance. 'I confess I find him an amusing companion. Whatever one says about him—and I cannot believe *half* the things that are said—he writes a very pretty line...

I had a dream, which was not all a dream.
The bright sun was extinguish'd and the stars
Did wander darkling in the eternal space,
Rayless, and pathless, and the icy earth
Swung blind and blackening in the moonless air...

Enough to send a shiver along the spine, is it not?'

'He visited us at Slough, once—it must be five years ago,' she said.

She had, she confessed, been disappointed in her first impressions of the famous poet. He had cut, she recalled, a somewhat graceless figure—tossing back bumper after bumper of William's best claret, and contributing little to the conversation at dinner beyond a few brusque remarks on the subject of a greyhound he was thinking of buying.

Only when, after dinner, he took his first view through the twenty-foot telescope, did she have cause to revise her opinion.

'I never knew before,' Lord Byron had cried, his face alight with wonder, 'that the Stars are Worlds. How do you live with the terror of that knowledge, Herschel? It would send me stark mad, I am sure...'

When she had repeated their distinguished visitor's words to Edward Pigott, he had smiled.

'It is my belief,' he said, 'that we astronomers are quite as conversant with madness as poets—only less given to writing about it...'

'I am sure you must be right.'

Although, in her experience, astronomy required one to be strong-minded.

After Poetry and Madness, their talk had moved, inevitably, to Time and the Stars. Fitting subjects for two astronomers, she supposes. In spite of all the years they had known one other, and all the sadness both had endured, they still could not bring themselves to talk about what was in their hearts.

Except that, in a way, perhaps they had, that afternoon. Sometimes it is not the words themselves, she thinks, that matter.

She remembers the softness in Edward Pigott's eyes; the gentleness in his voice, when the past was mentioned. 'One may live a moment not once, but many times,' he said.

She wonders whether, of all the hundreds of thousands of moments he might have chosen to live over again, some of them would have included herself.

For her own part, where he is concerned, there can be no question about it.

There are letters, of course. Always letters. How else would her love have been kept alive? A few conversations (mainly of an astronomical nature); a few looks and smiles; a few scribbled lines, and what might be read between them... it does not amount to very much. But she is used to making do with very little.

Here is another letter, intended for another—her brother, of course—and the last she has in her possession. Its tone of gentle reproach, for opportunities lost, still has the power to move her:

> Aug:t 24—1817
> Bath 15 Belmont
>
> My Dear Sir
>
> I write these few Lines to say how much I regret not having had the pleasure of seeing you for several times, when you passed through Bath; you must not I hope forget, we are very Old Friends, at least for 39 years past—as appears from the Astronomical Observations we made together in 1778 in King Street &c.—these are surely great Claims towards a continuation of our intimacy which I cannot easily give up...
>
> I remain, my Dear Sir, with the best of wishes
> yours most sincerely
> Edw:d Pigott

A fitting conclusion, perhaps, to their epistolatory romance—a romance spun almost entirely out of words meant for someone else.

It had been from dearest John that she heard the news of his death—her once-beloved. Appended to a long letter on John's latest findings with the twenty-foot telescope was a postscript:

> Sad news I fear about Father's old friend, Pigott. I heard from Dr Shepherd this morning that our learned colleague is no more. It appears he had been ailing for some time; as I may have mentioned to you, it was on the grounds of ill-health that he refused my offer of membership of our Astronomical Society four years ago. His death is a grievous loss to Science, and to Friendship...

She had sat for some time without moving or speaking. All she could think was, he is gone. I shall never see him more. Almost ten years had passed since she had last beheld his face, and yet it was hard to believe it could be so.

She recalled their first night together, star-gazing in the garden at New King Street. The night of *Messiah*. The night at the Assembly Rooms (O blessed night!) when they had danced. The night she had sung for him, at Slough. So many nights, and so many partings...

All gone, now.

Rising, at last, from the curious trance into which the news she had just received had thrown her, she began pacing up and down the drawing-room, which, connected by double doors to a room of equal size she had converted soon after her arrival into a library, took up almost the entire ground floor of the house. It was here she had set up the seven-foot telescope—handsome relic of her days in Bath; here, too, that the pianoforte she had bought, at considerable expense, from Berlin, stood open.

On the music-stand was the piece she had been playing a few nights before, when Dietrich and his wife had come to dinner. For she still sang a little, then...

Sah ein Knab ein Röslein stehn,
Röslein auf der Heiden...

Reaching the instrument, she had paused, in her restless agitation, and picked out the opening bars. The old airs were the best. Nothing she had heard in recent years could compare with the beauty of this—neither melody, nor words.

War so jung und morgenschön,
Lief er schnell, es nah zu sehn,
Sahs mit vielen Freuden...

Suddenly, she could not see for tears.

I am a foolish old woman, she thought, and there is no help for me.

XXXI

It has stopped snowing, for the time being. Soon it will be snowing again. The world outside her window is covered in a thick crust of white, which reflects the light from a small, pale Sun as if in a giant mirror. Branches of trees, roofs, church-spires, and cobblestones appear as if partially rubbed out. A new world might be drawn in their place. Pristine. How she would like to see that world! It has been years since she went out in the snow, but the memory of its coldness—so cold it burned the skin—remains with her. That is all she has left to her now: the memory of sensation, rather than the thing itself—like the sweetness left at the bottom of a cup of chocolate, after the cup is empty...

As she watches, a yelling child in a red muffler throws a dirty snowball at another child. The missile traces a pleasing arc through the wintry air, before hitting its target with some force. A predictable shrieking ensues.

She remembers a game of snowballs with her little brother, Dietrich—it must have been a good eighty-five years ago. His aim had not been very accurate at first, and she had laughed at him. Then he had caught her—smack!—on the back of her neck. She can still feel the shock of it, and the chill of the icy morsels slipping inside her blouse, though the child she was has melted away with the snow of that long-ago winter.

It is strange, she thinks, that she, of all the Herschels, had lived the longest, when, more than once in her early life, she had seemed the most like to die. For although the smallpox had not killed her, the typhus she had contracted a few years later, at the age of eleven, had almost done so. Several in their street had died; and she herself had stayed in bed for many weeks, too ill to move or speak. Perhaps Death, having come so close to claiming her for his own, had grown tired of the game, and decided to let her alone for the next eighty years or so...

Still, it does not seem possible that she should be so old. When she looks in the mirror—as she must, from time to time, to adjust a cap, or fasten a brooch at her throat—she does not recognise the face that she sees. With its pale wrinkled skin, sunken cheeks, and thin lips, which part to reveal the yellowing teeth of a hag, it seems a hideous travesty of all she once was. Her hair, too, of which she was once so proud, has grown thin and colourless. Her neck... but why continue with this anatomy of decay? In any event, it does not distress her unduly—she, who was never a beauty.

If she considers it at all, it is with a scientist's curiosity, which itemises the signs of ageing as it would the particular features of a dying star.

She adjusts the cap, and fastens the brooch, and puts the glass aside. She has no more need of it: she is as 'presentable'—her mother's word—as she will ever be. For when 'company' is expected (another phrase of Anna Ilse's), one must make at least the barest effort to show one's best face to the world. Un-brushed hair, and what Anna Ilse called her 'sulky' look, had earned her many a whipping... Her poor, cross mother! Caring for nothing but what the neighbours would think, if her steps were unscrubbed, or her rooms un-swept, or her roses un-pruned, or her child unkempt.

'I will not have you disgrace me!' she had cried, between slaps. '*Ach, Gott!* What it is to have a wayward girl...'

She had taken away the books and forbidden the music lessons and frowned when Isaac took his little daughter outside to look at the stars. 'She will catch her death!' Anna Ilse had said. She had not caught her death. What she *had* caught was the trick of seizing the moment. Because when you have a great deal you want to do, and very little time in which to do it, it makes you quick at picking up essentials.

If Anna Ilse had but known it, she was giving her daughter a great gift—which was the gift of making a little go a long way. Thanks, perhaps, to all those slaps and shouts and repeated injunctions to hurry up and finish whatever it was she was doing, she—Caroline—has never wasted time. For this she has her mother to thank—a woman who detested learning, and music, and all the things to which her daughter has devoted her life.

'Unnatural child! Changeling!' she remembers her mother crying, driven to distraction by some piece of folly on Carolina's part. (Desiring on one such occasion to perceive the world upside-down, she had borrowed Anna Ilse's precious pocket-mirror, and had walked about all day in a topsy-turvy universe, in which the sky with its swirling clouds had become the ground beneath her feet; unfortunately, she had not been looking where she was going, and had fallen over the door-sill, breaking the mirror, and gaining herself some fine bruises, not all of them self-inflicted.)

Changeling. She must have been a changeling, she decides. How else to explain what she was later to become: a woman, with a man's mind; a child, whom even the great looked up to?

Her ghostly brothers and sisters, she can feel them hovering at her shoulder; hear the baby murmur of their voices, calling her home. Johann Heinrich; Anna Christina; Maria Dorethea; Frantz Johann... Although all the others are dead, now—even those who lived long enough to bring children of their own into the world. She is the last survivor of the ten. Sophia, the eldest, and herself the mother of six, worn out by her long years of widowhood; Jacob—murdered (a terrible business); Alexander—poor, dear, unhappy Alexander—and Wilhelm (most beloved): these last two dead within a year of each other. The shock of it remains with her still.

Last to die was Dietrich—her pet, her little brother; thrower of snowballs. Dietrich for whose sake she (foolishly, as it turned out) returned to Hannover—gone, too, these twenty years and more.

She is quite alone, now...

Although not *quite* alone, if the truth were told—for there are still Dietrich's daughters, her nieces, even though she never sees them... well, not more than once a week, at most. Then when they *do* come, passing by on their way to dinner or the theatre, they sit yawning and glancing at the clock all through the visit.

She would rather be alone than in such company.

And of course there is John—beloved boy... although of course by now well over fifty. Well, he would always be a boy in her eyes, no matter what age he was—for all his proud achievements of journeying to the Cape, and the observatories he has built, and learned Societies founded.

She has had a letter from John, she recollects. He is sending her his completed observations from the Cape, he says. These—an entire mapping of the Southern skies, to complement his father's mapping of the northern hemisphere—will be his lifetime's achievement.

When it reaches you, he has written, *you will then have in your hands the completion of my father's work.*

Dearest John. So devoted a son; and no less devoted a nephew... How he puts those simpering nieces of hers to shame. They have not the least idea which end of a telescope is which. *They*, who grudge spending even five minutes in her company, have no conception of the dedication it takes to give one's whole life to another... as John (bless him!) has done. As she—no less blessed, for all that—has also done.

Yes, John is a good boy. Clever, too—although not as clever as his father. Her dearest Wilhelm. *William*, as he later became, just as she became *Caroline*, not Carolina. *Lina*. That was his name for her, always.

Dear William! Dearest Brother! How she misses him still... Those last few years, when he was growing old, had brought about a change in their relations. Now, he was the weak one; she the strong. He depended upon her, he said. She was, as ever, his trusty right hand. She was to preserve all his papers for Posterity: a colossal task, with material going back almost fifty years. For nothing was in order—his library was in a state of utter confusion, with papers stacked upon papers, without the slightest regard for Chronology. Bills for mirrors purchased thirty years before were mixed up with sheet music, and with notebooks filled, in his meticulous hand, with every observation he had made of every star.

Then there were all the notes and diagrams relating to his inventions: designs for telescopes, and experiments to do with the construction of specula. Not to mention the letters—O, those letters!—from everyone he had ever met, and a good many he had not... all of it tossed about together and covered in dust.

Even when he was able to persuade John—devoted Son—to quit his studies at Cambridge, in order to carry on his (William's) work, it did not significantly lessen her own contribution to the endeavour. For if John were to take over his father's career—which of course he would, for when did he ever refuse the old man anything?—then there were mirrors to be polished for the twenty-foot telescope, and an assistant (herself) to stand in readiness for when he (John) made his observations.

She thinks of the day when the two of them, brother and sister, had assisted the young man with his first sweep. It must have been June or July of 1822, a few months before William died—having made it into his eighty-fourth year; the same span of time as it took his planet, Uranus, to complete a single revolution around the Sun... It must have made a quaint picture, she supposes: the venerable white-haired old man, wrapped in shawls, directing operations from his bath-chair; whilst she herself—scarcely less Ancient a specimen—shakily ascended the ladder of the scaffold which supported the instrument, in order to make some necessary adjustment...

A tear runs suddenly down her cheek. She wipes it away with the back of her hand. It would not do to let anyone see that she has been crying.

For they are to have Company today. Her great-nephew, Friedrich—eldest child of the niece she dislikes least—is coming to tea, with his Intended. Friedrich she does not mind; he is less foolish than his sisters, whose names she can never remember, and has just returned from university in Wittenberg. She will enjoy seeing Friedrich. She likes the young, she thinks, more than their elders. They have had less time to turn into fools and dullards. She wonders what the girl—Fräulein Gottlieb—will be like. Not too silly, she hopes. She cannot abide silliness in young girls...

But where is Gerda with the tea-things?

It is nearly half-past three, she is dressed and ready, and still the table has not been laid, nor the fire banked up. A thought strikes her: perhaps her guests have already arrived, and are being detained downstairs by the talkative Gerda. She strains her ears. She swears she can hear voices...

She bangs her cane upon the floor, until Gerda appears.

'Bang, bang, bang! What's all the fuss?' grumbles the maid, setting down a tray laden with cups and saucers and plates upon the gate-leg table.

'Are they here yet?'

'No, they're not here. You said four o'clock—the *English* style,' says Gerda, with an ironical curl of the lip. 'It's only just struck three. And I've still the *spunge-cake* to make, and the *sandwiches* to cut…' She pronounces these alien words with the same lightly satirical accent.

'But the fire, Gerda—the fire needs repairing…'

'There's only me here, isn't there?' is the retort. 'Don't see as how I can be in two places at once, nor do the work of two people, neither…'

But, after the usual huffing and puffing, she gets down on her knees and, with the judicious application of a shovelful of coals and a sheet of the previous day's newspaper, soon has the bedroom fire blazing nicely.

Because of course it is to her bedroom they must come, the visitors; her bedroom which is now parlour, study and sleeping-chamber in one. It is two years since she last went downstairs; the rooms are all shut up, now. Apart from the yearly Spring-cleaning to which Gerda subjects them, there is no reason for anyone to enter them at all.

The empty rooms, with their dust-sheeted furniture, resemble her own life, she sees. Once, they were busy and bustling and full of visitors (well, maybe not exactly full; but certainly more in use than they are now). Once, she walked through these rooms, gazed at the pictures upon the walls, and ran her fingers over the keys of the pianoforte. Now she has retreated to just one room. It has all she needs: a bed, a table, a fire.

Soon, even these necessities will no longer be required.

Fräulein Gottlieb turns out to be very pretty indeed, so that her silliness can be endured with equanimity. She exclaims with delight when she sees Fritzie, the dachshund, and kisses him repeatedly upon the muzzle. She has never seen such a dear, sweet, precious, pet in all her life, she says. She praises the sandwiches, and the spunge-cake—thereby endearing herself to Gerda—and remarks politely upon some of the more interesting objects in the room. What a lot of books and pictures there are! She is sure she has never seen so many. She is very fond of books—although she has to confess that the books she likes best are novels, not scientific treatises... And what a charming tea-service! She supposes it must have come from abroad. It is so much prettier than anything she has seen in Germany…

'Is it not pretty, Mama?' she remarks to that lady.

Frau Gottlieb—a handsome woman in late middle-age, dressed all in black (a widow, Caroline surmises) agrees that the tea-service is very pretty.

'Such charmingly painted roses! When I am married,' Charlotte Gottlieb throws an arch glance at her Beloved. 'I should like to have cups and saucers like these, all covered in roses…'

When told that the tea-service she so admires has been brought from England, Fräulein Gottlieb is all curiosity.

Had Fräulein Herschel lived in England very long? she wants to know. She herself has never been there, but she has been told it is delightful…

'That is a picture of England,' Caroline replies, directing her young visitor's attention to the drawing which hangs above the desk. It is of the house at Slough; she looks at it almost every day.

'But how wonderful!' exclaims the vivacious young lady. 'Look, Mama! Friedrich, do come and look!'

'I have seen it before,' says her lover. But with her standing there smiling at him so prettily, he cannot resist going to look at it again. 'Yes, that is the house—a funny, old-fashioned place, is it not? Do you see that curious structure in the garden?' He places his finger upon the spot. 'That is Great-Uncle's telescope—the largest ever built. For you know he was a famous Astronomer…'

'Yes, that is the forty-foot telescope,' says Caroline. 'Alas, it is all dismantled now…'

'…nor was he the only famous person in the family,' continues Friedrich, with a wink at his fiancée. 'My Great-Aunt is too modest to say, but she was once the most celebrated woman of the Age. She has won several Gold Medals for her services to Astronomy.'

Charlotte Gottlieb's round blue eyes grow rounder still.

'But that is marvellous!' she cries. 'Think of it, Mama! A Female Astronomer!'

'She has found ever so many comets—have you not, Aunt?'

'A number, yes. But I was never a great astronomer,' says Caroline. 'Although I have been privileged to know several—my brother, William, of course, being foremost amongst them. But there were others—M. Messier, for example. Mr Edward Pigott…'

'Pigott? That is an English name, is it not?' says Frau Gottlieb.

Caroline concedes that it is. 'I had many English friends,' she says. 'The late Mr Pigott being one of them. A very *dear* friend to me indeed,' she adds—for who is there to hear her? When she was Charlotte Gottlieb's age, she would have blushed to have made such a confession; now that she is old, none of it matters anymore…

Patterns. It is all to do with patterns, she sees. If she thinks back on her life, she can see that it has been made up of patterns of many different kinds. There are those which are to do with family—with Bad Brothers and Good Brothers; with a Father who loved her, and a Mother who did not. That the One she loved above all others could not love her was also, perhaps, a part of this pattern… As were the places: Hannover, Bath, Slough, Hannover. She had not loved Hannover, nor anything about it, and yet she had returned here to die.

Music. That was another kind of pattern. The neat black marks—strokes, dots and curlicues—which made up any given page of a musical score were a pattern in themselves, as well as an ordering of units of Time, and Sound. And what a glory these little scratchings of pen and ink held within them! Only thus could Music—which was of its nature transient—be captured, for the edification of future generations; its patterns of notes, rests, and time signatures recorded, with perfect fidelity.

Numbers. Their intricate relationships, too, had governed her life. Without them, she would not have been able to record all she had seen of the movements of Stars and Planets, nor calculate, with such pleasing accuracy, recurring patterns of astronomical phenomena.

For things happens but once; only when it is written, or noted down, can it be experienced anew.

She thinks of the famous composer, her countryman, who—as his deafness worsened—could experience his Symphonies only through the medium of the written score—and is glad of the existence of patterns.

When Gerda comes up to tell her of her visitor, she is at first surprised, if only because it seems a little soon. But then she sees how it is: yesterday's visit was pleasure; today's will be business. When a marriage is in prospect—even between two young people evidently as romantically attached as her great-nephew and his fiancée—there are many unromantic matters to be settled. Financial matters, in fact. She supposes it is about these that Johanna Gottlieb has come, in the absence of a husband to act for her; although it does cross her mind that surely it is Friedrich's parents, rather than his elderly aunt, who should more properly be approached...

Perhaps they *have* already been spoken to, and have made a difficulty about the size of the girl's portion? She knows already from Friedrich that Fräulein Gottlieb is not rich. 'We are marrying for love, Aunt,' he has said—as if that cancelled all debts (of which, she happens to know, he has quite a few). In which case, his prospective mother-in-law might have been sent to put the case for love, as against cold lucre...

Well, well. She will soon know all.

And so she composes her features into an agreeable smirk, and invites her unexpected visitor to sit down.

The long silence which follows the conventional pleasantries with which their colloquy begins, is perplexing. Instead of getting straight to the point, Frau Gottlieb stares at the fire; then at her hands; then at the pattern on the carpet.

Out with it, woman, Caroline wants to say. I am not such a dragon as all that. Whatever your worries about pretty little Fräulein Blue-Eyes your daughter, they cannot be so great that we will not be able to reach an understanding. Why, if that niece of mine and her pompous husband have made an awkwardness about the dowry, I will pay for the wedding myself...

'I am sure you can have no idea why I am here,' says Johanna Gottlieb at last. There is a tremor in her voice, which makes Caroline look up sharply. 'But I confess that since Charlotte and I returned from seeing you yesterday, my mind has been in turmoil...'

'She is your youngest child, is she not?' interjects Caroline.

Frau Gottlieb seems mildly surprised at the question. 'Yes. A "late lamb", as they say. There is ten years between her and her eldest brother.'

'Are they all married, your sons?'

'The eldest two. My youngest son is training for the priesthood. For you know, we are Catholics...'

Ah, thinks Caroline. Perhaps it is not about money at all, but on a matter of religious scruple she has come to consult me.

'I assure you,' she begins, 'that on matters of religion I am at one with that great Atheist, Voltaire...'

'I do not know anything about that,' interrupts Frau Gottlieb, in some agitation. 'That is... I am sure it is all very fine, but...'

She is silent a moment, as if trying to order her thoughts.

'Yesterday,' she continues in a low voice, 'you mentioned that you were a friend of Mr Edward Pigott.'

For once Caroline can think of nothing to say.

'I think that it must be the same one... that is, it is not such a common name as all that, even in England...'

'I do not understand you.'

'Forgive me.' She makes a visible effort to compose herself. 'Mr Pigott was a friend to me, also,' she says.

When Caroline says nothing, the other continues:

'By "friend", I mean benefactor. It was he who paid for my education. When I married Gottlieb...'

'I do not believe Mr Pigott was ever in Hannover,' interrupts Caroline.

'You are right. He was not. The only times I ever saw him—and they were not many—were in Brussels.'

Caroline cannot suppress a start.

'I was born there,' says Frau Gottlieb. 'Although I never knew my mother...'

'He was certainly in Brussels,' says Caroline. 'He had, I believe, a sister there, in Holy Orders.'

'Yes,' replies Johanna Gottlieb. For a moment, she seems lost in thought. 'He never spoke of her to me. I have often wondered...' She breaks off, with a little shake of the head. 'But it makes no difference now. I was bought up by an elderly couple,' she continues. 'My name then was Jeanne-Mathurine Warens. I came to Hannover in the year '15, after I married Gottlieb...'

'You say Mr Pigott visited you in Brussels?'

'Yes. The first time was when I was seven years old. I remember that he took me out to look at the stars...'

Caroline is silent.

'There was one, I recall, which seemed to wink—flashing brighter, then dimming again. He called it the Demon Star...'

'Beta Persei. Sometimes called Algol...'

'That is right!' For a moment, Frau Gottlieb's pale face grows animated. 'But of course, as an astronomer, you must be familiar with all such things...'

'When was the last time you saw him?'

'A year after I was married. He gave me a gift, of money. He was always generous...'

'Why do you suppose that was?' Caroline's tone is sharper than perhaps she had intended.

'I believe he had an interest in me.'

Caroline looks at her visitor, as if for the first time. It cannot be, she thinks; and yet it might be so... There is something about the shape of the face; the colouring (for although Johanna Gottlieb's hair is streaked with grey, it must once have been dark); the eyes, above all... Yes, certainly, the eyes...

'Are you saying he was your father?'

Frau Gottlieb hesitates a moment.

'At one time I thought so, yes.'

The fine dark eyes hold Caroline's gaze. Yes, she thinks, it must be so; feeling, in the same moment, both happy and sad. To think that he...

'Now I know that he was not.'

She opens the reticule she has been clasping and takes out what it contains: a letter, evidently; and something else.

'I did not see Mr Pigott again after that day,' she says. 'But I received this from him...'

She hands the letter to Caroline.

'It was six years after I came to Hannover. I was expecting Hubert, my third... Please,' she says. 'Read it. Then you will know as much as I.'

Caroline unfolds the letter—a single close-written sheet, surrounding another, which she sets aside. It is the covering sheet she reads first. She knows the hand at once.

Brussels—19th April, 1821

Madam

a Lady, who is very dear to me, and who—for reasons which will become clear—has been restrained from making herself known to you until now, has made it her last request that the enclosed Letter and Picture should be conveyed to you.

I do so in the knowledge that the information contained in the letter may be abhorrent to you; but I pray that you will not judge either the writer or the sender too harshly, since both were guided by the same principle—which was their concern for your happiness and safety.

As for the picture—it is of One who was dear to both of us, but whom a cruel Fate tore from those that loved him before his time.

Indifferent health prevents me from giving these things into your hands in person; I trust that you yourself are well, and remain

Your hum:l & obed:t Servant

Edw:d Pigott

The letter awakens thoughts and feelings she had supposed long dead.

Do you suppose that, in some shape or form, we continue? he had said, the last time they met.

To have had a child was one kind of continuation; although not one that either he or she had ever known.

She raises her eyes once more, and sees that Johanna Gottlieb's are full of tears.

'After that day, I heard nothing more from him,' she says. 'Until yesterday, when you said his name…' The tears spill over, and run down her face, unchecked.

'My dear,' says Caroline. 'You are not well. I will send for tea…'

She reaches for the bell, to call Gerda, but her visitor shakes her head.

'No, no. I am quite well, truly. It is only that…'

The door opens a crack.

'Thank you, Gerda,' says Caroline. 'When we require tea, I will ring…'

But it is not Gerda, but the third member of the household, who makes an appearance. Sharp little nails make a clicking sound upon the floorboards. A velvet muzzle thrusts itself against its mistress's hand.

'Good boy, Fritzie,' she murmurs.

In the brief interval provided by this interruption, her visitor seems to have mastered her emotions. 'To think that you and he were friends!' she says, with a tremulous smile. 'And that, all these years, you have been here in Hannover, and I never knew…'

'The world is a smaller place than we imagine.'

'So it would seem. But you have not yet read *her* letter…'

Caroline unfolds it. A faint scent, as of dried rose-petals, arises from the single sheet of paper, which has been folded in two, and then folded again, to form a kind of packet. On the outside of this is written, in a hand so faint it betrays the writer's infirmity: *M:elle Jeanne-Mathurine Warens, c/o M. Edward Pigott*. The initials on the seal—which has been cut, not broken—are distinctive: M de V.

It is then that—just as on those long-ago nights in the dark garden, an apparently formless Shape in the sky would resolve itself into a definite Object—the whole pattern becomes clear to her at last…

My Beloved Child,

For so I have always thought of you, even though I gave up all claim to your affections a long time ago. I never laid eyes on you but once, when you were taken from my arms to be given to that good couple whom you have called parents, and to whom a duty of gratitude must be paid.

But close to Death as I am, I could not forbear from telling you the truth about your origins. I have lived a long time in the knowledge that my only child did not know me; to die, being known at last, is my one consolation.

This, then, is your history, dearest Child: albeit a sad one. You were born to a Mother who could not keep you, and to a Father who died before you were born. That your mother—poor, foolish girl!—was already married to another, need not concern you; the man in question being long dead, and the connexion an evil one. Suffice it to say, that if I have sinned in betraying such a one, then I have paid the price for it a hundred times over.

To have given up everything I loved in the world has been hard; all that has kept me from despair has been the Love of God, and knowing that you, my daughter, are safe and happy.

Of your late Father—Beloved Soul—I will only say that he was an English Gentleman, of an old and respected family. The enclosed is his likeness—the only token I have to remember him by—which I now give to you, in remembrance of us both.

I am, dearest Child, in Christ Jesus,
Ever your affectionate Mother,
Mathurine de Valois

'Here is the picture,' says Johanna Gottlieb. She holds out the object she has been concealing in the palm of her hand all this while: a picture, painted on ivory and framed in gold, about two inches in diameter. It shows a young man of surpassing beauty, aged about twenty, and dressed in the quaint fashions of sixty years ago. His lightly powdered hair is swept back, above an unlined brow, and tied with a ribbon at the nape. His gaze is direct; bright blue eyes regard the viewer from beneath fine-drawn dark brows. His lips are curved in the faintest of smiles.

Caroline looks at the portrait for a long time without speaking. There he is, just as she recalls him on the one occasion they met: the man who had stolen her beloved's heart. Such a sensitive face, she thinks—and so young. They had all been so young. Such a lot of heartbreak he had caused, so long ago.

Ach, but it had all been so long ago…

She hands the miniature back, with some reluctance, and turns her gaze towards Johanna Gottlieb's face. This, too, she studies for some time, thinking that perhaps she discerns a likeness to the painted image. There is something about the straightness of the nose, the curve of the mouth, which seems echoed here. The eyes, however, are unmistakeably Edward's; that is, his sister's, whom she had never met...

She sighs.

The pattern, she sees, has to do with variable stars. How their light, although remaining constant, appears to dwindle, and then grows bright again, as the Star's companion passes in front of it. It had been her Fate to be eclipsed by another; just as the man she loved had found himself eclipsed by a brighter Star's appearing in the firmament of the one he loved… Yes, yes. It all had to do with the stars.

For a while the two women sit in silence: the one absorbed, it appears, in her thoughts; the other attempting to marshal hers into some coherent form—to find words which will express all that is in her heart. Words of consolation, perhaps.

But (Caroline thinks) what is there to say, that will mean anything to this poor woman, who has lived with her secret for so many years? That this was a man who—although he and Caroline met but once—had changed her life forever? That without him, she might have had a chance of being happy? To say such a thing would be unkind—and she is not even sure, now, if it is true.

It was all so long ago. And she is tired.

She thinks instead of the night she found her first comet. A Summer's night it was, and glittering with stars. How her heart had leapt, when she knew what it was she saw! Nothing in her life, before or since, could ever compare with that moment.

She smiles at Johanna Gottlieb. She knows now what it is she has to tell her.

'Your father, too, was a great astronomer,' she says.

Acknowledgments

I should like to thank Paul Murdin, of the Royal Astronomical Society and the University of Cambridge, for his invaluable advice at an earlier stage of this novel; and Carolin Crawford, at the Institute of Astronomy, in Cambridge, for showing me the historic telescopes in their collection. Mark Hurn, the Librarian at the IOA, was equally generous with his time. Phil Charles, at the Observatory in Cape Town, and Brian Warner, at the University of Cape Town, also provided valuable assistance—not least in organising a visit to the South African Large Telescope, at Sutherland, S.A. Thanks are also due to Colin Bundy, Principle of Green Templeton College, Oxford, for showing me around the Radcliffe Observatory; and to Peter Hingley, the Librarian at the Royal Astronomical Society, for letting me use RAS resources. Of these, the most inspirational were the biographical studies of John Goodricke and Edward Pigott, and of Caroline and William Herschel, by Michael Hoskin—on which Dr Hoskin was kind enough to offer further comments in person. Adam Mars-Jones's remarks on more literary considerations were—as ever—wonderfully precise and helpful; while Tim Binding's editorial advice was unfailingly illuminating. I must also thank John Wilson, who offered many insights into the character of John Goodricke, drawn from his experience, as a Deaf actor, performing in Brightness Altered, a play about Goodricke's life; I am grateful, too, to Jane Dewey, who wrote it.

In a novel such as this, which sets out to dramatise events of historical record, a balance has to be struck between what can safely be asserted, and what is merely a matter for conjecture. With this in mind, I have speculated least where most is known, and allowed myself the license of invention where little or no documentary evidence exists. The decision by Caroline Herschel to destroy ten years' worth of her journals provided one such opportunity for the novelist; as did the single fact of Mathurina Piggot's date of birth: the only proof she ever existed. My thanks are also due to the Society of Authors, whose generous assistance at a critical stage enabled me to finish the novel.

Lightning Source UK Ltd.
Milton Keynes UK

172483UK00001B/6/P